The Couple at the Table

Also by Sophie Hannah

Little Face
The Truth-Teller's Lie
The Wrong Mother
The Dead Lie Down
The Cradle in the Grave
The Other Woman's House
Kind of Cruel
The Carrier
The Orphan Choir
Woman with a Secret
The Monogram Murders
A Game for All the Family
The Next to Die
Closed Casket
Keep Her Safe
The Mystery of Three Quarters
Perfect Little Children
The Killings at Kingfisher Hill

Nonfiction

How to Hold a Grudge
Happiness: A Mystery

The Couple at the Table

A Novel

Sophie Hannah

wm

WILLIAM MORROW

An Imprint of HarperCollinsPublishers

HarperCollins books may be purchased for educational, business,
or sales promotional use. For information, please email
the Special Markets Department at SPsales@harpercollins.com.

Originally published as *The Couple at the Table* in the United Kingdom in 2022
by Hodder & Stoughton.

A hardcover edition of this book was published in 2022 by William Morrow,
an imprint of HarperCollins Publishers.

FIRST WILLIAM MORROW PAPERBACK EDITION PUBLISHED 2023.

Library of Congress Cataloging-in-Publication Data has been applied for.

ISBN 978-0-06-325771-9

23 24 25 26 27 LBC 5 4 3 2 1

Some books are harder to dedicate than others, so . . .
this one is for Bounds, which actually feels just right
for so many reasons.

The Couple at the Table

Dear Whoever Killed Jane Brinkwood,

Dear Jane's Murderer,

Which do you prefer?

This is a first for me: writing to someone while not having a clue who they are. I've no idea how to approach doing something so strange, but I'll have to figure it out as I go along because I need to write this down.

I don't actually refer to you in my mind as either "Jane's killer" or "Jane's murderer." Both sound too formal. I tend to call you "whoever did it," especially if I'm talking to someone who knows what "it" means.

You might be surprised to know that I sometimes think of you as the second most likely person in the world (after me) to murder Jane. I didn't kill her, but I'm still the person most likely to have done so.

Anyway, these words have been circling my brain for months and I need to get them out of my system. When I wrote my long letter to William in September, it really worked: I felt an amazing lightness in my chest, an instant easing of pressure. It didn't matter that I had no intention of sending the letter any time soon, if at all. I didn't care that William would probably never read it, and I don't much care if you never read this.

And yes, I know that you, Jane's killer, might be William. There are so many levels of oddness here. Oddness and endless uncertainty, which leads to superstition—like my preposterous belief that waking up two hours before my alarm this morning means that now is when

I am "meant" to write to you, and that if I do it at this perfect time that's been preordained by the universe, it will somehow lead to me finding out who you are.

I'm guessing that, for you, there was a moment on 2 July, after eight in the evening but before nine, when it felt like the perfect time to stick a knife into Jane Brinkwood's back and then repeat the action. Two separate stab wounds, the police said. Whether you planned it or not, there must have been a reason why you did it when you did, not sooner and not later.

I'll probably never know the why, or the why-at-that-moment—or your name, address, age, sex, job, marital status . . . The list of what I don't know about you is almost endless. Most of these details are probably quite boring, but there's one question on my "unknowns" list that nearly ruptures my mind whenever I think about it: Are you Unknown Level 1 or Unknown Level 2? (I've only just invented these names for the two possibilities, roughly five seconds ago.)

Level 2 means you're a stranger to me. We've never met and I wouldn't recognize you if we did. I've never heard of you. I don't know that it was you who killed Jane, and I also don't know you in any other capacity. You're the unnamed intruder we've all speculated about.

I'm convinced you must be Unknown Level 1. I wonder if you could—or can, if you read this, which you won't—work out what that means. How clever are you? Have you, so far, got away with Jane's murder because you're brilliant and ingenious, or might you be stupid and lucky?

Unknown Level 1 means that, although I have no idea that you're Jane's killer, I do know you. We've met: either for the first time in the summer, at Tevendon, or else we knew each other before then.

And the flip side of that? You might know a lot, or nothing, about me. Or somewhere in between. Maybe you only know the official version: Lucy Dean, thirty-eight, engaged to Pete Shabani, mother of one girl (Evin, two years old), founder of a medical tech start-up that I rarely bother to explain to people because when I do they either look confused or make lame jokes about not knowing one end of a test tube from another.

No, that can't be all you know about me. If you know that much, then you know considerably more—by the time Jane was killed, everyone at Tevendon knew the "Poor Lucy" story: Poor Betrayed Brave Lucy Dean, divorced from William Gleave, who'd left her (and their newborn daughter—let's not forget that detail) for Jane Brinkwood, Lucy's former employee and, more than that, a close friend—someone she'd hired, paid extremely well, trusted.

While we're at it, let's hear it for Poor Brave Me's alter ego, Amazing Enlightened Lucy, who, after finding happiness with Pete, forgave both William and Jane for their treachery and formed a new friendship with them as a freshly minted couple, as if they'd never done her any harm. The worst of the lot, if you ask me, is Careless Idiotic Lucy, who booked a holiday for herself and Pete at the Tevendon Estate Resort without first thinking to check that William and Jane wouldn't be there at the exact same time (on their honeymoon, as it happens). This version of Lucy really should have known it was a distinct possibility because Jane was not only the daughter of Lord Brinkwood of Tevendon, owner of the entire estate that contained the resort, but also the person who had raved endlessly about how idyllic Tevendon was and how there was no more stunning or perfect place on earth as far as she was concerned.

Guess what Careless Idiotic Lucy did next? Having discovered her colossal error, did she leave Tevendon immediately? Strangely, no. Instead she declared that staying would be the proportionate and mature thing to do. Of course, she had no idea at that point that she would end up getting entangled in a murder investigation.

If you're not a stranger, Whoever Killed Jane, then you'll know all of these things about me already. Maybe more, if you and I are or have ever been close. And I confess: I'm harboring the deeply irrational hope that somehow, as a result of opening this line of communication between us, I'll get to hear your Jane Brinkwood story one day.

I wonder whose is more horrifying: yours or mine.

Why did you kill her? What had she done to you? I've been obsessing over these questions since July, and also doing a fair amount of self-soothing by choosing to believe, completely without evidence, that eventually I'll know the answers. I'd like to hear them from you, not secondhand. I listened to a podcast the other day about how to trust new happiness after terrible betrayal—my specialist subject—and one of the guests said that we always get back, magnified and multiplied, whatever we put out into the world. Maybe she's right and one day I'll get something back from you, like an explanation.

Let's face it, there's a lot to explain. Jane was stabbed to death, and the person who did it must have been someone who was at Tevendon that night. Must have been, yet can't have been. And the unknown intruder theory just doesn't work. There's no way someone who wasn't one of us could have got in that night. Either they'd have been picked up by the security cameras near the main entrance gates if they'd come in that way, or else they would have had to climb over the high wall and into the back garden of either William and Jane's cottage or maybe the office building. There are no other ways that a stranger could have got themselves into the resort, and it had rained hard the previous day, so they couldn't have done the over-the-wall entry method without leaving footprints in the damp flower beds.

There was a whole report about the state of the soil in those beds and all the other beds at Tevendon. The police showed it to me. The upshot was: no shoes or boots had trodden in that mud on the night Jane was killed. All of the resort's cottages have private gardens apart from Numbers 4 and 5, but if the killer had got in over the wall via one of those and walked from there to William and Jane's cottage, they would have been picked up by a different security camera: one of the ones on the main resort path.

Which seems to rule out a stranger and leaves only those of us who were officially at Tevendon under suspicion. Of that group, nine of us were together and in a different part of the resort when Jane was stabbed, one was Jane—the victim, though it kills me to have to call her that—and two were DC Simon Waterhouse and his wife Sergeant Charlie Zailer. Outside of preposterous TV dramas, police couples don't generally use their annual leave to murder honeymooners they've never met before, so they can be ruled out.

Which leaves only William. My ex-husband.

And now I'm going to write down what I've thought at least a thousand times since July: How can you possibly, Whoever Killed Jane, be anyone but William? He was inside the same four walls as Jane when she was murdered. Yet we've been told many times that it can't have been him—and actually, if by some remote chance you are a complete stranger (Unknown Level 2), then you won't know why DC Waterhouse and his colleagues concluded that William couldn't be guilty, so let me tell you: the blood evidence—the angle, size, and shape of a few splashes of Jane's blood on the back of William's shirt—proves beyond doubt, according to the police forensic experts, that he and Jane must have been at least a meter and a half apart when she was stabbed. He was in front of her with his back turned to her, and probably sitting down while she stood behind him. Therefore he couldn't also have been standing behind her and stabbing her in the back.

That's the full picture: one of us exonerated by the landing pattern of a few drops of blood, two by dint of being police officers, nine of us together and elsewhere at the relevant time, and the intruder scenario made impossible by the absence of footprints in some damp mud running alongside a wall.

And then there's you: Jane's murderer. You who, somehow, in spite of all this, managed to kill her. I like to think that you and I will one day sit face-to-face across a table and you'll show me how all the things I've written above can be reconciled and made to make sense.

I should probably be embarrassed to admit that I'm attached to you—to the idea of you and the meaning I've given you. I get attached quickly and easily compared with most people I know. Last week I heard a story about a family that got rid of their nine-year-old dog because they were about to move into an immaculate new-build and they didn't want dog hair all over the place. They'd had the dog since he was an eight-week-old puppy, and they gave him away to some acquaintances in order to have cleaner sofas and carpets.

When I heard that story, I thought, wow, some people obviously don't form emotional attachments in the way I do. To their wives, to their pets . . . Further evidence: I have a green aventurine palm stone that my mum gave me as an extra birthday present last year. Within days I was carrying it around with me wherever I went, making sure to put it on my bedside table before I went to sleep, even talking to it sometimes when no one was around. Nothing substantial—I wasn't asking it for complicated tax advice or anything—but I'd occasionally say things like, "Where's my palm stone? Oh, there you are." I know it's only a stone and has no feelings, but I love it. I wouldn't dream of ever moving anywhere without it. (I've just remembered that when I was a child I had a battered old book, a hand-me-down from my older sisters, about a girl whose family were horrible, so she formed a bond with a stone and turned it into her doll and best friend.)

I guess that makes you my stone doll equivalent. I'm putting this message out there into the world in the hope that it reaches you. (How? I have nowhere to send it. So my best answer has to be "Somehow.")

Also, I want you to know that I still can't decide if I'm pleased or not about what you did. To Jane, I mean. Whatever your reason was, I don't blame you, and there are times when I feel closer to you than to anyone else in the world.

Lucy x

1

Saturday, January 4, 2020

LUCY

My first thought when I open the door and see William standing there is about the bell, of all things. It makes a repellent noise: loud and harsh-sounding—more so than any other doorbell I've ever heard or lived with—and there are times, like today, when I seriously consider ignoring it because I'm too busy and mentally overloaded to contend with any unexpected visitors. I never do ignore it, though, because the prospect of it ringing again is too awful. I always hurry to open the door to whoever it is, and this time it's him, and it's the bell's fault, and I hate it and I'm going to rip it off the wall with my bare hands as soon as I can.

And now here he is—and my house is open to him, no barrier—because I couldn't stand to hear that shrill blare one more time.

William. William Gleave. His full name drags in my mind, clogging and cumbersome. He's tarnishing so much with his presence: my doorstep, the brickwork his right hand is touching as he waits to be invited inside, the home that I love, where I live with Pete and Evin, where I've felt safe until now. He's ruining it all by being here. When I gave him this address, we were divorced but on good terms. I was the one who made that happen, and I was proud of myself. In spite of everything he'd done, I liked him again. I never dreamed that one day I'd develop such a strong aversion that an unexpected visit from him could make me feel this bad.

Get a grip, Lucy.

The scene in front of me breaks up into shades and shapes that I can't interpret. Then, slowly, the elements start to define themselves again: the newly resurfaced road, its tarmac still wet and sticky in places; Audis, Minis, and Land Rovers on the other side; pairs of semi-detached yellow-brick Victorian houses with pale stone bay windows in a row behind the cars. The picture is irretrievably broken by its central corrosive element, which now takes a step towards me.

His breath touches my face. Neither of us has spoken.

This is bad. He shouldn't be here. He can't be.

"Hi," he says, as if this is nothing unusual—as if he popped out to the shops half an hour ago to stock up on the ingredients for his regular breakfast: two Weetabix with skimmed milk, an apple, one slice of toast with butter. Does he still have it every day? Probably. His dress sense hasn't changed since I first met him—still some permutation of the thin-striped shirt and the tweedy jacket and trousers combination, all of it the color of wet, muddy moorland in autumn.

I try to force from my mind the image of the two of us eating our very different breakfasts together. I don't want to think about William sitting at a table, either with me, as we used to, or with Jane at Tevendon the day it happened.

Me and Pete sitting nearby . . . Nearby, but not the nearest. None of our tables was any nearer to Jane and William's than any of the others. That was what made no sense. One of the things.

The couple at the table.

But which couple?

Stop, for God's sake. Stop before you get caught up in that old familiar thought loop that leads nowhere but craziness and frustration. That's what Pete would say. Has said, more than once. He used to follow it up with "Leave it to DC Waterhouse. I'm one hundred percent sure he'll give us all the answers in due course." He stopped saying that last reassuring part towards the end of last year. Even optimistic Pete had to concede that the sudden drop-off in activity and communication from the police wasn't a good sign.

I can hear his footsteps upstairs. Oh, God. Any minute now, he'll bring Evin down and—

"Luce?" he calls out at the exact moment that William says, "Lucy? Are you all right? I expect it's a shock, my being here."

"Luce? Was that someone at the door? Is it my Oliveology stuff?"

The jumble of words makes me feel faint, as if everything solid is collapsing beneath me.

"Can I come in?" William asks, walking in at the same time. "I need to talk to you. Sorry, I should probably have rung or texted." He heads towards the door to the lounge, then changes his mind and leans against the hall wall, knocking a picture frame and tilting it to the left. Should I straighten it? If I do, will he notice it's a new painting, not one I owned when we lived together? William and I would never have bought any of the pictures that Pete and I have bought together. This one's a big, colorful mess of block colors that suggests, while not actually depicting, pink flowers in a mint-green jug against a cobalt-blue background.

Why should William need to talk to me after all this time? I haven't spoken to him since last July. Since Tevendon.

Please let this not be about Evin. She's nothing to do with him any more. He agreed. Surely he can't go back on—

I cut myself off mid-hope, aware of the absurdity.

Footsteps thud down the stairs, accompanied by giggles from my daughter. Any second now she and Pete will appear.

This isn't fair. I'm not prepared. I never imagined that this was something I had to fear: a move on William's part from the past into the present. It's the most impossible thing that's happened so far. His desertion of me and Evin, even Jane's murder . . . both of those events, though shocking, were somehow easier to fathom and less implausible than him being here now. One of the few things I know for certain is that, given the choice, I would never have sought out William Gleave again, no matter how long I lived. I was sure, so sure, that he felt the same way about me.

Does this mean he is braver than I am?

The letter I wrote him . . . I can't believe I've only just thought of it. I wrote it for precisely this moment—so it can't be true that I didn't anticipate him reappearing in my life. I must have known there was a chance he'd turn up eventually.

I wrote the letter so that I wouldn't have to think about him or the two of us or Jane ever again—so that, if the worst happened, I'd be able to hand it to him with a quick "Oh, it's you. Here are my final words on every subject that concerns us both. My closing statement. Take it, leave and don't come back."

I know exactly where the letter is, even though I wrote it and stashed it away last September and haven't seen it since. It's tucked into my copy of *Appetites* by Geneen Roth, on the shelf above the sink. So why aren't I saying to William, "I've got something for you"?

I remember how furious I was when I wrote it. Would I still stand by every word? I'd like to check it through before handing it over, just in case I'd be horrified by my own vitriol. And . . .

Shit. Why didn't I anticipate that I might respond this way if William ever came back into my life? I want to feel safe again, as safe as I did before he rang my doorbell. How can I if I give him the letter and throw him out without first finding out what he wants? That's not an acceptable option. I need to know why he's here, or I'll be stuck with this unsettled feeling for longer than I'll be able to bear.

"Luce? Oh!" Pete stops halfway down the stairs. "William. Hello."

"Pete. Hi. Sorry to barge in on you all like this. I . . . I need to talk to Lucy."

I nod and give Pete a look. Luckily, he understands the silent message: *I'm fine. Please get our daughter out of here and far away from this, whatever it turns out to be.* "No problem," he says. "Evin and I were just going out, so we'll leave you in peace. Right, then, so . . . Luce, text me if you want to join us at the park, or in town." He gives me a pointed look. He knows today's a do-all-the-work-I-can-while-alone-in-the-house day for me— or rather it should be. Would have been.

I nod to show him I've understood. *Thank you. I'll call if I need you.*

William seems to notice none of this silent signaling. He's terrible at subtle communication and believes his every utterance to be crystal clear, even when it's ambiguous bordering on unintelligible. Once I texted him "Shall I buy bread or have we got lots?" He texted back: "no need." I took this to mean there was no need for me to stock up, and later discovered he'd meant the opposite: no, we did not have lots of bread. We had none, and needed some.

"It's obvious that's what I meant," he snapped at me, annoyed not to be able to make himself the lunch he'd been eating every day for his whole adult life: a sandwich consisting of Hovis Best of Both bread, thinly spread butter, six small rectangles of mild cheddar cheese, and nothing else: no pickle, no salad, no ham. No variation, ever. It's hardly surprising, really, that I didn't expect him to leave me for another woman.

Normally I'd kiss Evin goodbye, but Pete has bundled the two of them and her buggy out of the door in record time. He's probably explaining to her now why they had to hurry. William didn't even glance in her direction as Pete swept her past him. Does he really have so little interest in his own and only child?

Except she's not his child any more. Pete's her dad now. William's the past. All that matters is sending him back there.

"What do you want to talk about?" I'm not going to be a gracious host. No offers of comfortable chairs or hot drinks.

"Shall we . . ." William gestures towards the closed lounge door.

"No. Just say it, whatever it is."

"All right." His wire-rimmed glasses have slipped down his nose and he pushes them up. "I hope you'll forgive me. I thought I could . . . well, get away with not asking you this, but it's been bothering me. I need to know, Lucy. The truth."

"Yes, knowing the truth is nice, isn't it?" I say before I can stop myself.

William nods. "I deserved that, I suppose."

"You *suppose*?" I make a noise that sounds like disgust. I can't help it.

"I'm willing to offer you a lot in exchange for the truth."

"I've no idea what you mean," I tell him. "Are you trying to bribe me? With what?"

He opens his mouth. I wait. Then I notice that he seems to be waiting too.

"Are you offering me money, William?" He never had much when he and I were together. His only income comes from teaching maths part-time at a small, mismanaged private school with about fifty pupils in total and no outside space, fields, or playgrounds apart from a kind of weird balcony on stilts that hovers over the staff car park. The salaries are an insult: nowhere near what state school teachers are paid. Most teachers unfortunate enough to work there leave within two years at most, but William never did, probably for the same reason that he insisted on eating the same lunch every day. "Teaching is a good, reliable job," he repeated like a mantra every time I complained. "My salary is good too, relatively speaking." I used to wonder if he said this—and genuinely seemed to believe it—because his parents had been on the verge of going under financially for most of his life. They ran, and still run, a small fish and chip shop in Lancashire that barely makes enough money to stay open from one week to the next.

Jane, on the other hand . . . The only daughter of Lord Brinkwood of Tevendon. No money worries there. It's likely that William would have inherited significant wealth from Jane when she died.

He says, "Please answer the question I'm going to ask you as if your life . . . no, as if *Evin's* life depended on your honesty."

I feel sick. How could I have married a man who thinks it's acceptable to say that about the daughter he abandoned, to her mother? Bandying her life about like that. I wish whoever killed Jane had stabbed him to death too.

No, you don't.

But I do hate him.

"Did you know?" he says.

"Know what?"

"That we'd be there."

"You're going to have to be a bit less cryptic if you want an answer."

"Did you know that Jane and I had booked a cottage at Tevendon for our honeymoon on those particular dates? Did you deliberately book a holiday there for you and Pete, knowing we'd coincide?"

I laugh. It's such an anticlimax. Scorn surges up inside me, a frothing tide of it. "You know I didn't. Don't you remember when we first bumped into each other and couldn't get over the coincidence? Couldn't you see that my surprise was genuine?"

"I thought so at the time, but in retrospect it struck me as unlikely. And if you did it deliberately, you can tell me. A lot of time has passed. There's no point keeping any secrets now. I won't think less of you, but I do need to know."

"Why? Also, I couldn't give the slightest shit what you think of me."

"I can see I've made you angry, and I'm sorry," says William. "I know I have much to apologize for. But I've lost so much—everything, really—and I think I have a right to know."

"Do you really think I'd deliberately gate-crash your and Jane's honeymoon? Why would I want to subject myself to that particular torture?"

"I can't think of a reason. That doesn't mean there isn't one. And you didn't leave when you saw that Jane and I were there."

"No, I didn't. By then I was happier with Pete than I'd ever been with you, and the four of us were friends: you, Jane, me and Pete. Weren't we?"

"Yes, we were," William concedes.

"So why would Pete and I abandon the amazing holiday we'd booked and look for a new one, fork out extra money? I thought there was no need, since we were all friends at that point. I wanted to show you and Jane that I could be perfectly happy on holiday with Pete even if she and you were on your honeymoon nearby—because that was the truth. It felt like the best, most mature and practical way to handle the situation."

William looks disappointed. "I'm not sure I believe you, Lucy."

"And I'm sure I don't give a shit whether you do or not. Maybe it was naive of me—clearly it was—but the idea that you might have a honeymoon didn't even cross my mind. I think

I probably assumed that couples who get together in as shitty a way as you and Jane did don't bother with honeymoons."

He stares at me. "I *will* get a truthful answer from you, you know. However long it takes."

"Or however short. You've got it already: I had no idea you and Jane would be at Tevendon. Sorry, were you hoping I'd admit to some kind of secret plan to ruin things for you? I don't understand what difference it would . . . Oh!" Suddenly I see what this is about. I'd have got there quicker if I'd been in a normal frame of mind. "This is a gateway question, isn't it? What you really want to ask is: Did I murder your wife? Admit it."

William says nothing. A look of distaste appears on his face; I have been crass and used the M word. This is how he must look immediately before giving one of his pupils a detention.

"It's fine. You might as well admit it," I say. "At Tevendon, you were quick to accuse me. Then Waterhouse told you I couldn't have done it and you backtracked and apologized. But you've had time to think about it since and, let's face it, no one else has been caught for it, and detectives make mistakes. Police aren't infallible. So, you brood and stew for a few months and come back to your original hunch: 'Maybe it was Lucy after all. I know: I'll go round and ask her! Wait, I can't do that. I've already had to apologize for accusing her once, and it'd be a bit much to ask her outright, so what could I ask instead? Ooh, I know: What if I ask her if she knew that Jane and I would be at Tevendon for our honeymoon and planned the whole bumping-into-each-other thing? Because that's what she'd do if she was intending first to torment Jane with threatening anonymous notes and then to kill her.'"

"For Christ's sake, Lucy, stop!"

"Okay," I say breezily, glad to have got to him.

"Did you or didn't you?"

"Know you were going to be at Tevendon? Or . . ."

After a small pause, he says quietly, "You know what I'm asking. And . . . you won't believe me, but I mean it, I've thought about the pros and cons: you have my solemn promise that I won't take it any further, whatever you tell me. If you did kill Jane, I'd regard myself as being the true guilty party."

"Right. So, what, I'm just a robot with no real agency in this fantasy scenario? Programmed by you?"

"What?" He looks confused.

How did I ever manage to have regular conversations with him? He's like a computer that's only had a quarter of its software installed.

He shifts away from the tilted picture and leans against a different part of the wall. "Squabbling won't get us anywhere," he says eventually. "I've been over and over that night and the time we all spent at Tevendon, and . . . I think it must have been you."

"Thanks for sharing," I say flatly.

"You were the only one who had a motive. Why would anybody else there want to kill Jane?"

"So you want me to confess to stabbing your wife to death, and in exchange for my cooperation, you're offering me amnesty? Immunity?"

"Yes." I hear relief in his voice. Does he believe he's going to get what he came here for: a full confession?

Is it the truth about Jane that you need so urgently—about her death and what caused it—or the truth about me, my character? My pride would never allow me to ask him that, not if we were to stand here for a hundred years.

"Knowledge matters to me more than justice," he says as matter-of-factly as if he were talking about the weather. "And as I say: I believe I'm the root cause of all of it. If I hadn't fallen in love with Jane . . ."

"Knowing matters to me too. More than anything." As I

say this, the barrier I've so carefully built up comes crashing down, and I'm overpowered by it: my own need for the truth. Who have I been trying to kid? Before Christmas, I promised Pete that I would try to shut it all down in my mind. I thought I'd been doing so well too, but obviously not. William's intrusion today has torn down the wall I'd imagined I was building between the past and the future. Now, I have to find out.

William must have killed her. No one else could have. He was in the room when it happened. He doesn't deny that part.

But it can't have been him, remember? Blood spatters don't lie.

Even police experts can make mistakes. There's only one problem: William adored Jane. She had, to use the exact words he used when he told me he was leaving me, turned his life from "drab monochrome to the most radiant Technicolor." Why would he murder her? For her money? I've never met anyone who craves wealth less than William; it doesn't add up.

I haven't had this argument with myself for a long time. It's like meeting up with an old friend.

"How about you tell *me* the truth and *I* won't go to the cops," I say. "You killed her, didn't you? And for some reason you're keen for me to believe that you didn't, and this is part of that, this act of being desperate to know. Clever."

"Forget it," says William. "I should leave. Your face has given me the answer I need, anyway. I know you didn't do it. I can see it in your eyes. There's no guilt there."

I can't help laughing at this. William Gleave, claiming to be able to read someone else's emotions? It's too much for me.

"You could never kill a person," he says. "I couldn't either, for what it's worth, but . . . I can hardly object if you don't trust a word I say."

I hate myself for the gut feeling that tells me I ought to believe him, if only about this one thing.

Then who did it, if not him?

I want, more than anything, to go back to being the person I was before he rang my doorbell. I had resigned myself to never knowing. I was fine. I'd stopped pestering DC Waterhouse for news and feeling a spike of agonizing disappointment each time he told me there was none. It was over for me—firmly jammed into the never-think-about-it-again box, with the lid welded shut, a lid that no one but William could have opened.

He says, "I had a dream about it, you know. I've never told anyone. I certainly didn't tell Jane. It would hardly have been the perfect start to our honeymoon."

"A dream about her murder?"

"No. Not quite, but . . ." He looks embarrassed. "The night before we set off for Tevendon, I dreamed about the two of us sitting at a circular table, just like the ones there. Cutlery neatly laid out for several courses."

"Why are you telling me this?" I don't know if I want him to stop or carry on.

"We were about to eat dinner, except we couldn't because we were both dead. Sitting with our backs straight and our eyes open, but dead. I . . . was scared of us. The part of me that was still alive was scared, I mean. And—I swear to you, Lucy, this is true—there were other couples sitting all around us, at similar round tables. None of them seemed to notice or care that we weren't alive. It was horrible. I mean, I know it sounds macabre, but . . . it really was hideously awful."

"Am I meant to feel sorry for you?"

"No. That's not why I'm telling you. I don't think we'd been murdered, come to think of it." His tone suggests that this is something we might both be pleased about. "I suppose it's not that strange, really, apart from the detail of us both being dead at the table. God knows Jane had shown me the Tevendon resort website enough times, and there's probably a picture on there of the outside dining area and the tables. I must have taken it in subliminally."

"You should go," I say.

He nods and moves towards the front door. Halfway there, he turns back. "What about the police? DC Waterhouse and Sergeant Zailer. They weren't with the rest of you the whole time, were they? They must have separated off from the group in order to walk round to our cottage, where they found Jane dead, or . . ."

"Or what, William?" Is he this desperate, really?

"What if one of them killed her? Or both of them?"

"Oh, for God's sake. That's absurd. Why would they?"

"I don't know, Lucy. I don't know why anyone would do it."

"Neither do I." Suddenly, I feel brave. "You know what else I don't know? How you could have been there, in the room while she was stabbed, close enough for her blood to hit the back of your shirt, and not see who killed her. How the fuck was that possible?"

His face adjusts into the expression I know so well, the one that says, *This is too hard, therefore I'm opting out.* I had a nickname for it: "the official position." He used it throughout our marriage, to ward off any and all discussions I wanted to have that he didn't.

"It's a real shame you didn't see or hear anything despite being in such close proximity," I say, fighting back tears that seem to have come from nowhere. "If you had, you'd have known it wasn't me and there'd have been no need to come here and do a quick, midmorning, is-my-ex-wife-a-murderer check. I didn't kill her, William. I think you want it to have been me because that would make sense to you, but it wasn't." I hate myself for hoping that he believes me.

"I know. I can see you're telling the truth. I'm sorry I bothered you. You're a good person, Lucy. You deserve a good life."

Fuck off, fuck off, fuck off. I'm really not that good. You should see the inside of my head sometimes.

Once he's gone, I shut the door and lean against it. Despite my certainty that he's not a murderer, I'm furious, suddenly, with DC Simon Waterhouse. If he'd sorted this out by now, William would know who killed Jane and wouldn't have come around and pressed his finger down on my doorbell. How dare Waterhouse never contact me again after I stopped chasing him? It's his job to chase up everything and everyone until the case is solved.

I ought to tell him about what's just happened. It might be relevant. I'd much rather talk to his more approachable and chatty wife, Charlie Zailer, but it was Waterhouse's case. *Is,* not was. Charlie isn't even a detective, as she kept telling us all. Still, I'd love to know what she would make of William's sudden appearance in my life—his questions, his bizarre offer of his silence in exchange for my confession to a crime I didn't commit.

I'd love to know who she thinks killed Jane too. She had a theory at the time, one I couldn't persuade her to share with me. What was it? I wonder if she still believes it or if she's changed her mind since. Do she and Waterhouse even discuss the case any more? Do Waterhouse and the rest of his team—polite, charming Sergeant Sam and the slightly-too-friendly one with the sideburns—still talk about it? July last year was only six months ago. Surely a murder case isn't considered cold after that short a time?

I can find out, and I will. All I need to do is pay a visit to Spilling police station on the pretext of reporting William's strange behavior today. There's also the letter I wrote him, still in my kitchen. Maybe Waterhouse would be interested in seeing it. If I were a detective, I'd want to read every single word I could that might help me to gain new insight into the people and relationships surrounding my unsolved case.

Anything that's gone cold can easily be warmed up again. If I want it to. I need to decide if knowing the answer after all this time, assuming it's possible, will be worth it.

Which do I want more: to find out the truth, or for Jane Brinkwood's murderer to get away with it?

2

Tuesday, July 2, 2019

1:54 p.m.

Lucy was striding towards the open door, about to walk into Anita's office, when she heard a man say, "Just . . . beware?" Something about his tone made her stop. "Beware" wasn't a word you heard often in real life. Lucy associated it with grizzly monsters in children's books: fangs and claws, the ground shaking as the ogre thudded closer . . .

Just beware. The man, whoever he was, had said it slowly and deliberately. It had sounded almost theatrical.

Who was he? Apart from the kitchen staff who left after breakfast and didn't reappear until around 5 p.m., there were only four men at Tevendon as far as Lucy knew: Pete, William, Jack McCallion, and Mick Henry. The voice she'd heard was deeper than Pete's and William's, and neither broad Liverpudlian like Jack's, nor American, which ruled out Mick. The accent was unmistakably English.

Had it been a threat? If there was even a chance of that, Anita might need help in there . . . But no, it hadn't sounded sinister or aggressive. More like a question. *Just . . . beware?*

How strange. Lucy moved away from a window and closer to the edge of the building, partly to get out of the glare of the early-afternoon sun, but mainly because she was keen to hear whatever was about to happen next and didn't want Anita or the man to know she was listening. Come to think of it, the route to the resort office actively encouraged eavesdropping. The building's front door stood wide open for most of each day and the only way to get to it was through the gate from the outdoor eating area, which took you into the back of the office building's private walled garden. There was a back door, but it was always shut and locked, so you had to walk right around the building to the front, past the two wide-open windows behind Anita's desk, if you wanted to talk to her about anything. It was easy to feel as if you were sneaking up behind her back. If anyone was in the office with her already, you'd have to try hard not to pick up any of the conversation before you walked in.

Lucy let out the breath she was holding and, as if in response, she heard Anita repeat the words "Just beware," as if in answer to the man's question. She too sounded very deliberate. Declarative.

"And the second one?" That was the man again. "You said there have been two since she arrived?"

Lucy wondered if he might be the Tevendon Estate's owner, Lord Brinkwood. Jane's father. There had been no sign of him at the resort so far—which wasn't surprising. When she'd first told Lucy about her family's estate, Jane had said that her dad had nothing to do with the day-to-day running of the holiday cottage business, having hired Greg and Rebecca Summerell first to renovate it and then to run it. Anita, the deputy manager who covered for the Summerells when they were away, as they were now, had described Jane's father, when she'd first given Lucy and Pete the full resort tour, as "Lordian." "That's what I call him," she'd said in a tone that suggested it served him right. "His first name's Ian."

"There can't be many lords called Ian," Pete had said to Lucy later. Lucy had wondered if Anita called him "Lordian" to his face or only in his absence. She found it easier to believe in a lord called Ian than in one who allowed the staff on his estate to address him by an obviously mocking nickname.

Maybe the man with the deep voice was Greg Summerell, back unexpectedly from his holiday in Croatia. "Two since she arrived," he had said. Two of what? Since who arrived?

"Yes," Lucy heard Anita reply. "The first one must have been pushed through her letterbox the first night she was here, while she was asleep. She found it on the doormat when she came downstairs the next morning. The second one she found this morning, in the same place. This is it."

A few silent seconds followed. Then Lucy heard the man say, "Beware of the couple at the table nearest to yours."

She frowned. Something peculiar was going on. What were they looking at in there—some kind of note? What couple, at what table? Tevendon was a couples-only resort, but none of the couples had a particular table that was theirs, either officially or unofficially. Lucy and Pete had sat at a different table for every meal so far, and so had everybody else. The divine breakfasts and dinners were included in the price of the holidays here. For lunch, everyone was supposed to fend for themselves in their own houses. So far, Lucy hadn't bothered; the breakfasts were so generous that she was never hungry again until the evening.

If she walked into the office now, would she be able to join in the conversation, or would Anita and the man hide whatever they were looking at and pretend nothing unusual was happening?

"Something's been crossed out," said a woman whose voice Lucy also didn't recognize. "Very thoroughly, so there's no chance of reading what was there before. Why not bin it and write a new note?"

Lucy adjusted her mental picture of inside the office: not

Anita and a man alone together, but Anita with a man and a woman. It was bound to be Greg and Rebecca Summerell, Lucy decided. Clearly something was wrong, and maybe Anita hadn't felt qualified to deal with it.

Unless the whole "Beware" thing was a joke, or a game. It was hard to imagine anything seriously malicious or dangerous happening here. Who would need to tell anyone to beware in such idyllic surroundings?

Really? Are you that naive, still? Lucy's mind filled with the handful of non-idyllic aspects of her stay at Tevendon so far. None of them had been the resort's fault. Anita was lovely, and seemed to be one of those rare people who was naturally selfless and generous, without any resentment. She'd insisted on driving into Silsford to buy Lucy a bottle of factor 30 sun cream when it turned out that the office's "shop corner," as Anita called it, didn't have any in stock. Lucy had said to Pete at least three times, "I wish some of the people I interview for jobs had Anita's work ethic and attitude." Why was it so rare, that kind of happy, can-do approach? Lucy couldn't produce it herself half the time, so she had no room to talk. Maybe medical tech people were gloomier and grumpier than most.

It was fascinating to Lucy that Anita, who didn't get to spend any of her time at Tevendon reclining on a cushioned sun-lounger with a book by the heated pool, seemed more relaxed and jollier than all the people who had paid a small fortune to come here for the sole purpose of unwinding and enjoying themselves. Polly and Jack McCallion had been arguing yesterday, Lucy was pretty sure, and Harriet Moyle-Jones had been red-eyed at dinner last night; she'd clearly been crying. Mick Henry had rudely—in Lucy's opinion—marched away from her when she'd tried to chat to him near the woods behind Tevendon Mere, the resort's private swimming lake.

She couldn't help smiling at the memory of her telling Pete

about it later, indignantly accusing Mick of not even bothering to invent a credible excuse. "He said he had a *bus to move.* I mean, what the hell does that even mean? What bus?"

Pete had pointed out that Mick, being American, had probably said, "I've gotta bust a move." This had cheered Lucy up a bit, but still, would it have derailed Mick's day so much to stop and chat for two minutes?

Several people had seemed especially on edge yesterday. Pete had put it down to the rain, which no one welcomed when on holiday. Lucy had overheard Caroline and Harriet Moyle-Jones discussing whether or not they ought to regret not booking a holiday somewhere with an indoor pool that wasn't good-weather-dependent. One couple had left early—the couple from Number 6, the only ones who hadn't mingled at all. Lucy had overheard the wife saying to the husband at breakfast yesterday, "Are you finished? Because I cannot get out of here fast enough." Lucy didn't even know their names. Polly McCallion and Susan Henry had labeled them "Mr. and Mrs. Friendly" one morning, after they'd left the pool area without acknowledging anyone, and everyone else had made a studious effort not to call them that or laugh too much (well, Lucy supposed she could only speak for herself) because they didn't want to think of themselves as people who would give bitchy nicknames to their fellow guests or be amused by anyone who did.

Polly and Jack and Susan and Mick were evidently both couples who liked to befriend other couples on holiday. Harriet and Caroline joined in sometimes, as did Lucy and Pete. William and Jane noticeably did not. Mr. and Mrs. Gaze-Into-Each-Other's-Eyes-All-Day-Long-As-If-No-One-Else-Exists would have been an apt nickname for them.

Had Mr. and Mrs. Friendly left because of the rain? It seemed unlikely. Maybe they'd heard what Polly and Susan were calling them and weren't impressed. Susan obviously liked making up her own names for people and things. Lucy had twice heard her call her flip-flops "my flat spaniels." She'd asked why, and Susan had giggled and said, "You know what? I honestly don't know. There's no good reason. It just came to me one day and I liked it."

When Susan had found out that Lucy had once been married to William, she'd said in a shocked whisper, "Oh, my gosh, you were married to Professor Tweed? Does he always wear a tweed suit through the summer?" Lucy had told her that William wasn't a professor, he was a secondary school maths teacher, and yes, she'd admitted, his clothing choices had not changed since Lucy had first met him. "I *love* it!" Susan had replied.

Thoughts of William led to other less welcome thoughts about Jane. Determinedly, Lucy pushed them away. Equally insistently, they came back: Jane had been noticeably cool towards her since she'd arrived at Tevendon, even though Lucy had explained that her and Pete's presence there was pure co-incidence, and even though the four of them were meant to be friends.

After everything I've already forgiven her for . . .

Enough was enough. Lucy wasn't going to think about William or Jane any more this week, apart from simply as "the other guests," like everyone else at Tevendon. If Jane wanted to withhold smiles and warmth, let her. Lucy would shrug it off from now on, and retaliate with relentlessly friendly and understanding thoughts. Of course Jane was a little thrown. This was her honeymoon, and Lucy was William's ex-wife, and no one liked to be ambushed by the unexpected. Jane could hardly be blamed for having a little wobble. And if she wanted to blame Lucy, that was up to her and also her problem. As Pete said, she would be the only one to suffer from her unfriendly, uncharitable thoughts.

Lucy inhaled deeply. This was her and Pete's holiday and

nothing could be allowed to spoil it. Jane had been right about the perfection of Tevendon as a holiday destination—in the Culver Valley, of all places (and why, by the way, had Jane raved about it to Lucy in the first place if she hadn't wanted Lucy to be tempted?). Lucy had been to Mauritius on her honeymoon with William ten years ago, to Bali for her mother's sixtieth birthday, to San Francisco for a conference . . . In none of those places had she found the level of luxury that Tevendon offered. Every tap, every light switch, each square foot of landscaped garden and pool terrace looked as if it had been chosen after someone had asked, "But haven't you got anything rarer, smoother, more perfect and more expensive that we can use instead?" All the aesthetic choices had clearly been made by someone who understood, on a level that went beyond interior design and quite far in the direction of art, how to create beauty.

Lucy knew how to make a house look good in an ordinary kind of way—Persian rugs, white walls, not too many colors or patterns in each room—but she wouldn't have known where to begin to create anything as stunning as Number 7, the cottage she and Pete had booked for the week. She had also briefly been inside the McCallions' cottage, Number 2, which was equally gorgeous.

Pete had pointed out, and he was right, that Anita never said "Number" when talking about the houses. She'd thrown open the door and said, "Welcome to 7," as if that was its name.

Lucy realized she'd been lost in her thoughts and neglecting her eavesdropping when she heard the words "contact the police." It was the woman who'd said it, the one who wasn't Anita.

"We *are* the police," the deep-voiced man said irritably.

Not Greg and Rebecca Summerell, then.

"Yeah, and we're on holiday," said the woman. "We're here for a break. If you're worried, there's no harm in ringing Silsford police station and asking someone to come over and look at these. How does the guest feel, the one on the receiving end? Is she worried?"

"She's angry. She thinks it's a malicious joke rather than a serious threat," said Anita.

"Probably right," the woman agreed. "Does she have any idea who's sending them?"

"I mean . . . I don't know. When I spoke to her she was in a state, so . . ."

"I'd contact the police and ask their advice on next steps." The woman sounded as if she was keen for the conversation to end. "Can we go to our cottage now?"

"Yes, 6 is all ready for you," said Anita. "Thanks for the advice. And sorry to land this on you when you're on holiday. It's just that when your husband said he was a detective—"

"It's fine," said the man. "You were right to mention it."

The talk turned to sets of keys, and breakfast and dinner times, and soon the voices moved nearer. They were on their way out of the office. Lucy took a few steps back so that she could walk forward again and pretend to be only just arriving now.

Anita came outside first. She waved and said, "Hi, Lucy! Did you want me? I'm just taking these lovely people to 6. Lucy, meet Detective Constable Waterhouse and Sergeant Zailer!"

"Simon and Charlie," the woman corrected her. "I'm Charlie and I'm on holiday so please don't call me 'Sergeant.'" She smiled. She was tall and thin with chin-length hair, brown and wavy. Lucy liked her outfit: white linen wide-legged trousers with an orange top and orange and white raffia sandals. Much more presentable than her husband, who was wearing badly fitting faded jeans and lace-up brown shoes that didn't go together at all.

Lucy smiled at Charlie and tried not to feel belittled by the way Anita had introduced her. *Just plain old Lucy.* She'd made the booking under the name Dr. Lucy Dean, but it was ridiculous to imagine that Anita would still think of her as "Dr." The two of them had become a bit more than resort office deputy manager and guest since Anita had found Lucy crying near the fountain the other day and asked if there was anything she could do to help. The whole story of William and Jane had soon come flooding out, and Anita had listened carefully and, instead of showering Lucy with pity as so many people did, she'd suggested going to the restaurant immediately for some "special medicine," which turned out to be a delicious Negroni, though it was only midday. The building that housed the kitchen and indoor dining room was closed and locked, and no waiters or kitchen staff were there, but Anita had a special key for "situations like this." She'd told Lucy not to worry and that she certainly wasn't the first guest who'd needed the "emergency Negroni treatment," as she called it.

Lucy normally hated drinking in the day, but not on this occasion. She'd loved talking to Anita. There had been hardly any "Oh, how awful for you and what a tragedy for Evin" and quite a lot of Anita pronouncing, tipsily (in response to Lucy saying maybe it was her own fault for not knowing all along that William was the kind of man who might do this), "Yes, it was really silly of you not to realize, let's face it. I mean, his surname is *mainly* the word 'leave,' isn't it? William Leave. With a 'G' in front of it to hide his true intentions."

"Yeah. The 'G' probably stands for 'Gonna,'" Lucy had said with a straight face. "William Gonna Leave."

"And there's the title of your first album as a country music star, right there."

They'd then had another Negroni each and written some of the lyrics of the album's title song. Pete, hearing Lucy's report later, had said, "Wow, talk about five-star service. Free cocktails for distressed guests *and* a therapeutic song-writing session. You wouldn't get that at the Premier Inn in Rawndesley."

"I'll be back in ten or fifteen minutes, once I've taken these lovely people to their house," Anita said now, nodding towards DC Waterhouse and Charlie Zailer.

"No problem," said Lucy. "I'll wait." What had she come here for? Oh, yes, to ask if she could use the office printer. Again. She sighed. Founders of start-ups didn't get to go on holiday and leave it all behind in the way that normal people did. Lucy envied Pete his job at the hospital, which could be properly put out of mind whenever he was somewhere else.

"How have I lived in the Culver Valley for most of my adult life and never known this place was here?" Charlie Zailer looked around. "Isn't it amazing, Simon?"

Waterhouse shot her a quizzical, slightly disapproving look, as if she'd said something that made no sense. She gave up on him and turned to Anita. "Apparently there's a private swimming lake somewhere?"

"Yes, Tevendon Mere," said Anita. "The wild stuff is on the other side of the road: the mere, the woods. All totally private and exclusively for the use of our guests. On this side we have nature tamed and manicured, and a gorgeous heated pool. Full disclosure: Tevendon Mere is chilly at the best of times, though lots of our guests brave it."

"I'm heading over to the wild side as soon as I've unpacked," said Charlie. "Can't wait. I love cold-water swimming if it's hot like today."

"Oh, the mere's definitely cold," said Lucy. "I lasted about four minutes. Pete, my fiancé, did slightly better."

"After yesterday's downpour it might be significantly colder now, no matter how sunny it is today," said Anita.

"You're not going to put me off," Charlie told her as she and Waterhouse followed Anita around the side of the building.

The office door had been left open. Lucy went in, hoping to find either one or two "Beware" notes conveniently positioned on Anita's desk for her to have a nosy at. No such luck. She wandered in a slow circle around the office, glancing every now and then at the large mirror on the far wall to check that no one was on their way in from outside who might catch her on the prowl. The mirror was absurdly big for an office, and looked better suited to a palace's ballroom. At the top of the frame there was an ornate crest: the Brinkwood family crest, Anita had told her when she and Pete had checked in. Lucy had thought that, as crests went, it was an ugly one. There was some kind of creature on it with a hairy tail, and two disembodied yellow hands at the bottom. The only aesthetically pleasing part of the design was the two green leaves, one in each of the crest's top corners.

Lucy pushed open the door between the two desks that were both larger and messier than Anita's. Both had been unoccupied since Lucy arrived; presumably they belonged to Greg and Rebecca Summerell.

Wow. This was a surprise. She'd walked into what looked like a large, high-ceilinged traditional family drawing room, except that the sofa by the window was evidently in use as a bed: there was a sheet and a folded duvet on it, and two pillows at one end. Maybe the room had once been a family's lounge. This and Number 1, where William and Jane were staying, were the only two older buildings in the resort: Edwardian, red-brick, lots of stained glass. Both were big enough to be decent-sized family homes. All the other houses were sleek, modern constructions and on one floor only.

It was funny, thought Lucy, that they were all called cottages when two were Edwardian villas and the rest were luxurious modernist bungalows. She smiled to herself: the Tevendon Estate Resort would presumably rather close down and declare itself bankrupt than describe anything here as a bungalow.

Lucy resisted the urge to open a window. The room smelled of heat, dust, and sleep. It struck her as being simultaneously used and neglected. There was a small glass chandelier in the shape of a dandelion head hanging from the center of the ceiling. The flimsy, unlined pink and white flowery curtains were closed, but the sun was having no trouble getting through them and illuminating several thousand dancing motes of dust.

Apart from the sofa acting as a bed, the room contained two glass-fronted cabinets full of leather-bound books, a chest of drawers with a blue and green Tiffany-style lamp on it, and a dark-wood table positioned beneath a large framed painting of a woman in profile with her hair in ringlets. Five high-backed armchairs, three gray-green and two the color of dark mustard, occupied the middle of the room and faced in random directions, as if they'd been abandoned after a frenzied round of musical chairs. Lucy wondered if this was a sort of storage area. If it was, then who had been sleeping here?

"Ah, you're in here!"

Anita was back.

Lucy decided to brazen it out. "Sorry," she said with a smile. "I can never resist exploring houses."

"Me neither. As you can see, I've explored as far as actually sleeping here." She laughed and nodded at the bedding on the sofa.

Lucy couldn't imagine someone as neat and well groomed as Anita, with her sleek, glossy, angular hairstyle, sleeping in such ramshackle surroundings. "How come?" she said.

"I was planning to be in 4 on the nights I stayed over. That's the one that's reserved for whoever's in charge—usually Greg and Rebecca—but then one couple had a problem, and I decided to help them out by letting them use 4 as well as 5. While the cat's away . . . By which I mean, *please* pretend I haven't told you, because I shouldn't really have done it. Greg and Rebecca would have a fit if they found out. 4 is meant to be for staff only, and I'm not supposed to give our accommodation away for free. Oh, bloody hell! You don't mind, do you? As a customer who's paid for her accommodation, I mean."

"I don't mind at all, no."

"Thank God," said Anita.

"Remember, I got the free Negronis and the country song. You really do go above and beyond to keep guests happy, don't you? Giving up your own bed!"

"Well, it's not really mine. And it isn't only guests," said Anita. "I'm like this outside of work too. I need to try and make people happy—myself too, actually. I have this kind of weird compulsion to solve problems if they can be solved and I can see that they can. Because, you know, some really can't."

"No, some can't," Lucy agreed.

"Right—and it's such a waste to get it wrong and think of really easily solvable problems as unsolvable, when it's not too late and when it's not impossible. It won't kill me to sleep on a sofa for a few nights, will it? And soon there'll be a twenty-six-room luxury hotel standing on this very spot, and we'll be able to keep a few rooms free in case of emergencies and still make heaps of profit. Well, not me personally." She rolled her eyes. "They'll be Lordian's profits, not mine. Though I will get to be manager of the new hotel, so that's exciting! Greg and Rebecca didn't want the extra responsibility—they want to keep their focus on the cottages—so I got the job, and soon I'll have my own little empire in the form of a hotel. Anyway . . . some of the other guests might mind about me letting 4 be used for free, so would it be okay if you didn't say anything to anyone?"

"Of course," said Lucy. "Won't breathe a word."

"Thanks. To be honest, I hate my dingy little flat. Sleeping on a sofa here is preferable—so I've solved my problem as well as the guests'. Speaking of problems—what do you need?"

Lucy didn't feel she could ask which couple had the problem or what it was. "It was just some printing I need doing, but actually . . . can I ask you something?"

"Sure. Fire away."

"I couldn't help overhearing some of the conversation you were having with the police couple before I turned up. It sounded pretty serious, and not the kind of thing you'd want someone barging in on, so I waited outside."

"Oh. Yes." Anita seemed to be bracing herself.

"Has someone been sending threatening notes?" It struck Lucy that perhaps this might be connected to the couple who'd had the mysterious problem and needed Number 4. And . . . hadn't Anita said "As well as 5"? Mick and Susan Henry were in Number 5.

"I don't mind you asking. In fact, I was going to come and warn you . . ." Anita looked over her shoulder. "Tell you what, let's go and talk about this somewhere more private. I really do need to keep my massive gob shut, don't I? If you overheard that . . . I mean, I could keep the door and all the windows closed, but it just gets too hot in here and there's no air conditioning. Greg and Rebecca have been begging the mighty Lordian to install it for years, but there's no point now that he's revealed his master plan. This building and 1 are coming down to make way for the new hotel, which is why there's all kinds of junk—"

"Cottage Number 1's going to be demolished?" asked Lucy.

"Yup. Apparently it and this building are a bit of a money pit: constantly in need of maintenance, energy-inefficient. Why do you ask about 1?"

Because that's where William and Jane are staying and I love the idea of it being reduced to a heap of rubble.

Lucy realized that Anita was waiting for her answer. "I just thought older houses that are part of a historical estate would probably be listed on the national heritage register and protected from demolition."

"No. Lordian's massive manor-house mansion is Grade I listed, but none of the other buildings on the grounds are list-worthy. Right, follow me. I warn you, upstairs is even worse than my makeshift bedroom next door, but we should find somewhere to perch."

The word "warn" reminded Lucy. "You mentioned before that you wanted to warn me about something," she said, following Anita up a gray-carpeted wooden staircase.

"Yes, just to be on the safe side. I don't want to scare you, but I can't not tell you. It's about Jane. Jane Brinkwood."

3

Monday, January 6, 2020

Detective Constable Simon Waterhouse's day was derailed, all his plans and good intentions trashed, as soon as he stepped out of his car at 6:50 a.m. and saw a face he hadn't expected to see this morning, though since last July she had never been too far from his mind.

Today was supposed to be a new start: that's why he'd come in so early. New year, new start. He'd even told Charlie to hold him to it if she saw signs of him slipping. He had a mountain of work to catch up on—everything he'd been neglecting in favor of his obsession, which, let's face it, was getting him nowhere. Enough. He had to start tackling the terrifying inbox. Today.

Being the man he was, he had no intention of abandoning his obsession with Jane Brinkwood's murder until he got a result that satisfied him, but he was hopeful of being able to keep it more contained. Maximum two hours a day, in his own time rather than during his shifts, that sort of thing.

He was confident of being able to catch up fairly quickly as long as he faced the problem and didn't put off tackling it any longer. It had to be today, early, right now. Except that his "now" had just taken on a very different shape and flavor, and suddenly he was confident of absolutely nothing. It was definitely her: Lucy Dean, leaning against a car—her car. Simon remembered it from Tevendon.

What was she doing here? If she wanted a progress report—or lack of progress, to be more accurate—wouldn't she have rung up like she had all through the autumn last year? None of the others had; only Lucy.

She raised a hand in greeting and started to walk towards him. Now he saw her more clearly as the police station's security lights flashed on, chasing away some of the dark. Her hair was different: dyed a sort of silver-blonde color and cut very short. When Simon had last seen her it had been long and brown. Now it clung flatly to her head, as if someone had pasted it in place. It made Simon think of a silver acorn. And why was she wearing a Space Invaders . . . Simon screwed up his eyes. No, they were supposed to be white snowflakes against the coat's dark gray background, not those little creatures from the only computer game Simon had ever played, when he was about twelve. Did anyone play it any more?

The weird coat made her look otherworldly, Simon thought. It had a high neck and the folds of wool hung around her like a robe. There was a name for coats like this that weren't proper coats but Simon couldn't remember it. An arm emerged from beneath the wool and he saw that Lucy was holding something. An envelope.

With what inside it?

Simon's mouth was dry, suddenly. *Hurry up*, he thought as she crossed the car park. This might be everything he'd been waiting for—useful new information—but that didn't mean he wanted to wait any longer than he absolutely had to.

If Lucy had something for him that might be a game changer . . . Simon cautioned himself not to get his hopes up but it was useless. They were rocket-to-moon high already. No way she'd come, not this early, unless she had it: the crucial missing piece. People who turned up at police stations this early in the morning with envelopes in their hands, six months after a still-unsolved murder that everyone except Simon had secretly given up on, surely . . .

He tried to squash down his hopes, knowing how childishly naive they were. There was hardly ever one crucial missing piece that no one could find at first that then subsequently turned up to great fanfare and admiring gasps, just as you were about to jack it all in. Never, in fact.

Not that Simon had been planning to admit defeat. Ever. And even if the contents of this envelope weren't a big deal, that didn't mean they were nothing. And maybe Simon could use them to get a bit further. That was all he needed and wanted; to be inching closer . . .

"I bet you're surprised to see me," said Lucy with a small smile.

"Yes, and no."

"Explain the no?"

Should he just tell her? Did he care if it sounded corny?

"I've always thought: one day I'll know the full story of what happened at Tevendon. Didn't know how I'd get there, but . . . this is a way it might start. You, or one of the others, coming in to tell me something, or"—he nodded at the envelope—"give me something."

"I've always believed that too." Lucy smiled. "That we'll know. But I'm afraid you're going to be disappointed on this occasion. Now I feel guilty. I'm mainly here to tell you that William came to see me on Saturday. Turned up at my house uninvited."

"Why?"

"Ridiculous as it sounds, he wanted to ask me if I'd killed Jane."

"What?" Simon frowned. "That sounds like a pretext for something else."

"Not if you know William. You very kindly explained to him last July that I couldn't possibly have killed her. Remember?"

Simon nodded.

"And I think he believed you at the time, and maybe for some months afterward," said Lucy. "But then the days passed, and the weeks . . . and he's all on his own, and probably turning it all over in his head. Somehow he ended up circling back to his original suspicion: that I did it. And bizarrely, he seemed to believe me immediately when I said I didn't. Said he could see from my face that I was telling the truth."

"Sounds like he's just lonely and desperate," said Simon. He nodded at the envelope. "What's that?"

"A letter. It's funny, I was just thinking as I drove here . . ."

Don't bother. Just hand it over. Simon was aching to grab it from her hand.

"I've always had the sense that this really, deeply matters to you," Lucy went on. "Solving Jane's murder. But maybe I'm wrong, because you haven't contacted me for ages. Yet here I am feeling bad because my latest offering is going to be a huge letdown, when it should be you trying to cheer me up and . . . what's that horrible, manipulative phrase? Manage my expectations. I'm the one who's stuck wondering whether or not my ex-husband, my daughter's biological father, is a murderer. Am I ever going to find out? Are you still investigating?"

"Can I see what's in there?" Simon answered with a question. Lucy passed him the envelope. He felt himself relax a little as soon as it was in his hand.

"It's a letter I wrote to William last September, with no serious intention of sending it."

"Then why bother?"

"Free therapy, I guess. The best kind. I wanted to put all my

William pain behind me and properly move on. It's all explained in the letter. It felt important that I should have my say even if no one heard it."

"Right." It might still be useful, Simon tried to convince himself.

The envelope wasn't flat. Its bulk suggested there were several sheets of paper inside. The more words people let loose, the more insight you got into all kinds of things: their assumptions, their memories, their fears . . . Lucy Dean's "say" might well have informative as well as therapeutic value.

Don't give up on it before you've read it.

"That's actually a photocopy," she said. "I wanted to keep the original, but I decided you should have a copy. William coming round and stirring things up again made me realize: I'm *never* going to be satisfied with not knowing. And you drummed it into us all pretty hard at Tevendon that you wanted to know anything, everything, however tiny and irrelevant-seeming, so I thought you should have the letter. For the file—in case there's something in it that might help to stop the investigation from grinding to a halt."

"Thanks," said Simon. "You were right to bring it in. You didn't have to do it before seven a.m., though."

"I'm guessing you've never had a more-than-full-time career and a two-year-old at the same time?" said Lucy. "I don't have many opportunities to nip out for things that aren't either child- or work-related."

Simon tore open the envelope and pulled out the letter. It was dated 12 September 2019.

"I've never ground to a halt on the Jane Brinkwood case and I never will," he said. "If I'm not getting in touch it means there's nothing to report, Doesn't mean I'm not still on it. And by the way, he isn't. He really isn't."

"Who isn't what?" said Lucy.

"William. Isn't a murderer. He can't have killed Jane. We know that's impossible."

"So you've said many times, because you have to. I'm not sure you really believe it, though. And I've thought about it a lot since last July, and you're wrong. Technically."

"What does that mean?"

"Everything your blood-pattern people said—all it proves is that William didn't stab Jane while wearing his blue-and-pink-striped shirt that those blood drops landed on the back of."

"That's not true," said Simon. "Unless . . ." He shrugged. "Unless, all the things I've told you dozens of times already." The "unless" scenario was too ludicrous to be worth considering even for a second. Lucy ought to have known this.

"Yes, unless there was another person of William's height and build sitting in that chair wearing his shirt at the very moment that *William*, not wearing his shirt, stabbed Jane."

"That didn't happen. There are too many problems with that theory for it to be plausible." Simon had told Lucy this dozens of times too.

"Right, and I suppose there's no problem at all with the idea that none of us who were at Tevendon that night could have murdered Jane, and nor could it have been an intruder, and yet she still ended up dead?"

"There's a massive problem with that too," Simon conceded. It was hard, now, to remember the version of himself that he'd been ten minutes ago: stressing about his inbox and all those neglected tasks and emails. Lucy's visit had reminded him of his priorities. The whole think-about-Jane-Brinkwood's-murder-in-his-own-time plan would never have worked anyway. Simon remembered something he'd overheard Polly McCallion say at Tevendon about losing weight: that alternating between sensible-eating days and "treat" days was the worst method.

She'd called it "The Balance Delusion." Simon couldn't remember anything else she'd said about it, but he was sure he'd have ended up among the casualties of The Balance Delusion if he'd got as far as trying to put his sensible time-division plan into action.

Thanks to Lucy's surprise appearance and her letter, he now had a new plan.

"I'm glad you came here today," he told her. "Everything helps, everything I can get. Soon as I have something to report, or more questions to ask, I'll be in touch."

4

Tuesday, July 2, 2019

2:36 p.m.

Five minutes later, Lucy and Anita were sitting on blue-painted kitchen chairs with straw seats in a corner of an upstairs room that was otherwise full of boxes, piles of paper, poster tubes, and odd items of furniture: two tall lamps with discolored shades, a cupboard, a dresser, a footstool. Anita had closed the door and instructed Lucy to pay no attention to the mess. "I know, it's easier said than done," she'd said. "Greg and Rebecca seem happy to work out of what's effectively become a giant bin in the last few months." There had been an edge to her voice as she'd said this, and Lucy had wondered if she disliked her bosses. "If only I were in charge . . ." She'd laughed. "Well, I am, but just until they come back."

Lucy had done her best to appear patient until now, but Anita was taking far too long. "You wanted to tell me something about Jane Brinkwood, something that might scare me," Lucy prompted.

"Yes. Look, I'm really sorry about this, but . . . you heard me telling DC Waterhouse and Sergeant Zailer, so you know Jane's been getting these slightly menacing notes?"

"I heard about the notes. I didn't hear who was on the receiving end of them. Jane?"

Anita nodded. "The first was just one word: 'Beware,' which at least makes sense even if it didn't give any detail about what to beware of. The second note made no sense at all. It said 'Beware of the couple at the table nearest to yours.' The 'yours' was obviously a correction, though. It was written above a word or maybe two that had been crossed out."

"Right." Lucy couldn't see why any of this meant that she, Lucy, needed to be warned. "That sounds as if it makes more sense than just 'Beware' on its own."

"No, it makes less." Anita tucked a stray strand of her glossy black hair behind her ear. "No one has a particular table here. You've seen for yourself: each couple sits wherever they fancy sitting, for breakfast and dinner. It's different every day. But the really strange thing is the layout of the tables. I mean, you've seen them, right? Were you at breakfast this morning? I can't remember."

"Pete was. I wasn't. I had a lie-in after staying up too late to finish the book I was reading."

"When I arrived at six this morning to set up for breakfast, the tables had been moved."

"All of them? To where? Pete didn't say anything."

"He might not have noticed or, if he did, he might have assumed we'd done it—me and the staff. Can you picture the tables as they were at dinner last night?"

"Which ones—outside or inside?" Lucy asked. "Dinner was inside last night because of the rain."

"True, but all the other meals have been outside, right? It's the outside tables that were moved. The indoor ones are where they've always been."

"I think . . . The outside tables were kind of in little rows of two or three, weren't they?"

"Exactly," said Anita. "Three near the dining room, then two in the middle of the terrace on either side of the slightly raised bit, you know? Then another two were near 5, by the top of the path."

For a second, Lucy thought she meant that two tables were near five tables. But no, she was talking about Cottage Number 5. "That sounds about right."

"That's how they were last night, when I left," said Anita. "Someone moved them overnight. When I went over there this morning they'd been put in a circle, with one table actually on the raised bit in the middle. Until today, there's never been a table there. Now there is, and the other six are arranged in a ring around it. And it kind of makes sense—we should have done it ages ago, given that the paved area is circular. But I can't work out who would go to the effort of lugging all those tables around, and why. It had to be a man, I think. Or a very strong woman. The chairs are easy enough to move, but the tables are fairly hefty."

"It could have been a man *and* a woman. Or two women," Lucy added, thinking of Caroline and Harriet Moyle-Jones. "A drunken nighttime prank, maybe?"

"I thought of that but . . . I mean, really? A prank? Making the outdoor dining area look a bit better than it did before?"

"Yeah. Unlikely," Lucy agreed. None of the guests at Tevendon struck her as the midnight prank type. She'd had conversations with at least two of the women about how blissful it was to be somewhere that was so silent at night, where you could get into bed at half past nine and guarantee a long and peaceful sleep. There were no mischievous young couples in their early twenties among the guests. "Are you sure it wasn't any of the waiters or kitchen staff?" she asked Anita.

"Positive. I mean, unless one of them's lying, but I can't see why they would."

"What about the couple that left yesterday—the ones who were in Number 6? If they left because they didn't like it here, might they have . . ." The thought was too outlandish to be worth completing, Lucy decided.

"What, come back and moved the tables around for revenge?"

"It's not the most brutal revenge, to be fair." Lucy smiled.

"No, it's not," said Anita. "And they loved the resort. She made that very clear, the wife."

"So why did they leave early?" Lucy asked.

Anita gave her a curious look. "How do you know they did?"

"I heard her saying she couldn't get out fast enough, or words to that effect."

"That was . . . a personal thing. Nothing to do with Tevendon. She was apologetic about not staying for the full week they'd booked—as if she'd let me down, poor thing." Anita shook her head. "The table-mover must be a guest or guests, but I can hardly ask anyone, can I?"

"Why not?" said Lucy.

"I don't want to freak everyone out. There's no way I'm going to admit that furniture's being moved around mysteriously in the middle of the night and I have no idea what's going on. It's not exactly polished and professional, is it?"

"I'm a guest, and you just told me," Lucy pointed out.

Anita smiled. "It's hard to think of you as a regular, common or garden guest now that we've written a country ballad together. And to be honest, it's too weird for me to discuss it with *no one*. Do you think I should tell DC Waterhouse and Sergeant Zailer? I only told them about the notes. I didn't say anything about the tables because . . . I mean, there's nothing inherently sinister about tables being arranged in a different order, is there? I didn't want to bombard them too much when they've just arrived for their holiday."

Lucy thought she'd guessed why Anita had felt the need to warn her about Jane, even though the warning had not yet been delivered. "She thinks it's me, doesn't she? Jane thinks I'm the one sending her the 'Beware' notes."

Anita's expression told her she was spot-on. "I'm sorry, Lucy. I told her that in my opinion you were the least likely person to do something like that—"

"What exactly did she say? And when?"

"She accosted me before breakfast this morning with the second note, the 'couple at the table' one. It had been posted through the letterbox in the night, she said. She was in such a rage and . . . oh, God, Lucy, I'm so sorry about this."

"Sorry about what? Tell me. I can take it, whatever it is." Whether or not this turned out to be true, it made Lucy feel better to say it.

"She insisted that it must be you sending her the notes, and demanded that I ask you to leave. I'm obviously *not* going to do that, which I told her quite bluntly."

"How did she react?" Lucy was able to produce words, despite having been overtaken by numbness: an echo of how she'd felt when she'd first found out about William and Jane.

She was grateful for the reminder of that terrible moment, the worst of her life so far, because it mattered. The passing of time had shaved off none of its significance. It mattered in its own right, still, and it also mattered seriously and deeply in conjunction with this, what was happening now. Jane had done everything that she'd done already—right up to and including being cold and remote with Lucy since she'd arrived at Tevendon—and now she'd added one more thing to the list: one more offense. A false accusation and an attempt to cut short Lucy's holiday. Two more offenses.

"I couldn't not warn you, could I?" Anita looked anxious. "You're bound to run into her soon, and who knows what she might say to you? She really did seem convinced it was you. I did everything I could to talk her out of it but she wouldn't be persuaded. Maybe if you tell her yourself—"

"She and William might leave," Lucy said without much hope. "Surely a honeymoon without creepy anonymous notes would be more enjoyable for them."

It would be so perfect if they left. Lucy's friendship with Jane was clearly over, and for good this time. It couldn't recover twice. Correction: Lucy didn't want it to recover. The numbness was receding; hurt and indignation thrummed through her body.

"I'm afraid that's unlikely." Anita voiced what Lucy already knew: Jane would never admit defeat. "She made it clear that she had no intention of being driven out by an anonymous coward. Lucy, you have to understand that I *know* it's not you, okay? You might hate Jane enough—"

"I certainly do now. Again." Had she always, deep down, at some level—ever since Jane stole William, and throughout the Foursome Friendship phase?

"—but you seem too . . . thorough to send an ambiguous note like that," said Anita. "Aren't you? I mean, wouldn't it frustrate you to think that someone might read a note from you and have no clue what it was on about?"

"It would. It really would." Lucy couldn't help smiling at this. "I'd be more like, 'Beware. And now let me tell you *why* you should beware and *how* you should beware, and then I'll talk you through your various options for bewaring in a satisfactory manner . . .'" Lucy couldn't carry on; Anita's giggling had set her off.

"So who, then?" she said when she'd stopped laughing. "I didn't write those 'Beware' notes, which means someone else did—but who? And do you think there's a connection between that and the moving of the tables?"

"That's what I've been puzzling over," said Anita. "I kind of think there must be, yeah. The tables are the connection: a note saying 'Beware of the couple at the table nearest to yours,' and the fact that Jane got it on the same day that all the tables were rearranged for no apparent reason by person or persons unknown. But here's the problem: if that's the connection, then it's one that makes no sense."

"How do you mean?"

"Before this morning, several of the tables were nearer to each other than to any of the rest. All four that were in the two rows of two, for example. Any that were in the same row were closer to each other than to any of the ones in the other rows. See what I mean?"

Lucy nodded.

"So 'the table nearest to yours' might have made sense in that context—to somebody, at a particular meal. You and Pete could have said, 'Oh, look, Polly and Jack are the couple at the table nearest to ours tonight.' With the current arrangement, though, that's not true of any of the tables. The one on the raised platform in the middle is exactly the same distance from all the ones in a circle around it, and each of the tables in the outer circle are an equal distance from the table in front of them and the one behind them. It's as if . . . No, that's crazy," Anita concluded.

"Almost as if the tables were repositioned so that Jane *couldn't* identify a particular table as the one nearest to hers, no matter who sat where?" Lucy guessed.

"Yes! That's it, exactly! But then why send a warning note about a couple if you know you've moved the tables in such a way as to make the note effectively meaningless?"

"But even if the tables hadn't been moved, no one ever knows who's going to arrive at which meal first, who's going to sit where . . . The note-writer couldn't have known in advance who the couple at the table *would have been* at the next meal, even with the tables arranged as they were before."

Anita sat up straighter in her chair. "I can hear someone walking around downstairs, in the office. I'd better go and see who it is."

"Yeah, we should . . ." Lucy didn't know what she should do. Go and find Jane, try to sort this out and make her see sense? Not in order to preserve any kind of friendship, but purely so that Lucy and Pete could enjoy the rest of their time at Tevendon in peace. However determined Jane was to stick it out, Lucy resolved to be even more so. She had no intention of running away from anything or anyone. She'd done nothing wrong and, after all, what could Jane do to her that was anywhere near as shocking or devastating as what she'd already done?

Anita made her way down the stairs, having pointed Lucy in the direction of the upstairs bathroom, which turned out to be pleasingly clutter-free, if a little dust-coated in places. Lucy splashed cold water on her face and on the pulse points on her wrists. She thought about Pete waiting for her by the pool. He must be wondering where she'd got to, and was probably busy preparing a pep talk about how she mustn't let work take over too much of the holiday. He was right; the printing could wait till tomorrow, Lucy decided.

Should she tell Pete about the notes, the police, the tables, Jane's accusations? He would have a far more relaxed rest-of-holiday if she didn't, but Lucy hated keeping anything from him. His calm and cheerful perspective on almost everything felt as essential to Lucy as breathing; she was unwilling to deprive herself of it.

She arrived downstairs in the office to find Mick Henry perched on the edge of Anita's desk. He greeted her enthusiastically: "Hey, there, stranger! We missed you at breakfast this morning—unless you were in much earlier than us."

"No, I missed it today. Needed a lie-in. Normally I get up at five thirty with a two-year-old, so I made a vow: no alarms on this holiday. I wake up when I wake up."

"Hey, I hear you," said Mick. "Susan and I went through it all with our two. Boy, did we go through it. Nothing worse than sleep deprivation, but thanks to Anita here . . ." Mick bowed in her direction. "Seriously, Anita, you've saved our vacation. Susan adores you. Lucy, Anita rescued my poor long-suffering wife from my snoring that was keeping her awake all night. You probably won't need that kind of rescuing for a while yet. Pete's younger and fitter than I am. Anita: thank you." Mick bowed again, then saluted. "You're a hero."

Anita laughed. "It's my pleasure." Once Mick had gone, Lucy said, "You've given up your accommodation and you're sleeping on a sofa because of . . . a *snoring* emergency?"

"Yup. To be honest, I wasn't getting much sleep anyway, listening to them arguing and roaming around half the night, every time Mick's snoring woke Susan up. She got really upset with him about it, and he got upset because he obviously doesn't do it on purpose. I took pity on them. And on myself—I sleep much better in there." She nodded at the closed door to the adjoining room. "It's my little escape haven. I'm a bit of an escape addict, to tell you the truth, and here's where I escape to. It always has been. I really, really love it here."

"What, the office?" With Greg and Rebecca's messy desks jutting out, and all that clutter upstairs?

Anita rolled her eyes. "No, silly. I meant Tevendon—the estate, the resort." Seeing Lucy's questioning expression, she said, "You're wondering what I need to escape from. Long story— maybe over more Negronis some time."

Lucy opened her mouth to express enthusiasm for this sugges- tion, and then forgot everything when she noticed Jane Brinkwood standing outside in the garden, staring into the office.

There was no doubt that she was staring at Lucy, though she made no move towards her. Lucy refused to feel intimidated. "I've got to go," she muttered to Anita before striding out to get it over with, whatever "it" might turn out to be.

I've done absolutely nothing wrong, she told herself as she made her way over to where Jane was standing. "Jane. Hi. Listen, can we possibly have a quick chat? I've heard about—"

"Save it," said Jane coldly. "I don't *chat* with people who pretend to be my friend and then send me anonymous letters designed to gaslight me and traumatize me. I honestly didn't think it could be you at first. You're supposed to be my friend! I suspected every single other woman here before I suspected you—I mean, let's face it, men are direct and aggressive, not sneaky and spiteful—but I was wrong to suspect them all, wasn't I? It was you."

"No, it wasn't," said Lucy. "I haven't sent you any—"

"I'm not interested in listening to your lies, Lucy. You're going to listen to me. I'm on my honeymoon, with my husband, whom I love very much and who loves me. And nothing you can do will ruin it for us—don't you realize that? William doesn't love you any more and he never will. For your own good, you should stop fighting reality and just accept it. You'll never succeed in breaking us up, no matter what you do: gate-crash our honeymoon, send me horrible letters—"

"None of that is true," said Lucy. "I didn't—"

"William thinks you're pathetic, if you really want to know. I've always defended you until now, but not any more. Not after this last week. If you had any self-respect, you'd leave Tevendon immediately, but you plainly don't, so I'm sure you'll be staying put, won't you? And do you know what? I don't care if you do. That's how insignificant you are to me. Do what you like. Just don't come anywhere near me. From now on, we're two people who happen to be at the same resort and nothing more. Nothing to do with each other. Agreed?"

Jane raised her eyebrows. She seemed to be waiting for an answer.

Lucy turned away. She couldn't bear to look at Jane, let alone say anything. She saw DC Waterhouse on the other side of the wall by the landscaped gardens. It was clear from his face that he'd heard every word Jane had said.

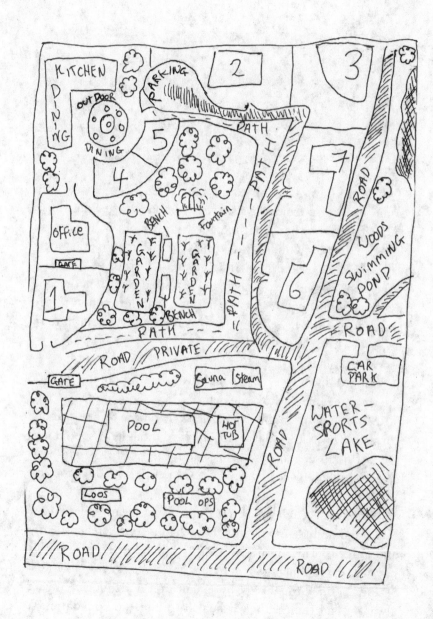

5

Monday, January 6, 2020

Two hours later, having totally forgotten his plan to grab some breakfast from the canteen, Simon was feeling dizzy, suffering from what Charlie called grainy brain. He'd read Lucy's letter to William three times and decided it was interesting but not useful in any immediately obvious way, so he'd gone back to his map-drawing. He stared down at the one he'd just finished. It wasn't perfect, but he couldn't face starting again. This was his best so far, and it would have to do, at least for today.

"Waterhouse!"

Simon didn't move. What had disturbed his thoughts? Not the voice: he knew who and what that was. Something else had flitted through his mind. That's right, he'd been thinking about correcting mistakes on his map, and he'd thought of something: the last note sent to Jane Brinkwood, the word that had been crossed out. Replaced. Corrected. Or perhaps made incorrect. What if . . .

"I thought I'd find you here." Detective Inspector Giles Proust was standing by Simon's side. How had he got here so silently and quickly? This always happened: Simon lost his grip on his physical environment whenever his mind was racing like this. Grainy brain, brought on by exhaustion and hunger, wasn't always a bad thing either. It helped to blur the boundaries. A few grains of an unreachable idea might float by and it was easier for them to get in, somehow—to mingle and swirl around with everything that would normally seem solid and well defined. Sometimes you ended up with a whole new picture or range of possibilities.

Was now one of those times?

"I see you've resolved your swimming pool problem," DI Proust said.

"What?"

"You drew one last week that was at least twice the size of any of the cottages."

"The scale's wrong on this too. And I took the hedge too far here, so it looks like it blocks the gates to Cottage 1, which it doesn't at all . . . but apart from that, it's accurate enough."

"Not as accurate as the accurate map in the file, drawn by someone who knows how to draw maps," said Proust. "I know you think that writing 'PATH, PATH, PATH, GATE, GATE' everywhere makes a world of difference."

"The paths and gates matter. To get to Cottage 1—"

"Please, Waterhouse. We don't need to repeat it every day as if it's the Lord's Prayer and we're novitiates in a convent. To get to Cottage 1 from the outdoor dining area, you'd take the path all the way round, but only if you didn't know about the much quicker way, and the gate, which evidently the murderer did . . . We all know it by heart, and yet here we are. Here *you* are: six months later, stuck on a dead-end capital-P-A-T-H to nowhere."

"Sir, look at this." Simon picked up a black pen and leaned in. He was about to start writing when Proust snatched the pen from his hand and threw it at the farthest wall.

"I wish it didn't always fall to me to be the bearer of disconcerting news, Waterhouse. Crazy-crayon playschool hour is over.

You have work to do—which is bad enough, I know, but worse still is that I'm actually going to make you do it."

"This is work." Simon nodded down at his map.

"No, this is what we could call a hobby if we wanted to be charitable," said Proust. "Or we could call it a life-ruining obsession with a murder you'll never solve. *Never*, Waterhouse."

"The case isn't closed."

"You're right. It isn't. Not officially. But neither is it what you're supposed to be working on this morning. Work, when one has a boss—and you do, and I should know because I'm it—work means doing what you are told to do *by that boss*. Which is not Jane Brinkwood's murder, not today. Face it: you failed. The longer you carry on with this nonsense, the longer that defeat will bother you. Can't you see how you're dragging it out? Instead of drawing a line and moving on, you're making this one failure—rare for you—last an unseasonably long time. Dipping into it over and over again, every day, like a slice of stale toast endlessly probing a rotten egg yolk."

Simon, who had stopped listening early in the diatribe, realized he'd made another mistake with this latest map in addition to the more substantive ones: he'd left no room for extra information to be written around the edges. Stupidly, he'd allowed the drawing to cover the whole page.

Swearing under his breath, he reached for a blank sheet of paper from the pile on the table and placed it so that it lay immediately above the map. The black pen being out of reach, he picked up a blue one and began to draw lines that ran from each of the dots inside the two circles in the map's top left-hand corner up to the new sheet of paper, where he had room to write. At some point he'd tape them together, but this arrangement would do for now.

It might be nothing. It's probably nothing.

Starting with the solitary dot inside the inner circle—the only table on the slightly raised, mosaic-paved platform, around which the other six lower tables were arranged; Simon could picture it as clearly as if he were at Tevendon and staring at it now—he extended the line a little and, at the end of it, wrote "Jane Brinkwood and William Gleave."

Now for the six tables in the outer circle. He wrote:

Lucy Dean and Pete Shabani
Polly and Jack McCallion
Caroline and Harriet Moyle-Jones
Simon Waterhouse and Charlie Zailer
Anita Khattou
Mick and Sus—

Proust grabbed the blue pen from between his fingers and threw it at the wall. It landed not too far away from the black pen.

Simon said, "All this time I've been thinking: it's a contradiction. Someone moved the tables before Anita Khattou arrived at the restaurant area in the morning, on the day of the murder. They moved them into an arrangement that made the second note—'Beware of the couple at the table nearest to yours'—make no sense. Whichever table Jane Brinkwood had ended up at that night, there would have been at least two tables exactly the same distance from hers."

"It's hardly the only contradiction," said Proust. "Someone there that night must have done it, yet none of them physically could have done it."

"Right, but look at this." Simon picked up the last pen left on the table—a red one. He took a clean sheet of paper from the pile and drew a large circle on it, then a smaller one inside the big one. He drew the tables, not as dots this time because he had more space, but as circles. Inside the table-circles, he wrote the names of the people who had been sitting at each table on the night Jane Brinkwood was killed. Then, around this configuration, he drew in Cottages 4 and 5, the kitchen, the indoor dining room, the parking area, and a tree that ended up looking more like a strange, hovering cloud. He wrote "TREE" on it in small capital letters.

"And with a flourish, the demented man embarked upon his three thousandth hand-sketched map of the Tevendon resort site." Proust sighed. "Can't you see why it won't work, Waterhouse, however many times you do it? The problem is that *you're* always the person doing it. Come to think of it, this disincentive must apply to all your endeavors, but let's stick with this one for the moment. You keep drawing the outer and inner circles—the six tables around the one table—and then you stare and stare, hoping to find something new, but you won't because there's nothing in your drawing that *you* haven't drawn. So unless you know something that you're pretending not to know, or that you're not aware of knowing—"

"Look at this map properly, sir. Tell me if you notice anything."

"I notice the symptoms of an increasingly tedious personality disorder. Is it because you were there when it happened? Is that why you can't let it go? Do you feel responsible? *Are* you responsible? Don't think the thought hasn't crossed my mind."

Simon pointed at his picture. "Why do you think I've included all these other things?" he asked Proust. "Why have I drawn this one tree but none of the others?"

"I shudder to think. Did you form a special bond with it?"

"The tables in the outer circle might all be the same distance from Brinkwood and Gleave's table on the raised platform in the middle, but each of the six is closer to *something* than any of the others is. Look . . ."

Simon bent over his work so that Proust couldn't see it until it was ready. He drew connecting lines and arrows where necessary. Then he stood back.

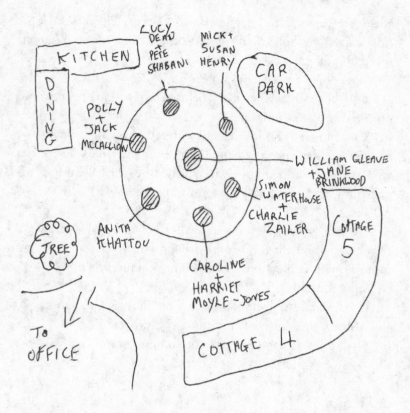

"See? Lucy Dean and Pete Shabani are nearer to the kitchen than anyone else is. Polly and Jack McCallion are nearest to the indoor dining area, restaurant bit, whatever you want to call it."

"Present tense, always present tense." Proust shook his head. "This was *six months ago*. They're not still there now. Only you are still there now."

"Anita Khattou is closer than anyone else to this tree—not any of the other trees, but *this* tree. It's right behind her table. Mick and Susan Henry are nearest to the car park. Caroline and Harriet Moyle-Jones are nearest to Cottage 4, and Charlie and I are closer than anyone else to Cottage 5. Every table is *closer to something* than all the others, and it's a different something in each case."

"Marvelous. So what?" said Proust.

Could he really not see it? "The note sent to Jane Brinkwood on the day of her murder—"

"Waterhouse." Solid ice had entered the voice. Proust—nicknamed the Snowman by Simon and the other detectives who worked under him—was beyond the playful hurling of pens now, and he wanted Simon to know it.

"Yes, sir?"

"Are you going to stop—immediately, right now—drawing these maps and diagrams and driving yourself ever closer to insanity with endless beside-the-point permutations?"

"Sir, it's not—"

"It's a simple question." The ice in the voice expanded: a thick sheet, through which nothing could break.

"No, sir," said Simon. "I'm not going to stop."

6

Charlie was determined to conceal her excitement from Simon as they walked along the path that led to the restaurant terrace. She couldn't wait to see what was on tonight's menu. Swimming in Tevendon Mere had given her a powerful appetite, and dinner was bound to be heavenly. Everything else at Tevendon had been so far, right down to the translucent shine on the polished, flat cobbles beneath her feet. It was hard to believe that somewhere so perfect existed in the Culver Valley, where Charlie had lived all her highly imperfect life. She was already panicking about how she'd be able to tear herself away at the end of her and Simon's three nights here.

Obviously she couldn't risk letting him see how she was feeling about their surroundings. Excitement about a holiday wasn't a component of Simon's universe, and he was generally uncomfortable in the presence of too much enthusiasm.

They passed another sleek wood-and-glass building like the one they were staying in, except this one was L-shaped. Charlie couldn't see a number on the door, but she remembered Anita, during the extremely thorough resort tour, saying that this was "7." ("The numbers are the houses' names," she'd explained, and, no, the L-shape wasn't intended to represent a 7: that was a coincidence.)

Charlie and Simon's cottage was Number 6, so it made sense

that 7 should be the next one they came to, but then beyond that were 3 and 2, in the wrong order. Cottages 4 and 5 were the only two that weren't detached. They shared a party wall and stood between the outside restaurant terrace and the formal gardens. Number 1 didn't look like the other cottages at all. It was a large, redbrick Edwardian villa. Instead of a "1" on display, it had a plaque above its front door with a name on it that had been too far away for Charlie to read from the path.

She'd asked Anita about it, and Anita had nodded as if she'd been expecting the question. "Everyone asks that. It says 'Heaversedge House.' That was its original name, before the resort was here, when there was only this house and the other Edwardian one next door that later became the resort office-cum-storeroom-cum-shove-everything-into-it-that-doesn't-belong-anywhere-else. That had a name too: Graves House. Lord Brinkwood—he's the owner of the estate—agreed to that sign coming down because we needed to put one up saying 'Tevendon Estate Resort,' with the company branding and logo on it, but he insisted on this one staying put. Something about heritage and legacy and tradition—which is absurd, if you ask me, since both of the old buildings are about to be demolished to make way for the new hotel that I'm going to be grand manager of." Anita had done a little twirly dance on the spot at that point to demonstrate how thrilled she was. Charlie nearly laughed as she remembered Simon's horrified face. Going on holiday was a big enough stretch outside his comfort zone. Charlie wasn't sure how long she'd be able to keep him here if the resort staff were in the habit of breaking into impromptu dance routines.

"That's not going to be my actual title," Anita had added quickly, already apparently embarrassed by her celebratory outburst. "Not the 'grand' part anyway."

Once they had turned the corner and walked past a few more houses, Charlie risked asking, "So, what do you think?"

"I'd still rather go back and eat some of the food we brought with us," said Simon.

Charlie gritted her teeth. *How many times?* "Everyone has dinner at the restaurant. It's included in the price, and everyone on Tripadvisor says it's the best part."

"Yeah, well, I'm not everyone—and presumably it's not compulsory if you'd rather—"

"Simon, we're going to the restaurant for dinner, as we agreed we would," Charlie said in her best, breeziest, not-letting-him-get-to-me voice.

"Then why ask what I think?"

"I meant the holiday in general. This place. Never mind. I'll find a leaf to talk to instead." She pulled one off a tree as they passed it. "Much easier and more relaxing. Hello, leaf. How do *you* like being at the Tevendon Estate Resort?"

"I like our house," said Simon.

Charlie stopped walking. "Fine, Simon. Fine! Shall we just pack up our stuff and go home, then? Fucking hell."

"I meant our house here."

"Oh. Did you?" Charlie answered her own question silently: yes. Yes, he had. His intonation had made that clear: "I like our *house*," not "I like *our* house." And now she'd sworn at him. *Well done, Zailer, you numbskull.*

"Yeah, I like it," said Simon, walking ahead—in the direction of the restaurant terrace, which had to be a good sign. "That's why I'd rather we had our meals inside it."

"No, you'd rather we had our meals inside it because you're a weirdo who doesn't want anyone seeing you eat your food." Charlie followed him.

"There's a massive indoor dining room next to the kitchen," Simon said hopefully as they approached the terrace. "Ask if we can eat in there. Everyone else can eat outside if they want, but we don't have to."

"Fine, but I'm not asking," said Charlie. "You ask, if it bothers you so much. I'd prefer to eat outside. It's the perfect weather for it. Hi, Anita!" Charlie waved, though she wasn't yet near enough to be heard. But, God, the relief of spotting someone in the vicinity who was less of a pain to talk to than Simon Waterhouse. In certain moods, Charlie could make herself cry thinking about all the women married to men who weren't Simon, and the blissfully easy lives they must be having.

"The weather's not going to be ruined by me looking at it through a window," Simon muttered, and Charlie knew she'd won. His quiet mumble-grumble voice always signaled his acceptance of being overruled.

Anita and three waiters in white shirts and black suit trousers were hurrying back and forth between the tables and the L-shaped building that housed the kitchen and the indoor restaurant. Of the seven tables, five in the outer circle were already taken: four by actual people, couples, and the fifth by Anita's pile of accessories—clipboard with papers attached, pen, mobile phone—that sat neatly between her knife and fork.

Two tables were free: one in the outer circle and one on the raised circular platform at the center of the terrace. As a joke, Charlie asked Simon, "Which one do you fancy?" The table in the middle was his nightmare: to be up on display, on a stage-like structure, surrounded by other couples. The fact that it wasn't a stage and this was a restaurant and not a theater in the round made no difference; Simon would still rather starve. He indicated as much by ignoring Charlie's question and heading for the lower table in the outer circle. They sat down.

"Look, they've even got the family crest on the silver cutlery. Simon, look."

He was looking at Anita instead, who had just sat down. "Her table's set for one, which means she's eating alone," he said. "Good."

"What do you care who the resort manager eats with? Don't you like her?"

"I don't like or dislike her. I don't know her. But it's embarrassing if everyone at every table's in a couple. All these couples . . . The whole idea of a couples-only resort." Simon shook his head. "Why not let whoever wants to come, come? There should be families here: old people, kids, unmarried people."

"Why not start a new career in the travel and tourism industry?" Charlie suggested. "I wonder which'd be most holidaymakers' favorite: Tevendon, or the Simon Waterhouse resort where dinner is a quickly made sandwich in the kitchen of your villa and there's no restaurant or room service?"

"It's the last thing I'd want to do," Simon said, as if she'd been serious.

Charlie looked at him, considering her next move. Finally she said, "Okay, I'm just going to ask you straight out. Say no politely if you want to, but don't sneer at me as if I'm evil for suggesting it. Do you want to gossip with me about the other couples?"

"No. I'm not interested in them." Simon picked up the small menu card on the table and studied it, mouthing the words as if revising for an exam.

Charlie looked around. Lucy, the woman she and Simon had met outside the office earlier, was sitting at one of the tables in a white dress. Her long, dark hair was loose and fanned out, covering most of the back of her chair. She was holding hands across her table with an archetypal romantic hero type: tall, dark, handsome, charming smile. Not of Indian heritage, Charlie suspected—maybe Middle Eastern. When Lucy caught Charlie's eye and waved at her, the Romantic Hero waved too. *I bet he'd be happy to gossip about the other couples*, Charlie thought.

At another table there was a super-glamorous couple of roughly the same age—late thirties, early forties—who both looked as if they spent at least twenty-two hours of their daily twenty-four on a treadmill. His bulging arms and chest muscles were visible beneath his linen shirt, and her short clingy dress didn't cover up any more than was strictly necessary. She had a diamond stud in her nose and hair that was dyed candy-floss pink from about one inch down, with very visible dark roots. On her wedding finger was a stack of rings that reached up to her knuckle: engagement, wedding, eternity, even more eternity. Charlie heard the man call her "Poll."

The next table in the circle was occupied by a youngish black woman with very short cropped hair and an older white woman with long wavy auburn hair in a low-hanging ponytail. They were both leaning over in a way that looked uncomfortable in order to read the menu card that lay flat on the table between them. "Just take turns to look," Charlie murmured. They also seemed to be having a quite intense conversation, which, annoyingly, wasn't close enough for Charlie to overhear, though she heard the older woman call the younger one "Caro" a couple of times. Were they talking about the food options? Surely no one would furrow their brow quite that much over a choice between "tea-cured salmon with seaweed salt" and "ham hock croquette with sauce gribiche and pickled onions."

At the loudest of the occupied tables, a middle-aged American woman—midfifties, Charlie guessed—was telling a story to her weather-beaten man. His leathery face creased as he chortled at the story. Every so often he said something like, "Oh, boy" or "That is *off the hook*."

The American woman's voice carried well, so, after giving her and Simon's starter order to a waiter, Charlie was able to hear most of the story. It wasn't exactly riveting: a work colleague had needed some papers from the office and the

American woman had agreed to drive them around to her house. Only then had this woman revealed that she lived in Laramie, Wyoming. Mrs. American thought her colleague should have known that this fact rendered her request instantly invalid and deeply unreasonable. Her husband agreed with her.

"I wonder if the honeymooners are going to turn up for dinner," said Simon.

"Ah, so you *do* want to gossip about the other couples."

"No, I really don't. Forget it."

"Which honeymooners? How do you know who's on their honeymoon? Did you get chatting to people while I was swimming today?"

"No. Forget it. Anyway, here they come."

Charlie could hear a faint clack of heels in the distance.

"How did you find out about this place, anyway?" Simon asked her. "You were cagey when I asked you before, and you changed the subject."

"I heard about it from my mum. What exactly do you think I'm trying to hide from you? Me wanting to go on holiday doesn't need to be a cause for suspicion. It's only three days, for God's sake. If you could just bring yourself to relax—"

"Yes, here I am!" a woman's shaky voice cut through the conversations at every table. "I'm sure you're all *delighted* to see me."

Bitter. That was Charlie's first thought. Sarcastic, and undoubtedly angry, but not out of control, reined in. Was she angry with everybody? It sounded like it.

Charlie turned and saw a woman with wavy, golden-blonde hair and a face that was almost doll-like in its prettiness. She appeared to be dressed in some kind of fairy-princess outfit— or maybe it was simply that Charlie really wasn't the girly-dress type. Perhaps dresses like this were regarded by most women as normal for special occasions.

The woman was visibly shaking with . . . definitely rage, thought Charlie, but something else too. Triumph or pride, perhaps. She was smiling very purposefully and even defiantly, turning to face everyone in turn so that they could all see her smiling.

"Did your mum tell you this place was full of psychos when she recommended it?" Simon muttered to Charlie.

Anita Khattou stood up. She looked scared. "Jane . . . ," she said, but then didn't follow it with anything.

Right, thought Charlie. So Mrs. Honeymoon was Jane Brinkwood, recipient of two anonymous letters. Unless there was another Jane.

Beware.

Beware of the couple at the table nearest to yours.

In her gold stiletto heels, Jane headed straight for the table on the raised platform at the center of the terrace. "Didn't expect me to still be here, did you?" she said to the assembled group. "Well, I'm sorry to disappoint you." She performed an exaggerated bowing gesture before pulling back a chair and sitting down.

The man who had been trailing after her reached the table a few seconds later and also sat. Charlie wouldn't have predicted this man as the fairy-princess's husband. He was tall and skinny with sandy hair, glasses, and a sharp chin. His face was sallow and his cheeks were concave. He looked intelligent, and about forty-five years old. His wife was probably around the same age. Absurdly, given the heat, Mr. Honeymoon was wearing a heavy tweed suit. Charlie winced at the expression on his face. The only word she could think of to describe it was devastated. As if something terrible had happened to him, and recently.

"Look at him. Condemned man," Simon whispered.

"Uh-huh." The honeymooners must have had the most horrendous row, Charlie decided, just as they were about to head out for dinner. That would explain both their lateness and his ravaged expression.

"You!"

Charlie looked up. No, she wasn't imagining it. Jane was talking to her, her and Simon. "Who are you?"

Might as well answer. "My name's Charlie."

Simon said nothing.

"Jane, can we go somewhere to talk?" said Anita.

"Charlie? Charlie what?" Jane stood up and walked over to the edge of the platform. What was she going to do, jump onto the table and attack them? It felt possible.

Charlie stood up. "I'm sorry you're upset," she said, "but I don't really have to tell you anything about myself. I'm a guest here just like you."

"Oh, you're nothing like her, honey," said the American woman loudly. "Be grateful for that every single day of your life."

Jane kept her eyes on Charlie. "I know you're a guest here, but why?" she said. "Why here? Why now? Ha! I can see you getting ready to lie to me."

Simon was on his feet. "I'm Detective Constable Simon Waterhouse. This is my wife, Sergeant Charlie Zailer, and if you don't stop being rude to her, you're going to find—"

"Detective Constable?" Jane interrupted him. "Detective Constable and his wife the sergeant? Oh, please. You don't expect me to believe that, do you?"

Damn. Charlie had been eager to hear what Simon's threat was going to be.

"It must be fun, pretending to be a big, scary policeman, but we both know it's not true. And *she's* no sergeant either. So come on. I'm all ears. Why don't you both tell me who you really are?"

7

Wednesday, January 8, 2020

LUCY

I watch from the lounge window as Charlie Zailer gets out of her car. She's got an unlit cigarette in her mouth that I didn't notice at first against the backdrop of lipstick screaming for attention. It's the same garish color she wore that night at Tevendon. I'd seen her earlier in the day with no makeup on and been surprised when she'd arrived at dinner with the shiniest, reddest mouth I'd ever seen. I remember feeling vaguely envious, and thinking that if I were more like her, if I were the sort of woman who had the confidence to wear that lipstick, maybe William wouldn't have left me. I'd never think something like that now, which I suppose is progress.

She's fifteen minutes early. That's good. It isn't as if I'd have been able to focus on anything else while I waited. Since dropping Evin at nursery, I've been pointlessly pacing up and down, running through several possible versions of what might be about to happen. What will I say when she asks me why I've invited her to my house? I should have decided this by now, but I haven't. If I tell her the true reason, will she get indignant and leave?

It's not too late to change your mind. You don't have to do this. You can text later and apologize, say you realized it was nothing and didn't want to waste her time . . .

I'm about to leave the window and head for the front door when Charlie pulls her phone and a lighter from her small, weird bag—black hairy material with silver blotches on it at the top, purple leather middle section, green leather bottom. She lights her cigarette, then puts the lighter back in her bag and taps at her phone with her free hand. She's facing away from me, unaware that I'm watching her.

It's strange to think that before 2 July last year I'd never laid eyes on her. The police weren't part of my life; I didn't visit them at work and they didn't visit me at home.

Before 2 July last year I'd never... I could start so many different sentences with those words. Such a vast distance was traveled—from one part of my life to another, with the two feeling eons apart—in one day: first my eavesdropping, then meeting Simon Waterhouse and Charlie, then Jane viciously accosting me and everything that led to. And later the trouble at dinner and Jane's murder and everything that happened afterward.

The day before, 1 July, almost nothing had happened. It had rained all day. Pete and I had stayed in, read our books, made an amazing lunch for ourselves—lemon sole with potted shrimp butter and creamed spinach, followed by Pete's special ginger-biscuit and orange trifle for pudding—and gossiped extensively about why the couple who'd had Number 6 before Waterhouse and Charlie had left so suddenly. We'd entertained ourselves by inventing ever more outlandish theories. It's strange, now, to think of us then, happy and relaxed, unaware of what the next day had in store.

When I see Charlie drop her cigarette end on the pavement, I move towards the front door. It's open before she has a chance to ring the bell.

"Lucy." She's at my house, so I don't know why she looks faintly surprised to see me. Maybe I'm imagining it, or it's because my hair's different. Do I look that much worse than I did in July last year? I know I've lost too much weight, and I could do with sleeping at least three hours more every night, but I've made an effort today: washed my hair and put on a bit of makeup.

"Hi. Sorry to lurk and ambush you," I say. "I've developed a bit of an aversion to the sound of the doorbell since William came round unannounced on Saturday. Thanks so much for coming. How . . . how have you been since I last saw you?"

"I'm good, thanks." She smiles.

"We've got the place to ourselves," I say, ushering her in with a stream-of-consciousness about Evin's nursery (known as "Noo" in our house—I include this detail too). I don't know why I'm chattering nervously like this. She's only a police sergeant, not the Queen.

I show her straight through to the lounge and even tell her which chair to sit in. I've planned it all, control freak that I am: I'll get her settled, then offer her a drink in a way that makes it clear she should stay put while I'm in the kitchen. When we were first looking for a house, Pete assumed I'd want a huge kitchen with room for sofas and a dining table. "God, no," I told him. "The kitchen's where I go to escape when I want to get away from everyone and get my head straight. A kitchen that's only spacious if one person's in it alone—that's my perfect kitchen."

"So no table or chairs at all?" he said.

"A small table with only two chairs," I said decisively. "Otherwise we'll never eat in the dining room. I *really* want a house with a gorgeous, proper, traditional dining room. With a fireplace and a mantelpiece and picture rails." He teased me about how old-fashioned I was.

I shiver, remembering my innocent words: *a small table with only two chairs*. William's description of the scene from his dream comes back to me: him and Jane seated at a round table, cutlery neatly laid out in front of them, both dead. Surrounded by other couples at other tables.

He had no right to put that image in my mind. Why did he? I'm sorry, but you don't get to tell your ex-wife, the one you abandoned less than two weeks after she'd had your first baby, all about your disturbing dreams. It's inappropriate. Was he trying to establish a new closeness between us?

I offer Charlie a drink and she asks for builder's tea with milk, no sugar. I tell her to "sit tight" (that's what we control freaks say when we mean "Do not move from that chair" but want to sound welcoming, not scary) and head for the kitchen. Before she arrived, I filled the kettle with fresh water and laid out two mugs, a teaspoon, the coffee jar, and all the boxes of teabags in the house.

Finally—it seems to take an age—we're sitting opposite each other in the lounge. "So," she says, "you said there was something you wanted to talk to me about?"

I nod. "I assume DC Waterhouse has told you I spoke to him on Monday."

"He mentioned it, yes. You gave him a copy of a letter you wrote to William."

"Did you read it?"

"I skim-read it. But, Lucy, I'm not a detective. This isn't my—"

"I know. I just thought . . . Did he also tell you that William came here on Saturday, uninvited?"

"Yes, and asked you if you murdered Jane. You told him you hadn't. He believed you."

"Right."

He'll have told her the briefest possible version. The key points—which are pretty much all I told him.

Charlie's watching me. Waiting.

"I just . . . I wasn't sure DC Waterhouse would tell you about William coming round, or show you the letter. After I'd seen him, I thought, *I'd actually really like to tell Charlie Zailer what happened on Saturday* and just . . . well, just talk to you properly about everything. I don't feel I can do that with DC Waterhouse. He's often either firing questions at me or disappearing into his own head, so that I feel he's not listening to me properly."

Charlie smiles. "Yes, I know that feeling."

"And despite the fact that it's his case and he's a detective, he hasn't solved it, even though it's been six months. And I haven't heard anything from him since Monday."

"It's only Wednesday."

"I know, but . . ."

"Were you expecting him to get in touch so soon? About what?"

"I don't know," I say, imagining how vague and silly I must sound. "I hoped my letter to William might at least make DC Waterhouse want to ask me more questions. Please don't take this as an insult to your husband, but I have a strong hunch that this case might actually get solved if I can talk to you about it. I know you're not officially involved, but you were there when Jane died, and . . . At the risk of sounding sexist, you're not an impatient man. I think that might help. Please can I tell you exactly what happened when William came round on Saturday?"

"I mean . . ." She seems to be considering it. Finally she says, "Okay."

"Thank you."

"You said before that William came round uninvited on Saturday. Is he ever invited?"

"Never. He and I haven't had any contact since Tevendon. No calls or texts or anything. I'd have kept it that way forever. I was convinced he would too, but evidently I was wrong."

Charlie nods slowly. "So tell me about Saturday, then."

I might have forgotten the odd detail, but I don't think so. I have a pedantic memory. Everyone close to me teases me about it.

Charlie listens without interruption until I've finished. Then she says, "Why do you think he told you about his dream?"

"I don't know. To manipulate me in some way? I'm not sure I believe that he even had the dream. He could have made it up, to have something to confide in me that he supposedly hadn't told anyone else."

"Why would he want to do that?"

"Maybe to charm me into confessing to Jane's murder. Perhaps he's been on edge all these months wondering if DC Waterhouse is ever going to arrest him. Me confessing would solve that for him."

"But if he did it, then he knows you didn't," says Charlie. "He'd therefore also know that you wouldn't confess to it."

"Maybe. Or he might have thought I'd confess anyway, to earn his forgiveness and maybe also his love, and perhaps the chance of us getting back together. Who knows what he's thinking? He said very clearly that if I confessed, he'd blame himself and forgive me. It was like he was trying to win me over. I mean, who says that about their wife's murder? It felt manipulative."

"Aren't you married to Pete now?" Charlie asks.

"No. Still engaged." I hold up my left hand, show her the ring. "We delayed the wedding. It didn't seem right to start planning it immediately after Jane's death. And . . . I don't know, Pete still wants to, but I've kind of lost my appetite for it. Bad things seem to happen to people who get married."

"Not always."

"Yeah, to be fair, I think what I mean is: bad things seem to happen to people who marry William Gleave."

"Can I ask you a personal question?" Charlie says.

"Please do."

"If William said that leaving you for Jane had been a terrible mistake, would you take him back? I won't judge you whatever your answer is. Nobody believes people who say that, I know, but I promise you, I'm in no position to judge anyone when it comes to personal relationships."

"He wouldn't want me back. Ever. There's no question of that."

"But hypothetically, if he expressed sincere regret, told you that you were the one he truly loved and the Jane thing had been nothing more than infatuation, would you take him back?"

"Not in a million years." It's comforting to contemplate—to inhabit, imaginatively, as if it were a real danger—how awful it would be to have to kiss William again, to share a bed with him, to have to ask him about his day at work and listen to his news and his worries. The prospect makes me shudder. "Never. But if we can go to Wishful Thinking Land for a second, I would absolutely love it if he asked."

"Just so that you could reject him?" Charlie asks.

"No. I wouldn't get a kick out of causing him pain."

"Then why would you want him to ask?"

"For the effect it would have on me if he did. I'd take it as official acknowledgment from him that leaving me was a mistake. That it had made his life worse. That Jane Brinkwood was never better than me—not a better person to be with, and not more deserving of love than me."

Charlie nods. Then she says, "Lucy, I don't really understand why I'm here. I mean, don't get me wrong, I'm happy to talk— it beats working—but I don't think us discussing your feelings about William or your marriage . . . I don't think it's going to help Simon to find Jane's murderer."

"It's still an open case, isn't it?" I say. "He told me he hadn't given up on it."

"That's an understatement," says Charlie. "It's still his main preoccupation. If anyone can solve it, he can."

"Okay, great." This reassures me a little. "But then . . . something needs to happen, and it seems as if nothing is. None of the detectives had been in touch for ages. And since Saturday, I've had this . . . this craving for the truth. Before then, I honestly thought I was fine with not knowing. I'd promised Pete I'd banish it from my mind. William ruined all that on Saturday. I've been trying to work out why, given that I could have pushed it all away again as soon as he left. If I wanted to do that before, then why wasn't it also what I wanted after I'd seen William?"

Charlie waits for the answer.

"I think it's that, before Saturday, there was no part of me that suspected William. I had, at various points last year. He was the only person at Number 1 with Jane when she died, so it was hard not to. But he'd been cleared by the blood evidence, I was told over and over, and no one knew better than I did how much he adored Jane. It was more a kind of cultlike worship than what I'd call love, actually, but even so . . . Her death destroyed him—destroyed his happiness completely. You saw what he was like immediately afterward. I just can't see why he'd kill her."

Charlie takes a sip of her tea, leaving a red imprint on the side of the cup. Her face is unreadable.

"When I made my resolution to stop thinking about it, I decided that I knew William hadn't done it, and I knew that I hadn't, and Pete hadn't, and . . . It sounds cold, and maybe it is, but I didn't mind that Jane was dead. By that stage I truly loathed her. I suppose I convinced myself that I was fine with never knowing because at least then there would be the consolation of the murderer getting away with it."

"But then William came round on Saturday . . . ," says Charlie.

"Yes. And by the time he left, I was desperate to know. Looking at him, listening to him, I kept thinking, *It* could *have been him. It must have been. It has to be possible that the blood pattern experts were wrong.*"

"Right," says Charlie. "So it's more of a need to know if William's a murderer than a need to know who killed Jane? That's why you went to see Simon on Monday?"

"I guess. But, no. Because even if it's not William, I still want to know who it is. I think I never stopped wanting it, really. Whoever the killer turns out to be . . . It's hard to explain, but they mean something to me."

Should I carry on? I'm not yet past caring what anybody thinks of me, but for the first time in my life, I can imagine getting there. Everything I did until the age of thirty-six was entirely appropriate, conventional, and well behaved, and look where it got me: abandoned, along with my two-week-old daughter, by my husband.

Her father.

No. *That's what he was then. Not any more.*

"I used to think no one could ever hate Jane as much as I did when I first found out about her and William," I say. "On 2 July last year, I discovered that I was wrong about that, or at least potentially wrong. There might be someone else: whoever did it."

"A kindred spirit?" says Charlie.

I'm not going to back away from it now. "Yes. And I started to wonder what Jane might have done to that person."

"That sounds a bit like 'Murder victims deserve to be murdered,'" says Charlie.

"Only if you weren't listening properly." I try to soften my words with a smile. "Hey, I'm a scientist, so forgive me for being a stickler, but . . . no one deserves to be murdered, and no one deserves not to be."

"Meaning?"

"Deserving isn't a fact in the world. It's something humans have invented to make us feel better, and we each get to make it mean whatever we want it to. Forget it," I say, seeing that my explanation has failed to clarify anything for Charlie. "I agree with you that murder's always wrong, if that's what you're asking. But even if Jane didn't deserve to be stabbed to death, that doesn't mean that there wasn't something she did at some point that adversely affected her killer. That person, whoever they are, might be—probably is—the only person on the planet who's ever felt that violent hatred that I've felt towards her. I need to know who it is. If it's William, I'll be disappointed, but I still need to know."

"Disappointed because then your kindred spirit would be sullied by his past history of also being someone who betrayed you?"

"Very well put."

"Lucy, can I make an observation without offending you?"

"Make it and we'll see," I say.

"You're very changeable."

A burst of laughter escapes before I can stop it. "I'd have said I'm boringly set in my ways and *un*changing. I'm one of those old-fashioned fools who thinks marriage should be forever, and acts as if it is."

"One minute you're happy for Jane Brinkwood's murder never to be solved. The next, you'd give anything to know who killed her. Today you hate her so much that you've formed an emotional attachment to her killer without knowing his or her name, but not too long ago you'd forgiven her betraying you and nicking your husband, and you were all great friends: you, Pete, William and Jane. Or at least that's what you told me at Tevendon."

"And it's true. The friendship didn't start immediately after Jane and William got together. It was several months later."

"But by the time we all left Tevendon, you no longer had any friendly feelings for either Jane or William, did you? You were quite open about it."

"No. I mean, yes, that's true."

"So can we get the chronology straight?" says Charlie. "They betrayed you, you hated them, understandably. Then you decided to befriend them—"

"Yes, I did. I made it work." I'll always be proud of this. Most people couldn't have done it.

"But then at Tevendon you decided you hated them both again?" Charlie says.

"When you put it like that, it makes me sound erratic. I suppose I think of myself as stodgy and stable because I was when William and I were together. In reality, ever since he left me, it's like . . . I mean, not every day, but some days it's as if someone's put all my emotions into a cocktail shaker and just . . ." I perform a frenzied gesture with my hands. "Pete thought I'd gone mad at first when I suggested we invite William and Jane round for dinner. But it *worked*, that was the incredible thing. I wasn't sure it would, but it really did, until they ruined it. It made me feel so much better about everything. More in control."

"How did they ruin it?"

She's trying to drag me deeper into something I don't want to think about today. This isn't the conversation I want to be having. "Can I ask you a question?" I say. "I asked DC Waterhouse a few times and he never gave me an answer. How thoroughly were the kitchen staff and cleaners at Tevendon investigated? I know none of them were there when Jane was murdered, or so everyone believes, but has anyone looked into who they are? Their backgrounds? And what about Lord Brinkwood, and the Summerells? And the couple who were in Number 6 before you, Mr. and Mrs. Friendly?"

"Is that what you called them?"

"Not me, but others did. They weren't exactly sociable. And they left in some kind of strange and dramatic circumstances, from what I overheard. I think that's worth looking into."

Charlie sighs. "Look, all I can tell you is that, knowing Simon, he'll have investigated the bejesus out of everything there was to investigate."

"How come you and he knew about Number 6 suddenly being available to rent?" I ask her. "I've thought about that a lot. Do you know Mr. and Mrs. Friendly? Was that how you found out 6 was about to be free?"

"I heard that Number 6 was available from my mum, not from the couple who left—and my holiday arrangements are neither here nor there. I promise you, Mr. and Mrs. Friendly didn't kill anyone."

"How can you know that if you don't know them?"

"I know—*we*, the police, know—that nobody was at the resort when Jane died apart from all the people we know about. Kitchen staff and cleaners had all left before the murder happened."

I nod and try to look satisfied because I don't want to seem ungrateful. It's frustrating that Charlie can't see what's so obvious: if "the people we know about," as she calls them, have all been ruled out as well, then that invalidates the ruling out of the people we don't know about. Whatever the film from the security cameras and the blood spatters and the eyewitness testimony seem to prove, it's an undeniable fact that someone—insider or outsider—murdered Jane Brinkwood on 2 July last year.

"Can I ask you something else?" I say. "You might not know, but—"

"Ask away."

"Had Jane made a will?"

Charlie nods.

"Did she leave everything to William?"

"I can't tell you that. Sorry." Seeing my expression, she says, "I can't, Lucy. Imagine if you blurted out to William that you'd been told the details of his late wife's will by DC Waterhouse's wife."

Something she said earlier comes back to me. "What did you mean before, about not being in a position to be judgmental about personal relationships?"

"Nothing exciting. Just, you know, I'm an ordinary, complicated person like we all are. I don't always behave perfectly."

"So what's your best guess about who killed Jane? Someone must have done it. At Tevendon you said something about having a strong hunch that was unprovable."

She laughs. "See what I mean about me not always behaving perfectly? If I said that in front of you, I shouldn't have."

"Actually, I was kind of eavesdropping," I admit. "If it's just a hunch, how can it do any harm to tell me? You wouldn't be alleging anything or accusing anyone. *Please.*"

After a pause of a few seconds, she says quietly, "William Gleave"—as if I need to be told his full name, as if I wasn't married to him for thirteen years. "I've been sure in my bones that it was him since the moment Simon and I found Jane dead. Oh, I know I'm wrong, I have to be, but . . . I can't shift my hunch. It seems not to give a toss about the blood evidence."

This new information buzzes around inside me in search of a settling place. *She thinks it was William. She believes William did it.*

"What about DC Waterhouse? Does he agree?"

"Nope." Charlie's faint and slightly weary smile makes me think the two of them must have discussed it at length.

"He doesn't?"

"Simon's as convinced as I am, except in the opposite direction," says Charlie. "He's one hundred percent certain that William's innocent."

8

Simon couldn't believe he'd allowed himself to get caught up in this mess. Holiday? This was like being trapped in a nightmare. He didn't care about crests on towels or memory foam mattresses or any of the things Charlie enthused about endlessly. On the contrary: he almost resented them. Towels weren't supposed to be embroidered; mattresses weren't meant to remember stuff. And if Simon had obeyed his gut instinct and stayed at home, he wouldn't now be getting screamed at by a deranged newlywed.

At least she wasn't yelling specifically at him and Charlie any more. She'd turned her attention to Anita and was busy telling her that "Hester," whoever that was, was not really called Hester at all: "She and her so-called-husband-more-like-sex-toy-in-human-form were also here under false names."

Also? Like Simon and Charlie—was that what she meant? Who the hell did she think they were? Simon thought it ought to be obvious to everybody that there was zero chance of him ever being, or ever having been, anyone but Simon Waterhouse.

"It wasn't exactly hard to work out," Jane told Anita. "I called after her more than once, called her Hester, and she completely ignored me. At least she and her bit on the side weren't pathetic enough to pretend to be detectives."

"I can show you my ID card if you want," said Charlie.

"IDs can be faked, as you'd know if you were a real police sergeant."

Charlie laughed and shook her head. Was she enjoying this?

"Hester? Do you mean Mrs. Friendly?" the American woman asked Jane. "How did you find out her name?"

"You really expect me to answer your questions?" Jane spat back, still glaring down from her elevated position. "I can barely stand to look at you."

"Jane, stop," Anita pleaded with her. "Let's go inside and talk."

"No, I won't stop. Why should I do anything for you? Did you help me today when I asked you to? No. Quite frankly, Anita, you can go fuck yourself." Jane turned back to Charlie. "Maybe you are the real police, who knows? Maybe you're going to have me arrested for the crime of marrying the man I love. Well, do your worst, because, d'you know what? I don't care any more. None of you matter to me—not your shitty little lives, not your opinion of me, none of it. You don't deserve to take up any more space in my brain."

Having finished her speech, Jane sat down and started to chat brightly to her husband about the various menu choices and something about a bottle of champagne. He had his head in his hands so Simon couldn't see his face. Anita sat down too and picked up her phone.

At all the other tables, chairs were shuffled closer in and heads leaned forward as people started to discuss, in their pairs, the evening's drama so far.

"I give up," Charlie said.

"On what?"

"If you want to leave right now, I won't argue. I can't really pretend any more that this is likely to be the relaxing break I wanted."

"I'm staying," said Simon. "With us here, it's less likely that anyone'll do anything stupid. I'm glad they all know we're police."

"Do you honestly think—"

"That there's a potentially dangerous situation brewing here? I do, yeah. Two anonymous notes in block capitals, and now this? I know my experience of holidays is limited, but I'm guessing this is abnormal."

"Just a bit—from what I can recall. I haven't had any holidays, really, since I shacked up with you. Not a complaint." Charlie held up her hands. "Just stating a fact."

Their starters arrived. As he ate, Simon wondered why Anita was allowing Jane to stay and have dinner, given what she'd just done. Why wasn't she being forcibly escorted out of the resort? Where was the duty of care to the other guests?

The answer came to Simon straight away, or at least a possible answer: Jane was the daughter of Ian Brinkwood, aka Lord Brinkwood of Tevendon, who owned not only this resort but the entire estate surrounding it. Anita had explained this when she'd told Simon and Charlie about the "Beware" notes, and it very likely meant that Jane couldn't be thrown out by a mere staff member like Anita, no matter how badly she behaved.

To Simon's relief, nothing remarkable happened while the starters were being eaten, nor as the plates were cleared away. People spoke quietly to their other halves, everyone seemingly taking care not to be overheard. Jane's tweedy husband stood up and walked towards the door to the L-shaped building that housed the kitchen and indoor restaurant. Simon caught a glimpse of his expression as he turned: no happier than before.

What was wrong with him? Was he upset, in a much quieter way, about the same thing that had angered his wife? Unlike her, he hadn't had the benefit of the cathartic relief that came from screaming at everybody like a tyrant on speed. Or perhaps he was disgusted with himself for marrying a woman who could behave so outrageously in public. Either way, he was probably heading inside to lock himself in a bathroom cubicle and bang his head against the wall.

"So what do we do about this messy psychodrama we've wandered into?" said Charlie. "Anything? Nothing?" She smiled. "Wouldn't it be funny if it turned out to be all staged—some kind of at-table immersive theatrical experience? My last excruciating holiday with my extended family involved after-dinner entertainment in the form of an Alison Moyet impersonator. I mean, I was as big a fan of 'Love Resurrection' as anyone but—"

"Oh, my word!" Jane cried out suddenly. "Insult to injury!"

"She's on the move," muttered Simon.

Jane had pushed back her chair and was attempting a precarious gold-stilettoed climb-down from her platform. Was she about to follow her husband into the kitchen building? Unlikely. She'd been sitting alone for a good minute at least since he'd gone. Simon hadn't noticed anyone insulting her during that time.

Once she was down on the same level of the terrace as the rest of them, she marched over to the table at which Lucy sat with a man who looked as if he'd been designed in a factory that produced perfect alpha males. "Every time I think you can't sink any lower, you surprise me," she said to Lucy.

The perfect man stood up. "I don't want to say anything unpleasant or get into an argument with you, Jane, but you're being very unfair to Lucy, and I think, deep down, you must know that."

"Must I? Do you even know who your fiancée is? Do you know what she's trying to do to me? You're clueless!"

"I know what you and William did to her," he replied. "And I know what you, without William's help, did to some other people as well, because you told me yourself, remember? At the hospital?"

"Fuck you! You can't even hear how self-righteous you sound, can you?"

"Do you think I want to bring this up here, now, in front of everyone?" Lucy's partner maintained his soft, reasonable tone throughout. It made Simon suspicious of him. "Because I really don't, Jane. Nobody wants that. It's ruining this beautiful place and this beautiful night for all of us. Look, why don't you go back to your table, and maybe we can have a proper conversation in the morning—"

"Count me out," Lucy said.

"—to try and clear the air in a more constructive way. What do you think?" He had the kind of smile that most people would find hard to disagree with.

Jane Brinkwood wasn't most people. "I'd love to be able to admire your noble stance, Pete, I really would. There's only one problem: you're a fucking thief."

"What?"

"You've taken—*stolen*, like a thief—our champagne. Mine and William's."

Simon's attention switched from the faces around the table to the bottle at its center.

"No, I haven't." Pete looked confused. "Why would you think that?"

"That bottle you're halfway into, the Krug Clos D'Ambonnay 1995?" Jane said. "It was a present from my dad on my twenty-first birthday. I've been saving it ever since. Specifically for my honeymoon. I gave it to Anita earlier to put in the fridge in the kitchen, ready for tonight. William's in there looking for it right now." She pointed to the L-shaped building. "No wonder he can't find it."

"But . . . this can't be . . ." Pete picked up the bottle, then put it down again. "I ordered a bottle of champagne and this was the one the waiter brought."

"I thought it tasted a bit too amazing," said Lucy with a sigh. "And . . . it turns out to be hers. Perfect."

"Jane, I'm so sorry," said Pete. "If this is yours—"

"Oh, he's *so* sorry, everybody. Course you are. Pull the other one!"

"We had no idea. Lucy said as soon as she took a sip: this tastes a bit too good even for a hundred-and-fifty-quid bottle."

"A hundred and fifty? Not even close." Jane looked as if she could murder him.

"If there's been a mix-up, I'll happily buy you a new bottle," said Pete.

"You can afford to do that, can you? I doubt it."

"If it was one of our kitchen people who's responsible for the mix-up, then we'll buy the replacement bottle," said Anita, who had hurried over to the table as soon as the trouble had started.

"You're missing the point," Jane snapped at her. "Even if a waiter made a mistake, are you seriously asking me to believe these two didn't notice that the bottle that turned up wasn't the one they ordered? The waiter must have repeated the name of the champagne when he delivered it to the table. They always do."

"Jane, I promise you, I'm as far from a champagne buff as it's possible to be, and I had no idea this bottle was yours." As Pete spoke, he was dialing up the soothe factor in his voice. He'd make a good hostage negotiator, Simon decided.

"The waiter came over, he said something French-sounding . . . I'd forgotten the exact name of the bottle I'd ordered by that point . . ." Pete reached for the menu card on the table, but Jane got to it before he did.

She made a big show of inspecting it. "Oh, of course! You'd have to be a real buff, a real expert, to spot the difference between 1995 and 2006."

"I didn't, though," said Pete apologetically. "I honestly,

genuinely didn't. My mind was on other things. I think we've all been a bit . . . preoccupied since your dramatic arrival earlier."

Simon picked up his and Charlie's menu card and had a look. Under the heading "Tonight's Recommended Champagne" was something called Clos Lanson Millesime 2006. Simon passed the card to Charlie. "Also French," she whispered. "And contains the word 'Clos.' Easy mistake to make."

"Give me that!" Jane leaned in and grabbed the bottle, then put it down on the table again almost immediately. "No, actually, first you can pour what's still in your glasses back into it. Go on. I'm waiting. Pour the stolen champagne from your glasses back into the bottle. You first, Lucy."

"No," said Pete firmly. He stepped back and covered Lucy's glass with the flat of his hand. "I'm sorry to have to say it, Jane, but this is getting undignified."

Getting?

"You're not thinking rationally. Come on, you don't want the contents of our glasses, complete with our germs. Wouldn't you rather have a new, unopened bottle?"

Jane didn't answer at first. Slowly, she moved in closer so that her body was pressing against the edge of Lucy and Pete's table. She pulled the bottle towards her, then picked up Pete's champagne glass and poured the pale gold liquid back into it—deliberately messily, by the look of it, making it clear that she didn't actually care about this valuable drink for its own sake. This was all about proving a point.

Hardly any of the champagne landed in the bottle. The rest splashed on the table, spilled down the front of Jane's dress, dripped down the menu card that she was holding in her other hand.

All around this little drama, people were standing up: the American couple were both on their feet and hovering, evidently with great intent in the case of the woman—but to do what? The young black woman with the cropped hair had pushed back her chair and looked ready to spring out of it. The muscly woman with the nose stud and the dyed pink hair was tapping her husband's upper arm repeatedly as if she expected him to take some sort of action. Simon wondered what they all had in mind: taking a run at Jane in unison as soon as someone gave the signal that she'd finally gone too far? Who was in charge of deciding what too far meant?

Simon was intrigued by the sudden clumsiness of Jane's movements. He guessed it was deliberate and that she was right-handed; she'd picked up the menu card, and was still holding it, with her right hand. She'd used her left to pour the champagne, as if to say, "Look how little I care."

"The thing is," she said in a quiet, sharp voice, "I *would* rather have a new, unopened bottle, Pete. Yes, I would. But I'd also rather you didn't drink a single sip more of this bottle because it was never yours to drink in the first place. And I'd like to hear you admit it."

"He already has," said Lucy. "It's funny, I've spent so long wondering if you're an evil monster disguised as a human, but maybe you're just profoundly thick."

Jane staggered back from the table. She started to scream at Lucy, "You will *not* be allowed to make this about me and what I did *years* ago, as if you're an innocent victim! Nuh-uh, sorry. You're not at liberty to do that, not any more. I want to hear you admit, in front of everyone here, that you *knew* you were stealing my champagne. You *knew* how special that particular bottle was to me—"

"Are you still on about the champagne?" Lucy laughed in her face. "Oh, my God. I mean . . . it's just a fucking drink! Who cares?"

"*It wasn't yours! It was ours!*"

There was a loud bang. Simon was up, out of his chair. "What was that?" he asked Charlie.

She pulled him back into his seat. "Calm yourself," she whispered in his ear. "It was the door banging shut. Look: the return of the unluckiest man in the world." She nodded towards the kitchen building. "Husband of the world's biggest cham-pain in the arse. Sorry, that sounded cruder than I meant it to."

Simon turned and saw that she was right: here was the unfortunate Mr. Honeymoon. William, that was his name. When yelling at Lucy outside the resort office earlier, Jane had referred to her husband, Lucy's ex, as William.

His miserable expression was still in place. Given the performance that he'd interrupted when he reemerged onto the terrace, it was hardly surprising that he'd neglected to close the door quietly.

Jane finally noticed his arrival. "Well?" she said to him, shaking as if electricity was coursing through her body. "Are you going to say anything, or just stand there?" She took a few steps towards him.

William's face convulsed. The unhappiness was gone in an instant. His new expression, as his wife continued to approach him, was one of absolute horror. It was as if he'd . . . It was too absurd even to consider it, Simon knew, but it was as if he'd just found out that he was about to die, or something equally shattering. He looked terrified for his life.

What the fuck could it be? Nothing had happened to change anything. Jane had taken some steps in his direction. That was all. Simon was dimly aware of Charlie's finger prodding his arm. He stood up, ready to move quickly if necessary.

William strode towards Jane. Two things happened at once. The champagne flute she was holding in her left hand fell to the ground and smashed. In the same instant, William snatched the menu from her other hand and started to rip it into small pieces.

When he couldn't rip any more, he let the pieces fall to the ground. Then he put his arms around Jane and started to mumble something in her ear. Simon couldn't catch any of it.

A few seconds later, Jane pushed her husband violently away from her with both her hands. "Oh, my God," she said, her voice trembling. "I can't . . . I can't believe it!" She looked as horror-struck as William had a few seconds earlier.

She backed away, across the dining terrace. "Get away from me!" she yelled at William. "Do *not* follow me. Just . . ." She seemed to have run out of words, and was moving as fast as she could, as fast as anyone could in those heels, towards the path that led away from the restaurant area, the same one Simon and Charlie had taken in the opposite direction on their way to dinner.

"Jane, please," William called after her. He was crying. "Jane, I'm sorry, please! Come back."

Too late. She was gone. William stood still for a few seconds. He clutched at the top of his hair with both his hands. Simon couldn't remember ever seeing a man look more desperate. He noticed that Lucy was also crying. Pete had pulled his chair up so that it was next to hers. He'd put his arm around her shoulders.

William seemed to come to a decision. Ignoring Jane's instruction not to follow her, he set off at a brisk pace towards the path. Presumably he was on his way back to their cottage where he expected to find her. No doubt he hoped to be granted the opportunity to beg for her forgiveness.

For what, though? Simon knew something momentous had occurred—something life-changing, maybe even life-destroying. He'd been right here, mere feet away, watching and listening as it happened. That was how he knew he wasn't wrong.

There was only one problem: he didn't have the slightest clue what it was.

9

Wednesday, January 8, 2020

"This is totally safe, right?"

"It's *extremely* safe. Don't worry: in a minute, once the nurses have got you sorted, I'm going to give you all the information you could possibly want and need about exactly how safe it is. You'll feel as if you've researched the subject yourself." Dr. Pete Shabani smiled down at the woman who had asked the question: a thirty-seven-year-old mother of two who was about to have an elective C-section. Mother of three, Pete corrected himself. It didn't matter that this latest one hadn't yet made his or her official entrance into the world. That was why they were all here; it was about to happen.

Pete loved his job most when an elective C-section was on the schedule. He'd been an anesthetist for seven years now, and still found it incredible that babies could be safely removed from wombs and placed in their excited mothers' arms without either mother or baby experiencing any pain or distress. It struck him as a widely underappreciated miracle—and all the better for being one that took place in thousands of hospitals all over the world, every single day.

Spinal block patients didn't always ask about safety, but about half of them did. More than epidural patients, anyway. Pete never minded, or interpreted it as a lack of trust in him. He understood that it seemed profoundly unnatural and risky to allow a substance to be injected into your spinal fluid that would render you temporarily unable to feel any sensation in the lower half of your body. Pete had recited his "If it wasn't safe, I wouldn't be doing it. Let me tell you how safe it is . . ." spiel thousands of times in his career so far, and he saw it as a crucial part of his job. He'd worked with doctors in the past who'd got irritated whenever they were required to switch their focus from a medical procedure to the feelings of a human being. Pete found that attitude unfathomable. He'd always thought it was an amazing perk of his job that he could cure unnecessary anxiety with a few words and a smile.

On this occasion, he was allowed to get all the way through his reassuring presentation of statistics. More often, he was interrupted around halfway through by women saying, "Wonderful, that sounds great!" and insisting that they were quite reassured enough already, thank you. This mother of three—Deborah Holroyd, she was called—waited and listened patiently, expressing her gratitude only once he was finished. Her manner was serious and cautious. In this respect alone, she reminded Pete of Lucy. He said, "This isn't strictly relevant, but . . . it might interest you to know that I was the anesthetist at the birth of my own daughter, Evin."

"Really?" Deborah Holroyd said. "I wouldn't have thought that would be allowed."

"It's . . . complicated. When she was born, she wasn't yet my daughter. She was . . . well, she was someone else's daughter at that point. I told you it was complicated!"

Deborah Holroyd laughed. "Sounds it," she said, and Pete could tell that she was no longer worrying about her own safety or her baby's.

Pete's own mother liked to remind him every time they spoke on the phone that Evin "isn't actually yours, darling." Only once or twice had she put it so bluntly. Mostly she was more subtle about it, finding less explicit ways to remind Pete of the lack of a blood relationship between him and Evin. One of her favorite tactics was to bundle it up in a thick wad of concern, so that if Pete were ever to challenge it, she could make a watertight case for herself as the kind, well-meaning party and him as the troublemaker.

Bernice Shabani was the queen of plausible deniability—all that "just checking you're okay" that she did in the aftermath of Jane Brinkwood's murder: "I can't begin to imagine how worried you and Lucy must be. With Jane gone, well, William might see his situation very differently. What will you do if he decides he wants to reestablish contact with Evin? He might, you know, darling. She's not only his flesh and blood but also, since the murder, all he has left. How will you and Lucy feel if he decides he wants to step back into the father role? I mean, can you prevent that, legally, when he hasn't been convicted of any crime?"

"Don't worry, Mum," Pete had replied with what he hoped was convincing cheeriness. "No point fretting about disasters that haven't happened. If it *does* happen, Lucy and I will do what we always do: make the best plan we can, look after Evin as best we can, and be as happy as we can."

"Hmm" had been Bernice Shabani's distracted reply, before she'd changed the subject. She tended to lose interest quickly once she saw that an emotional manipulation attempt had been unsuccessful.

Pete had himself been dreading the scenario she'd outlined so avidly, but he'd learned at around the age of eleven or twelve that it was a terrible idea to confide in Bernice anything that mattered to you. His father, Ibrahim, seemed to have adopted a similar policy. Though they still lived together, Pete's parents had separate bedrooms and barely spoke to one another these days. When Pete visited them in Cardiff—usually leaving Lucy and Evin safely at home to avoid having to witness Bernice's "Do I really have to pretend this child is my granddaughter?" face—he socialized with each of them in turn and vastly preferred the "Dad" part of his trips to the "Mum" element.

Ibrahim Shabani's natural tendency was to be upbeat and exuberant. "That must be where you get it from," Lucy had told Pete early in their relationship. She'd added, "You're easily the most comforting, reassuring person I've ever known."

"Yeah, well I had the best possible upbringing for that," Pete had said. "An always-cheerful dad who was and is genuinely able to be happy no matter what, and a sinister, doom-predicting mum. It was like: pick between these two opposites. No contest."

"You're the perfect blend of the two" was Lucy's verdict. "Much more heavily weighted towards the optimistic side, but not crazy-to-the-point-of-denying-reality like your dad. You wouldn't continue to share a home with someone who was as vile to you as your mum is to your dad and insist that you were perfectly happy, would you?"

No, Pete wouldn't. He held his father in higher esteem than his mother, but Ibrahim's imperviousness to reality sometimes infuriated him. For how many more years would he doggedly believe that Bernice's unwavering dedication to both causing and experiencing emotional anguish was a temporary state?

Lucy was fond of saying, "Well, I'm delighted they met and embarked upon a disastrous marriage. If they hadn't, there'd have been no you. And after a certain point, no me either. I'm not exaggerating. If you hadn't come along when you did, I wouldn't have survived. I'd have died of a broken heart and rage and betrayal. Don't tell me people can't die of those things." Pete hadn't been planning to. It might be called "heart failure" in the textbooks, but as an experienced medic, Pete knew only too well that unhappiness and loneliness were lethal.

While Deborah Holroyd and the nurses were busy discussing

which outfit or outfits to bring to the operating theater—she seemed to have brought a whole wardrobe full of sleep-suit options—Pete slipped his phone out of his pocket to have a quick look at the notifications. There were dozens: all Lucy. He sighed. He'd had a feeling this would happen. Charlie Zailer had been around to the house this morning and Lucy had no intention of waiting for Pete to get back from work before telling him all about it. Her first message said, "I'll tell you the full story this evening," and her next began: "Key points, though."

Quickly, Pete scrolled through the rest. It was almost impossible to concentrate, and he soon gave up, but not before he saw the message that said, "Charlie Z's convinced William killed Jane. Simon W equally convinced that he didn't."

"Dr. Shabani?"

Pete turned around. One of the nurses was holding up two sleep-suits: one white, covered in bright green caterpillars and bright red strawberries; the other black leopard print against an orange background. "What's your vote for baby's first sleep-suit?"

"Definitely the caterpillars and strawberries," Pete said. "Irresistible."

"Outvoted, doctor!" The nurses giggled. "Three to one!"

Leopard print, for a newborn baby? Awful idea. Pete smiled and said, "Well, you're the experts!" One of his talents—another reason to be grateful to his mother—was his knack of saying nothing negative, ever, that did not absolutely need to be said. Most people he'd known in his life so far seemed to lack that skill.

Pete had been practicing it a lot since Tevendon last July, and it had paid off. Lucy had promised him before Christmas that she was going to draw a line and move on, and for a few blissful weeks, the subject of William and Jane, and Jane's murder, had barely cropped up at all. Now, though, thanks to William's unexpected visit on Saturday, Lucy was as preoccupied with the past as she'd ever been.

Pete was finding it hard to bear. He felt as if he'd been pushed off the summit of a mountain that he'd expended almost super-human levels of effort in order to reach, and was now rolling painfully down its jagged slopes, headed for suffocation in the mud at the bottom.

Why couldn't William have stayed away? Wouldn't that have been kinder to them all? Knowing who killed Jane couldn't bring her back, after all. Pete had never understood the relent-less need, so often expressed by the protagonists of TV shows and movies as well as by real people, to know the whole truth no matter what. Obviously one needed to be able to trust loved ones and to know a great deal of the truth most of the time or else life would be impossible, but all of the truth all the time struck Pete as being a strange thing to hanker after. Yet, since William's visit, Lucy was full of a new, frenzied craving to know everything. She'd spent most of Sunday trying to work out what William's visit had meant, whether his sudden decision to ask questions about her possible guilt might have been an ingenious ruse designed to trick her into believing he couldn't have killed Jane himself.

Pete hadn't dared say, "You're not planning to do anything rash, are you?" because, in all honesty, the likelihood that he'd get an answer that was some version of "yes" had seemed very high and, coward that he was, he'd wanted to pretend that the whole Tevendon nightmare wasn't about to get stirred up again and that he'd finally succeeded in liberating his life and his family from William Gleave's stifling grip—a grip that William, infuriatingly, didn't care about having or even know that he had, in all probability. That somehow made it worse.

Pete sighed. Who was he kidding? There was no more rolling

down the slopes of the mountain. He was already at the bottom, flailing in the mud.

Quickly, he clarified to himself that the situation was the mud in this metaphor, not Lucy. Lucy was amazing and beautiful, clever and loyal—she was every possible brilliant thing. Pete needed to trust her more. She was passionate, yes, but not reckless. And her need to know who'd killed Jane was understandable, except . . .

Did she really not know? How was that possible? To Pete it was obvious who must have done it, and if it was obvious to him then, whichever way he looked at it, it must surely be obvious to Lucy as well. And yet it wasn't. Her puzzled ignorance was entirely genuine—of that Pete had no doubt.

There was no question of him saying anything to the police, since he might be mistaken. Lucy would certainly tell him in no uncertain terms that he was. She'd explain that the person he suspected couldn't possibly have done it, that they'd definitely been elsewhere at the time, that she'd *seen* them herself. Still, it was hard—almost impossible—to disregard the firsthand evidence of one's own eyes: what you see, what you don't see; what's there and what isn't there.

Jane's killer had to be the person Pete thought it was, no matter what Lucy believed. So why did he feel absolutely no inclination to contact DC Waterhouse and tell him? Did he, deep down, believe Jane had deserved what she'd got?

No, it wasn't as simple as that. It was true that he'd never met as disgraceful and unethical a person as Jane, but her depravity did not excuse her murder. All the same . . . he was in no doubt that the world was a better place without her, and so he'd decided to believe, also, that Lucy's eyes were as functional and trustworthy as his own. And if the police were somehow wrong about the evidence—which was possible, Pete kept trying to convince himself—then the person he suspected might well be as innocent as he was.

"You know what? I've changed my mind," said Deborah Holroyd. "Dr. Shabani's convinced me. Let's go with the caterpillars." A look passed between the two nurses, who evidently had concerns about whether a proper democratic process had been followed.

"Right, then." Pete grinned. He needed to drag his thoughts away from unsolved murders and back to the safe delivery of babies. *No more looking at your phone at work—and this time, stick to it.* "Caterpillars it is! Let's get this baby-delivery show on the road, shall we?"

His phone buzzed in his pocket.

Not now. It can wait. Let it wait.

Unimpressed by his own lack of resolve, Pete pulled his phone out of his pocket. As he'd suspected, the new message was from Lucy: "I've had the most brilliant idea that might solve everything," it said.

As he prepared to give Deborah Holroyd her spinal block, Pete did his best to ignore the churning sensation in his stomach and reminded himself that, all other things being equal, the word brilliant was a good sign and nothing to worry about.

10

Tuesday, July 2, 2019

"Why did she turn on him like that?"

"Simon, I've no idea," said Charlie. "Just like I had no idea last time you asked me, three seconds ago. Or the time before."

Had Jane expected William to hurry over and start screaming at Lucy and Pete alongside her? Perhaps his failure to do so constituted disloyalty in her eyes.

Were all the couples at all the tables on the terrace having their own version of this conversation? Simon didn't see how anyone could be talking about anything else in the circumstances. The atmosphere—he couldn't tell if it was real and tangible in the air or only in his mind—was heavy with a combination of relief and a new guardedness. Yes, the scene they'd all witnessed had been horrible, but now that William and Jane had gone, there was a possibility of the rest of the night being calm and uneventful. Yet somehow the drama felt very much still in progress. Simon knew it was a symptom of trauma: waiting for the next bad thing to happen.

"She wasn't angry with him at first," he said to Charlie. "And he wasn't scared. When he first came out and she started walking towards him, there was no indication she was even upset with him. Upset in general, yes, but not especially with him. I mean, am I wrong? Was she?"

"Not as far as I could tell, no. She was angry with Lucy and Pete."

"Right. And then nothing happened, nothing at all, except she got a bit closer to him . . . and suddenly he was petrified. And then he tore up the menu. Why, for fuck's sake?"

"Asked and answered: don't know."

Simon closed his eyes and tried to reconstruct the scene.

"He wasn't looking at her face, I did notice that," said Charlie. "He was looking at her . . . waist, or maybe her hands. Or more likely the menu, since he grabbed it and tore it up. So . . . doesn't it seem as if the tearing up of the menu must be what made Jane so angry with him?"

"No, it can't have been that. He put his arms round her—she let him do that. And he whispered something to her. The whispering went on for a good few seconds. Did you overhear any of it, by any chance?"

Charlie shook her head.

"Me neither, but whatever he whispered, that was what made her push him away violently—whatever he said to her, not the ripping up of the menu. There's nothing to say she gave a toss about the menu one way or another. Was the one William tore up any different to any of the others?"

"How do you know his name's William?" Charlie asked.

"I heard her say it."

"When?"

"Earlier."

Charlie looked suspicious for a few seconds. Then she said, "Yeah, the menu Jane was holding was different from the others. It was soaked in spilled million-dollar champagne." She rolled her eyes. "Look, instead of pointlessly speculating, we should go after them." She gestured towards the path. "What happened was public enough that we'd be totally justified in checking everything's okay."

"Hold up." Simon was looking over Charlie's shoulder. Anita Khattou was on her way over. When she reached their table she said, "I'm so sorry to disturb you, and even sorrier about everything that's happened here tonight, but . . ." She started to cry, wiping the tears away quickly as they fell. "I don't know what to do. And now I'm crying and looking like I'm totally out of control, and it's true." She had lowered her voice, presumably so that no one else would overhear. "Nothing like this has ever happened before at Tevendon. *Ever*. I don't want to bother Greg and Rebecca with it while they're on holiday, let alone Lord Brinkwood, but . . . I just want to run away. I can't let anything like this happen again, but it's so hard. Jane's Lord Brinkwood's daughter. What can I do? And now I'm dumping all this on you two and you're supposed to be guests."

"We actually *are* guests," said Charlie. "Checked in under our real names and everything, no matter what Jane thinks."

"Let me get you a chair." Simon walked over to the raised platform and pulled down the one Jane had been sitting on.

"Thank you," said Anita. "I'm so glad you're both here. I can't apologize enough, for everything."

"You already have," Simon told her, knowing it probably wouldn't do any good. Over-apologizers never considered, in their floods of contrition, that it was draining for their apologizees to have to say "It's fine," "Don't worry about it," "It's nothing," "You're forgiven" for three hours straight.

Two waiters were approaching. "Shall we bring out the main courses?" one of them asked Anita. She looked lost for a second or two before finally nodding and saying, "Yes. Serve the main courses. Not the high table in the middle, they've gone, but all the other tables can have their mains. And then you can go home. I'll take care of the rest." The waiter asked if she was sure and she told him she was.

Once he'd gone, she said, "Should I go to 1 and check if Jane's okay? And poor William—he seemed so devastated. Do you understand what happened? I mean ... something obviously went wrong between them, but ..."

"I don't think anyone knows what it was," said Charlie. "No, you stay here. Simon and I were going to check on Jane and William, weren't we, Simon?"

He nodded. "Hopefully they'll have put the kettle on and be well on the way to sorting things out by the time we get there." *Yeah, right.* Simon didn't believe it for a minute, but it was the sort of comment that made everyone feel better, and Charlie was always telling him he ought to make more of those.

Seeing that Anita was keen to do something useful, he said, "Why don't you go and check Lucy's okay? It can't be pleasant to go through what she's just experienced."

"I will." Anita nodded but didn't move. "I'm almost too ashamed. I mean, I stood there and let another guest lay into her."

"Not just any old guest," said Simon. "The one who's just married her ex-husband."

"Yes, exactly," Anita stifled an anguished noise. "How negligent does that make me? I *love* Lucy too. We're actually ... I mean, she probably hates me now, though."

Simon noticed that Charlie was giving him The Look—the one that signaled a time-consuming argument in the near future. "Sorry, I didn't mean to make you feel worse," he said to Anita, hoping it would make The Look go away. It didn't.

"It's okay," said Anita. "You're right. I just ... part of me can't believe the way Jane's been this week so far. In the past she's been such a good friend to me, or I thought she was. She and her dad, Lord Brinkwood, rescued me. Without them, I probably wouldn't even be here now. Which in no way excuses what she did tonight."

Simon wondered if, in Anita's mind, the categories of counselor/ therapist and police detective had become confused. Why was she talking in this way to him and Charlie? It was hard to gauge how old she was. She dressed like a smart, professional middle-aged woman, but her face was unlined and youthful and her manner was often naive and unworldly. She could have been anywhere between thirty and forty-five, Simon thought.

"I can see that it'd be hard to think too badly of someone who'd rescued you," said Charlie.

"But I *do*." Anita sounded as if she was trying to convince herself. "What she and William did to Lucy . . . And this week she's attacked me constantly and treated me as if I'm her enemy."

"She's attacked you?" said Simon.

"Not physically, but yes." Anita lowered her voice again. Simon and Charlie had to lean in to hear her. "Ever since the first 'Beware' note arrived. Jane insisted it was Lucy and started demanding I throw her and Pete out. When I explained that I couldn't because they were guests and I *knew* Lucy hadn't done anything wrong, Jane just turned. It was like she thought I'd taken Lucy's side against her. Since then she's been relentlessly vile to me. But maybe she's right. Maybe I didn't take the notes seriously enough. You told me this afternoon to phone the police—other police, not you—but I haven't. I didn't. Maybe if I had, Jane would have seen that I was taking it seriously and not been so aggressive tonight."

"You know what?" said Charlie. "You could just let yourself totally off the hook. How about you think like this: it's been a horrendously difficult situation and you've managed it as well as you could. Give Lucy and Pete a new bottle of posh champagne on the house and move on."

"That's a good idea." Anita looked slightly mollified.

"Right. Come on," Simon said to Charlie.

Once they'd set off on the path and were far enough away from the restaurant terrace, Charlie grabbed Simon's arm. "Well?" she said.

"What?"

"'*What?*' Don't give me 'What?' William, Psycho-Jane's husband, used to be married to Lucy?"

"Yeah."

"How the fuck did you know that?"

Simon told her about the confrontation outside the resort office earlier in the day.

"And you didn't think to mention it to me?"

"Not at the time, no. Why would I?"

"Because you knew I'd be interested? One guest who's here on her honeymoon with the former husband of another guest? Simon, that's the best holiday gossip *ever*. Don't look like that! Holiday gossip is a thing."

"I wish it wasn't," he said. "I'd rather be eating my dinner, even in public, than checking the honeymooners aren't beating the crap out of each other."

"Obviously you're totally fine with us keeping things from each other, then," Charlie said ominously. "Great. Handy to know."

"Are you keeping something from me?"

"Yep. And now you can't complain about it," she said.

She started walking again. When they arrived at Heaversedge House, or "1" as Anita called it, Simon rang the doorbell.

Nothing. No response.

"What if they didn't come back here?" said Charlie.

"Where else would they go?"

"I don't know. The pool? Walk in the woods, by Tevendon Mere? That'd be an atmospheric place to have a big bust-up."

"No one walks in the woods wearing the shoes Jane was wearing," said Simon.

"She could have come back and got changed. I'm going to have a look round the back of the house. Ring the bell again."

Simon did so. He left his finger on it for longer this time. Again, there was no response. He was about to look through the window to the right of the front door when he heard Charlie call his name in a way that made him run.

The house's back door was standing wide open. He walked in. Immediately, he smelled the blood. Charlie was standing in the kitchen, looking through another open door into a lounge. Simon saw what she was looking at: Jane Brinkwood, lying on her front, one arm outstretched. There was a pool of blood around her body. And something in front of it, something Simon couldn't quite see because her head was blocking it . . .

Slowly, he entered the room. Charlie followed, calling for backup at the same time. "Ambulance?" she said to Simon.

"Yeah," he said, though he could see it was too late—Jane was dead. A few more steps into the room and he noticed that there was an alcove off to the right: one that contained the still-breathing body of William. There was a small writing desk in the alcove. He was sitting in a wooden chair with a curved, slatted back and fabric padded arms, facing the wall. His tweed jacket was lying on the floor by the side of the desk. Simon noticed the splashes of blood on the wooden slats and, between them, on the back of William's striped shirt. There were blood splashes on the carpet too.

The object Simon had spotted on the floor, the one that lay immediately in front of Jane's dead face and between her body and William, was a large carving knife. It looked spotlessly clean.

"William?" said Simon, walking around to the side of the desk so that he could see his face.

William didn't move. He said nothing.

"Are you all right? William?"

"Gleave," said William.

"Sorry?"

"G-L-E-A-V-E. That's my last name."

"Are you all right?" Simon asked him.

"No."

"Right." He seemed physically unharmed. "I meant, are you hurt, physically?"

"No." His face was completely blank. "Is Jane all right?" he asked after a few seconds.

Simon and Charlie exchanged a look.

"Where do you think Jane is?" Simon asked him.

"Here in the house with me," said William. He hadn't moved his head at all since Simon and Charlie had arrived.

"Whereabouts in the house?" asked Charlie.

"I . . . I don't know."

"Is she here in this room with us, do you think?"

"I don't know." Still, he didn't turn.

"Who else is in the house, apart from you, me, Jane, and DC Waterhouse?" said Charlie.

"No one." His voice trembled.

"Has anyone else been in the house with you and Jane, before we got here?" said Simon.

"I don't know," he half whispered.

"Did you hear or see anything?" said Charlie.

Finally, he moved. His head turned slightly, not towards Jane's body—in the opposite direction, towards Charlie. "No. I . . . maybe. I wasn't really . . ."

"When did you last see Jane?" asked Simon.

"Here, in the house. I don't remember when."

"William, is there a reason why you looked at Sergeant Zailer when you addressed her but you won't look at me now?"

"I don't know."

"Is it because you know I'm standing near to where something else is, something you don't want to look at?"

"No." He stared straight ahead, at the wall. "Why are you asking me these questions? Where's Jane? Has something happened?"

11

Wednesday, January 8, 2020

DC Colin Sellers was doing his best, but where the fuck were Gibbs, Charlie and Sam? Six o'clock in The Brown Cow meant six o'clock in The Brown Cow. Last time Sellers checked it was nearly half past. If they were on their way, fine, but they were normally reliable, all three of them. So far no one had texted anything about being held up.

Waterhouse was oblivious, as usual. He forgot about things like where he was and what time it was once he got going on one of his rants. There was a good chance, Sellers thought, that he wasn't even aware he was talking to only one person instead of the four he'd been promised. He was too busy proclaiming about his latest breakthrough (which might or might not turn out to be one; so far, it wasn't looking promising) while staring aggressively across the table as if challenging Sellers to disagree.

"I don't know why it took me so long, or why none of the rest of you saw it either, but I think I'm right this time," he said.

This meant nothing. Waterhouse always thought he was right.

"The note that was sent to Jane Brinkwood on the day she died—what did it say?"

" 'Beware of the couple at the table nearest to yours.' "

"Right," said Waterhouse. "But *did it* say that?"

"Yeah. It did." Sellers wondered how soon he could ask permission to go to the bar and get another pint in. Technically he didn't need to ask—he was a free agent—but . . . no, he couldn't. Not yet. He'd only be ordered by Waterhouse, who had an untouched pint of Coke in front of him, to sit his arse down and listen. Better make the dregs of this pint last, then.

The pub was filling up. Soon the bar would be unreachable, obscured by a sea of bodies.

"*Eventually* the note said that," Waterhouse conceded. "But not at first."

"Oh, you mean the 'yours' was crossed out?"

"No, the 'yours' had been added."

"You know what I mean." Sellers allowed his impatience to show on his face. "Ah, here they are! Gibbs!" He waved across the room, a gesture of emergency. "Get us a pint in, will you?" he mouthed. Gibbs nodded.

" 'Yours' wasn't crossed out, was it?" Waterhouse ignored the arrival of Sam Kombothekra and Charlie at their table. Keeping his eyes on Sellers, he said, "Something else had been crossed out—whatever was there before 'yours.' The 'yours' was added later. That's the opposite of what you said."

"It's what I meant."

"Are you sure?" Waterhouse asked. "Think about it. Really think. This is important."

Sellers looked at Charlie, who had taken the chair beside his. "No need to fill us in," she muttered. "I live with him, so . . . yeah. I can easily imagine how the conversation has come to this."

"How come you're so late?" Sellers asked her.

"We were intercepted," said Sam Kombothekra wearily.

"Snowman?"

"Yeah," said Charlie. "Short version? He guessed we were

coming here to meet Simon and hear his new Jane Brinkwood theory, and he wasn't in favor of the plan."

"Great," said Waterhouse. "A DI who actively obstructs his team from solving a murder case."

"I don't think he sees solving as the main activity," said Charlie. "More like obsessively indulging to no noticeable effect. Don't look at me like that: I'm conveying his views, not mine."

"As you can see, we paid no attention to him, because here we are," said Sam. "It was quite funny—eventually Gibbs just started walking away from him while he was still speaking—"

"Yeah, like someone who doesn't give a fraction of a shit," Charlie chipped in. "Sam and I ran after Gibbs, with Sam turning round every few seconds to call out, 'Sorry, sir, bye, sir.'"

"He was worse than usual." Gibbs had arrived at the table with the tray of drinks. "Like he'd written a speech specially for the occasion."

Charlie laughed as she reached over to take her drink from the tray. "Give me gin. I need it. Oh, gin, how I love you!" She took a long sip. "So, guess what the first thing he said was? 'Sergeant Zailer, Sergeant Kombothekra, DC Gibbs...'—he said our names one by one, as if he was taking the register. 'Tell me, what would you say if someone asked you if you were a conspiracy theorist?' We all told him we'd say we weren't one. Turned out to be the wrong answer. 'The world these days seems to be full of two kinds of people: those accusing others of being conspiracy theorists, and the accused, who deny that they're any such thing. Can nobody think properly any more? In a world where people were sane and rational, it would make no sense either to be or *not* to be a conspiracy theorist.'"

"I'm always going to remember it as his Hamlet moment," said Sam Kombothekra.

"Stupid dick," Gibbs muttered into his pint. It wasn't entirely clear who he was referring to.

Fueled by another gulp of gin, Charlie continued with her impersonation: "'Sensible people, a category in which I would include myself, are conspiracy theorists when there's an undeniable conspiracy staring them in the face, and not when there isn't one. Nobody calls weathermen rain theorists, do they, or sun theorists, as if they're somehow determined to find rain or sun where there isn't any? The simple fact is: people *do* conspire with other people—and they don't like to have it pointed out, which, in my opinion only makes it more obvious what's going on.'"

"Why was he talking about conspiracies?" Waterhouse asked.

"That's what he thinks this is," said Charlie. "Us coming here to meet you and Sellers."

"Which we admitted to," said Sam. "At which point Gibbs asked him if he thinks the world's run by lizards, and Charlie and I didn't laugh or smile or breathe for a few seconds. And then we ran away from him."

"Ran for our lives and didn't stop running till we reached the border." Charlie raised her glass. "Happy ending."

"No doubt we'll pay the price tomorrow," said Sam.

"The Snowman's never going to do anything apart from make our lives a misery in the way he always has," said Gibbs. "He loves us too much, in his fucked-up way."

Charlie muttered something Sellers couldn't hear.

"What was that?" said Gibbs. "I ought to know, did you say? About what?"

"About loving people in a fucked-up way, but forget I mentioned it." She gave Gibbs the benefit of her widest smile. It looked incredibly fake. She had a problem with Gibbs: that much was clear. Had for so long now, Sellers couldn't even remember when he'd first noticed it. Years ago. Four years at least. He had no idea what it was about and had given up trying to find out. Neither of them seemed to want to talk about it, and Waterhouse had looked affronted and walked away the one time Sellers had asked him about it. At least Sam was clueless too; Sellers wasn't the only one in the dark.

"So. Jane Brinkwood, eh?" Charlie said brightly. "As Simon's probably already told you, Lucy Dean summoned me to her house this morning. I mean, she'd describe it as an invitation rather than a summons, but trust me, she didn't make it sound optional."

"I've filled them in," said Waterhouse.

"From what Simon said, it sounds like she was questioning you rather than the other way round," said Sam.

"She's suddenly impatient for answers," Charlie told him. "Popping down to the police station to see Simon, then ringing me less than forty-eight hours later—"

"I'm clearly not working fast enough for her," said Waterhouse.

"To be fair, everyone's waited six months already for an answer that might never arrive," said Sam.

"I'm not waiting for it to arrive," Waterhouse told him. "I'm hunting it down. Lucy Dean has no idea. No one's more impatient than me."

"It's not like we haven't done our best," said Gibbs. "Why's it her chasing, though? William Gleave hasn't pestered us once, and it's his wife that got murdered."

"Do you think it's suspicious, this sudden activity from Lucy?" Sam asked.

"No," said Sellers, who hadn't admitted to anyone how much he hoped Lucy Dean was innocent. Most shameful of all: he was pretty sure he'd rather the case remained unsolved than for it to turn out that Lucy had murdered the woman who had (as she must see it) stolen her husband. Two years ago, Sellers had left his wife, Stacey, to move in with his girlfriend, Sondra. It had felt necessary for his survival when he'd made the move, but Stacey had taken it badly and things had rapidly turned acrimonious. Currently, Sellers's two children were refusing to see or speak to him, which was getting him down. The last thing he needed on top of that was to worry that Stacey might decide to attack Sondra in some way. So far she'd confined her attacks—still only written and verbal, thank God, rather than physical—to Sellers. He knew, of course, that the Jane Brinkwood case had no direct connection to his own situation, but it very much didn't feel that way. If Stacey were to do anything to Sondra, he'd never forgive himself.

"Can we talk about the note sent to Jane Brinkwood on the day she died?" said Waterhouse. "Sellers just told me, before you all turned up, that the word 'yours' was crossed out. Except it wasn't. 'Yours' was there, written above another word or words that had been scribbled over, hard, so that you couldn't see what had been there before. Now, ask yourselves: Why would Sellers say the 'yours' had been crossed out when it hadn't? The *opposite* had happened, right? The word 'yours' had been added."

"I always knew what I meant," said Sellers. "You're making something out of nothing. I was knackered and beer-deprived, that's all."

"*Or* . . . you meant something you didn't know you meant," said Waterhouse. "Maybe you assumed the scribbled-out word was also 'yours,' or a failed attempt at 'yours.'"

Sellers looked at Gibbs, who shook his head as if to say, *I haven't got a clue either.* "No one knows what you're on about, Simon." Charlie yawned.

A failed attempt at 'yours.' In his pre-Sondra days, Sellers would have used that comment as the basis for a crude joke. Not any more. His former self had been a twat in many ways, Sellers could see that now: a liar, a cheat, an entitled sexist pig. Still, there were moments when he missed him and this was one of them.

"Whoever wrote the note crossed something out and wrote

'yours' above it," Waterhouse pressed on. "What was there before? What was crossed out and why?"

"We've no way of knowing," said Sam. "Nothing that came up in the investigation gave us any pointers."

"Maybe Sellers assumed the first 'yours' was messy, or misspelled," said Waterhouse. "The rest of the words in the note were neatly written. Excessively so."

"They were," Sam agreed. "Like a handwriting teacher making a special effort."

"Or someone writing in very neat capital letters, not joined up, to make their writing unrecognizable," said Charlie.

"The first note sent to Jane was also in neat capitals, the one that just said 'Beware,'" Waterhouse went on. "Yet the black scrawl that covered up the word or words beneath the 'yours' in the second note wasn't neat or tidy at all. It was a big scrawly mess. So does the writer care about tidiness only when he's writing words and not when he's deleting them? That seems unlikely."

"I think you're making an issue where there isn't one," Charlie said. "The note-writer's tidy and cares about presentation, all other things being equal. When scribbling over whatever they'd written originally, though, things weren't equal. Hiding their first attempt so no one would ever be able to read it was the priority, not neatness, therefore lots of black scribble was needed."

"Maybe," said Waterhouse. "Either way, and whatever Sellers and the rest of you have been thinking, I realized today that *I've* been half assuming the crossed-out word was 'yours.' It'd make sense: When you sit down to write a threatening poison pen letter, don't you plan what you want to say well in advance? It's not like a thank-you note to your grandma, where you'd be like, 'What shall I say? Shall I say "thank you for the pajamas" or "thank you for the thoughtful gift"?' How many people change their minds about what they want to write in a piece of anonymous hate mail?"

"You're assuming way too much." Gibbs took a sip of his pint. "Hate mail? You don't know the letter-writer wasn't trying to warn Brinkwood. Save her life, even."

Waterhouse looked at Sam. "What do you think? Threat or warning?"

"Threat," said Charlie without hesitation. "That's not how you'd warn anyone you cared about. You'd be like, 'Hey, listen, I need to talk to you about something...' Face-to-face. An anonymous note's obviously going to freak someone out as much as help them."

"We're getting sidetracked," said Waterhouse. "Point is, until today, I'm pretty sure I was taking for granted that the crossing-out was covering an attempt to write 'yours' or 'your table' that for some reason had gone wrong. That changed when Lucy Dean turned up on Monday with a copy of a letter she'd written to William Gleave last September. It wasn't the letter itself, it was her bothering to come all that way to give it to me. It fired me up again. I drew a new map—"

"Oh, God, not more maps." Charlie groaned. "Please not at home, okay? I feel as if I've only just got my lounge wall back."

"Let me show you this." Waterhouse pulled a folded piece of paper out of his pocket. "It's not like all the others. It's not the whole site, just the top corner. Move your drinks." He unfolded the paper and laid it down on the table. It was a drawing of the outdoor dining area at Tevendon, with some of the rest of the site drawn in around it: the L-shaped building that housed the kitchen and dining room, Cottages 4 and 5, the car park, the resort office, some of the gardens, a tree. Inside each circle that represented a table, Waterhouse had written the names of the person or people who had sat at that particular table on the night of Jane Brinkwood's death.

"Careful, mate," said Gibbs. "You'll be giving David Hockney an inferiority complex if you carry on like this."

"Look. This table here, where Lucy Dean and Pete Shabani sat? Nearer to the kitchen than any of the others. Mick and Susan Henry were nearest to the car park. Anita Khattou was sitting alone here"—he pointed—"at the table closer than any of the others to this tree here, next to the entrance to the office building's garden. Caroline and Harriet Moyle-Jones's table was nearer to Cottage Number 4 than any of the others. Polly and Jack McCallion—the indoor restaurant. Me and Charlie—Cottage 5. See what I'm saying?"

Charlie pushed his hand away from the paper. "Move your beefy mitts and let me look."

Sam Kombothekra said, "All right. So each table was closer to something than any of the other tables was to that same thing."

"Exactly," said Waterhouse. "Which made me think: What if what was crossed out, in the note to Jane Brinkwood, was 'the tree,' or 'Cottage 4'? That would have identified which couple were a danger to Jane, wouldn't it?"

"No," said Charlie. "There are so many holes in that theory. First and biggest: everyone sat somewhere different every night. So the note-writer wouldn't have known who'd be nearest to the tree, or the kitchen, or anything. And then . . . What, you're saying they wrote 'Beware of the couple at the table nearest to the kitchen'—not knowing which couple that would be—then changed their mind and decided they wanted to write 'nearest to yours' instead, when all the other tables turned out to be exactly the same distance from Jane Brinkwood's? Makes no sense. Why change from one message that doesn't clarify which couple to a different wording that also doesn't? What's the point?"

"To terrorize Jane, maybe," said Waterhouse. "Scare her,

make her think she's going mad. If that was the aim, 'nearest to yours' works better. Jane arrives for dinner, immediately sees that all the tables are an equal distance from the only one free for her and William . . . What's she going to think?" He looked at Charlie. "What would you think? Remember, even if she'd turned up to find the higher table in the middle already occupied, none of the tables in the outer ring was closer to one particular table either. All the outer circle tables were an equal distance from the one on their left and the one on their right."

"What would I think?" Charlie repeated his question. "I'd think someone hated me and was trying to mess with my head. Whereas if the note said 'Beware of the couple at the table nearest to the parking area,' I'd think, *Huh. Susan and Mick Henry. Okay. Who wants me to beware of them and why?* Hopefully if I had my brain switched on I'd also think, *But how could anyone have known Susan and Mick would sit there?* Which might lead me to the same conclusion in the end: someone's messing with my head."

"I think it's reasonable to assume that the purpose of the note was to torment Jane, since it didn't effectively warn her of anything," said Sam. "There was no nearest table, so . . ." He shrugged.

"The note-writer's target is Jane." Waterhouse stared down at his drawing. "Jane alone. And writing 'nearest to the tree' or 'nearest to the dining room' would have been inviting Jane to suspect *someone* . . . So here's a theory: maybe the plan was for the note-writer to make sure to arrive early and sit at the same table they'd warned about. It might have given them a thrill to think of Jane suspecting them when she couldn't prove anything, and maybe they weren't going to do anything and just wanted to freak her out. But then, immediately after writing the words, they realized there was no guarantee that another couple wouldn't get to that table first, and they didn't want Jane suspecting someone else—that wouldn't have been fair to the third party. So they changed it to 'yours.' Sorted. Jane's having a shit time, probably pretty scared, and no one's specifically implicated."

"That theory's a mess," Charlie told him. "Random, plucked out of nowhere. I don't like it."

"Anita Khattou," said Gibbs.

"What about her?" Sellers asked.

"I reckon she did it."

The rest of them exchanged a puzzled look. "You've never once said that," Sam pointed out.

"Yes, I have. Just now. Anita's the only one at the dinner that night who wasn't part of a couple. If she's the note-writer as well as the killer, she's cast suspicion on every single other person there that night apart from herself, hasn't she, by writing 'Beware of the couple'?"

"Anita's—" Charlie broke off. "I was going to say she seems really nice, but so do plenty of people who aren't, so who knows. Lucy Dean, on the other hand . . ."

"Lucy's all right," said Waterhouse, as Charlie had known he would. Lucy was as intense and obsessive as he was.

"I'm not sure she *is* particularly all right," she said. "I don't dislike her and I don't believe she's a killer, but . . . who would want to scare Jane away from the resort and from her own honeymoon more than the betrayed ex-wife? We can't ignore that." Charlie sighed. "I still think William Gleave did it, by the way. I know I'm not making much sense. But Lucy Dean isn't in good shape mentally, that's for sure. Changing her daughter's name . . . I mean, come on! She had a baby, called her Zoe Amelia Gleave, and then a few months later changed her name to Evin Amelia Shabani-Dean? A person who was on good psychological form wouldn't do that."

"It's like the 'yours' in the note." Sellers tried not to laugh at his own joke. "Crossing it out and replacing it with another 'yours.' Lucy Dean changed her daughter's middle name from Amelia to Amelia."

"Shut up, Sellers," said Charlie.

"Pitiful, mate." Gibbs shook his head.

"I need to read Lucy's letter to William again, more carefully this time," said Charlie.

"Why?" asked Waterhouse.

"I'm not sure, really." She looked as if she was trying to work it out. "The fact that she wrote it months ago, kept it, didn't send it to him, still hasn't, but suddenly thought she needed to make a copy to bring to you . . ." Charlie shook her head. "I've never quite believed in good old straightforward Lucy, the hard-done-by ex-wife."

"What are you hoping to find?" asked Sellers. "A hidden confession, written in invisible ink under the words 'Dear William'?"

"I don't know." Charlie shrugged. "That's a question I'll only be able to answer once I've read the letter again."

September 12, 2019

William,

I've put off writing this letter for a long time. I have no desire to send it to you and I hope I'll never have to.

So why am I bothering? Two reasons:

1.) It's been cluttering up my head from the moment I first thought, "Maybe if I wrote him a letter, got it all down on paper . . ." That was when I realized that there was an "it all"—tons of horrible, angry baggage that I'd been carting around with me. It was eating me up. So often, I said to myself, "Get over it, move on, forget it," but it wasn't working. I was becoming more and more obsessed. I felt bitter the whole time. So I thought, what if I do the opposite of trying to silence my anger? "What if I allow myself to be loudly angry, on paper?" That's when I first pictured myself writing this letter, and just the thought that I could—that I could have this outlet, this release—made me burst into tears of relief. I imagined myself letting all the poison finally flow out of me, but safely. Safe because (hopefully) you will never read this letter, so my harsh words won't harm you. I can rid myself of all the rage without upsetting you. (Please also take this as a warning that I'm not going to hold back. If I'm doing this, I'm going to do it properly.)

It sounds a bit hackneyed to talk about "closure," but, in relation to you, I crave it. I long for the day when I'll know for sure that you will never touch my life again, even in the most minor way. This is where I found myself running into problems. If somehow I could have extracted from you a formal agreement—"We will never see or contact each other again, and if we happen to meet by accident we will pretend we are strangers who have never met"—signed by both of us . . . but no, that wouldn't have worked for me because I wouldn't want to sign anything you'd signed. I don't want to be part of anything that you're part of ever again. And, though I strongly suspect that you're as keen as I am for us to steer clear of one another, I can't guarantee that you'll always feel that way. I can't know with 100 percent certainty that you won't, in ten years' time, think, "You know what? I quite fancy getting in touch with Lucy. Surely by now everything that happened between us will be water under the bridge." Here's the thing: I need to know beyond doubt that our old water will never flow back in the wrong direction. If you contact me in 2029, I don't want my head to fill with thoughts of you, or you and Jane, as I wonder how to respond. Writing this letter is the very last thinking about you that I'm prepared to do in my life, ever, and it's going to be my closure. I'll keep it somewhere safe, only to be produced in an emergency situation—but if I need to, I'll use it. In the future, if you ever try to communicate with me or reenter my life, I will send or give you this letter. And you'll read it and understand that these were my last words for you and thoughts about you, these words from 12 September, 2019.

William, I think you've misunderstood something incredibly impor-tant. If someone were to ask you why you and I haven't been in touch since Tevendon, I think you'd most likely say, "There was too much pain between us—first the divorce, then Jane's murder . . ." You'd give your charming little shrug at that point before carrying on: "We would only have served as unpleasant reminders for one another of all the misery we'd been through."

The thing is (and I don't know whether you've noticed this), friends who go through unpleasant experiences together don't usually avoid each other afterwards. They normally support each other. If I was your friend—and I was, right up to when Jane was killed and for some hours after that too, even though I was your ex-wife as well—why wouldn't I give you all the support I could when you were widowed and apparently devastated? Your wife was murdered, William. On your honeymoon. Didn't you think it was strange that, once the police let us go, you got nothing but silence from me? What kind of good, true friend wouldn't have been all over you in that situation, offering whatever comfort she could? And yet I didn't contact you at all once we'd left Tevendon and gone back to our real lives—which only makes sense if, by the time the police set us free, I no longer thought of you as a friend.

I wonder what you'd say if we were face-to-face and I asked you for your best guess as to why. You might say, "I've always assumed you thought I was guilty of Jane's murder—after all, I'm by far the most likely person to have done it." Though, actually, I don't think you've ever considered that I might believe you killed her, which is infuriating in itself—so, no, that's not how you'd respond. You'd prob-ably mumble something like, "Maybe you were angry with me for suspecting you of killing Jane, even though I apologized for it." And that would drive me mad, for reasons I'll explain.

Yes, you apologized. Over and over again: "I'm so sorry I suspected you, Lucy. I'm sorry I ever believed for a second that you might be capable of . . ." etc.

For a clever person, you're really stupid, William. Of course I'm capable of murder. Everyone is. Well, most people. When there's enough at stake, or they care enough and/or think there's a decent chance they'd get away with it. And of course you suspected me, just as there must have been moments when you suspected everybody else: Polly and Jack, Mick and Susan, Caroline and Harriet, Anita. Even lovely Pete. Even DC Waterhouse and Sergeant Zailer and the mythical stranger-intruder figure we've all imagined. When we don't know, we suspect. When we can't rule anyone out, we doubt everyone. I was luckier than you, and able to eliminate all the people I was in a room with when the murder happened, but you couldn't be sure where anyone was when Jane was stabbed because you weren't with any of us. You were only with her, in the lounge of Number 1, your holiday cottage. And, let's face it, who but me, the ex-wife, had anything even vaguely resembling a decent motive?

So of course you suspected me, and it's not that quite natural and understandable suspicion that turned me from friend to enemy, William. (God, I hope you can understand the subtlety of what I'm about to say, even though you'll probably never read it. You know all about how to solve quadratic equations and find square roots, but will you be able to get your head round this?) Here's what I can't forgive: when you have years-long personal knowledge of someone and you know them to be a nonviolent, ethical person and generally a force for good in the world, then, yes, certain exceptionally horrendous circumstances like the ones we were in might just lead you to suspect them of murder, or at least to ask yourself, "Could it be them?" and from there, maybe, to go even further—to think, "Who else had any kind of motive? No one. Now I'm really, seriously suspicious." I thought all of these things about you, almost straight away. The rest of us were all together. You and Jane were alone in your cottage, and she ended up getting stabbed to death.

Sorry: you, Jane, and The Unknown Murderer were alone together— The Unknown Murderer, that random stranger who must have pushed his or her way through thick woodland, scaled a high wall, landed in Number 1's garden without leaving any footprints in the mud . . .

It's ridiculous. That story is obvious bullshit. Please be in no doubt, William: my suspicion of you was and is huge. But I'm a decent and fair person, so guess what I didn't do? *I didn't accuse you, as if my suspicions were facts that had already been proven true.* You see,

I know that it's inexcusable, utterly morally repugnant, to decide that someone "must have" viciously stabbed to death another human being, or even Jane Brinkwood. (Sorry, I couldn't resist. Allow me this one moment of extreme bitchiness.) It is unacceptable to accuse someone of this when you can't possibly know for sure that they've done it. And in this case, I didn't do it. Oh, but that didn't stop you! You looked me in the eye, in front of DC Waterhouse and Sergeant Zailer, and you said, "Lucy, you and I both know it was you. You killed Jane. You need to stop lying and admit it. Not for my sake—for yours. So that you can sleep at night."

Writing this, I'm feeling it again: the volcano of rage that erupted in my chest when I heard those words. I couldn't speak or move.

DC Waterhouse rather awkwardly pointed out that I couldn't have done it because I'd been with all the others the entire time.

"So that you can sleep at night." No one who says that to someone who's done nothing wrong deserves to get a wink of peaceful sleep for the rest of their life. Can't you see that it is grossly, disgustingly out of order to miss out on that crucial stage in your deliberations where you say to yourself, "Hang on a minute. Yes, I suspect Lucy . . . but what if I'm wrong? How certain can I be that she killed Jane? Did I see her do it? No. Do I have any evidence against her? No. Hm. I really can't be at all certain, can I?"

The next day, you approached me with a sheepish expression on your face and said how sorry you were for *suspecting* me, when to have done so was natural and understandable. You have never, not once, apologized for the only truly unforgivable aspect of your behavior: *accusing me as if you had concrete knowledge of my guilt when you didn't—believing it's okay to treat possibly guilty people as if they're definitely guilty.*

Instead, you could have thought, "I don't know for sure, and meanwhile, I do know Lucy, and my knowledge of her character, formed over many years, tells me that there's at least a chance I might be wrong. Maybe, instead of accusing her, I ought to ask her."

"So that you can sleep at night." You said that to me, William. After all your appalling behavior—leaving me not for some random woman but for Jane Brinkwood, lying over and over again, even once you'd already abandoned me and your own child. Using our daughter as a bargaining chip. I won't go on. Your roll of dishonor is so long, I might run out of paper.

Oh, and then, once you'd apologized for suspecting me, while I was still dumbstruck and too full of fury to splutter out any words in response, you said chirpily, "Still, it's lucky I accused you when I did! If I hadn't, DC Waterhouse might not have explained to me how he knew you were innocent, and I'd have suspected you for longer." Fuck you all the way to hell and back, William, for saying that to me and actually seeming to believe that you were offering me a genuine consolation—something we could both be pleased about.

(In case you care, by the way: writing this is really working for me. The poison and the pain are well and truly flowing onto these pages, which are probably radioactive by now.)

I've just read through what I've written so far and it's never been clearer to me that you are not worth a second more of my time, so I'm going to stop now. I'm going to choose to believe that you've had time to think since we last spoke, and that you are now full of guilt and horror at your behavior towards me. I can only hope that both are strong enough to keep you away from me forever. And I'm so, so tempted to send you this letter so that you can know how terrible you are and suffer the shame you've earned, but I won't, not unless you provoke me. I'll be compassionate, even if I don't currently feel it. So that I can sleep at night, you see. Unlike you, I don't think it's okay to package up vicious words and send them out into the world, like a spite bomb through a letterbox, when you could just as easily not do that. Not ever, really. Not even to someone who has done all the things you've done to me.

Lucy

12

Tuesday, July 2, 2019

Almost the worst thing was that everyone's untouched or in some cases half-eaten dinners were still on the table when Simon and Charlie got back to the restaurant terrace. *Grotesque.* Simon knew he ought to be starving, but even the thought of picking up his fork made him feel nauseous. Everyone else was in the same position: half-finished meals in front of them, no one eating.

Simon half listened as Charlie asked for the names of all those present and wrote them down. Mick and Susan Henry—that was the American older couple. Polly and Jack Something—the pink-haired nose-stud lady and her muscly husband. Caroline and Harriet Something Double-Barreled—the big-age-gap couple. Lucy and her flawless-and-straight-from-the-factory boyfriend Pete with whom she didn't share a surname. And Anita, whose surname sounded as if it would be hard to spell.

Thank God Charlie was able to be more practical-minded than he was. She stood on the raised platform, in front of the abandoned table at which William Gleave and Jane Brinkwood had briefly sat, and explained that she was a guest, yes, but now that something serious had happened, she was acting in her capacity as police sergeant. Yes, serious in a not-good way, and yes, that had been police sirens and an ambulance that the other guests had heard. They had been heading for Tevendon, yes.

Lucy stood up. "Is William all right? Is he . . . hurt?"

"William hasn't been hurt, no. Physically, he's fine," Charlie told her.

"Then . . . is Jane . . . ?"

"Please, sit down," said Charlie firmly. "You'll all be told what's happened as soon as possible, okay? For now, though, let me ask the questions."

Simon wanted to bring his authority to bear and back her up, but he felt strangely frozen. He hated the way he was feeling: as if a filter—a thick sheet of some heavy, invisible, warped substance—had slid between him and the rest of the world. He'd felt this way before, but rarely. It was as if there were two of him: the outward, visible version that needed to be propped up to maintain appearances, and his true self, too scattered to be presented in a public setting.

He knew what this was: a reaction to knowing full well what was real and, at the same time, being absolutely convinced that it couldn't be. That a woman had been murdered? Real. In these precise circumstances? Impossible to believe—as was the fact that now, after everything that had happened in such a relatively short space of time, Simon was back here, at the restaurant, looking at the same food.

It was as if time had gone into reverse. Here he was, sitting in the same chair he'd sat in originally, when his biggest problem had been the prospect of eating dinner in front of strangers. Same chair, same table, surrounded by most of the same people. Same warm, peaceful, still night it had been then, except it wasn't.

Most of the same people . . .

Not William Gleave. He was with Sam Kombothekra and the scene of crime team at Number 1. And his new, dead wife. She was there too.

Charlie was in no doubt that Gleave had killed Jane; Simon

knew that without her needing to say a single word. ("Who else?" he could imagine her asking incredulously. "I mean, he was right there when we walked in, sitting next to her still-warm body. The knife was on the floor just behind his chair. Come on, Simon.")

It was only then, when he imagined Charlie chastising him for his typically contrarian unwillingness to submit, that Simon realized what he himself believed: William Gleave was innocent. He might be disloyal—to his first wife at least, and maybe he would have been eventually to Jane too if he'd had the chance, since that seemed to be the way of these things—but, in Simon's opinion, Gleave was no murderer.

He surveyed the faces at the tables. *Faces.* From the start, faces . . .

Simon frowned to himself. What was the thought he'd just had? Too late: already escaped. He tried to grasp the tail end of it . . . The word "murder" had not been uttered, either by him or by Charlie, and no reference had been made to death either, which was strange, because . . .

Why was it strange? Simon cursed under his breath. Now the idea, whatever it was, had fully slipped away. His brain wasn't working properly. Not his fault. The murder scene he'd just come from hadn't been working properly either. It made no sense: the clean knife on the floor instead of replaced in a drawer, William Gleave's apparent failure to notice that someone had stood behind him and stabbed his wife to death . . .

Simon looked again at the expressions on the faces around him. That was all he had to go on: the word that had felt significant for a fraction of a second. *Faces.* Everyone was looking shaken and frightened. He remembered the fear on William Gleave's face earlier in the evening . . .

"Not a single one of you?" Charlie asked. For a second, Simon imagined he was included in the question. No, she'd been asking about them leaving their tables. She knew Simon had left his; she'd been with him throughout.

"None of us," said Lucy Dean, who seemed willing to act as spokesperson for the group. "From when you and DC Waterhouse left to go and check on William and Jane until you got back: we've all just been sitting here, waiting, talking. Wondering what the hell's going on. And . . . the sooner you can tell us, anything at all, the better."

"Nobody went in there to use the bathroom?" Charlie nodded towards the kitchen building. "No one nipped back to their cottage? Anita, you didn't go to the kitchen to get any more drinks for anyone?"

"No one went anywhere," Lucy said again. "We all stayed right here, where we are now." Several other heads nodded in confirmation of this.

"We tried to have a nice dinner as if nothing had happened," said Muscly Jack, whose last name Simon still couldn't bring to mind. McSomething.

"Frankly, drinking was the last thing we wanted to do at that point," said Harriet Double-Barreled.

"Speak for yourself," said American Susan. "After all that drama and hysterics, are you kidding me? I definitely wanted to drink, and drink I did." She held up her empty glass in one hand and an empty bottle in the other. "See? All gone!"

"But you didn't go in search of more alcohol?" said Charlie.

"No, I didn't," said Susan. She laughed, then shook her head. "We all sat tight and speculated wildly, in our little groups of two, about what had just happened."

"I wasn't in a group of two," said Anita, looking directly at Simon. "I sat here and wondered what the hell was going on— what was taking you so long? I expected you to be back long before you were. Eventually, I thought, *Well, I'd better go and look for them and check myself that everything's okay at 1.*"

"Yeah, I saw you stand up," Caroline Double-Barreled said to Anita. "And then you saw DC Waterhouse and Sergeant Zailer coming back, so you sat down."

"All right," said Charlie. "So you were all within sight of each other from the moment DC Waterhouse and I left this area until we returned to it. Yes?"

Most people either nodded, said yes, or made affirmative noises.

"Listen, Sergeant Zailer, this sounds a hell of a lot like an attempt to establish our alibis," said American Mick. "Which, I'd say, means a crime has been committed. So . . . would you mind telling us what exactly is going on? If we're being asked to account for ourselves, then surely we have a right to know."

"As soon as we're able to tell you, we will," Charlie assured him with a smile.

"I'd say we know already," said Jack. "William is physically unhurt, right? Yet more police are here and an ambulance is here, and, as Mick says, we're being grilled about our where-abouts during a very specific time. So unless I'm missing something, Jane, William's wife, has either been attacked or, worst case, murdered."

Harriet Double-Barreled made a whimpering noise. Caroline, who was not only quite a bit younger but also looked tougher and more robust, reached for her hand. To Simon, the gesture gave the impression of being as much about restraint as comfort.

"If Jane's been hurt in any way, William's the only person who could have done that to her," said Caroline.

"Not necessarily," Lucy said quietly. She turned to face Anita and asked, "Were the main resort gates shut, or locked, while we were having dinner?"

"No. I suppose someone could have driven in . . . though I'm sure I'd have heard a car, and we weren't expecting anyone." Anita looked doubtful. "Someone might have walked in, I suppose, if they parked across the road, in the car park for the mere and the woods."

"And there's CCTV next to the main entrance, isn't there?" said Simon.

"Yes. If anyone did come in, by car or on foot, it'll be recorded."

"Good," said Charlie.

Simon said to Anita, "There's lots of questions we'll need answers to from you: about locks on doors, access to cottages, that kind of thing."

"Of course. I'll help in whatever way I can. God, I can't believe this is happening," she muttered.

"We don't know what's happening," American Susan reminded her.

"I know it's nothing good," Anita said.

"We have questions for everyone," Charlie told the group. "Anita, are there some private rooms Simon and I can use to talk to all the guests, and to you, one by one?"

Lucy Dean said, "Please can I be interviewed first?"

"Why?" asked Charlie.

"Isn't it obvious? Something has clearly happened to Jane— some kind of attack, I'm guessing. Who at Tevendon this week is most likely to want to harm Jane?"

Charlie glanced at Simon, then turned her attention back to Lucy. No one else would have known what the look meant, but Simon had understood: it was Charlie's "Well, well" look, the one she gave him when she thought things were about to get interesting.

"Me, obviously," Lucy announced. "William's a waste of time—he could never see the truth about her. He's like a brain-washed member of the cult of Jane Brinkwood. I don't think it's arrogant of me to assume I'm likely to be the person here with the most to say about her that might prove useful to your investigation, since I actually knew her before we all came here: first as a doula, then a close friend. Then an enemy, a betrayer, then a friend again—"

"What's a dooler?" Simon asked her.

"A woman you hire to help you during pregnancy," said Caroline.

"That's right." Lucy's laugh had a hard edge. "I can't tell you how many times I've looked up the definition since Jane did what she did to me. It gives me a kind of sick satisfaction, I guess, to see how far she strayed from what she was professionally obliged to do and from what her honor and integrity as a professional should have ensured that she did."

Lucy had given this speech before, Simon guessed. It was word perfect, with outraged emphasis in all the right places.

"A doula's job is to provide practical, emotional and psychological support to a pregnant woman," she went on. "Her job is to prioritize the mother's emotional well-being throughout pregnancy, birth, and postnatally. And, though it doesn't explicitly say so on any of the websites, her job is *not* to ensnare and then make off with the pregnant woman's husband and end up married to him."

"Lucy . . ." Pete tried to reach for her hand.

She pushed him away. "No, I want to say this. I want the police to hear me say it, so they know I'm holding nothing back." She stood up and stepped away from the table. "It is *not* part of a doula's job description to sneak out for secret romantic dinners with the soon-to-be-new-mother's husband, at extremely expensive restaurants where he spends hundreds of hard-earned pounds from his joint marital bank account—to which he contributes *next to nothing*, by the way, as a craply paid maths teacher—on cocktails and lobsters and steaks for the doula, which, if his heavily pregnant wife were to have bought them *for herself* at a dinner *she was paying for with her own money*, he would have said, 'Er, shouldn't we consider a cheaper option? No dinner needs to cost more than fifty pounds in total. Some people in the world are starving.' He actually said that to me—more than once."

"I'm one of those people," said Jack, patting his stomach. "My dinner's gone cold and I'm starving."

"The kitchen staff went home ages ago," Anita told him.

"I know," said Jack. "I don't suppose there's a chance of Deliveroo round here either."

"I'm hungry too," said Mick. "I could eat a horse and its wagon."

Suddenly, Simon had it: the idea that had vanished into the ether earlier had crash-landed back in his brain. *Faces and food.* As he'd suspected, his subconscious mind had noticed something significant, and now he knew what it was. Was he totally wrong and making something out of nothing? Or were all these people lying, and planning to carry on doing so?

13

Friday, January 10, 2020

"It's not as simple as that."

Polly McCallion opened her eyes with a gasp. Had she just said that out loud? She'd heard of people talking in their sleep, of course, but she'd never thought it was something she might do. As far as she knew, she'd never done it before.

She groaned, closed her eyes again, and reached out to pat the bed behind her. No Jack, so she couldn't ask him if he'd heard her say anything or not.

In her dream, she'd been talking to Nina Lesser. She'd been explaining that, even if she tried her hardest, it might not be possible to put things right. Jack would have to agree—Polly couldn't possibly think about even trying unless he was fully on board—and Adler Communications would have to do an embarrassing U-turn, which they might not agree to, especially when they heard the true story of what Nina had done. If it were to come to that, Polly would very much hope that they *wouldn't* be willing to rehire Nina.

"Ja-aack!" Polly called out hopefully. If she was in luck, he'd still be downstairs and not yet on his way to the office.

No answer.

She rolled onto her back and opened her eyes again. On Jack's side, the bedding was thrown back as it always was: as if he'd leapt out of bed in a great big whoosh and not looked back. Light was streaming in around the curtains. It was after 9 a.m., Polly guessed. A quick look at her phone confirmed it: 9:26. Why did her stomach feel so hollow? Normally she didn't start to feel the first pangs of hunger until around midday.

She sighed, hoping that an extra cup of coffee would make a difference. Otherwise this morning was going to be a slog. "Nothing wrong with that," she muttered to herself. "I have chosen this slog." Her current eating window was 2 p.m. to 8 p.m., and she wasn't about to break her promise to herself. The rule was that she was only allowed to create a new eating window once a month, on the first day of the month.

She smiled. Just thinking about the rule and how meticulously she'd obeyed it made her buzz with pride. "I'm someone who honors my commitments—to myself most of all," she said out loud, just as she taught her students to do, and was immediately aware of a dragging sensation in her stomach. This wasn't hunger; it felt more like guilt.

The word "honor" had brought to mind a face Polly tried not to picture if she could help it: Jane Brinkwood. If ever there was anyone who was a complete stranger to the concept . . . even Nina Lesser was nowhere near Jane Brinkwood's league when it came to appalling behavior.

And what about you? What about what you did to Nina? And to Jane, for that matter. If it weren't for the game that you went along with so enthusiastically, might Jane still be alive? Would she have been quite so incandescent with rage that night? And if she'd been calmer, would she have stormed off like she did? Because if she hadn't done that, if she'd only stayed at dinner with everyone else . . .

It was pointless to think that way, Polly knew, and impossible to know the answer to questions about how the past might have been different if this or if that. The trajectory of cause and effect wasn't a single, clear, straight line in any case.

"It wasn't *my* game," Polly muttered to herself as she pulled on gray jogging pants and a blue and green T-shirt. She hadn't proposed it as a plan or been the first to take it seriously. Quite the opposite, in fact: she'd needed a lot of persuasion. So why, six months later, couldn't she put it all behind her? Was it because the killer of Jane Brinkwood still hadn't been caught and perhaps never would be? Or was it guilt about Nina? It was too easy, sometimes, to get the two situations mixed up, so that anger and guilt from one spilled over into Polly's thoughts about the other until she couldn't get her bearings at all.

She was sick of the running commentary that was constantly playing inside her head. It was going to end, she decided. Today. She needed to do a proper guilt and blame audit: write it all down, get clear about what was her fault, what wasn't, and what she could do to make things right, so that she could feel better once and for all. Then she would finally be able to move on instead of having to make a new effort every day to peel back the fingers of anxiety that, too often, held her mind in their grip.

Grabbing a red scrunchie, Polly put her hair up and out of the way, and drew back the bedroom curtains. Jack's car was still there, parked across the street next to hers. That was annoying. If she'd known he was still home, Polly would have texted him the word "Coffee" and he'd have brought her up a cup. Unless he'd cycled to work today. Come to think of it, hadn't he said last night that he was planning to do that? Anyway, it didn't matter. Polly was up and dressed now; it was just that persuading herself to get this far was always so much easier if she had the first cup brought to her in bed.

Ever since the early days of their relationship, Jack had teased Polly about her belief that what Jack called "getting up in the morning like a normal, healthy person" was one of life's major traumas. Reciprocally, Polly had teased him about his inability to keep his eyes open after 11 p.m., no matter what was happening. Jack could fall asleep in the middle of a vigorous argument if it was past his bedtime.

Polly moved away from the window, having seen quite enough of their annoying street, with its unreasonable lack of off-street parking. She'd made some headway in her attempt to persuade Jack they should move, but nowhere near enough. Where they lived was, in most respects, lovely, but Polly would have preferred a detached house with a garage and a little bit of land, and, now that her business was taking off, she was sure they could afford it.

Some days she was content to tell herself that where they lived was fine for now, but today wasn't one of those days. It was because she'd dreamed about Nina, and then started thinking about Jane: the worst possible start to a day.

Still, any day that wasn't over could still be saved. Reset. That was what Polly taught, and it was a point of honor for her to ensure that she practiced all the tools and concepts that she preached in her program.

She headed down to the kitchen and grimaced when she saw the state Jack had left it in. He appeared, with his bike helmet slung over his arm, just as she was slotting the last dirty fork into the dishwasher. "Don't do that," he said in a tone of great regret, as if he'd missed out on a trip to the best funfair ever. "I was going to do it."

"Uh-huh," said Polly with a grin.

"You don't trust me, I can tell."

"Oh, you can tell? How can you tell?" She walked over and kissed him.

"It's the subtle clues you give off," he whispered in a mock-sexy voice into her ear. "Like all the times you say, 'Jack, you lazy fucker—why don't you ever do any housework?' Have you seen my speaker?" He disentangled himself. "Aha—there it is!"

He grabbed a black blob-shaped thing that Polly hadn't seen before. Wasn't his speaker a tall, green, cylindrical object? And not too long ago it had been a square red thing. Why couldn't he use cheap earphones that, every now and then, decided to stop sending your music to one ear for no apparent reason? If it was good enough for Polly . . .

"Right, I'm off to work," he said. "See you at about seven. Shall I bring back a Thai takeaway?"

"Yeah, perfect. Remember, *rice* noodles for me. Vitally important." Seeing his mouth open, she raised a finger and said, "Do *not* tell me that a noodle is a—"

"—noodle is a noodle," he raced to finish the sentence before Polly could.

"I'll hit you, I swear."

"Love you, hon. See you later."

Don't go. Don't leave me alone with the inside of my head.
"Jack?"

"What?" He leaned back into the kitchen. "If this is about rice noodles—"

"If you had to choose—"

"I'd choose any old noodle. I'm not scared of leptin, me!" he teased her. "Poll, I've really gotta go."

"I know. Sorry."

"What were you going to say? If I had to choose . . . what?"

"Let's say you could turn back time—"

"That would be useful today."

"—or a genie popped out of a lamp and gave you a choice: either you could bring Jane Brinkwood back to life—like, make it so that her death never happened—or she's still dead, still murdered, but Nina has her old job back, which would you choose?"

Jack frowned. "Well, obviously, I'd choose Jane not dead," he said.

"Why?"

"Same reason you would."

Polly looked away.

"You *wouldn't*? Are you serious? Yes, Jane Brinkwood was a nasty piece of work, but no one deserves to get killed like that. And, like . . ." He shrugged. "If we'd wanted Nina Lesser to keep her job, she'd still be in it. She lost her job because of us—and rightly so."

"True." Polly wished she could feel as certain as Jack sounded. "I guess that's my issue, though. At least someone else killed Jane. Not either of us. We weren't the ones who stuck a knife into her, whatever else we may have done. So if I had to undo one of the two, I might opt to undo the bad thing that I personally was responsible for. Then I wouldn't have to feel as guilty." *Which proves how utterly selfish human beings are: your own easy conscience is worth more to you than someone else's life. Or maybe it's just me.* "Actually, I feel guilty for Jane's death too. Don't you?"

Jack snorted. "Not even remotely."

"But we—"

"No, Poll. Like you said: we might not behave brilliantly every second of our lives, but we didn't murder anyone, and that counts for a lot. There's a red line." He shook his head. "With murder on one side of it and us on the other. I tell you what . . ." He pulled his house key out of his pocket. "If that genie ever pays me a visit, I'm definitely going to choose Jane not getting murdered, for one entirely selfish reason: the police still don't know who did it. That means we must still be suspects, at least to an extent."

Polly shut her eyes tightly. *For fuck's sake, why did he have to say that? Another lump of dread to add to the pile.* "That's not true. They know neither of us could have done it." But let's face it, you heard all the time about people who were sent to prison for twenty-five years for crimes they didn't commit. And Polly, so far, had never worried about this in relation to Jane's death, but she probably would from now on. She could almost feel the nightmare-scheduling software in her brain book a slot for a horrific dream tonight, all about rotting in jail and being separated from Jack forever.

He'd blown her a kiss and left the room. Polly heard the front door, then "Oh! Sorry, mate!" and something about signing. The postman. Something about a parcel for the neighbors who weren't in. Would Jack mind? "Not at all, mate. My pleasure. I'll drop it round later, when I'm home from work." Cheery chatter drifted towards Polly as she filled the kettle: the weather, Jack's bike, were those new wheels? Yes, they were. Ah, the postman had thought so. He'd been right.

This was something Polly had never understood about her husband. He seemed positively to relish small talk with casual acquaintances and even complete strangers. Lighthearted banter was his favorite mode of communication. He hated what he called "anything deep." Knowing this, Polly would probably never raise the choice-offered-by-a-genie conversation again, though she'd have liked to ask Jack if he really believed that Jane hadn't deserved what she'd got. What that woman had done to Lucy Dean . . .

Polly shuddered. She'd tried several times since last July to imagine her own equivalent: doing to one of her students what Jane Brinkwood had done to Lucy. Unthinkable. She knew that one could never say never—or so they said, so said people like Jack who preferred never to think too deeply about anything— but Polly happened to believe that sometimes one could say never, and this was such an instance. How could Jane have had such a complete lack of professional integrity?

The front door slammed suddenly. Polly assumed it was Jack leaving, but then she heard him in the hall. "What the *fuck*?"

"Jack?" Had the postman gone? Polly realized she hadn't heard his voice in a while.

She put down her coffee and went to investigate.

"Look at this," he snapped, waving what looked like a small card and a letter in her direction. "She sent it Special Delivery, for fuck's sake!"

"Who did? What is it?" Polly asked.

"Here, read it."

She took the card and letter from him. Looking at the card first, she read the first few words aloud: "Dear Jack, this is not an accusation . . ."

"It is, though, or else she wouldn't have sent it," said Jack angrily. "Of course it's a fucking accusation!"

"Shush, let me read," said Polly, her heart pounding. She was halfway through the letter when Jack, looking at another envelope from the pile the postman had brought, said, "Oh, my God. She's sent one to you too."

"You can relax. I just want to try it out on you," said Caroline Moyle-Jones. "It's entertainment, not an ordeal. I mean, I hope it's entertaining."

Harriet, her wife, nodded. She looked nervous. She sat forward in her chair across the room, with the palms of her hands planted on her knees as if to keep her firmly anchored in place.

"Harri, I'm not doing this if you're going to get stressed about it. There's no point."

They were in Caroline's garden-room office at the back of the kitchen. Harriet was fidgety, and kept looking out towards the garden as if she was searching it for something.

"Well, I know, but . . . you want feedback, don't you?" She

allowed her eyes to land on Caroline, finally. "I need to pay attention in order to—"

"No, I don't want *feedback*. That sounds as stodgy as a customer services email from the dullest company in the world. I want you to listen, and then tell me what you think. What's wrong with you today?"

"Nothing!" Harriet's trying-to-sound-jolly voice was proof as far as Caroline was concerned. So was the outfit: smart black trousers, peach-colored cashmere cowl-neck, the earrings. Harriet didn't normally dress up to give feedback—ugh, there was that awful word again—and Caroline would have preferred it if she hadn't. The symbolism of being the only one in your pajamas at 2 p.m. was annoying, especially when you'd been up and working since six.

Was she planning to go out somewhere later? Caroline had asked and the reply had been a slightly shrill "No, not at all."

Something was definitely up with her. And Caroline could see that Harriet had no intention of telling her what it was.

"I'm not sure I'm the best judge, that's all," Harriet said. "I don't think I've got much of a sense of humor."

You used to have one. Before Tevendon.

"You'd be better off trying out your work on other comedy sketch-writers."

Comedians, Caroline corrected her silently. "Comedy sketch-writers" made it sound like an adorable hobby.

"And you always hate it so much if I make the slightest suggestion for improvement. You know you do. You like to think you take criticism in your stride, but it always upsets you—and then you pretend not to be upset."

"Yeah, because *you* insist on living your entire life as if someone getting upset about something is the biggest tragedy that could befall the world!" Caroline sighed. "Look, forget it. If it's going to be this much hassle—"

"No! No, I . . . I'd really like to hear it. I just . . ."

And now you're going to make heavier weather of it if it doesn't happen than if it does. So we might as well get it over with.

Caroline mustered all the enthusiasm she could. "Okay, so, the first scene is a woman driving in her car along a motorway. Yawning. Maybe we see her slap herself in the face a few times."

"Why would she do that?" asked Harriet.

"So as not to fall asleep."

"Is that what people do?"

"Yes. I've done it more than once."

"Caroline. You shouldn't—"

"So then she sees a sign. One of those overhead signs, you know, the ones that say, 'Don't drive while tired,' with kind of computerized writing and messages on them?"

"Right, yes. Yes." Harriet nodded vigorously.

"The first sign says: 'Take a break. Don't drive while tired.'"

"What do you mean the first sign? Is she going to see more signs?"

Caroline forced down her impatience. "Yes. Try to imagine the scene flowing, as if you're watching it on TV and can't interrogate the scriptwriter."

"Oh, God, sorry. I told you I'd be rubbish."

"You're not rubbish. We see the sign, then we cut away from it and back to the woman's face. She looks a little bit annoyed or frustrated. She drives on for a few seconds. Then we're seeing things through her eyes again and we see another sign in the distance. As she drives on, we see it get closer and then closer still, until finally we can read it, and it says . . . Can you guess?"

"No."

"No idea?"

"None whatsoever."

"Okay. Good. The second sign says, 'That's a terrible excuse.

Public transport exists, for one thing, and you could also maybe go to bed earlier.'"

Harriet frowned. "Oka-ay."

She evidently didn't get it. Caroline pushed through her embarrassment and carried on. "Then we cut to an external shot—"

"External as in outside the car?" Harriet asked.

"No. I don't know. Just, outside the woman. We're looking *at* her, not through her eyes. We see her getting even more annoyed. She drives a bit further. Then we're in her point of view again, and we see another sign getting nearer. This is the third sign she's seen, right? It says, 'Right. But unfortunately this is real life, and in real life something usually has to give. And safety should never be that thing.'" Impatient for encouragement, Caroline said, "Don't you think that's genius? I laughed for nearly ten minutes straight when I first thought of it."

"So the joke is that the road signs can read her thoughts and it's as if she's having an argument with them as she drives along."

"Yes! The fourth and last sign, just before the sketch ends, would say something like, 'Oh, well, that's very mature, isn't it?'"

"Doesn't it bother you to have all that unopened post piled up on your desk?" Harriet asked, pointing at the pile by the side of Caroline's laptop.

"*What?*"

"I brought it in hours ago."

"You hate it, don't you?" Caroline sighed.

"Hate what?"

"The sketch idea. This swift change of subject is because you don't want to offend me."

"No, I . . . I like it. I think it's very clever."

"So it's too clever-clever?"

"No. It's clever in a good way."

Caroline didn't want to talk about it any more. She looked at what Harriet had called "all that unopened post." Harriet always opened anything the second it arrived, just as she always answered the landline and every message and email as soon as they came in. Caroline didn't understand how she could bear to be always at the beck and call of all the things that were supposed to be at hers.

Harriet was still staring at the unopened letters. There were three envelopes fanned out next to Caroline's laptop. Two were clearly bills. The other had a Special Delivery sticker on it and the name and address were handwritten on the envelope. Harriet stood up as Caroline reached for it, muttering something about needing to put some washing in the dryer.

Caroline opened the envelope, pulled out a small card, and started to read. What on earth . . .

She read the card twice, then turned her attention to the letter. Her confusion soon gave way to disbelief. This was incredible. Was it really happening? Did she need to pinch herself, or blink twice or something?

Harriet.

The various pieces slotted into place and, with a thud of the heart, Caroline knew: Harriet had received an envelope this morning just like this one, with exactly the same contents. Everyone who was at Tevendon last July must have got one. And, Harri being Harri, she'd have torn into it and read everything straight away. And—this was the truly incredible part—even knowing Caroline would work this out as soon as she opened hers, Harri had chosen to say nothing. Nothing at all. That's what she'd been nervous about, not hearing Caroline's latest sketch. It was also why she was smartly dressed; she'd probably assumed that Caroline, as soon as she read the letter, would insist they leap in the car and head for DC Simon Waterhouse's office. She'd wanted to be ready, knowing that Caroline would want to "do something."

Yet she had said nothing. She'd been so afraid of the "discussing it and then doing something" part that, instead, she'd sat nervously and waited for the inevitable, while no doubt trying to convince herself that perhaps it was avoidable. And then she'd realized that was making her more anxious, hence her blurted-out question: *Doesn't it bother you to have all that unopened post piled up on your desk?*

Unfathomable. Caroline wondered if it was a generational thing, something to do with women of Harriet's age and the way they'd been socialized.

She looked down at the card in her hand. No, it hadn't changed. Those ominous words were still there: "PLEASE READ THIS FIRST. This is not an accusation . . ."

14

"Do we have to do this in here?" DI Giles Proust had opened the door and now stood in the corridor, looking in. He was doing his best to demonstrate his reluctance to enter. He'd arrived late to the venue: Spilling police station's Sir Robert Batchelor Room. Simon, Charlie, Sam, Sellers, and Gibbs had all been waiting for him for ten minutes.

"This is the room we've got booked for it," Simon told him. "We're all here now, and we're running late, so . . . do you want to come in and sit down?"

" 'Want' is a stretch," said the Snowman.

No one asked him what his objection was. Everyone knew: he'd been against the police station's refurbishment project—against even the tiniest drop of style or comfort being introduced, against having any rooms that looked "designed for lounge-lizard dilettantes, not police officers," and particularly against the naming of any part of his workplace after someone he disapproved of. Simon couldn't remember what precisely the late Sir Robert Batchelor had done in the mid-1990s to put the Snowman's nose out of joint, but he had known at one time. To the best of his recollection, he'd been on Batchelor's side insofar as he'd cared at all.

"You'd better have good news for me," Proust warned as he sat down.

"If you mean progress on Brinkwood then, yes, there's some news," Simon told him. "Not sure how good it is or if it gets us anywhere."

"And what's Sergeant Zailer doing here?"

"You want me here," Charlie told him. "I was at Tevendon when Jane died, remember?"

"Who could forget such an extraordinary coincidence?" said the Snowman. "Your mum, wasn't it, Sergeant, who just happened to mention that a cottage at the resort was available at short notice?"

"Yep." Charlie smiled at him. "Feel free to ask her if you don't believe me."

"Can we get on with what we're here for?" said Simon. "Charlie and I had nothing to do with Jane Brinkwood's death. You know we didn't."

"Do I?" said Proust.

Don't rise to it. Deprive him of his twisted pleasures.

"All right, I'll start with the basics," said Simon. "We know where Jane Brinkwood was murdered: Cottage Number 1 at Tevendon. She wasn't moved there postmortem. It's where she was killed. We know it happened on Tuesday, 2 July, between eight fifteen p.m. and nine p.m. She and Gleave would have arrived at the cottage at eight fifteen, and nine was when Charlie and I found her dead on the floor at Number 1.

"Between those times, thanks to the weather and the security camera footage, we know three important things. One: no one climbed over the back wall into the office building's garden or Number 1's garden. They'd have left footprints in the mud, and there were none, so we can rule that out. Two: no one we don't know about, no stranger or intruder, entered the resort in the usual way, via the main gates—they'd have been caught on the camera there. Three: no one got in over the resort's boundary wall into any of the other cottages' gardens. Whichever one it was, they couldn't have got from there to Number 1 without being caught by one of the two other security cameras. Now unfortunately, there are no cameras that cover the area directly surrounding Number 1—"

"Very unfortunately," Proust agreed. "Sod's Security Camera Law."

"—so we can't see who entered the house, but I think it's safe to say that Jane Brinkwood's murderer must be one of the paying guests that we know were there that night—more about them in a minute—or Anita Khattou, the acting resort manager for the week. All the kitchen staff left between eight and ten past, after serving the main courses. Anita was going to be clearing away after the mains were finished, and taking it from there."

"So that puts who at the scene at the right time?" asked Proust. "By scene, I mean the resort as a whole."

Simon picked up a pen and started to write the names on the whiteboard, saying them as he wrote them down:

Anita Khattou (acting resort manager)
William Gleave (husband of victim)
Jane Brinkwood (victim)
Lucy Dean (ex-wife of William Gleave)
Pete Shabani (fiancé of Lucy Dean)
Mick and Susan Henry (married couple)
Caroline and Harriet Moyle-Jones (married couple)
Polly and Jack McCallion (married couple)
Simon Waterhouse and Charlie Zailer

"You and Sergeant Zailer are a married couple," Proust pointed out. "Aren't you going to put it in brackets?"

"No." Simon stood back and looked at the list he'd made. "Those were all the bodies, alive and dead, at the resort at the relevant time. Now let's talk about who wasn't there: Lord Ian Brinkwood—not there. Greg and Rebecca Summerell—not there. Housekeeping staff—not there. Hester and Chris Arthur—not there."

"Hester and Chris Arthur?" said Proust. "I don't recall hearing those names before."

"The couple who'd been staying at Cottage Number 6 before me and Charlie, the ones who left three days early. But their names don't matter because they weren't there on the evening of 2 July. Unlike Lord Brinkwood and the Summerells, Hester and Chris Arthur don't have a confirmed alibi, but the same applies to them as applies to our hypothetical nameless intruders: the only way they could have entered the resort and got to Number 1 without being picked up by one of the cameras is if they came over the back wall, and the undisturbed soil in the beds shows that they didn't."

"Couldn't someone have made the soil appear undisturbed, after disturbing it?" Proust asked. "Could they, for example, have stabbed Brinkwood, climbed back over the wall again, then from the top of a ladder they had waiting on the other side, leaned over with a rake and eliminated their footprints?"

"Out of the question," Simon told him. "All areas of the soil beds that run alongside the wall of Number 1's back garden and the office building's back garden were in the same condition as the other parts. There's a five-page report explaining it, if you want to read the science. The killer would have had to do whatever he did in terms of compensatory raking not only to the patch of the flower bed where he landed but to all the beds in both gardens. I'm happy to believe the experts on this: that earth hadn't been disturbed by anything but rain and the usual creatures that live in flower beds."

"There's only one conclusion we can reasonably draw," said Charlie. "Whoever killed Jane must have been one of the names on this list." She pointed at the board. "Problem is, there's not a single one of them who could have done it."

"That would be an insurmountable problem if it were true," said the Snowman. "Which it can't be."

"Nine of the ten possibles were together on the restaurant terrace when Jane was stabbed," Charlie told him. "They all swear that none of them left that spot, even for a second, between when Simon and I left and when we returned. That leaves only William Gleave as a suspect. Simon, you can do this bit because you know I don't believe it." Charlie held up her hands. "To me it seems obvious that Gleave must have killed Brinkwood."

"Except he didn't," said Simon. "Can't have. Charlie and I found him facing away from her body, sitting at a table with his head in his hands, his back turned to the scene. He seemed completely unaware of his surroundings. Didn't have a clue what was going on or what had happened."

"Just the kind of fugue state a murderer would fake in order to avoid a long prison sentence," said Charlie.

"He wasn't faking it," Simon told Proust. "I knew it straight away and forensics confirmed it. It's all in the file, if you don't want to take it from me, which I know you won't. There were splashes of blood on the back of his shirt—blood that flew through the air during the attack on Jane by someone else, someone standing behind her, not sitting in front of her with his back to her. Gleave told us the truth: when his wife was stabbed, he was sitting in the position Charlie and I found him in. Must have been, for the blood spatters to land on his shirt as they did."

Proust made a noise of dissatisfaction. "How did the killer get into Cottage Number 1?"

"Back door, we think," said Charlie. "It was standing open when we got there at nine, and Jane was stabbed from behind."

"We think the killer came in through the back door into the kitchen, took a knife, then crept up behind Brinkwood and stabbed her."

"So, they didn't bring the murder weapon with them?" the Snowman asked.

"We don't think so, no. All the cottages had the same cutlery in them. Each had one knife of the sort that was used for the murder. Number 1's was missing from the kitchen drawer and is likely to be the one we found lying on the floor in front of the body."

"Therefore, whoever it was, you don't know if they arrived at Number 1 planning to kill Jane Brinkwood or not?" said Proust.

"If it was planned, it can't have been planned too long beforehand," Simon told him. "I can't see how anyone could have predicted Brinkwood would storm off the way she did, back to her cottage. I suppose they might have planned to kill her that night somewhere else, or later, but . . . My guess is it was pretty spontaneous, but who knows?"

"Not you, Waterhouse. Not you. To summarize: you know nothing and all the suspects have been eliminated."

"Yep, that's about where we are," said Simon. "It's a problem. I'm not going to deny it."

"Why did they leave early, the couple in Number 6 before you and Sergeant Zailer? I've forgotten their names already."

"Hester and Chris Arthur. Dubbed Mr. and Mrs. Friendly by some of the other guests because of their unsociable behavior."

"Who wants to make friends with a load of strangers on holiday?" Gibbs sneered.

"Quite," the Snowman agreed.

"No one knows why they left early," Sam Kombothekra told him. "They told Anita Khattou that it was nothing at all to do with them not loving the resort, which they apparently did.

Lucy Dean overheard them talking at breakfast one morning, though, and apparently Hester Arthur said that she couldn't get out of there fast enough."

"Interesting," said the Snowman. "And we don't know why?"

"No," said Simon.

"And they overlapped for quite a few days at Tevendon with Gleave and Brinkwood," Sellers told Proust. "So there might be something there."

"We don't know what, though," said Gibbs. Then his face broke into a grin and he said, "I think it's going to be a long, long time before we find out too."

Proust chuckled. "No tune?" he said.

Gibbs started to sing: "And I think it's gonna be a long, long time, till touchdown brings me round again to find, I'm not the man they think I am at home, oh, no, no, no . . ."

Shortly after leaving his wife, inspired by his new girlfriend Sondra, Sellers had turned vegetarian. Last week Gibbs had caught him eating a sandwich in which rocket was one of the main ingredients and had immediately christened him "Rocket Man" and taken to serenading him with snatches of the famous Elton John song at every available opportunity.

"Mate, it wasn't funny the first time," said Sellers, who, nevertheless, turned red whenever Gibbs sang his new theme tune.

"I have to say something," Sam Kombothekra announced. "I've been trying not to say it because I know how it'll be received but . . . Gibbs, you've got an amazing voice. You're a brilliant singer."

Gibbs looked affronted. Sellers laughed. "Cheers, Sam. Now he'll stop doing it, guaranteed."

"Can we not have this crap now, and can we instead focus on this?" Simon pointed at his list.

"Spoilsport," Charlie murmured.

Simon ignored her. "I'm going to come back to Hester and Chris Arthur in a minute, but first let's look in more detail at the people we know were at Tevendon when Jane was murdered. Anita Khattou, temporary resort manager. Stays at the resort sometimes. Her official address is the Wynstanley Estate in Combingham."

"She has my sympathies," said Proust.

"Yeah, she hates it. It was her parents' place, which she inherited. No love lost between her and them, from the sound of it. She stays at Tevendon as much as she can—one of the cottages, Number 4, is for staff, and Greg and Rebecca Summerell hardly use it. They prefer their big house in Spilling, so I think Anita gets to live at Tevendon quite a lot.

"William Gleave, Brinkwood's husband, is a secondary school maths teacher." Simon moved down the list. "Lives in Silsford, in Jane Brinkwood's house—lived with her there before she died. Was married to Lucy Dean first. They had one child, now called Evin. Lucy changed her daughter's name shortly after she and Pete Shabani got engaged. William has no contact, though he's the biological father. He and Jane Brinkwood fell in love when Jane was working as a doula for Lucy during her pregnancy. A doula is—"

"I know what they are," Proust cut him off. "My wife was of the view that our daughter needed one when she was pregnant."

Simon could imagine what Proust's own view had been, as well as the outcome of the disagreement.

"It's pure charlatanism, Waterhouse. Doulas, personal fitness trainers, all these . . . vitamin people. You can't move these days without bumping into them. Crooks."

Charlie was trying not to laugh: nodding solemnly as if in response to profound wisdom.

"Pete Shabani and Lucy Dean now live with Evin in

Rawndesley," said Simon. "Lucy's CEO of a start-up, her own start-up, that does something techy to do with medical trials and biological samples. Pete's an anesthetist at Rawndesley General Hospital. He was Lucy's anesthetist, in fact, when she gave birth to Evin. They subsequently got together as a couple, after William had left Lucy for Jane."

"So, William Gleave and Lucy Dean are both in the habit of trawling routine medical appointments in search of potential future paramours?" said the Snowman. "They should have stayed married. It sounds as if they have much in common. Why haven't you put on your list which cottages everyone was staying in, Waterhouse?"

"Good idea," said Simon. As he wrote on the board, he recited, "1: Gleave and Brinkwood. 2: Jack and Polly McCallion. 3: Caroline and Harriet Moyle-Jones. 4: First Anita Khattou, then, after the snoring issue, Mick and Susan Henry—"

"Ah yes, the Great Snoring Crisis of 2019," said Proust.

"5: Mick and Susan Henry."

"It's fucking outrageous that the Henrys got two houses for the price of one when all the others were paying full whack for one," said Gibbs.

"6: me and Charlie," Simon went on. "7: Lucy Dean and Pete Shabani."

"All right, so tell me about the others," said Proust. "Some of these couples still feel rather shadowy. The McCallions, the Henrys, the Joneses?"

"Moyle-Joneses, sir," said Sellers.

"No one needs more than one surname," came the reply.

Simon pulled himself up into a seated position on the edge of a table. "Polly McCallion runs her own business," he said. "An online coaching program that helps people lose weight in a healthy way. Her husband, Jack, is the MD of the ConnoisseurCuisine restaurant chain that seems to be taking over the world at the moment. Well, the UK, anyway. Mick Henry retired early from the US navy and now runs an antiques business, and his wife, Susan, is CEO for some kind of network of shared-work-space office buildings in Fort Collins, Colorado. That's where she and Mick live. Oh, Polly and Jack McCallion live in Twickenham, by the way."

"Two CEOs, out of ten guests." Proust sounded unhappy about this, as if it might augur badly.

"Three, really," said Charlie. "Though Polly McCallion doesn't describe herself as a CEO. She prefers 'Founder and Visionary.' She told me she thinks that sounds less management-bureaucratic."

"Yes, it sounds more like an unwashed lunatic with a cult following," said Proust. "Carry on, Waterhouse."

"Caroline Moyle-Jones is a stand-up comedian and comedy TV creative person. Her wife, Harriet, is an academic at the University of Sheffield, which is where she and Caroline live."

"Harriet's specialist research field is the relationship between mental health and the way people are treated at work," Charlie told Proust. "You know, the way bosses treat their underlings," she added pointedly. Simon had resisted the temptation to mention that detail.

"Of course." The Snowman sighed. "That's what people in Sheffield want to learn about these days, is it? Well, I suppose it had to happen. That's the way things are going. Unstoppable decline."

Simon wondered if he blamed the Vitamin People.

"What can you tell me about Hester and Chris Arthur?" Proust asked. "I'm almost more interested in them than in the others at the moment. Why were they in such a hurry to leave, I wonder?"

"Yeah, well . . ." Simon looked at Charlie, who gave him an encouraging look. "That question's probably linked to the most recent development, and I guess it's a promising one. It's suspicious if not informative."

"Don't talk in riddles, Waterhouse."

"When Jane Brinkwood arrived at dinner on 2 July, she accused Charlie and me of not being real police officers. She also told Anita that Hester wasn't Hester Arthur's real name. We thought that was worth looking into, even though it seemed likely to be rubbish that Jane had dreamed up, like the rubbish she was spouting about Charlie and me—but in the case of the Arthurs, she was spot-on."

"Explain," said Proust.

"There's no married couple by the name of Hester and Chris Arthur living at the address they gave Anita when they booked. They paid in cash in advance too. Phone numbers, email addresses—all the information the Tevendon resort had about them was false. Fake."

Now Charlie was giving Simon a funny look that he couldn't interpret. She probably wanted him to get on with it, so he did. "As things stand, we have no idea why the couple calling themselves Hester and Chris Arthur lied, or who they are," he said.

15

Friday, January 10, 2020

LUCY

The doorbell rings at two o'clock, just as I'm about to start work again after lunch. Not that I've been achieving much on the work front. I can't concentrate on anything apart from Jane's murder, can't stop thinking about the letters—letter, I suppose, though I made multiple copies—that I sent out yesterday, and what might happen as a result.

Surely now something will happen.

The bell rings a second time, reminding me that I've made no move towards the door. I'm expecting no one. It would be easy to catastrophize and imagine it's William again— another unexpected visit—but for some reason I don't think it's him. And I'm going to go and check, like a brave person would (which I must be—a coward wouldn't have sent those letters), instead of hiding away in my office at the back of the house.

For William to come back this soon after Saturday would be too . . . too something for him, I don't know what. I can't find the right word.

I'm right: it's not William. It's Charlie Zailer. She smells of cigarette smoke and also, faintly, of something else that I'm not prepared for. It takes me a moment to work out that I smelled this same perfume on her at Tevendon: a metal-mixed-with-flowers kind of scent. An unusual flower—not roses or lilies. Maybe geraniums.

The red lipstick is faded today. "Can I come in?" she says.

My first thought is: *She knows about the letters.* Someone has reported it, thinking it worth ringing the police about. Oddly, this makes me less anxious. It means we're likely to discuss it. Which is fine. I'm bursting with the weight and also the surprise of what I've done. Part of me still can't believe I did it, and I'd welcome the chance to explain it to someone.

What's the worst Charlie can do—yell at me? Technically I've done nothing wrong. Ethically? Unconventional and potentially upsetting are not the same as wrong. I've accused no one: that's what I keep coming back to whenever a frightened voice in my head tells me I've gone too far.

I wonder which of the Tevendon crew contacted the police. Harriet Moyle-Jones, probably. I can imagine her hoping to pretend Tevendon never happened and being unable to cope with a reminder from me that it did. Seeking reassurance and protection from authority feels like a very Harriet thing to do.

I make Charlie a cup of tea, letting her follow me through to the kitchen this time. She asks about my egg cup collection, and I take it as a sign that she doesn't want to broach anything too serious until we're sitting down. I don't either. Luckily, I am able to witter on about egg cups at length, a skill I didn't know I possessed.

Once the tea's made, Charlie walks ahead of me into the lounge and sits in the same chair she sat in on Wednesday. I sit on the sofa, waiting to have to justify myself, and am surprised when she says with a half smile, "I've been studying your work since we last saw each other."

"How d'you mean?"

"Not your work work," she says. "I'm talking about the letter you wrote to William last year—the one you gave Simon on Monday. I've been reading and rereading it."

"Oh."

"You seem surprised."

"No, I . . . It's fine, it's just . . . I wrote it months ago, so . . ."

I've had other letters on my mind. Is it possible she doesn't know? That none of them has contacted the police?

"If you don't mind, I'd like to ask you about the whole you, William, and Jane being friends thing," says Charlie.

Waterhouse must have sent her. This has to mean he's focusing on the case again.

"Go ahead," I say.

"Explain to me why exactly you tried to be friends with them after they'd betrayed you so horrifically. Were your friendly feelings towards them ever genuine? I'm impressed if so, but . . . I just know I could never do that. And I don't get why anyone would want to. If it were me, I'd have hated them passionately forever. I wouldn't even have considered a reprieve." She sounds proud of this. "They didn't deserve one."

I close my eyes for a second as I store away her words for safekeeping, knowing I'll want to revisit them over and over. It means more to me than it probably should to hear unambiguous condemnation of what William and Jane did to me—especially from someone who's virtually a stranger. So many of William's and my mutual friends, after the breakup, didn't feel able to say anything that was unequivocally condemnatory. I understood completely: William was their friend as much as I was, and they didn't want to turn against him simply because he'd fallen in love. And if they hoped to stay friends with William, they could hardly slag off Jane either. For their own convenience, I'm sure they all decided to make that, in their minds, The Thing That William and Jane Had Done: fall in love with each other.

Nothing more than that. No need to think too hard about the other inconvenient details.

I lost count of the number of friends, relatives, and acquaintances who said things like "Poor you" and "I can't begin to imagine how hard it is." There were lots of pointless and unfinished expressions of shock: "I can't believe . . . I mean, I just can't . . . I mean, William?"

Until now, only one person has ever said anything that I found genuinely consoling: Pete. The first time he came around, he said solemnly, "They're the lowest of the low and the scummiest of the scummy, and this isn't just my opinion. It's an objective fact in the world, like gravity and the existence of kangaroos." Months later, when we were on our first official date, I asked him why kangaroos. He frowned and said, "I think it's because they've got pouches. Like, they have *pockets as part of their bodies*. It's almost unbelievable, yet we know they really exist and we haven't made them up because no one would make up a creature that has a body with a pocket. No one's imagination is that bizarre." I remember laughing—and then even more at his inability to understand why I found it so funny. That night was when my brain did a complete about-turn, from "Love and men are finished for me now that William's abandoned me" to "What if something better, happier, more fun is possible?"

At Pete's and my engagement party, my mum asked me, "If you'd met William and Pete at the same time and they'd both asked you to marry them, which one do you think you'd have chosen?"

"Pete," I said. Ridiculously, I felt a pang of guilt for creating an imaginary past in which I betrayed William before he betrayed me—even though that made no sense because, in the thought experiment, he and I weren't a couple yet.

It means more to me than it probably should that Charlie Zailer doesn't believe all is fair in love and war. It makes me want to answer her friendship question honestly. "I looked at all my options. William and Jane were madly in love, and there was every reason to think it was solid. Forever. And I was really falling for Pete by then, and . . . even, astonishingly, starting to feel glad that William had left me. If he hadn't, I wouldn't have had this amazing experience of new love—the exciting kind, the kind where you're buzzing and on a high every second of every day. I honestly never thought I'd get to have that experience again, could barely believe it was happening. I think it was that—the massive impossibility of this amazing thing that had transformed my life—that made me believe I could do anything. It made me more ambitious."

"With Pete's love behind you, you could do anything?" says Charlie.

"Yes, and fueled by the intensity of my feelings for him. I thought, *How can I be even happier? How can I just be all happiness, with no sadness and no anger, no horrible burden to carry around?* The answer seemed obvious: I needed *not* to have two enemies I was committed to hating forever."

"That's . . . an enlightened approach." Charlie sounds suspicious.

"Maybe, but that's not what I was aiming for. All I wanted was relief and peace of mind. It took me a while to brainwash myself, but I did it. I persuaded myself: Jane and William had fallen in love because they were meant to be together. And they'd done me and Pete a favor, because we were meant to be together too. And, yes—this was what I told myself at the time—yes, they'd behaved appallingly, but who hadn't? Over and over, I listed all the times I'd behaved badly for selfish reasons. There were plenty! So, was I really all that different from them?"

"So what happened?" Charlie asks. "Did you formally suggest a new start? New friendship?"

I can't help smiling at the memory. "I had to win them over,"

I tell her. "They didn't trust my desire to befriend them at first. Understandably. But in the end . . . I mean, I was persistent. And finally, I think, they worked out that a reconciliation, a friendship, would suit them too. All our mutual friends would think—*did* think—*Oh, look, it's all turned out for the best. These things happen, everyone's fine now, and that's all that matters.* Much easier for William and Jane than having me tell everyone I meet that they're a pair of morally bankrupt shits. They were able to kid themselves, with my collaboration, that what they'd done hadn't been a friendship-ending offense."

"And then Jane was murdered, and William accused you of killing her," says Charlie. "You explained very eloquently in your letter why that turned you against him."

"Even before then, the friendship was doomed. Jane behaved shockingly from the second she arrived at Tevendon and found me there. Until then, she'd been perfectly lovely to me since the official start of our new foursome. As she should have, after what I'd already forgiven her for. But from the minute she decided I'd deliberately gatecrashed her honeymoon, she took every opportunity to flaunt her relationship with William—smooching all over him, reaching for his hand, stroking his face, right in front of me. Deliberately hoping to make me jealous."

Charlie puts her empty mug down on the carpet and leans forward. "Is it really, honestly true that you had no idea they'd be there on their honeymoon on the exact same dates that you and Pete had booked?"

"Really true. They didn't go on a honeymoon immediately after their wedding. It was delayed because of William's school's term dates—and then, when they finally booked it, they didn't mention it to me or Pete—though Jane claimed she'd told me. If she did, it must not have registered with me."

Charlie looks unconvinced. "And you just happened to pick the same dates for your holiday with Pete?"

"Yes. Coincidences happen. All the time. This was one."

"Why did you choose Tevendon? Presumably you knew the owner of the resort was Jane's father, Lord Brinkwood?"

"Yeah, of course. Jane told me all about it when she first—" I stop. For a second, the revulsion is too much. "When she first entered my life under false pretenses. She made Tevendon sound absolutely amazing—the perfect, luxurious, rural retreat. I looked at the website and decided on the spot that I had to go there one day. Pete agreed. It's a pretty special place, you must admit—and it was right on my doorstep, almost. Why trudge through airports when you can set off from home by car and arrive somewhere so beautiful and peaceful forty-five minutes later?"

"Did William and Jane invite you and Pete to their wedding?" Charlie asks.

"Oh, that part was all very civilized. As soon as William's and my divorce came through, I told Jane that she and William probably wanted to get married immediately, and that they mustn't feel the need to invite me and Pete, despite us all being friends by that point. She was really grateful, I could tell. Said it was so incredibly thoughtful of me. In the end, she *did* invite me and Pete to the wedding. She insisted, and . . . we went. We had a nice day!"

Charlie's eyes widen. "Seriously?"

"Uh-huh. Obviously I felt emotional at times, but I still managed to be happy for them, I think."

"Wow. You're a better woman than I am, that's for sure."

"Charlie, can I tell you something?" I can't believe she'll never find out about the letters I sent yesterday, and I don't want her to look back on this conversation and wonder why I didn't tell her something so important. She's going to find out, and I'd rather she heard it from me. "I did something yesterday that might stir things up a bit. Not because I want to make trouble or upset anyone, but . . . I do want to get things moving so that we can all finally find out the truth about who murdered Jane."

"What did you do?"

"Wait here. It's easier if I show you." I go to the kitchen and pull my bulging copy of *Appetites* by Geneen Roth down from the shelf. It falls open in my hand and three envelopes fall to the floor. I need to find a better place to keep my unsent letters.

You've got to give Pete the one that's for him. You have to, however much you don't want to. It's the only fair thing to do. It must be all of them or none at all.

I put the letters addressed to William and "Jane's killer" back in the book and replace it on the shelf. The third envelope, the one with Pete's name on it, I take into the lounge and give to Charlie.

"Before you open it, I need to explain," I say. "The letter I wrote to William last September, the one you've been studying . . . It's not the only letter I've written and not sent since Jane was killed. I also wrote a letter to her murderer. It's inside that envelope."

Charlie's eyes widen. "Are you telling me that Pete killed Jane?" she says.

"What? No!"

"This is addressed to Pete."

"No, you don't understand. I wrote a letter last November— not to Pete. To Jane's killer, whoever that is. I didn't intend for anyone to see it—but then, everything's felt so different since William came round last Saturday. And I started to think . . . maybe this could be a way to shake things up, to provoke someone into saying or doing something that gets us closer to the truth. So, I printed nine copies of my letter to Jane's killer, added a covering note to go with it, same note to everyone, and sent a copy to each of the people there that night: William,

Anita, Polly and Jack McCallion, Mick and Susan Henry, Caroline and Harriet Moyle-Jones. And Pete too, except so far I haven't had the heart to give him his. That's why it's still here. Most of the others will have got theirs this morning, Special Delivery—all apart from Susan and Mick, who are in the US."

"So, to be clear: you sent everyone but me, Simon, and Pete, everyone who was at Tevendon when Jane died, the same covering note and letter, yes? A letter you'd already written, last November?"

I watch as she unfolds the pages. "Yes."

"A letter you wrote to Jane's murderer."

"Yes. You'll understand a bit more once you've read it. In case you're wondering why I'd bother writing to a murderer I don't know."

Waiting while she reads is agony. When she gets to the end of the letter, she looks a little stunned, and I think she's going to say something, but she doesn't. Instead she picks up the small, pictureless postcard: my disclaimer note. I handwrote each one, to make it more personal, I suppose. At the bottom of Pete's, I added a "PS" that the others didn't get: "I love you so much, and I know you're not the person I was writing to when I wrote this letter. I'm only sending it to you because I sent it to all the others—to be fair and thorough. Please don't be angry."

After what feels like about a year, Charlie looks up. "So, for the couples—McCallions, Henrys, Moyle-Joneses—did you send one per household or one each?"

"One each. The letter I wrote to Jane's killer is addressed to an individual, not two people. There's no reason to assume that a couple killed her. Together, I mean."

"Right." Charlie shakes her head. I sense that she's playing for time, that she genuinely doesn't know how to respond. "So, each of the couples would have been, what, sitting across from each other at breakfast this morning, opening their separate his 'n' hers or hers 'n' hers envelopes, quickly discovering that the contents of both were exactly the same?"

"I suppose so."

At least I've done something. What are the police, the people whose job it is to find answers, doing to find the killer?

Charlie says, "I'm not often lost for words, Lucy, but . . ." She leaves the sentence unfinished.

A strange sense of calm spreads through me. It's okay. There have probably been enough words said for the time being. I, at least, don't feel a need to offer any more.

Eventually, swearing under her breath, Charlie pulls her phone out of her bag. "Simon needs to know about this," she says. "Right now."

16

"So Hester and Chris Arthur booked in under false names?" said Proust.

"Yep," said Charlie. "And, somehow, Jane Brinkwood found out."

"We have no idea who they are," said Simon. "We're looking into it, but no luck so far. All the other guests, though, and Anita—they're all legit. Real names, real addresses. They're all who they claim to be."

"Why wouldn't they be?" Gibbs sounded irritated.

"Ask Jane Brinkwood," said Charlie. "She's the one who assumed Simon and I were lying about our identities too."

"Why would she extrapolate like that?" said Sam.

"No idea, but here's what I do know: whatever their real names, the Arthurs were all about the adultery. Both married to other people. How much do you want to bet?"

"Why'd you say that?" asked Sellers.

"Rocket Man's ears prick up at the mention of adultery," muttered Gibbs.

"None of you will have heard of it, but there's a famous book called *The Scarlet Letter*," said Charlie. "The heroine, an adulteress, is called Hester. And the guy she's in love with, who makes all the adultery feel so worthwhile? His name's Arthur. Any woman who picks the fake name Hester Arthur—"

173

"I'm not interested in why she chose the name, Sergeant," said Proust. "Could she have killed Jane Brinkwood? If not, then I'm not interested in her at all."

"She could have put someone else up to it," said Sellers. "Though how does that help us if no one there on the night could have done it? That gives us nowhere to go."

"We examine every possible weak point in what we currently believe is true until we find the one that won't hold," said Simon. "It can't be the case that no one could have done it, because it got done. Either someone left the group of nine on the terrace without being spotted, or they were spotted by one or some of the nine who are now covering for them, or all nine are lying. One of those things must be true."

"I love the way you leave out the overwhelmingly more likely option," said Charlie. "William Gleave killed Jane, and the forensics people are wrong. He took off his shirt, draped it over the chair, then a bit later he found himself standing behind Jane and he stabbed her. The blood landed on his shirt when he wasn't wearing it."

"Except that's not what the evidence showed," Simon told her. "Evidence said the blood would have landed differently if Gleave hadn't been sitting there *wearing* the shirt when Brinkwood was stabbed. There's no getting round it."

Proust said, "If we're assuming the killer came and went via Number 1's back door, did he or she have a key?"

"Didn't need one," said Simon. "William Gleave was pretty sure the back door was unlocked. He'd spent some time on the afternoon of 2 July reading a book in the garden, and he doesn't think he locked the door when he went back inside. Tevendon's so private, and he knew, or thought he knew, that no one would be anywhere near the house apart from him and Jane."

"That's such a lie," said Charlie. "He didn't think anyone would go near the house even though his ex-wife had turned up on his honeymoon and his new wife, by that point, had received not one but two sinister notes telling her to beware?"

"Fair point," said Sellers.

"Maybe," Simon conceded.

"So, if the murderer got in by the back door, he or she was in the back garden," said Proust.

"Yeah, and since the mud by the boundary wall was undisturbed, that leaves only one way for our killer to get into Number 1's garden: by first going through the office building's garden, which they must have got into from the restaurant terrace area. Unfortunately none of the cameras are in the right position to have caught anyone doing that. Crazy as it sounds, there are no cameras near the office."

"There's a gate between the office building's garden and Number 1's garden," said Sam. "It was unlocked. Anita tells us it's never used, and couldn't tell us where the key was. Neither could the Summerells when we asked them. From what we could gather, that gate might have been standing unlocked for years, with no one ever going through it."

"Until now," said Proust. He tapped the side of his head with his middle finger a few times. "My first thought is that the killer must be someone who was sitting at a table on the restaurant terrace when Waterhouse and Sergeant Zailer left to follow Brinkwood and Gleave to Number 1."

"They'd have had time," said Charlie. "Not loads, but enough. From the terrace, though, through the office garden you could get to Number 1 much quicker. They'd have had time to kill Jane, clean the knife, put it down on the floor in front of her body, and leave before we turned up."

"Wait," said Proust. "Did all the guests know they'd find that gate between the two back gardens unlocked? Because if not—"

"They didn't, but that doesn't mean what you think it means," Simon told him. "It's a metal gate with bars. Anyone reasonably agile could have climbed over it. And they'd all have known that because they'd all seen it. It's clearly visible through the largest of the office's windows."

"My second thought is that William Gleave might not be a murderer but he's certainly a liar," said Proust. "I don't believe he failed to notice someone standing behind him murdering his wife."

"I don't either," said Charlie, as Simon had known she would. "He's both: murderer and liar."

"Here's an interesting angle," said Sam. "Let's say Gleave didn't kill Jane—sorry, Charlie. Why did the killer risk killing her in front of him? Didn't they mind if he turned round and saw them?"

"They might have been working together," said Sellers. "Gleave and the murderer."

"There were no prints on the knife," said Simon. "It had been cleaned to within an inch of its life." Simon shook his head. "Which makes no sense at all, because—" He interrupted his own explanation to pursue a thread that interested him more.

"I quite like the Gleave-and-the-killer-working-together theory," he said thoughtfully. "Let's go with it for a minute. Let's say Gleave starts that evening with a plan to get Brinkwood back to their house and kill her. And someone else at Tevendon knows about it and is cheering him on."

"Lucy Dean?" Gibbs suggested.

"Maybe. Whoever it is . . . the plan's going well. Gleave makes Brinkwood angry, knowing she'll storm off back to the house. He follows her—but he doesn't plan for Charlie and me following him. His confidant and supporter sees us go, though, and knows what it means: we're going to get there before Gleave has a chance to do the deed. So they hurry to Number 1 and do it themselves, quickly, before we can arrive and stop them.

And miraculously, Gleave's then in the clear—because the blood lands on his shirt, proving he can't have done it."

"Right, but then the actual killer wouldn't be in the clear," said Sellers. "There's no way everyone at the restaurant would cover for them, not when something as serious as a murder's involved."

"Even if the killer, William's coconspirator, was Lucy?" said Charlie. "Everyone knew what Jane had done to Lucy—everyone at the resort. They were all firmly on Lucy's side."

"No," said Sam. "I agree with Sellers. That many people wouldn't all lie in such a serious situation, not to protect someone they'd only met on holiday a few days previously. It's just about feasible that one or two of them would, but more than that? I don't think so. And no one could have left that terrace without everyone seeing. Think about it. Think what had happened already: all the drama and to-ing and fro-ing. They'd all have been extra aware of any movement in any direction, in case it was Jane coming back or someone else storming off in a tantrum."

"Also, when I think about Anita Khattou's statement . . ." Simon got up off the desk and walked over to the window. "Anita was the only one eating alone with no one to talk to. She was able to do a lot of listening. She overheard snatches of conversations from all the other tables that she relayed to us—"

"Yeah, probably in more detail than we needed," said Charlie. "Definitely in more detail than anyone else offered when we first asked them what they talked about at their tables in that crucial window of time. But when we asked them if they'd said X or Y—what Anita had heard them say, basically—they all looked a bit sheepish and basically went, 'Oh, yeah, come to think of it, I did say that.'"

"Lucy had been telling Pete how much she regretted befriending Jane after she'd done what she'd done, and how mad must she have been, and why hadn't Pete tried to stop her. He said that he had, but she'd insisted it was a good idea. Polly and Jack had been talking about someone called Nina, who'd lost her job," said Simon. "And the other two couples—the Henrys and the Moyle-Joneses—were talking about things they'd have preferred no one to overhear and report to us, by the sound of it," Charlie said. "High blood pressure in the case of Mick and Susan Henry—"

"High blood pressure?" Proust looked confused.

"Yes. Eventually they admitted to having discussed, briefly, some medication Susan was taking, Lisinopril, but they were both huffy about it and asked why they had to tell the police about their private medical business. Caroline and Harriet Moyle-Jones had been discussing two people called Lindsay and Davina. Like the Henrys, they didn't at first volunteer this information and looked a bit shocked when Simon told them they'd been overheard and asked who Lindsay and Davina were. Then Caroline admitted they were parts she and Harriet had played once, in some kind of embarrassing parlor game. They'd been talking about how the tables on the terrace had been moved, and whether it was maybe part of a silly game like that one. Anyway . . . none of that matters much, except that I was convinced they'd all been there, talking, and Anita had been there eavesdropping."

"Does anyone have any thoughts about the moving of the tables?" asked the Snowman.

"No new ones," said Simon. "Someone moved them early morning on 2 July. In their new arrangement, no table had any one table that could accurately be described as 'the nearest table.' Which obviously makes the warning note to Jane Brinkwood meaningless, wherever she and Gleave might have ended up sitting that night."

"So someone moves the tables, then sends Jane Brinkwood

an anonymous note, warning her about no one in particular?" said Proust.

"It seems that way, yeah. I mean, we don't know the order: the note might have been written and posted before the tables were moved."

"Wait. Didn't the table-mover get caught on any of the security cameras? Or the note-poster?"

"No," said Simon. "The tables were moved before Anita went over to the restaurant area at six a.m. No cameras caught anyone doing anything before then on 2 July. Which I guess makes sense. If you were sneaking around at the crack of dawn, you'd probably duck down and make sure you were out of shot if you knew you were about to pass a camera."

"Tell him about the will," said Sam.

"Yes, what did Jane Brinkwood leave, apart from a mess for us to sort out?" asked the Snowman.

"She was worth about five hundred grand in savings and investments," said Simon. "Plus her house in Silsford, which she owned outright, and another house in Suffolk—all left to her by dead aristocrat relatives. She'd made a will, but not since her marriage to William Gleave. And as we know—"

"If you marry, it invalidates all previous wills," said Proust. "Which means William Gleave gets the lot."

"Oh, what a surprise," said Charlie.

"It's not as simple as that," said Simon. "I just heard back from the Brinkwood family lawyers about an hour ago: Gleave doesn't only inherit the five hundred grand and the two houses. Jane's got an aunt: Adrienne Brinkwood. She's ninety-seven years old. Jane was due to inherit thirteen million from her, give or take, and I can't imagine she's got long to live, can you?"

"But Jane's dead," said Sellers.

"Yeah, which means the thirteen mill will go to Ian Brinkwood. His Lordship," said Simon. "Except guess what?

He made it clear to the lawyers yesterday that he intends to give most of it away: five mill to William Gleave—because he's oldish himself, seventy-seven, and already wealthy. What's he going to do with it? And he said he knows that's what Jane would have wanted, for it to go to William. And the remaining eight mill's going to be gifted by his generous lordship to guess who?"

"Who?" asked Charlie. Simon heard indignation in her voice. He knew she'd be annoyed he hadn't told her first, and alone. *Tough*. There'd been no time.

"Anita Khattou."

"*What?*" said Sellers.

"So, Anita's soon going to be eight million quid richer because Jane's dead?" said Sam.

"Hang on," said Gibbs. "That can't be right. No one gives away eight million to some random employee, even a good one."

"Well, as it turns out, he's not going to be giving her any money," said Simon. "Or his palatial manor house, or his farm-house in Essex, or his fancy London flat."

"Why not?" asked Charlie.

"Because she said she didn't want any of it. All she wants from Lord Brinkwood after he dies, apparently, is a normal-sized house that feels like home—that she loves and can live in for the rest of her life. The rest? She's not interested. She's currently saying she'll refuse to accept it—she'll give it to a charity instead."

"How quickly can I become a charity?" Sellers quipped.

"She's already got one in mind," Simon told him. "Some outfit that helps abused children."

"Wow," said Charlie.

"Also, she's not a random employee. She's Lord Brinkwood's rock these days, according to the lawyers. That was the word they used: his rock, since Jane died. He nearly fell apart. So far, Anita seems to be keeping him together."

"Didn't want eight million quid?" Gibbs snorted in disgust. "All these people are fucking mental."

"Maybe that's just a posture, and she'll end up keeping it," said Charlie.

Simon smiled. "You sound suspicious."

"Yeah, I am."

"Good. This is the first sign you've shown of being willing to suspect someone other than Gleave. Allow me to make you even more suspicious of Anita Khattou."

"How?"

"Not that this extra detail adds anything, really," Simon argued with himself. "Since she's planning to give away all the money—"

"Tell me," Charlie snapped.

"Yesterday—just two days after Jane's murder—Ian Brinkwood summoned the lawyers to his manor house. Did he and Anita want to talk about the will so soon after Jane's death? Yes, they most certainly did. Keen to lay down some parameters—that was how Lord Brinkwood was described to me."

"Two days after his daughter had died?" Charlie wrinkled her nose in distaste.

"Lord Brinkwood also had an announcement to make to the lawyers at that same meeting," said Simon. "One that was to be strictly a secret until they were told otherwise. Or until a murder investigation blew all secrecy out of the water."

"What announcement?" Sellers asked.

"On 3 July, only *one* day after Jane was killed, Ian Brinkwood asked Anita Khattou to marry him. And she said yes."

17

Saturday, January 11, 2020

"Can we come back here some time?" said Charlie. It was a dry, bright, freezing cold day. She and Simon, wrapped in jumpers, coats and thick scarves, were reclining on cushionless sun-loungers beside the Tevendon resort pool, which was covered by a blue tarpaulin.

This was Simon's idea, of course. Anita Khattou had given them full access—they could have been snug and warm inside any of the cottages now instead of here freezing their arses off, but Simon had mumbled something about physical discomfort being as good for their brains as luxury and warmth would have been detrimental, as if he were a scientist who'd researched the topic. Anita had said, "No problem," and tried to disguise her incredulity when Simon had refused her offer of cushions and blankets that would have made the loungers more bearable.

"I'll be coming back here constantly," he told Charlie. "Until we solve Brinkwood. Come with me whenever you want."

"Right. I meant: Can we come back here properly one day? For a holiday."

"*Here?*"

"Don't look like that. It's a holiday resort. Or rather it was." Ian Brinkwood could have reopened the resort by now if he'd wanted to, but according to Simon, he was adamant: it was staying shut until the police had found and charged whoever had murdered his daughter. Everything had been put on hold: the income the resort brought in, the plans for the new hotel. All deposits for future stays had been refunded with apologies and a distinct lack of "We'll make it up to you" promises.

"Do you think it'll ever reopen?" said Charlie with a sigh.

"Maybe. For the time being, Lord Brinkwood seems to want to forget the place exists, and I don't blame him."

"All right, forget it then. It'll never reopen and I can never have a holiday ever again, so I won't bother to try."

"What do you mean?" said Simon.

Charlie knew this was the worst possible time to raise it with him but she couldn't help it. "Normal people have holidays. *I'm* a normal person. I used to go on holiday before I got together with you. It was hard enough to get you to agree to a three-day break here, and then that break turned into a case for you . . . Even our honeymoon got interrupted by your work, if you remember."

"Look, if you want to go somewhere, we'll go somewhere, but I don't want to talk about it or think about it now."

"Fair enough. But can we agree that as soon as Jane Brinkwood's killer's been caught, we book a holiday—abroad, if this place still hasn't reopened? In fact, let's just say abroad. Portugal or Spain or somewhere like that?"

"Fine. Whatever."

"Really?" He couldn't be agreeing so readily. "You won't have a late-night chat with your mother and then ambush me with a load of plane crash statistics?"

"No one needs to fly to go abroad these days."

Charlie closed her eyes and did her best to imagine that she was on a baking hot beach in the Algarve, sand between her toes, a paperback book stained with sun lotion on her belly, the sound of waves crashing and children playing with beach balls nearby . . .

"Is it strange that so many of them came from so close?" Simon's voice cut into her fantasy.

"Huh?"

"Gleave, Brinkwood, Lucy Dean, Pete Shabani . . . they all live or lived in the Culver Valley, and they went on holiday—on their honeymoon, even, in the case of Gleave and Brinkwood—in the Culver Valley. Who does that?"

"We live in the Culver Valley, and we were there too," said Charlie. "Sometimes close to home is convenient, and this place is, or was, genuinely next level in terms of luxury and aesthetic appeal. I'd imagine Jane Brinkwood's attitude was 'Why go anywhere else when Daddy's resort has all the trimmings?' We know Lucy heard Jane talk often, while they were friends, about how amazing Tevendon was. I don't think there's any mystery there. I tell you where there is one, though."

She'd known that would get Simon's attention. "Lucy Dean's letter to William. I keep reading it—I think I've read it more than you have by now. Every time I do, I get a really uncomfortable feeling."

"Say more," Simon ordered.

"It's as if there's something I really need to notice about it that I haven't noticed yet. I know that sounds daft."

"Not necessarily."

"When we get back, I'm going to ask you to read it aloud to me."

"No way."

"What? I'm trying to help you solve your case, Simon. All right, how about if you listen while I read it aloud?"

"Yeah, I'll do that."

Charlie shook her head. *Face it, Zailer: you married a weirdo.*

"Speaking of letters," she said, "I wanted to tell you this yesterday after I spoke to Lucy, but you were agitating about coming here again and I knew you wouldn't be able to concentrate on anything else, so I decided to leave it till today."

"What? Tell me."

"Lucy's been busier on the correspondence front than you think."

"Meaning?"

Charlie smiled, enjoying the feeling of knowing something Simon didn't. Usually it was the other way around. "She obviously gets a kick out of writing letters she's never going to send. As well as the one to William, she wrote another one with no intention of sending it to its proper recipient—because she had no idea who that person was."

"I don't get it."

"She wrote to Jane Brinkwood's killer in November last year—without having a clue who that is, according to her. The letter begins, 'Dear Whoever Killed Jane Brinkwood.' Purely therapeutic value, I think. Nothing useful in it."

"You've read it? Have you got a copy?"

"Kind of," said Charlie. "I took photos on my phone."

"Show me."

"I will, but let me tell you first. On Thursday—as in, two days ago—Lucy printed out nine copies of this letter she wrote two months ago to an unknown killer and sent a copy to every single one of the Tevendon lot. Oh, except Pete. She made him a copy but hadn't given it to him yet—she might have since, I guess. With each copy of the letter, she included a covering note explaining that she wasn't accusing anybody individually. I've got a photo of that too—"

"I need to see all these photos. Now." Simon put out his hand.

Charlie handed him her phone. "I'd have shown you yesterday but you looked through me every time I tried to—"

"'This is not an accusation,'" Simon read aloud. "'It's really important that you understand that, and don't feel offended, unfairly accused, or personally singled out. I have sent a copy of this letter—which I wrote last November to Jane's murderer, whoever that is—to everybody who was at Tevendon on the night Jane was killed: Polly, Jack, Susan, Mick, Caroline, Harriet, Anita, William, and Pete. Yes, that's right—even to Pete, my fiancé.'" Simon stopped. "That's a lie, right? The part about sending it to Pete?"

"I'm not sure I'd call it a lie. She's definitely planning to give Pete his copy, and might well have done it by now."

Simon read on: "'The police insist that no one else could have entered the resort on 2 July, which means that one of you nine must be the person who stabbed Jane, since I know it wasn't me. I'm also ruling out DC Waterhouse and Charlie Zailer for obvious reasons. But please understand that I do not suspect, and am not accusing, any of you individually. This isn't personal or aimed at you specifically in any way. Having said that, if you read this and you happen to be Jane's murderer, please get in touch with me. I know this is a huge ask, and all I can say is: it would mean a lot to me to be able to talk to you about this.'"

Simon looked at Charlie. "And she's sent these?"

"Yup."

"Then we need to talk to everyone again. We might get new and different information from a few of them now, thanks to this. It's bound to be taken as an accusation by some and go down well with no one at all. Nobody's going to be happy to have this crazy shit pushed through their letterbox."

He gave Charlie back her phone, then stood up and started to walk slowly around the pool. From the other side, he called out, "Can we talk about the knife? It was clean as clean can be when we arrived at Number 1. No fingerprints, none of Brinkwood's blood."

Charlie nodded.

"Which means the killer gave it a thorough clean—at the kitchen sink, which is just to the left of the back door, no more than about seven footsteps away. So, why not put the knife back in the kitchen drawer once it's clean?"

It was a good question: one Charlie hadn't thought of.

"Instead, our man—or woman—takes the clean knife back to the lounge area, risking *again* that Gleave might turn round and see them, and places it carefully on the floor between the dead body and where Gleave's sitting with his back to the room. Why? Why would anyone do that?"

"Come back round here and I'll tell you," said Charlie, who didn't want to yell it across a swimming pool.

For once, Simon obeyed an instruction.

"I can only think of one possible reason, and it's annoyingly vague," Charlie told him. "The murderer wanted to make it look as if somehow . . ." How could she put it into words?

"Yeah, that's vague," Simon agreed.

"As if the murder was all about something between William and Jane. That's the best way I can think to express it. If they came back and placed the knife physically between William and Jane, it could have been some kind of symbolic gesture intended to show that the trouble that led to the stabbing was all about them, their relationship. I know that's weak, but it's the best I can do."

"How about this for a possibility: there are two knives."

"What?"

"The one we found was placed on the carpet between Brinkwood's body and Gleave because it wasn't the murder weapon—but we were meant to believe it was. The real murder weapon, a knife of the exact same kind from one of the other cottages, was removed from Number 1 by the killer—he or she took it when they left—and later cleaned and replaced."

"I mean, I suppose it's possible," said Charlie. "The lack of any trace of blood in the sink—"

"Exactly," Simon cut her off. "It might mean the killer's an exceptionally good crime scene cleaner, or it might mean the bloody knife, knife number two, was removed from the house and never cleaned in Number 1's kitchen sink at all. While we were keeping all the Tevendon gang busy on the terrace, Sam and the crime scene investigators were the ones who decided that knife was the murder weapon—"

"Which it might well be," Charlie reminded him. Her phone buzzed in her hand. She looked at the screen. It was a text from Lucy Dean, and it gave Charlie's heart a jolt.

"Tell me," said Simon.

Sometimes Charlie wished he weren't able to read her expression quite so easily. She'd have loved to say, "Oh, it's just my mum wanting to arrange dinner next week."

Lucy's message said: "What do you know about Mr. and Mrs. Friendly that you haven't told me?"

Charlie had no idea how she'd given herself away, but if Lucy was on to her then she could maybe use it as leverage. She'd have to tell Simon first, though, if she was planning to tell Lucy. It was funny: she had always known that this moment, and this conversation, was lying in wait for her somewhere in the future. Now here it was. She felt drained rather than scared, emotionally exhausted in advance.

"There's something I need to tell you," she said. "About the guests at Tevendon. The other guests."

"Char, if you've been holding something back . . ."

"I have. Nothing that's going to help you solve your murder, though, so don't look at me like that. Mr. and Mrs. Friendly—the couple who were in Number 6 before us . . ."

"The fake Hester and Chris Arthur? What about them?"

"I tried to give you a clue last year, at the briefing. Remember

I said Hester's the name of the heroine of *The Scarlet Letter*, and Arthur's the man she's in love with? You never picked up on it."

"A clue? What are you talking about?"

"Think about your favorite novel in the world."

"*Moby Dick*? What's that got to do with anything?"

"Think about a conversation at a barbecue in a garden, quite a few years ago."

"Just fucking tell me."

"All right, sorry." She sighed. "I know who Hester and Chris Arthur are. I've always known—since before Jane Brinkwood was murdered. Since before we arrived at Tevendon, even."

Simon seemed to be frozen. "You . . . you *know*?"

Charlie nodded. "So would you if you thought about it," she said. "It's kind of obvious."

18

Saturday, January 11, 2020

"Let me make sure I'm clear about what you're telling me," said Susan Henry in her slowest and most careful tone. She had her phone clamped to her ear and was leaning back in her red leather club chair, her bare feet up on her desk.

"Uh-oh," said her husband, Mick. He lowered his voice. "Someone's about to catch hell. Don't know who." Susan made a face at him that said *Keep quiet*.

Mick, who had arrived two minutes ago, when the call was already in full swing, was sitting on a less comfortable chair at the table in the middle of Susan's large office. They were supposed to be going out for dinner—Mick could see the restaurant he'd booked from Susan's office window: the Rodizio Grill on Jefferson Street—but who knew if their date night would happen now? Susan sounded as if she was about to start something with whoever she was talking to.

"You're telling me that Mr. Andrews has asked you to arrange for new professional photos to be taken of the house?"

Right: it had to be Zack, their Realtor, thought Mick.

"Professional meaning for his own sentimental value, to frame and put on the wall of his new home after he moves, or a different kind of professional?" asked Susan. "Uh-huh. I see. Photos for a new listing on your website, for the purpose of selling the house. I understand. Here's what I'm missing, though,

Zack: why is Mr. Andrews doing that when we all know where we stand?"

Was their holiday home purchase about to fall through? Mick hoped so. He'd never understood why Susan's dream-home fantasy was so focused on complete isolation in the Mojave Desert, with views from every window that contained no buildings, no people and not even the possibility of people. Mick preferred to be surrounded by life, bustle and other humans.

"I'm not proceeding with anything until the water results are back," Susan told the Realtor. "I've been super clear about that from the start. We need to check we have good access to clean water that won't poison us. Mr. Andrews seemed to understand this less than a week ago. He explicitly said he'd give us the time we needed for the survey, on the understanding that we were fully committed as long as there was no problem with the water. I'm sure it'll be fine and, assuming it is, Mick and I are all in. There was no problem with any of this last week, so why's there a problem now? Has someone offered Mr. Andrews more money, by any chance?"

Mick had his fingers crossed under the table. He was praying that it was a whole lot more money.

"Oh, he has? Well, the problem *there* is that he didn't need to agree to my offer, Zack, but he did. And I understand that he'd like more—and let's face it, he could always have gotten more—but he failed to take that into account when he agreed a sale price with *me*. And now, after a comment someone made in passing, he wants to list the house again as if we haven't got a deal? Listen, Zack, I'm going to go and have dinner with my husband now, before I say something I'll regret. Let's talk tomorrow. Goodbye."

Susan threw her phone across the desk. "*Fuckers!*" she said.

"We don't have to give them one single buck if we don't want to," said Mick.

"Right. I think that's the way it's going."

Hallelujah.

"I mean, we've got the most beautiful house right here in Fort Collins," said Susan. "We can wait for the perfect California desert holiday home, right?"

Mick nodded. *Happy to wait forever.*

"You know what really gets me?" Susan stood up and slid her feet into her shoes. "The slippery way Zack told me. Like, 'Oh, just FYI? Mr. Andrews asked me yesterday to arrange for some new professional pictures to be taken. You know, of the house.' It's so passive aggressive, forcing me to ask why Andrews wants new photos. When I ask if it's for real estate purposes, he says, 'Well, his strong preference is to do a deal with you this week if possible.' So crass and manipulative. He either wants to sell the house to someone else for more money, or he wants to hurry us along and seal the deal before the water results come in. He must think I'm too dumb to realize I'm being played. Remember how he laid on the charm when we first met him and all he wanted was to beat out all the other Realtors and get our business? And now he does *this*?"

"Let's forget it for now and go eat dinner," said Mick hopefully. Susan had got as far as putting both shoes and her jacket on but they weren't safe yet; instead of putting her phone in her bag, she was staring at it with a kind of fixed expression.

"Suze? What's up?"

"Strange email just landed. From Caro Moyle-Jones."

"Tevendon Caroline?"

"I can't really be any more precise than Caro *Moyle-Jones*, Mick. That ought to narrow it down for you."

"I never remember last names. What does she say?"

"Here, read for yourself."

Mick took the phone from her. He read Caroline's email, then the two attachments. Both were photographs of letters, both signed by Lucy Dean. "What the hell is this crap?" he said angrily.

"Caro's dead right," said Susan. "That's why she emailed me—not only to warn me about what's heading our way in the mail, but also because she knew I'd agree with her, and I do: Lucy getting obsessed about who murdered Jane Brinkwood is just a way of keeping herself stuck in the past. It's not really about Jane or who killed her; it's about William Gleave. She wants to carry on thinking and talking about him all day and night, and making her life all about him. And Jane's unsolved murder gives her the perfect cover, doesn't it? I mean, who wouldn't be obsessed with an unsolved murder, right? Especially if you were there when it happened. It sounds so natural and understandable to want to know the truth, but it's going to destroy Lucy if she doesn't watch out. If I were her, I'd be like: 'Listen: I don't care about anything that happened before today. The past is over. If I never think about it again, *it will literally stop existing for me*.' Come on, let's go eat."

As they were crossing the street a few minutes later, Mick said, "Maybe it's no surprise that William left Lucy."

Susan gave him a puzzled look. "Why do you say that?"

Wasn't it obvious? Apparently not. "Well, if she can do something like this . . ."

"Something like what?"

"That letter to Jane's killer. And sending it to all of us. I don't want to get that in the post! It's offensive and then some. Who the hell does she think she is?"

Susan looked amused. "Well, if you insist. But, I mean, that's such a boring way to look at it."

Mick didn't want to argue with his wife on one of their sacred date nights. Once they were seated at their table in the restaurant and he'd ordered a good bottle of wine and a *bife com parmesão*, he said, "You're right."

"Always." Susan grinned at him.

"About the past. How we need to dwell on it, or keep remembering it, in order for it to continue to exist for us."

"Right. Otherwise it's gone. Boof!" Susan made a gesture with her hands. "So, let's talk instead about the future. Why do you keep lying to me about ours?"

"What?"

"You don't want a holiday home in the Mojave Desert, Mick. That's obvious. You'd rather have somewhere more manicured and tame: with a golf club and a lake for sailing and other holiday homes around, maybe."

"A lake for swimming more than sailing," Mick dared to say, since Susan didn't seem angry. "The lake in the woods at Tevendon was spectacular."

"Oh, I know you thought so." She chuckled. "One holiday in England and you turn into a weird Britisher. Don't think I didn't notice you sneaking off into the forest to freeze in the icy waters, when there was a perfectly lovely heated pool you could have been enjoying. Mick, seriously, just be straight with me. If you don't want something, tell me you don't want it. It's much easier."

"But, honey, if *you* want it—"

"No." Susan shook her head. "That's not enough. You have to want it too. My dream home can't be one that isn't yours too."

"Aw, you're so sweet, Suze—"

"Please don't say that about me. I'm in the habit of making grown men weep when they cross me." She smiled at the waiter who had appeared at their table, and said, "Don't worry, you're perfectly safe, honey."

"I'm relieved to hear that, ma'am."

Once he'd gone, Susan said, "Speaking of Tevendon, since we have been . . . I've never told you before, but there's one detail that really sticks in my mind from that day, 2 July. And I bet you'll never guess what it is."

"Was it Jane Brinkwood getting murdered?"

Susan laughed. "Hilarious. No. Want a clue?" She waved her menu in front of his face.

"A menu?"

"Not this one, but yeah. The dinner menu that night, the night Jane was killed. There was one on every table. Now, that's all I'm going to say. Do you know what I'm talking about?"

Mick didn't. "I mean, I believe you about the menus on the tables but I don't see the significance."

Susan leaned in. "Okay, so, you know I was watching all the drama that night super attentively? I wasn't even pretending to mind my own business. You were, in your aspiring Britisher way—being all reserved—but I was all in, determined to enjoy the big honeymoon bust-up show. Couldn't have happened to a more deserving couple, in my view. You reap what you sow. Anyway . . . you know I'm a keen observer of detail when I want to be."

"For sure," said Mick.

"Right. So, here's what I saw happen: William Gleave went inside, into the kitchen building. Probably to use the restroom, or to hide somewhere and sob about the terrible life choices he'd made. While he was in there, Jane started an argument about the champagne, accusing Lucy and Lovely Pete of stealing her bottle deliberately, then she grabbed the bottle, picked up Pete's glass and tried to pour the champagne in it back into the bottle. She ended up spilling some of it on her dress. You agree so far? That's what happened?"

Mick nodded.

"Good. Now, all this time, Jane's holding the menu in her hand—"

"I didn't notice that."

"*What?* You didn't? It wasn't a big one like this menu. It was a tiny little rectangular card-type thing, all snooty and embossed. Covered in spilled champagne now too. Jane's holding it and, like, vibrating with entitled rage. This is the state William finds her in when he's foolish enough to emerge from his kitchen hiding place. He comes out looking dejected and grumpy, as usual—as no doubt anyone who'd just got hitched to the Brinkwood bitch would—but then something *happened*. It must have. Something changed for him, in a big way. And yet . . . I didn't see or hear anything happen, and I was watching carefully."

"What happened was that William whispered something in Jane's ear and then she started to say 'Oh, my God' and told him to leave her alone—"

"No, you're wrong. That all happened eventually, but I'm talking about before that. Something happened in William's mind, some internal shift, so that he went from looking the way he'd looked when he first came outside again—like a doom-fearing, slack-jawed basset hound that expects to get kicked by everyone it meets—to looking like he's seen his own ghost or something. Something terrible beyond imagining. It had to be related to the champagne somehow, but I can't think how. Can you?"

"No," said Mick. "Also, I don't understand why he grabbed the menu from Jane and tore it up. I've never understood that."

"I've replayed it in my head so many times and it still makes no sense," said Susan. "He really looked like he *hated* that menu when he ripped it up. I mean, let's be clear: I personally don't care who killed Jane Brinkwood. Good luck to them. I hope they get away with it. She was a monster and deserved everything she got."

"You don't really mean that, Suze."

She laughed. "You're so sweet and naive. Believe me, I mean

every word. I'm not nice and forgiving like you. Anyway, I don't want to argue about the Brinkwood bitch or slack-jawed William or any of them ever again. I want to put them in the past and leave them there."

"Then let's do that," said Mick.

"We will, soon. But first . . ." Susan gave him a pointed look.

"First what?"

"We need to go back to England. To the Culver Valley."

"Why?"

"Because it's all going to start up again. Everyone's going to be churned up by Lucy's latest mail-out and people might start to talk, to say things they haven't previously said. I want to be on the scene for whatever's about to go down. From all the way across the pond, I feel too much at the mercy of whatever everyone else decides to do."

"There's no point in resisting, is there? Do I at least get to swim in the lake at Tevendon again if we go back?" This was just like the Mojave Desert house: Mick wanted, badly, to say no. So why was he going along with it?

"The resort's been shut since Jane was murdered," Susan told him. "I'm sure we can find some other expanse of ice-cold water for you to dive into. Bear in mind this is going to be England, in the winter—probably too cold even for you."

"Not with my new Neoprene socks and gloves."

"You're insane."

"How do you know the resort's shut?"

"I like to keep abreast of developments," Susan said with an enigmatic smile. "I google Tevendon from time to time."

"Well, if you insist, then I guess I'm in," said Mick, trying to ignore the feeling of dread in his gut. "I just hope we don't regret it."

19

Saturday, January 11, 2020

"There you are." Lucy walked into her and Pete's bedroom where he'd been sitting alone for the past half hour, cross-legged on the bed, with her letter to Jane's murderer and the covering note in front of him. He couldn't believe she'd sent one to him too—treated him no differently from the handful of almost-strangers they'd met at Tevendon last year and not seen since. Come to think of it, he couldn't believe Lucy had sent these communications to anybody, or written them in the first place.

"Are you okay?" she said. "Was there a problem putting Evin to bed?"

"No. She's sound asleep."

"Then why haven't you come down?"

"I was reading and rereading these," said Pete. "Trying to get my head round it all."

"You've taken it personally, haven't you?" She sighed and sat down beside him. "I told you not to."

"No. No, I haven't taken it personally at all."

"Pete, come on. Don't be like this."

"Like what, Luce? How do you think I'm being?"

"You know I know you didn't kill Jane, right? In fact, I'd suspect myself before I'd suspect you—that I'd blacked out, stabbed her, and then deleted the memory."

Pete looked at her. "Is that a joke? Are you waiting for me to laugh?"

"Why are you so angry with me? I told you: I had to give you the letter too if I was going to send it to everyone else. Otherwise it's unfair to the others."

"I'm not angry, Lucy. I'm worried. Really worried."

"About?"

Pete hated having to spell it out, but he couldn't see a way to avoid it. Not if he wanted her to get better. "I'm worried for you. Your state of mind. Writing a long, heartfelt letter to a murderer in which you . . . I don't know, make a bid to be his or her best friend . . . And then, two months later, sending that letter to a load of people you *know* are innocent because you were with them at the relevant time . . ."

"What about it?" Lucy asked when Pete didn't finish his sentence. "Yes, okay, so I did all those things—though I'd dispute the part about trying to be the murderer's best friend. That wasn't at all what I was doing. But carry on. What's your point?"

"Luce, those aren't the actions of a mentally well person."

She stared at him blankly for a couple of seconds. Then she laughed. "You think I've lost my marbles? Are you going to come over all Victorian husband and have me locked away?"

"I think you've got more marbles than most people will ever have, Luce. In almost every area of your life, your brain is functioning in the same brilliant way it always has, but . . . I think you were quite understandably traumatized when William and Jane betrayed you, and you never had any therapy for it and—"

"Listen, I hired a doula to help me with my pregnancy and the birth, and look how that turned out. Who knows what'd happen if I hired a psychotherapist? She might steal my kidneys or put strychnine in my coffee."

Pete couldn't for the life of him understand why Lucy was

suddenly in such a good mood. "Can we be serious?" he said. "This is difficult for me to say, so I'm just going to get it over with: I think you're still unhealthily obsessed with everything involving William and Jane. Including her murder. These"—he pointed at the letter and note on the bed—"are evidence of that. I really think you need to get some help, Luce."

"Yeah, I can see why you'd think that," she said cheerily.

He wasn't sure what she meant, but he didn't like the sound of it.

Trying again from a different angle, he said, "You didn't even seem to care when Caroline Moyle-Jones rang and told you how much your letter to a murderer has upset and scared Harriet—"

"I didn't seem to care because I *didn't* care," said Lucy. "If Harriet wants to get in a state about nothing, that's up to her. I'm not taking the blame for it—I didn't accuse her of anything. I did the opposite. My note began: 'This is not an accusation.'"

"But . . ." How could Pete explain if she couldn't see it? "I don't think that's the real you talking when you say things like that, that you don't care if you upset people."

"The real me? You mean the more polite and considerate version of me that you'd approve of more? The version that doesn't express herself truthfully?"

"Luce, you texted a police sergeant and accused her of lying."

Lucy frowned. "No, I didn't. My text to Charlie said, 'What do you know about Mr. and Mrs. Friendly that you haven't told me?'"

"Why the hell should she tell you? Sorry, I don't mean to sound angry but—"

"Pete." Lucy put her hand on his arm. "If you're angry, there's nothing wrong with sounding like you are. And you're right, Charlie has no obligation to tell me anything she doesn't want to, but you've shifted the goalposts. Your original point—that I'd accused her of lying—wasn't true or fair."

"I know I can't win this argument," Pete said. "You're ten times cleverer than I am, and you can split hairs and justify your every move brilliantly, but to me it all sounds precision engineered to justify an obsession that's doing you no good at all."

"I can see that it looks that way to you." Lucy's tone was eminently reasonable. "Now let me tell you how it looks to me." She stood up and walked over to the bedroom window. "You want me to get therapy? Writing that letter to Jane's murderer, and the letter I wrote to William before that—"

"You wrote to William?"

"I didn't send it. But yes, I wrote to him, to put into words some things I'd been thinking for a while. It helped me massively to write it all down. Same with my letter to Jane's killer. I felt *so* much better, so much mentally lighter, after writing it. And I sent the copies to everyone as a deliberate strategic move— because the police were getting nowhere. They weren't going to solve the case. Nothing was happening. And I'm sorry but whenever I find myself thinking, *Someone needs to do something*, my next thought is usually *And who better than me?* I did it for us, Pete—so that we can be free of all this shit one day. William turning up on our doorstep last week made me realize how much I want to relegate him to the past once and for all and then never think about him or Jane again. I knew I wouldn't be able to do that until I knew who had killed Jane."

She turned to face Pete. "Look, I'm very aware of how obsessed I've been. I know how large the shadow of William and Jane's betrayal has loomed over my life, our lives. Please don't think for a second that I haven't noticed."

Pete nodded. He felt numb.

"I'll make a deal with you: if Jane's murder gets solved in the next . . . week? No, let's say two weeks. If we know who killed her within fourteen days of today, and if it's in any way down to my little mailing campaign that we gain that knowledge, then we'll agree my strategy worked."

"And if it doesn't work, and in fourteen days we still don't know?" Pete asked.

"Then I'll stop. I'll get therapy—whatever you want. But it won't happen, because my plan's going to work. We'll know the truth, long before two weeks have passed. I can feel it. Sorry if that sounds crazy to you. Who knows, maybe I am."

"Can I have a turn at sounding crazy?" Pete said. "There's a question I've wanted to ask you since Tevendon."

"Go on."

"Do you know—or do you strongly suspect you know—who murdered Jane?"

"No." Lucy looked puzzled. "Of course not. How could I know?"

"Well, you don't, so . . . you don't!" Pete smiled brightly, hoping that would be enough to draw a line under the matter.

"Do *you* know?"

"No." How obvious was it that he was lying?

Not lying. Knowledge and suspicion are two different things.

"Do you suspect someone? Fuck, Pete! You do, don't you? Tell me. Why haven't you told me already?"

"I don't. I really don't, okay?"

Maybe it was true, what he'd just said. He *had* suspected a particular person, on and off, sometimes quite strongly. But surely Lucy's answer to his question was all the proof he needed that he'd been entirely wrong to do so.

20

"Are you going to speak to me before we go in?" Charlie asked Simon as they pulled into the driveway of the house that Charlie's sister, Olivia, shared with her husband, Dominic. "I'd recommend it, if we want Liv to tell us anything. You know what she's like: if she gets wind of any trouble between us, she'll be totally focused on that and nothing else."

Simon didn't reply. He got out of the car and waited for Charlie to do the same.

Eventually she did, and slammed the passenger door. "Fine. I deserve it. I should have told you much sooner, blah blah. Can I just point out, though, that eventually we're going to have the discussion and sort it out. We always do. I'm in favor of having it sooner rather than later, so that we don't have to waste days or possibly weeks not speaking to each other."

"Easy for you to say."

Oh, thank God. Words at last.

"You've got no reason to not want to speak to me." Simon rang Liv's doorbell. "I haven't been lying to you since last July."

Did Charlie have time for a quick swipe back? She decided to risk it. "You've been ignoring my hundreds of apologies. What if that's worse? I think it is. Also, you've decided, as you always do, that pretending I don't exist is a legitimate way of expressing your annoyance."

"It's more than annoyance."

"Ooh, I'm scared. Honestly, you're *such* a child."

The door opened, and there was Liv with . . . What on earth was that, dangling from a chain around her neck? A pendant. It looked like a hot beach—waves, sand, and sky, in layers—inside a glass globule that was almost, but not quite, spherical. As well as this strange object, Liv was wearing her old favorite: a bright pink velour tracksuit that Charlie knew well. It had "Juicy" spelled out in small fake diamonds across the buttocks area. Liv's hair was balanced on top of her head in an odd style: a sort of fat bulb shape on top, with tendrils escaping off to the left above her forehead. "You've got an octopus on your head," Charlie observed.

Liv looked pleased. "Funny you should say that. It's a hairstyle I invented, and I called it guess what? 'The Octopus'!"

"Can we come in?" Simon asked. "Are you alone?"

"You'd think I might not be, wouldn't you, since it's Sunday?" Liv looked sorrowful. "Weekends aren't a thing for Dom. He works every second of every day that he's not asleep. It's barbaric. He seems to like it, but I don't see how he can, really. I've found this thing I want us to do together, called the Grown-Up Gap Year. It looks amaz—"

"Is Dominic at home or not?" Simon cut her off.

"Not. I told Char on the phone that he wouldn't be in." Liv dropped the self-pity and smiled again. "I'm dying to hear what it is that can't be discussed in his presence."

Really? You can't work it out? You really think this might be some fun gossip that we can all enjoy together?

"And—oh, my God! It's so lovely to see you both," Liv gushed. "I say to Dom all the time, 'I honestly think Charlie and Simon might be avoiding us.'"

"Not any more, apparently." Charlie managed to produce the semblance of a smile.

Liv beamed back at her. "It's so fab to see you, Char!" Now she was blinking back tears.

Incredible. She's going to fall in with my act and pretend nothing was ever wrong. Of course she is.

Charlie had given herself strict instructions to think only about the information she and Simon were here to extract, but, as they followed the bottom strewn with fake diamonds along the hall to the large dining kitchen, Charlie could feel her resolve crumbling. If she colluded in the pretense that all was sweetness and light and always had been, didn't that make a mockery of the stand she'd once thought worth taking?

Around three years ago, she'd decided that the effort she was putting into fighting down her anger whenever she spent time with her only sibling was simply not sustainable. She hadn't been prepared to do it any more, and Simon had shrugged and said, "Whatever. It's up to you." Before Charlie knew it, the decision had been made, and she'd felt only intense relief. From that point on, she had turned down Liv's invitations and rejected all her social overtures.

Liv was no fool, especially where interpersonal relationships were concerned, and had noticed the new policy within three weeks of its introduction. She'd ambushed Charlie outside work and demanded to know what was going on. Charlie had anticipated this move and prepared her response. "You and Gibbs," she'd said—a conveniently ambiguous explanation. "I can't do it any more, Liv: can't sit there at your and Dom's kitchen table and pretend I don't know about your relationship with another man—a man Simon happens to work with."

Charlie had known exactly what Liv would think she meant, and also that Liv wouldn't suspect she knew much more than that.

Liv had begged her not to be so "draconian"—that was the word she'd used, which still took Charlie's breath away whenever she thought about it.

The upshot was that Charlie had drawn a line and hadn't spoken to her sister for years. Until today. And instead of saying, "How dare you decide to reestablish contact exactly when it suits you, as if you didn't cut me off a few years ago like the judgmental bitch you are?," Liv was displaying no bitterness at all. No confusion either. Instead, she was skipping around her kitchen, producing fancy coffee pods for Simon and Charlie to choose between and pointing out local attractions in the high-pitched squeal of a tour guide on speed: "Look, this is new since you were last here: it's an actual bona fide pizza oven! I've been making the most amazing pizzas. And this is our brilliant Ninja air fryer . . . Oh, and you *have* to come and see the new summer house in the garden! Can I show it to you once we've finished talking about whatever you want to talk about?"

"Depends on time," said Charlie. An air fryer? Who the hell needed or wanted to fry air? Charlie and Simon didn't even have a working toaster any more—it had broken long ago. They'd also recently lost their cheese grater. It always felt like too much effort to think about replacing these supposedly necessary, offensively boring items.

Liv handed them their coffees in cups and saucers that looked as if they'd cost more than all Charlie's crockery put together. "Well? I'm all ears!" She perched on one of the tall, blue-leather-upholstered stools next to the white marble island in the center of the room. "What do you want to ask me about? I'm dying to know."

How could she not have worked it out? Or was her edge-of-seat curiosity an act? Could well be, Charlie decided. Liv was probably one of the most proficient liars in the country by now, if not the world.

"Jane Brinkwood," said Simon. "Specifically, her murder at the Tevendon Estate Resort on 2 July last year."

"Oh. Right. That." The eagerness drained from Liv's face.

"Yeah, that."

Had she really imagined she'd be able to keep her connection to it secret forever?

Of course. To live the way she does, you need a brain that believes only what's easiest and most advantageous at any given moment.

"You and Gibbs were staying at Cottage Number 6 under false names," said Simon. "Pretending to be a married couple: Hester and Chris Arthur. You named yourself after Hester Prynne, your fictional hero. I'd forgotten until Charlie reminded me: you told us your favorite book was Hawthorne's *The Scarlet Letter*—at a barbecue, just"—Simon pointed over his shoulder at the French doors that led out to the garden—"out there, a few years ago."

"Imaginative first-name choice on Gibbs's part," Charlie couldn't resist saying. "Chris. His actual, real name."

"We were gone long before anyone was murdered," said Liv.

"Yeah, we know that," said Simon. "Presumably you knew we took over your cottage soon after you'd left it?"

Liv nodded. "How did you know about it, though? Chris and I couldn't figure that out."

"Remember telling Mum and Dad you'd left early?" said Charlie. "I spoke to Mum just after you'd told her. She's always passing on your news to me in the hope that it'll make me want to get in touch with you and heal the rift."

"Any mum would do that," said Liv.

"Yeah, I'm not criticizing her." *Though I easily could . . .* She knew Liv would have told their mother that the Tevendon holiday was a her-and-Gibbs thing and not a her-and-Dom thing, and that not a word of criticism or question would have been offered in response.

Charlie had never expected her parents to cut Liv off for having a years-long affair while first engaged and then married to the completely oblivious Dominic—not even when they considered that Liv's lover was also married, and the father of twins, and a colleague of both Charlie and, more closely, Simon.

The idea of Liv being deserted and shunned by her entire close family was intolerable, even through Charlie's mists of fury and resentment, and she was positively glad that her parents had found themselves still able to stand the sight and company of Liv despite it all, otherwise she might not have felt so free herself to cut all contact. Still, though—and Charlie knew she couldn't make the whole world dance to her tune—her parents' attitude to Liv's antics sickened her. They were determined to view the situation as having come about as a result of Liv's uniquely romantic, abundantly loving character. Few people, apparently, had quite such a sensitive and original psyche. Liv had different needs from most ordinary folk, Charlie's mother, Linda, had tried to explain several times. She was less able than more conventionally minded others to subdue her true nature and submit to society's requirements.

Bullshit. Charlie would have had far more respect for her parents if they'd said, "Look, we know as well as you do that your sister's a selfish twat with zero integrity, but we love her too much to let ourselves give a shit about that."

Charlie noticed that Liv was waiting for her to say more. She dragged her thoughts back to the reason why she and Simon were here: Tevendon. "When Mum said you'd walked out of your holiday with three days left, I thought, *Why not?* Simon and I were both owed time off. Neither of us was particularly busy for once. So I rang and scooped up the suddenly available cottage for the last three nights of your week. Arrived just in time to have one swim, a third of a dinner, and then get caught up in a murder."

"God, Char, how awful for you to have been there when it happened."

"It was a stroke of luck, us being there," said Simon. "We were able to have firsthand access. Doesn't often happen."

"That hasn't seemed to help you much," said Liv. "Chris says this is the longest any case has dragged on without being solved since he and you have worked together."

"Shall we talk about what hasn't helped me?" Simon slammed his coffee cup down on its saucer. "Only finding out now that you were there. You know you could be charged with obstruction of justice?"

What Charlie knew and Liv didn't was that Simon was giving his anger free rein now to compensate for the fact that he would never confront Gibbs about his role in the cover-up. He'd be scared to do so, and unwilling to admit it to himself. When Charlie had cut off contact with Liv, Simon had continued his relationship with Gibbs exactly as before.

There was something about Gibbs, a kind of force field of menacing I-might-just-kill-everyone energy that surrounded him, warning you never to push him too far. And Charlie had noticed that Simon had recently—well, over the past few years—come to regard Sam, Gibbs and Sellers, and even Proust, with a new and almost religious loyalty. They were his team, and he liked having a team that was there no matter what, and that mattered more than anything they said or did.

"I haven't obstructed anything," Liv protested. "I wasn't there when that awful woman died and I don't know who killed her."

"Awful?" said Charlie.

"Yes! She was *horrible*, Char. Like, almost unbelievably horrible. And didn't seem to care. She threatened me."

"With what?" Simon asked.

"Somehow she found out that Chris and I had booked in using pseudonyms. I suspect she sneaked around and eavesdropped near our open windows. That's my best guess. She—"

"Pseudonyms," said Charlie. "Ha! Mark Twain, George Eliot,

and Hester and Chris Arthur. No difference between the three cases, really. Apart from the masterpieces produced—or lack thereof, but let's not get hung up on the details."

"Charlie, for fuck's sake," Simon snapped.

"It's okay. She's only joking. And actually, a timely reminder is always useful."

Charlie didn't want to take the bait but her willpower had been stuck on a low setting for the past few days. "Reminder?"

"That I've yet to produce my literary masterpiece." Liv grinned. "Still, plenty of time. I'm reading an amazing book at the moment, called *Repotting Your Life*, about how important it is to reinvent yourself and grow."

"What were Jane Brinkwood's exact words when she threatened you?" Simon asked. "Was it only you or did she say it to Gibbs too?"

"No, I was singled out for special persecution," said Liv. "I don't think she'd have dared go near Chris. She accosted me when I was walking in the gardens on my own and said, 'I know you're not who you're pretending to be. You're not a married couple at all—you're both married to other people.'"

"What an outrageous slur." Charlie feigned shock. She shouldn't have come; her self-control wasn't up to the job today. "Imagine telling you and Chris, of all people, that you *aren't a married couple*. The cheek! I hope you set her straight."

Liv looked perturbed. "What do you mean?" she asked.

"Did she threaten to tell someone you weren't who you were claiming to be?" Simon asked.

"Oh, yes. Everyone at the resort. And then she said she was going to find out who we really were and inform on us to our respective spouses. I said, 'Why on earth would you do that? Why don't you mind your own business? What have we ever done to harm you?' and she said, 'You tell me,' in a really knowing, weird way. My heart was pounding so hard I thought

I might keel over. I've never been threatened like that before, by someone who doesn't even try to conceal their . . . ill-wishery. When I said that I couldn't think of anything Chris or I might have done to offend her, she accused us of sending her an anonymous note telling her to 'Beware,' in capital letters. It was so silly, such an anticlimax, I actually giggled. Then she accused me of being a sociopath. Strange thing was, she wasn't mollified at all when I swore on my life and everything I hold dear that we knew nothing about the note and hadn't sent it. That seemed to make her even angrier. She screeched at me, 'Well, who, then? If not you, who?' To be honest, I think she was just very upset at the thought that someone had sent her a horrible anonymous message—which is understandable, I suppose, but that doesn't make it okay to go round threatening and accusing people."

"So was that it, the whole conversation?" said Simon.

"No. I told her I was sorry someone had sent her a horrid note, and especially on her honeymoon. She thanked me, as if suddenly we were friends, and started to say how stressed she'd been even before the note arrived. One of the other guests . . . oh, well, of course you know this. Her husband's ex-wife gate-crashed their honeymoon, with her new partner. Jane ended up kind of crying on my shoulder, while I made encouraging noises and gave her tips on how to enjoy her honeymoon despite the presence of the ex-wife."

"Great," said Charlie. "So you became pals. Good old husband-thieving pals."

Liv looked wounded. "That's not fair, Char. I very clearly *haven't* stolen Chris from Debbie, as we can tell from the fact that he's still married to her and living with her. I would never lure a man with children away from his family, so don't try and lump me in with Jane Brinkwood. I'm nothing like her: I don't threaten or accuse people. The opposite. I think the best of everybody and go out of my way to give as much benefit of the doubt as I can, always. I certainly don't march around trashing other people's precious summer holidays with eruptions of unpleasantness."

"So that's why you left Tevendon three days early?" said Simon.

Liv looked uncomfortable. She pulled the glass ball full of beach out of her cleavage and started rubbing it between her thumb and index finger as if hoping a genie might appear to answer the question on her behalf.

"If I tell you something that happened at Tevendon, do you swear you won't tell Chris?"

"No," Simon said. "I work with him. If it's important, he'll find out."

"But . . . I mean, I don't mind if you tell him the information. That's fine. Surely you don't need to tell him it came from me. Please?"

Unbelievable. She thought she was in a position to bargain.

"I didn't tell him at the time and I haven't since," Liv went on. "I made up other reasons for why I suddenly wanted to leave: bad atmosphere, the new wife and the old wife keeping their beady eyes on each other across the swimming pool while pretending not to. I mean, all that was true too. Honestly, Char, I kept thinking, *I wish Charlie was here so that we could gossip about it.*" Liv smiled. "And thanks to me, you *were* there—only a bit later. And here we are now, gossiping about it! Awww."

"So you lied to Gibbs about why you wanted to leave Tevendon?" Simon said.

"Well, I just thought, if I tell him the truth, he'll have to get all police-y about it, and I didn't want him distracted by anything. It had been so hard to find a week when we could both go, think of plausible excuses for why we had to be away from home . . . I didn't want to give up the rest of our precious full week together." Seeing the confusion on Charlie's face, Liv said, "Oh! We didn't sack the whole thing when we left Tevendon early. I booked us into a luxury five-star hotel in Sussex for our last three nights." Liv looked proud.

"Hope Dom didn't mind paying for that," Charlie murmured.

"When we got to the hotel, I considered telling Chris why I'd really wanted to leave Tevendon."

"But you didn't," said Charlie.

"No. I knew he'd be angry that I hadn't told him at the time. And then the same thing stopped me mentioning it later too, after Jane was—"

"What was your true reason for wanting to leave the resort?" Simon said briskly.

"I'm about to tell you." Liv sounded puzzled, as if she couldn't understand why he was in such a hurry. "It has nothing to do with Jane Brinkwood, so you might be disappointed. This is about Mick, the American guy."

"Mick Henry?" said Charlie.

"Yes. And Anita from the office. I was on my way to the office one day to ask about booking a chef to cook us a meal in our cottage, and . . . You know how you have to come up sort of from behind and go round the side of the building to get to the front door, and all the windows and the door are usually open?"

Charlie nodded.

"I overheard Mick talking to Anita and sounding . . . really agitated. He was in a flap about something. So I hovered and listened, not wanting to barge in if there was a scene going on—"

"But wanting to hear every word," said Charlie.

"Obviously." Liv tittered as if they'd shared a joke. "And I *did* hear lots of words—alarming ones. Mick was talking about finding some bones. Bones!" she repeated. "He kept saying, 'But what if they're human? What if they're human bones?' Anita was trying to reassure him that they couldn't be. She said she'd seen loads of animal bones since she'd started working at Tevendon and even before that, when she'd lived there—"

"Anita used to live at Tevendon?" said Simon.

"I don't know," Liv said. "I'm only telling you what I heard. Anyway, she reassured Mick that they were definitely animal bones. He kept insisting the police needed to be called because clearly someone had *hidden* the bones, and why would they have done that if they were just innocent old animal bones?"

Simon was scribbling in his notebook. "You're sure Mick Henry found these bones himself?"

"Um . . ." Liv considered it. "No, but . . . he and Anita were the people who knew about the bones, so one or both of them must have found them, I guess. I assumed Mick had, but I don't know for sure."

"Did he say where they'd been hidden?"

Liv nodded. "Chris tapped me on the shoulder at that point, though, and obviously I didn't want him to overhear anything—"

"Obviously," said Charlie. "He'd have gone all boringly police-y about the finding of possibly human bones. What a killjoy."

"Haha!" Liv took a break from her story to show her appreciation for the joke.

"Go on," said Simon, shooting a look of disgust in Charlie's direction. She hadn't been much of a help to him so far; she knew that. *Could do better.*

"I started chatting to distract Chris, but I was still listening to Mick with one ear too," Liv said. "So, yeah, I heard where the hiding place was, sort of."

"How do you mean 'sort of'?" asked Simon.

"I know Mick found the bones behind Tevendon Mere. I clearly heard him say that, and I *think* he then said 'in the woods'—which would make sense because there's nothing else behind the mere apart from the woods, is there?"

"Not for a few miles, no," said Simon.

"But what I didn't hear was why he thought what he'd found was a hiding place. I mean, why did he think someone had hidden the bones rather than just assuming they were the bones of an animal who'd died in the woods? I kept wondering: Were they half buried, or in a bin bag or something?"

Simon was shaking his head. "I needed to know this the second you heard Jane Brinkwood had been murdered. Not telling me then, straight away—"

"I know, I know." Liv pulled an apologetic face. "I'm really, really sorry that I couldn't and didn't. It's just . . . Chris would have been *apoplectic* if he'd found out I hadn't breathed a word about any of it before we left the resort, and . . . Well, actually, you can take it as a compliment!" Liv loved nothing more than to identify a hitherto-overlooked silver lining. "When I heard about Jane's death and you being on the case, I thought, *Thank God. Simon'll soon get to the bottom of it all, even without my help.*"

"It's January," Charlie said expressionlessly. "Six months later. That's not soon."

"So, just to be clear about what you're telling us . . . ," said Simon. "You left Tevendon because you heard Mick Henry panicking about the bones and Anita Khattou trying to reassure him?"

"Yes. And then, twenty-four hours later, both Anita and Mick were wandering around, chirpy as anything, looking as if nothing was wrong, but in a really fake way. I don't know, maybe I imagined the fakeness. But it was too weird for me. They were both behaving as if the whole bones thing had never happened. It made me feel uneasy, as if something really bad had been swept under the carpet. No police came to ask questions about any bones. And in a way I didn't want them to, in case Chris abandoned me and went to join in with them, but . . . why wasn't the fact of the bones having been hidden enough to make Anita call the police, if only to check and reassure Mick, who was a guest?"

It was a good point. Charlie could imagine the Tripadvisor review: "My accommodation was as luxurious as the website had promised, however the resort staff rudely refused to take my discovery of hidden bones seriously."

"I decided to trust my intuition, which was screaming *Enough, enough, enough*," said Liv. "It's hard to describe, Char, but I suddenly had a feeling of foreboding about Tevendon that was nothing like I'd ever felt about anywhere before. I just had to get the hell out."

21

Monday, January 13, 2020

LUCY

"How did you know?" Charlie asks as soon as we've got our mugs of mint tea in front of us. This time we're not at my house. We've met at Antívaro, a Greek café in Spilling that she said would be more convenient for her. She and I have now met three times. This is the third. The first was my initiative, the second was hers. This one's half and half. She suggested we meet, but only because I texted her first. And none of this matters or means anything, so why am I even thinking about it?

Remember: Charlie Zailer is not your friend. Neither is Jane's killer.

"How did I know what?" I say.

"That I knew something about Mr. and Mrs. Friendly, more than I'd told you?"

"I read the room, as they say. Ugh, I don't know why I used that expression. I hate it. It basically means: work out what everyone around you wants you to do and then do it."

Charlie's looking at me in a strange, unfocused way. She half whispers, "Read the room." Then her eyes clear and she says in her usual voice, "That's what I did: I *read the room*. And I didn't know it until just now."

"What do you mean?"

She smiles. "I owe you one. You've helped me work something out."

"About Jane's murder? What? Tell me."

"I thought you wanted to know about Mr. and Mrs. Friendly."

"I do, but—"

"I'm willing to tell you about them, but only if you'll answer a question first: How did you know I was keeping something back?"

"It's one of the advantages of being an overthinker," I tell her. "I've been replaying our conversations in my mind, and that part felt odd whenever I remembered it. I'd said something about the Friendlys maybe having something to do with Jane's death, and you shut me down so definitively and automatically, it was like, 'No, it *definitely* wasn't them.' Not in a defensive way as if you wanted to protect them, or in a straightforward 'They've been eliminated' way. The more I thought about it, the more I suspected you trusted them because you knew them personally."

"Excellent deduction," says Charlie. "I do know them. And I trust them not to have murdered anyone."

"So, who are they?"

"If I tell you, will you return the favor and tell me the truth you've been withholding?" She smiles faintly. "Don't look at me like that. I know you've been lying."

Fuck. Fuck, fuck, fuck.

"I don't think you murdered Jane," she says. "My gut instinct is screaming that you didn't."

"Good, because I didn't."

"Then this should be easy. Tell me everything you've lied about, and all of the truth. All the inconvenient parts of the story you've withheld so far. If you're honest with me now and from now on, then I'll tell you all about Mr. and Mrs. Friendly. Deal?"

My heart hammers in my chest. I daren't pick up my mug of tea. I'd spill it all over the table.

"Oh." Charlie makes a show of looking disappointed. "Not enough incentive? Okay, how about I buy you some baklava too? Look." She points to the glass display cabinet. "Looks good, right?"

"What do you want to know?"

"All the things, please. Someone like you? You know exactly what you've lied about. You've probably got a numbered list on your phone."

My memory's so good, I didn't need to write it down. Or type it up.

"While you're considering it, I have another question," Charlie says. "Why did you change your daughter's name from Zoe to Evin? No one does that."

"I don't care what anybody else does or doesn't do."

"Yeah, I can tell that about you."

"I wanted a fresh start—for Evin too, with a better father, one who'd never abandon her. Evin was Pete's grandmother's name. It's Kurdish."

Charlie nods. "Did you deliberately steal Jane's special honeymoon champagne?"

"No." I almost tell her that I'm unlikely ever to drink champagne again, that the word alone is enough to make me shudder. "We ordered a different bottle and a waiter brought us out that bottle. Honest mix-up by the kitchen staff."

"Fair enough. And how's your letter-to-a-murderer going down with the Tevendon gang?"

"Badly." I try to smile. "Pete thinks I'm well on my way to a padded cell. Caroline Moyle-Jones is angry and feeling protective of Harriet, who's apparently very upset. Jack and Polly McCallion sent a one-line, Jack-and-Jill message effectively saying, 'Thanks for sending us this very interesting letter, but please don't send any more.' And I haven't heard from William at all. Oh—Susan and Mick Henry are apparently flying back to the UK, according to Caroline. She sent me a text demanding that I tell her why, even though I don't know any more than she does and she was the one Susan contacted, not me. Okay then."

"What's okay?"

"I'll tell you everything I haven't told you already."

"Great." Charlie grins. I could imagine us becoming friends if the circumstances were different. "Baklava?"

"No, thanks."

"Just quickly," she says. "What's a Jack-and-Jill message? I've never heard of them."

"That's because I made it up on the spot ten seconds ago. You've heard of a Jack-and-Jill bathroom?"

"No."

"Doesn't matter. I just meant: a message that a couple writes together and signs from both of them, with an air of 'This is what we, a couple who are very much in love and agree about everything, wish to say to you, as one.'"

Charlie laughs. "I'm going to start using that expression immediately." She pulls a notepad and pen out of her bag. "Okay then, let's hear it."

"You guessed right. I have a list—"

"Of course you do."

"—of things that don't seem right, or that I can't find an explanation for."

"Such as?"

"There was a day—I can't remember which, I'm afraid—that I bumped into Mick Henry near Tevendon Mere. I was gearing up to chat to him, but he was really weird and unfriendly and just kind of grunted and walked off. I wondered if I'd done something to offend him. He was on his way for a swim in the mere, though, so maybe he was just in a hurry. The next time I saw him, he seemed totally fine. It wasn't a big deal but it was a bit jarring."

"Did he look miserable, angry, scared?"

"Couldn't tell you, sorry. The only thing I knew for sure was that he wished he hadn't bumped into me, and he didn't want to linger and chat."

"Noted. Go on."

"Second strange thing: the snoring." I feel pathetic even saying it. It can't be relevant.

"Snoring?" Charlie looks up.

"Yeah. Both Mick Henry and Anita Khattou told me that Mick's snoring was a problem—so serious that it kept not only Susan awake but also Anita, who was supposed to be sleeping in Cottage Number 4, the one that was just through the wall from the Henrys' cottage, Number 5. Anita said she'd had broken nights as a result of Susan yelling at Mick about his snoring wrecking her sleep. And then Mick confirmed it. He thanked Anita for moving into a back room in the office building so that he could move into Number 4 and not ruin Susan's sleep for the rest of the holiday."

"What's strange about that?" Charlie asks.

"It might be nothing. You'll probably think I'm inventing puzzles that don't exist, but . . . when you sit around a swimming pool with people all day, there's quite a lot of napping that happens—more so the older you get. I was within range of a snoozing Susan and a snoozing Mick quite a few times. Like, at least once a day each. Every time Susan fell asleep, she instantly started snoring like . . . the loudest train you've ever heard. Everyone was very polite and British and pretended not to notice. Mick would nudge her and then she'd stop for a while, but she'd always start again. I've never heard anything like it. It was really, horrifically loud. Whereas Mick? He could be fast asleep and you'd never hear a peep out of him. So . . . I don't know. It's just a bit odd, I reckon, that both he and Anita said that Mick was the snorer."

"And Anita definitely said she'd heard rows about *Mick's* snoring? Not just rows about snoring?"

"No, she definitely said that the rows involved Susan getting upset with Mick for snoring, and then him getting upset because it's not his fault and he doesn't do it on purpose."

"Interesting," says Charlie.

"That's what I thought. Probably irrelevant, though. And who knows, maybe when you fall asleep on a sun-lounger, your snoring habits are different from when you're lying in bed at night."

"Maybe." Charlie sounds unconvinced.

"The third and final thing is the one I feel worst about telling you, because, frankly, I feel as if I'm just being mean and bitchy. And I could easily have got the wrong impression."

"Go on."

"I read in the papers about Anita's engagement to Ian Brinkwood."

Charlie nods.

"Obviously the engagement happened after Jane's murder, which probably changed a lot of things for a lot of people, but even before Jane died, I'd thought to myself that there was something about Anita's attitude to Lord Brinkwood that didn't add up, somehow. One minute she was speaking about him adoringly—he was giving her this amazing opportunity to run a new luxury hotel once it was built, he'd let her live on the Tevendon Estate when she ran away from home when she was younger . . . She was full of praise and admiration for him. Except she also had a nickname for him that she seemed to use in a quite scathing, mocking tone every now and then— Lordian—as if she didn't think much of him at all."

Charlie looks up from writing in her notebook. "Anything else?"

"No. That's all. And I only kept quiet because each of the things, on its own, is nothing."

"That's always hard to tell." Charlie looks over at the display cabinet. "Sure you don't fancy some baklava? I do."

"Go on, then."

Ten minutes later, we're wiping honey off our fingers with napkins. "I guess it's my turn, then," Charlie says. "Mrs. Friendly is my sister. Her name's Olivia. Liv for short."

"Really? I'd never have guessed. There's no particular resemblance."

"No," Charlie agrees. "Especially not personality-wise, I hope. Mr. Friendly isn't her husband. She's married to someone else. So is he. He has twins. Oh, and he's a detective. He works with Simon. His name's DC Christopher Gibbs." Her voice hardens as she says it.

"Wow. That's . . . a lot." And not what I was expecting.

"Oh, there's more. A few years back, I found out that Liv and Gibbs were planning a secret wedding. Like, actual bigamy." Charlie shakes her head and looks puzzled for a moment. "Which . . . I could so easily not have told you, so why did I?"

Maybe the thought's also crossed her mind that in a different context the two of us might be friends. "Sometimes it's easier to talk to a virtual stranger," I say. She seems embarrassed. I don't want her to wish she hadn't told me.

"I guess."

"So . . . did they go through with it?"

She shrugs.

"You don't *know*?"

"I've never asked. I've been pretending to know nothing about it ever since I found out."

"Why? You could have told her you knew and stopped her

from doing something insane. Why did they want to have a fake, illegal marriage anyway? They could have just been two married people having an affair."

"Maybe I should have done more to stop it. I'm sure they went through with it. Liv would have loved the drama and the secrecy—she'll have decided it added to the romance or some such crap." Charlie looks sad. "Simon and I disagreed about what to do. And . . . he was so much more confident of his rightness than I was, and at the time I'm pretty sure I didn't actually want to be responsible for whatever decision we made. Simon said we absolutely shouldn't get involved. As police, it would compromise us to know that an illegal marriage had taken place, so . . . we needed to make sure we didn't find out. We needed never to ask. It was all about him not being able to stand the thought of Gibbs hating him forever, or hating me."

She attempts a smile. "So I've kept quiet, not asked, not snooped any further—and hated my sister and Gibbs and myself ever since. I'm afraid there's no happy ending. Well, not unless you count me and Simon going round to Liv's yesterday to talk to her about Tevendon. She was so happy to see me, and I was so livid . . . and then last night I found myself lying in bed and thinking all kinds of deranged things."

"Like?" I ask.

"Like that it had been nice to see her," Charlie says quietly. "That I miss her. That maybe I could decide I don't give a fuck what the law says about marriage, and get my sister back. 'Cause, like, I've only got one. So maybe, however flawed she is . . . I mean, I'm not exactly unflawed myself. I didn't tell Simon anything about Liv and Gibbs being in Number 6 before us. Even when Jane was murdered, I didn't tell him. I just . . . try to erase them as a couple from my mind as much as I can."

She hasn't told me the name of DC Gibbs's wife, the mother of the twins. It makes me wonder if there's anybody in a café somewhere in the world right now talking about William and Jane, and maybe Jane's unsolved murder, and referring to me throughout as "William's ex-wife" as if my name doesn't matter.

"So." Charlie looks at me intensely. "That's full disclosure from me. Way fuller than I needed to give you."

Why is she saying it in that way?

"Don't you feel bad?"

"Bad?"

"Guilty, for still holding out on me."

My face starts to heat up. *How the hell . . .*

"Lucy, I don't think you killed Jane. I really don't. So whatever it is, how bad can it be? Just tell me. You'll feel better. I do, having got all my sister shit off my chest. I know you take your commitments seriously, but there's no need to be quite so committed to deceit and withholding. It's not the way forward, trust me."

How can she know? What do I do now? Tell her?

No. Unthinkable.

"I'm not withholding anything," I say, trying to keep my voice level. "I've told you the truth. All of it."

22

Monday, January 13, 2020

"They left because of the bones?" Anita Khattou blinked a few times. "That's so sad. I wish Hester Arthur had spoken to me about it. I could have reassured her that there was nothing to worry about."

Simon hadn't told her that Hester and Chris Arthur's real names were Olivia Zailer and DC Chris Gibbs. He was interviewing Anita and her fiancé, Ian Brinkwood, at their home, the Manor House, which was at the other end of the Tevendon Estate from the holiday resort.

Lord Brinkwood, Simon knew, was seventy-seven years old. He looked much older, with short white hair and a pouchy pink face. He was dressed in a white shirt, mint-green trousers that looked like the bottom half of an ice-cream vendor's uniform, and a navy blazer with some sort of badge or brooch pinned on it. Simon couldn't see what it was from his current position. Lord Brinkwood was hunched in his chair and the badge, instead of sitting flat against his lapel, was hanging at an angle, pointing downward.

Beneath the green trousers, the socks were red and the shoes were bright white tennis shoes that looked as if they'd never been worn before. From the way Lord Brinkwood had shuffled slowly through the corridors of his home a few minutes ago, Simon guessed that it had been some years since he'd last played tennis.

Anita Khattou sat beside him, immaculately dressed and looking very obviously decades younger than her fiancé. Simon suspected it was unfashionable to disapprove of other people's romantic choices, but he nevertheless wished that Brinkwood and Anita had chosen separate chairs far away from each other, so that he could have felt less queasy than he did now, seeing them so close together.

The house made Simon feel nearly as uncomfortable as its residents did. He had never been inside such a grand building before. Until today, all his conversations with Jane's father had taken place at Lord Brinkwood's London flat, which was expensively done out but of much more normal proportions.

This old pile couldn't really be called a house; it was a mansion. Simon was trying not to stare: at the sculptures, the portrait collection, the grandfather clock . . .

"Would you like a tour of the house?" Anita asked him.

"No. No, thanks. Sorry. I mean . . . it's an impressive place."

"We're used to it," said Lord Brinkwood abruptly.

"You haven't lived here long, though, have you?" Simon asked Anita.

"No. Not long at all."

"You don't find it daunting?"

"Not even remotely," she said with a laugh. "It's just a place to live, isn't it? All houses are, unless they mean more to you than that, and as you say, I've not lived here long. It's a damn sight nicer to live in than my horrible, dingy flat in Combingham, and it might be a fancy manor house and all that, but . . . it's just a house, isn't it?"

"Yes, well, it means a great deal to *me*," Ian Brinkwood said indignantly. Immediately, Anita dropped the throwaway manner and started to pat and stroke him, and murmur reassuring things about how she too liked the manor house very much.

Simon thought back to his conversation with the Brinkwood

family lawyers, who had told him about Anita's insistence that she didn't want to inherit any of Lord Brinkwood's property when he died. Instead, she'd told him to leave anything he would have bequeathed to her to a charity. What was it called? Action for Children, that was it.

Simon frowned. Something was snagging at his mind, but he couldn't get a grip on it. Something messy that didn't quite fit . . .

Maybe it was nothing.

"Let's get back to the bones that Mick Henry found," he said.

"Foolish man!" Ian Brinkwood huffed. "Hasn't he walked in woods before? Woods are full of animal bones."

"Given the obvious truth of that, why do you think Mick Henry was so insistent that the police should be called?" Simon asked Anita.

"All I can think is that he thought the bones looked human," she said. "Which they really didn't."

"So, what happened?"

"Well, eventually, when he saw that I wasn't at all worried, he realized he'd overreacted. Pretty soon he was embarrassed about having made a fuss and he started making jokes about how he was a city type, not used to the ways of the country."

"When he came to the office to tell you about the bones, did he bring them with him?"

"No. While he still thought they were probably human, he did the sensible thing and left them undisturbed so as not to destroy any evidence." Anita rolled her eyes. "Once I'd persuaded him to calm down, I went back to the woods with him and showed him several other heaps of bones scattered around exactly like the ones he'd found. That reassured him."

"But the bones he found had been hidden, correct?"

"Hardly." Anita smiled at the memory. "He thought that at

first, but only because he found them in a pile behind a tree. I'm honestly not sure he'd ever been in woods before, unlikely as that sounds."

Ian Brinkwood cleared his throat. "DC Waterhouse, my daughter's murderer is still at large. Could we discuss that rather than the more trivial matter of American tourists and animal bones?"

"Sir, the reason I ask every single question I ask is because I'm trying to work out what happened at the resort that night— what happened to your daughter. I'm sorry if some of it seems beside the point. It's not. It's all important, or at least it might be."

"How much longer, though? Are you getting anywhere? Jane is *dead*."

His pain was as much of a presence in the room as he himself was. Simon felt for him.

"It's intolerable," Brinkwood went on. "All our lives are on hold. I don't mind so much for myself, but poor Anita—"

"Darling, I've told you till I'm hoarse. I don't mind."

"There was supposed to be a new hotel!"

"I know." Simon was still internally shuddering from Anita's "Darling." It was like hearing someone say it to their grandfather.

"Anita was going to run it—she was so looking forward to having her own little empire."

"I don't need an empire," she told him firmly. "I have everything I need." To Simon, she said, "Ian doesn't want to reopen the resort or go ahead with the building of the hotel, and he feels guilty about it for my sake, no matter how many times I tell him there's no need."

"Not only for your sake," Brinkwood corrected her. "Greg and Rebecca Summerell rely on the resort for their livelihood."

"Greg and Rebecca will be *fine*," Anita insisted.

"Yes, but the waste!" Brinkwood's face was getting pinker. "Holidaymakers loved the resort, didn't they? Am I going to keep it closed forever? And the missed opportunities, if we never build the hotel!"

Anita looked at Simon. "Please help me convince him not to keep torturing himself," she said. "Darling, your daughter was murdered at the resort. It's quite, quite natural for you not to like the idea of people going there to have *fun*." She said it as if fun were an abomination. "There's nothing wrong, nothing at all, with the resort remaining closed for as long as you want it to be, even if that's forever, as a way of remembering Jane and respecting her memory."

Simon could hear from the sagging desperation in her voice that Anita had made this speech dozens if not hundreds of times already. Lord Brinkwood shook his head, as if every word she said was an affront. To Simon he said, "Do you agree with my soon-to-be-wife that sacrificing the resort's future and other people's livelihoods in order to indulge my grief and misery is a sensible way forward, DC Waterhouse?"

"I think you should do whatever you want to do," Simon told him.

"Exactly what I've been telling him." Anita sighed.

This life couldn't be much fun for her. And if she also had no interest in inheriting the millions . . . Could it be that she really loved this much older man? Romantic love was probably the thing in the world that Simon understood least well. He knew he loved Charlie more than anyone else on the planet and that he'd happily hurl himself in front of a bullet or an oncoming train to save her life, but was that romantic? Or suicidal?

"I've just got a couple more questions," he said. "I hope they're not too upsetting."

"So do I," said Anita pointedly.

"Anita, I've been told by Lord Brinkwood's lawyers—with his permission—that instead of leaving any money or property or land to you, he's agreed to donate a large sum to a charity you chose."

"Right and wrong," she said. "Yes to the charity part."

"And that charity is Action for Children UK, correct?"

"Yes."

"So, what's the wrong bit?" Simon asked.

"Ian's not leaving me absolutely nothing. Some provision has been made for me."

"On no account will I allow Anita to return to her inadequate flat in Combingham after my death!" Lord Brinkwood said vehemently. "Place isn't fit to house a gerbil!"

"Ian insisted, and I do hate my Combingham flat. I think Ian's lawyers might have confused 'nothing' with 'next to nothing,' which is obviously a matter of opinion and depends what one's used to." Anita gave Simon a just-between-the-two-of-us look that clearly said, *You know what these aristocratic family lawyers are like.* "I'm sure they probably think of what's going to William as nothing too." A note of bitterness had crept into her voice.

"Anita doesn't approve," said Lord Brinkwood.

"That's not true, darling. I just worry. William was the only one with Jane when it happened. I know we've been told he can't have done it but . . . well, can we know that for sure?"

"I'm happy to take DC Waterhouse's word for it." Brinkwood nodded at Simon. "And Jane would have wanted William to be well looked after. She's very much approving from on high— that's how I look at it. And by the way, darling, my Jane would *never* have married the sort of man who would ever kill her."

Simon said to Anita, "Action for Children UK—why did you choose that particular charity?"

"What the blazes does that have to do with anything?"

Brinkwood asked. "Anita, you don't need to answer that. This is getting unpleasantly personal, DC Waterhouse."

"Darling, it's fine. I don't mind talking about it. I had a not-very-pleasant childhood," Anita said. "No physical abuse to speak of, but plenty of the emotional kind. It lasted well into my adulthood—until both my parents were dead, in fact. They were . . . it sounds awful but they were the kind of parents whose grip on your mind ruins your life until the day they die."

Simon knew what she meant and wished he didn't. His parents were a less extreme case; that was something to be grateful for.

"My flat in Combingham that I was slagging off a few minutes ago?" said Anita. "I grew up there. It was my family home until my parents died. Then it was mine, but . . . the atmosphere, the memories. Ugh. Horrible. It's strange: I thought I was okay living there until I moved in with Ian, but now? I'd rather die than go back to its stifling misery."

"You should never have gone back there in the first place!" said Lord Brinkwood.

"I had no choice, darling." To Simon, Anita said, "Ian is my knight in shining armor. He's rescued me twice—recently, when he proposed to me, but also many, many years ago. When I was in my early twenties, still living in the flat with my parents, I had a bout of severe depression. My doctor recommended more physical exercise as well as various other things, so I joined a yoga class. That was where I met Jane."

"Wait." Simon sat forward in his chair. "You knew Jane before you worked at the resort?"

"Yes, through yoga," Anita repeated as if he was being slow. "She was my rescuer before Ian was. I fell apart in a yoga class one day and Jane took me under her wing. I told her about my terrible situation at home and she said, 'Well, that's rubbish. You can't be putting up with that. Don't worry, we'll soon have you sorted out.' And then, as if by magic, she'd spoken to Ian and the two of them had arranged for me to come and work on the estate, and live here too. Ian gave me a roof over my head, financial support, friendship . . . everything I needed. I ran away from home, basically."

"And I should never have let you go back there," Ian Brinkwood said through gritted teeth.

"Unfortunately I was a complete basket case and couldn't really do any of the work I was supposed to be doing," said Anita. "I was meant to be helping the gardeners, but most of the time I just lay around crying while Ian tried his best to cheer me up. He was so kind. He made sure to come and spend time with me every day. We had these wonderful long talks." She smiled at the happy memory.

Simon was thinking: *Kindness from a man old enough to be her father, plus a psychologically abusive real father . . .* He was starting to see why Anita might have fallen in love with Ian Brinkwood, and how it could easily have had nothing at all to do with money, titles, houses, or land.

"But . . . after being rescued and coming here, you went back to your parents' flat?" he said.

Anita winced. "I heard from an acquaintance I'd kept in touch with that my mum was terminally ill. I couldn't stay away after that. And once I was back, their hold over me was stronger than ever. Then my dad got ill too. They died about four years later, within months of each other. Once they were dead, I got back in touch with Ian straight away," she said tearfully. "I'd missed him so much, but I hadn't been able to face having any contact with him while I was so focused on caring for my parents. So I kept my head down and did my duty. Had no social life whatsoever. When they were both dead, though, I went straight to Ian."

Lord Brinkwood took over the story. "I said, 'Tell you what, young Anita—why don't you come and work for this new resort we've created here at Tevendon?,' and that was exactly what she did! I should never have left her in that wretched flat, though. I should have proposed to her then and there. I didn't because I thought, *Why on earth would she want to marry an old relic like me?* It was the only unselfish decision I've ever made in my life! Then when Jane was killed . . ." He shrugged. "I thought, *What have I got to lose? It's now or never.*"

"So . . ." Simon looked at Anita. "You and Jane were friends, then? Ever since the yoga class?"

"Well . . . we remained friendly, I suppose, but we weren't close. I only really saw her when she came to Tevendon. She was always very busy . . . But I was loyal to her because she saved my life that day at yoga. That's not an exaggeration."

"In the days leading up to her death, did Jane confront or threaten you at all?" Simon asked.

Anita nodded and gave Simon a pointed look that was out of her fiancé's line of sight, while saying, "No, of course not. Like I said: we were friends."

Simon decided to play along. "Right," he said. "Well, thanks for seeing me, both of you."

Anita was on her feet. "Shall I see you to the front door?"

Once they were well out of Lord Brinkwood's way and there was no possibility of him overhearing, she said in a whisper, "Thank you so much for not making me tell you in front of him."

"Tell me what?"

She stopped walking. "Jane did threaten me," she whispered. "I don't think she meant to. That sounds stupid, I know, but . . . the thing is, I know she liked me a lot. I think she was just in such a state that she didn't really know what she was doing or saying, and—"

"What was the threat she made?"

"It was about the anonymous notes: 'Beware' and 'Beware

of the couple at the table nearest to yours.' She wasn't so bad after the first one but when the second one arrived . . . For some reason she got it into her head that Lucy Dean had sent them, and she demanded I kick her and Pete out of the resort, but how could I? I didn't want to." Anita looked stricken. "Even for Jane, I couldn't do that. My job was important to me, and I didn't agree with her. I don't think for a minute that Lucy sent those notes. She seems lovely."

"What was Jane's threat to you?" Simon asked again.

"She said that if I didn't make Lucy and Pete leave, she'd tell Ian I was siding with her enemies. She'd make him fire me, and then I wouldn't get the job at the new hotel, and Ian wouldn't want anything to do with me, and I'd lose everything, absolutely everything in the world that mattered to me and made my life feel worth living."

"She said all that, in those words?"

"Those words. And do you know what?" A tear rolled down Anita's face.

"What?"

"When she said that, I fantasized, for a fleeting moment, about physically harming her." Her face colored. "Leaning over and scratching her face or something like that. But I *didn't*. And like I say, it was fleeting. I'm not good at hating, DC Waterhouse. I'm really actually pretty awful at it. I can't imagine how anyone gets to the point where they hate someone enough to kill them."

Tuesday, January 14, 2020

Dear Charlie,

You must hate me. I hate me too. Despite being (as you pointed out) a liar, I inconveniently have a guilty conscience the size of a small continent that won't leave me alone—even when I've done nothing wrong, I find things to torment myself about. And when I know I've behaved badly to someone who's only ever behaved well to me, I can't bear it. Like now.

Do I want, in an ideal world, to write everything I'm about to write in this letter and send it to you? No. There are things I'd rather not tell you because they make me feel either guilty or ashamed or both, but I've decided I have to tell you anyway because not doing so has made me feel so much worse.

Lying to people isn't okay with me if they're people I like and respect, and you are. I should have told you everything I'm about to write when we met yesterday, but I didn't, so here goes.

You know already that William and I hired Jane to be our doula for my pregnancy and the birth of my baby. You probably assumed—I let you assume—that the order of events was 1) we hired Jane, 2) she and William fell in love and decided to hide it from me until the birth was out of the way in order not to upset a heavily pregnant woman, 3) they ran off together fourteen days after the birth, leaving me alone with a two-week-old baby and still barely able to move after my

C-section. Charming, right? So far, so bad. And for a short time, I also believed that was how it had happened. I didn't bother to imagine that the truth might be even worse. As far as I was concerned, there was no worse than that.

Then, three weeks after William had moved in with Jane, my doorbell rang. I opened the door and found a man standing there. I knew I'd seen him before but couldn't immediately place him. Then he introduced himself: Pete Shabani, the anesthetist who'd done the spinal block for my emergency C-section. He apologized for having looked up my address and turning up at my house, but he had something important to tell me. It was about Jane.

While I'd been trying and failing to give birth to my baby, William—and Jane, as my doula—had both been in the hospital with me most of the time. As we now know, they weren't only there because they wanted to be with me. They mainly wanted to be with each other. They were madly in love, though both were putting on an extremely convincing show of not being, and of being solely focused on me and my well-being and the baby. Pete, also, was in the hospital at the time because he works there.

There's a little branch of Costa Coffee in the hospital foyer. The day before my C-section, Pete went in there to get a coffee and saw a heavily pregnant woman screaming at another woman. The pregnant woman's husband was with her. Pete was struck by the fact that the husband wasn't doing anything to try and keep his wife under control. He had his arm around her shoulders, an enraged look on his face, and he just let her scream. She was saying, "You're a disgrace, you should never be allowed to practice again"—things like that. Pete thought this was odd because the woman who was getting yelled at wasn't wearing any kind of doctor's or nurse's uniform.

Eventually the screaming pregnant woman ran out of steam and she and her husband left Costa Coffee. The other woman, who'd been quite poker-faced until this point, burst into tears. Pete rushed to her side like the gentleman he is, offered to buy her a tea, sat down with her. He did all the things a lovely man would do. She seemed grateful, and although he didn't want to pry, she seemed happy to tell him all about it.

Here's what she told him: she was a doula (yes, you've guessed right, she was Jane Brinkwood). She had a boyfriend called William. They were desperately, madly, passionately in love and had been for *a year and a half*.

Yes, that's right. Well spotted. A year and a half. I'd only been pregnant for nine months. Which means that William and Jane had met long before I got pregnant and found myself in need of a doula. They'd met online initially—some kind of chat room—and very quickly formed an unbreakable bond, apparently. They were already in love months before I fell pregnant.

When I told William we were about to become parents, thinking it was wonderful news, he was already busy planning to leave me for Jane. As in: he'd planned the walk-out for later that same week (yes, Jane really did sit there and tell Pete all of this, sounding not in the least bit ashamed of any of it).

Suddenly William felt he couldn't leave, not just like that. He pretended to be thrilled about the baby. He and Jane decided that abandoning a pregnant wife was not ideal, and so they'd have to wait. How virtuous and saintly of them! Except the prospect of not being together for a whole nine months and perhaps beyond was unbearable, so they came up with a plan—after all, Jane was already a doula, so it was the easiest thing in the world.

William started to talk about how I was bound to need support during my pregnancy, especially if I was planning to work throughout, which I was. Had I considered hiring a doula? he wanted to know. You can imagine the rest. As soon as I said, "Ooh, what a good idea!" he offered to look into it (his work was much less pressured than mine, he said. The least he could do while I was carrying his child was take this task off my hands. Etc.). He was the one who "found" Jane. I had no idea that she'd been his lover for many months already.

Being my doula was Jane's dream come true. She got to almost live in my house throughout the pregnancy. Pretending to bond with me and genuinely care about me was a small price to pay for all that proximity to her beloved. But also, it was impossibly hard and painful for her, she told Pete, to be so close to William but not be able to be with him properly yet. The torment! And she was having a hard time professionally too. Various people were making formal complaints about her to her professional body, an organization called Doula UK. One couple she'd worked with about two years earlier had complained that she'd spent more time flirting with the husband than attending to the pregnant wife. They'd let her go almost immediately for that reason, calling her "outrageously unprofessional," and the wife had then had a late miscarriage. Jane told Pete they were crazy, this couple, that she hadn't flirted at all and how dare they blame her for the miscarriage.

Another complaint had come from a different couple, the people Jane was supposed to go to when William invited her to semi-cohabit with us instead. Jane let them down—just left them in the lurch. They'd never met her, but they'd got very attached to the idea of her. They'd corresponded with her quite a bit, seen her photo on the Doula UK site . . . and then she emailed them out of the blue to say, "Sorry, I've taken another position instead." This couple had had the temerity, as Jane saw it, to complain to Doula UK about her when all she'd done was treat them with a complete lack of consideration. How dare they, right?

She kept saying to Pete, who was fully aghast by this point, that it was the most stressful year of her life, that she might not be able to work as a doula for much longer if all these bastards kept unreasonably complaining about her. It turned out that the couple who'd been in Costa Coffee, the screaming lady and her husband, were the ones who'd fired her for flirting. At least they'd had a happy ending: pregnant again, plus well armed against Jane because they knew she was a monster and didn't feel any need to pretend otherwise.

Pete had been mightily relieved to escape from Costa Coffee and the conversation when Jane finally released him from her clutches.

Imagine his horror when, the next day, he found himself face-to-face with an emergency C-section patient and that patient—me—was accompanied by the very same monster he'd escaped from only twenty-four hours previously.

He realized that I was the woman whose husband Jane planned to run off with just as soon as they both felt it was feasible. He liked me too, which made it worse. Jane didn't even blink when he walked into the room to do my spinal block. She just smiled at him and said, "Oh, hi! It's you!"

What could Pete do? You can't say to a patient, "Lie down while I inject drugs into your spinal fluid that'll make you unable to feel your own legs—oh, and by the way, your husband and your doula have been shagging for ages and are planning to elope as soon as they can."

Pete kept thinking and worrying about me and the baby once we'd been discharged. Then he heard on the maternity ward grapevine that I'd been in again to talk to my favorite midwife, Rowena. I'd been in a terrible state (true), almost suicidal (not true—I had a now-fatherless baby who needed me), and asking for advice: Should I report Jane for professional misconduct? Pete didn't know what rules applied to doulas but he very much wanted me to report Jane and he knew from what she'd told him in Costa Coffee that two other couples had reported her for unprofessional behavior. So he decided to find me and tell me everything he knew. He came to visit me . . . and thank God he did, because it was exactly what I needed: a kind, good, unselfish man in my life. He really rescued me.

At first I couldn't believe what he told me about William and Jane having been in love and an item for so long before I got pregnant. When he was leaving, William had made his love for Jane sound very much like shiny new object syndrome: these strong, irresistible feelings were only weeks old, he told me. Not months. Certainly not more than a year.

Luckily, he'd neglected to take anything more than the absolute basics with him when he'd first moved out, so I was able to have a good, thorough look at his bank statements going back a few years.

Lo and behold, there was the proof that Jane had told Pete the truth. There had been lots of cozy dinners for two at all the most romantic restaurants in the Culver Valley, as well as trips to boutique hotels in London. That was when I realized that maths teachers didn't have quite so many nights out or conferences as I'd been led to believe.

Why am I telling you all this? Because it's a truth I've been withholding, one I hardly tell anyone. Even now that I'm happy with Pete and relieved not to be wasting any more of my life on William Gleave, I still can't bear the knowledge that they planned their betrayal of me in advance in the way that they did. I prefer to let people think it happened in the more normal way that these sorts of things tend to happen.

I can't see how you having this new information could shed any light on who killed Jane, but I owed you full disclosure and I want to behave honorably whenever I possibly can. I don't want to end up like Jane. (An utterly immoral shit, I mean—not dead. Though obviously I don't want to end up dead either.)

The only other things I've kept back are just self-indulgent crap from inside my head that I've thought it was better not to blurt out, as opposed to things that have actually happened. For example:

1.) I resent Jane's killer sometimes. That was my job. If anyone was going to do it, it should have been me.

2.) I love Pete. Nothing in the world could ever make me want to leave him and go back to William, apart from one thing: if I found out that it was William who killed Jane. If the good man I thought I married is still in there somewhere, if she duped him, if he grew to loathe and despise her so much that he decided she deserved to die for what she'd done to him and to me (and in order to stand even a tiny chance of getting me back), then I fear I might be able to love William again, even more than I did before. And that really scares me.

Lucy x

23

Tuesday, January 14, 2020

While Simon waited for William Gleave to make him a cup of tea, he thought about how ill-suited Gleave was to his own home. The brown-brick Silsford Victorian semidetached where he lived had once been Jane Brinkwood's and hers alone. Gleave had moved in when he'd left Lucy. Clearly he had been, and still was, content to live in this house that Simon—and, he was fairly confident, most men—would have run a mile from. The front-room wallpaper had given Simon an ache behind his eyes every time he'd come here so far, today included: green and pink birds perched on thin brown branches with white and orange petals protruding from them, open-beaked and seemingly chirping at one another against a pale blue background.

One whole wall was covered with floor-to-ceiling shelving that displayed small groups of books, huddled together with their pages facing the room instead of their spines, punctuated by dozens of glass ornaments that were all different shapes but the same shade of blue: vases, jugs, a couple of weird bowls that looked like wide-brimmed hats turned upside down. There was spot-lighting built into the shelves, creating a strange glow effect and making the rest of the room look a little too dark by comparison. The ornaments were all, Simon noticed, as clean and dust-free as they had been last time he'd come here in August.

Gleave reappeared with a mug of tea for Simon, looking like

an actor who had stumbled onto the wrong stage set. This room was clearly not the right backdrop for a bespectacled man in a tweed suit the color of the gunk at the bottom of your average kitchen bin.

Simon remembered the dress Jane had worn to dinner on the night that she was killed: gold background, pink lacy bits, a pattern of bouquets of pink flowers tied with pink ribbons. What had she seen in William Gleave, who was so evidently at odds with her preferred aesthetic?

"You said you had more questions for me?" Gleave sat down. He seemed ill at ease. More so than usual?

Simon couldn't tell. The man was hard to read. Perhaps that's what had attracted Jane to him: his air of ambiguity, of having hidden depths. Then again, would someone who appreciated those things have a living room that looked like this?

Simon was tempted to blurt out the big question, the only one that mattered: *Which is it, Gleave? Were the forensic experts wrong? Were you somehow not sitting where I found you, with your back turned, when someone stabbed your wife behind you? Was someone else wearing the shirt, maybe, and were you the one doing the stabbing? Let's not worry for the time being about who that someone else might have been.*

Or were you in your chair and in your shirt, as you claim? Because if you didn't kill Jane, then one of the others did— which has to mean they all lied when they told us no one had left the restaurant terrace.

This was something Charlie never factored in when she insisted Gleave was the guilty party: the relative likeliness of the only two possibilities. Which was more probable, that the physical evidence was lying, or that people were lying? Simon knew which one he was betting on.

Which didn't, of course, mean that William Gleave had told anybody the whole truth, or anything approaching it.

"You went round to Lucy and Pete's house recently, didn't you?"

"Yes."

"Uninvited."

"Yes."

"Why?"

"If you know I went, then you must already know why. I hadn't seen Lucy for several months before that." Gleave looked mildly puzzled—as if he'd intended to make a point, then heard his own words and realized he'd failed to make it. "In the absence of new encounters, one imagines things. I'd been getting it into my head that maybe Lucy was . . . responsible."

"For Jane's murder."

He nodded.

"So you went round to ask her if she'd done it?"

"Not initially. I mean, in essence, yes, that's what I wanted to ask her. Which she guessed—and was understandably upset by—and by that point, I knew I'd wasted my time."

"What do you mean?"

"I knew Lucy was innocent. It was clear from her manner and everything she said. I know her well enough to be sure."

"Did you receive a letter from her recently?" Simon asked.

"Yes."

"What did it say?"

"It was a letter she'd written to Jane's killer, without knowing who that is. With a covering note addressed to me. She wasn't accusing me of being the killer, which she made clear. I suspect you know all this already."

"Were you planning to let me know that you'd received this communication from Lucy?"

"No. Why would I?"

"Because I'm investigating your wife's murder. You didn't think I might find it useful to know that someone who was at Tevendon on 2 July had done something so unusual?"

"It wouldn't have been any use to you at all," said Gleave. "It might have caused you to suspect Lucy, but she isn't the guilty party. So, a distraction."

"Maybe," said Simon. "Do you care, any more?"

"What do you mean?"

"Do you want Jane's murderer caught and charged?"

Gleave sighed heavily. "Jane was the love of my life. How would you feel if someone had murdered your wife?"

"I'd want to kill them, and I probably would," Simon told him.

"Well, exactly."

Then why are you always so fucking calm, if this really matters to you? The palpably miserable, on-edge William Gleave from Tevendon was long gone. Simon couldn't recall the precise date, but at some point towards the end of July last year, this new, slower, calmer version of Gleave had appeared and seemed to have bedded in for the duration. Maybe he was taking some kind of antidepressive drug.

"I very much want Jane's killer to be *charged*," Gleave stressed. "And that requires the 'caught' part to come first, doesn't it?"

"I'm doing my best, and I'm not planning on giving up," Simon told him.

"That's not what I meant."

"What, then?"

"At the moment, I have Jane's death to . . . contend with," said Gleave. "Her absence, my life without her, the fact that she's never coming back. All of that. And also . . . *only* that. That and nothing else. Which is bad enough, believe me. If possible, I'd like not to have any more to deal with. As soon as I know who killed her, I'll have something else to get over— something in addition to the fact of Jane no longer being here. There'll be a story that I'll have to know: X person killed her for this reason or that reason. It'll be another thing to bear, another burden. I won't be able to get it out of my head."

"If that's how you feel, then you're unusual," Simon told him. "Most loved ones of murder victims find the uncertainty and the possibility of never knowing to be a far greater burden."

William said nothing for a long time. Then he said, "I suppose I'm just . . . different."

"It makes sense now," said Simon.

"What does?"

"Your not telling me everything. Withholding the full story."

"I'm not withholding," said Gleave easily.

"Yes, you are. I've asked you the same questions over and over and you dodge them every time: Why were you so upset when you and Jane arrived late for dinner on 2 July? You always tell me you weren't, that you were fine, but I was there. I saw your face. You were visibly not okay. No wonder you've never wanted to say why. The more you tell me, the more I have to work with. The more likely I am to find out what happened— and you've just admitted that you don't want to know what happened because you'd find it too upsetting."

"But I do want Jane's killer punished," said Gleave quietly, looking down at his hands.

"You say you do, but you don't. If you really did, you'd tell me everything."

They sat in silence for a few seconds. Then Gleave said, "I don't have any new or different insights for you. I'm sorry."

"I don't want insights, I want true answers. Why were you unhappy when you and Jane arrived at dinner on the night she died? She was miserable too, and angry, though not with you. But then suddenly she was. Here's my memory of what happened: First you went inside and were gone for a few minutes. Then you came back out again. Jane saw you and said something like, 'Well, are you just going to stand there?' It seemed as if she wanted you to weigh in and support her in her attack on Lucy and Pete over the champagne. Then your face changed and you looked terrified. Like you were facing a firing squad. You grabbed the menu card from Jane's hand and ripped it up. Then you whispered something to Jane that really shocked her. She started saying, 'Oh, my God, I can't believe it,' as if you'd done something unforgivable. Then she ran away, screaming at you to leave her alone and not to follow her."

Gleave didn't flinch.

"Do you remember what happened next?" said Simon. "You called after her that you were sorry. You sounded like you meant it. What were you sorry for?"

"I've explained this already, many times. I was sorry about the mix-up over the champagne. It might not have been my fault but I was sorry it had happened. And I was sorry more generally that Jane's honeymoon, our honeymoon, was proving so much less happy and relaxed an occasion than we'd both hoped it would be."

Simon shook his head. "I'm done with pretending to believe you."

"I can see that," said Gleave. "I've said this before but I'll say it again: not all apologies are admissions of guilt."

"What exactly did you whisper to Jane that night that made her so angry? Why did you tear up the menu?"

"As I've said before, my memory of the smaller details—"

"Is hazy. Right. Tell me about your dream."

"My dream?"

That had given him a shock: a question he hadn't been expecting. *Good.*

"The one you told Lucy Dean about when you turned up at her house ten days ago."

"Lucy told you about that?"

"She told Charlie. Sergeant Zailer."

"It was just a horrible dream. Why does it matter?"

"Can you describe it to me? As accurately as you can, please."

"If you insist." Gleave looked uncomfortable. "Jane and I were sitting opposite one another at a table. It was round. We were both dead, but we were upright. We couldn't eat our dinner."

"Because you were dead?"

"Yes."

"Was your dinner on the table?"

"Yes. As I said to Lucy, I don't think we'd been murdered. We were just dead. And there were other couples in a circle around us. They were all alive."

"It sounds a lot like the way the tables were arranged at Tevendon on the night Jane died," Simon pointed out.

"No. Jane's and my table that night was on a little terrace of its own, raised above the others, which were all on a lower level."

"I know," said Simon. "I was there, remember?"

"All the tables were on the same level in my dream," said Gleave.

"Why did you tell Lucy about it six months later? An old dream. Seems a bit odd."

"I don't know. I suppose I must have wanted to, in the moment."

"Why do you think you wanted to?"

"Maybe I missed how close we once were. I don't know. If I say I don't know, it means I don't know." A trace of impatience had crept into Gleave's voice.

"You wanted to confide in her, maybe? Now that Jane's no longer around, did you consider trying to—"

"No. To reconcile with Lucy? No, I could never want that. She's seen the very worst I'm capable of. Whenever I'm in her company, I see it too."

It was the most genuine-sounding thing he'd said since Simon had arrived.

"Did you find it disturbing, the dream?"

"It *was* disturbing. It was frightening, which is why I'd rather stop thinking about it if you're ready to move on to a new topic?"

A new topic? What did he have in mind: possible trade deals between the UK and Europe? The novels of Charles Dickens?

"What was so frightening about the dream, specifically?" Simon asked.

"Me and Jane."

"You and Jane were frightening? Or do you mean you were scared? You can't have been, though, because you were dead. Correct?"

"Have you never had a dream that contained illogical elements?" Gleave said smoothly. Whatever you threw at him, there was a sense of it bouncing hard against a blank, hollow object and coming back to hit you in the face. Charlie had said a couple of times that she thought Gleave might be "on the spectrum," whatever that meant.

"I was scared in the dream, and Jane and I were dead in the dream, and that was what I was scared of. I agree: it's inconsistent. I was both alive enough to feel fear and also dead. I had to get us both away from the dead version of us, but . . . I couldn't. It was too late. I knew that very powerfully in the dream."

Gleave cleared his throat and said, "I can't see what it has to do with anything. A dream I had six months ago is hardly going to tell you who killed Jane, is it?"

"It sounds like the kind of dream you'd have if you were feeling guilty," said Simon. "Your relationship with Jane had caused a lot of harm already—to Lucy, arguably to Evin too. Maybe your subconscious was trying to tell you that if you and

Jane carried on the way you were going, hurting people, something bad might happen to you."

Gleave shrugged. "Who knows why anyone has one dream and not another?"

Simon's mind, meanwhile, had moved on from Gleave's dream and was busy elsewhere. He was thinking about two words: about the similarity and the difference between them. If he was right, it would also explain another puzzling element . . .

Could it be?

It seemed so obvious—but then why had it occurred to no one but him? Why had he only thought of it just now?

The dead William and Jane at the table who were frightening. The still-alive William who was frightened of them, but knew it was too late. The illogicality of dreams . . .

This was it. Simon could feel it.

"Are you all right?" Gleave asked him.

His mind was already racing ahead to the next problem: making new links between what he thought he'd worked out and the many things that were still unknown. That could wait, though. For now, it was enough to know that the power balance between William Gleave and himself had shifted in his favor. Gleave had no idea that Simon was about to leave his house with a lot more knowledge of the truth than he'd arrived with.

"I'm fine," Simon told him with a smile. "You've been very helpful. Unintentionally."

24

Tuesday, January 14, 2020

Colin Sellers felt as uncomfortable in Polly and Jack McCallion's lounge as he had in their hall, their downstairs loo, and their kitchen. Which was his fault, he knew, and he ought to get over it but so far he hadn't succeeded. This house, and others like it that he'd seen before—generally only on TV or in the pages of magazines in the dentist's waiting room—made him think about his marriage to Stacey, now over, and his relationship with Sondra, still new and exciting. Yet the home he'd shared with Stacey, and the rented flat he now lived in with Sondra, looked nothing like Polly and Jack McCallion's house, and perhaps that meant something bad—about Sellers in particular. Didn't they say that your home was a reflection of your personality?

Sellers was in a bad mood, that was the problem. He'd had to get up at 4 a.m. to get here. For the life of him, he couldn't understand why Waterhouse thought that Lucy Dean sending out some freaky letters meant that all the Tevendon lot needed to be interviewed again urgently. And Gibbs, it seemed, wasn't being asked to get up at the crack of dawn and drive to Twickenham or anywhere else inconvenient, while making sure to hide it from the Snowman, who had no idea that his team had secretly made the Jane Brinkwood case top priority again. No, Gibbs was apparently allowed to carry on as normal, doing the work he was supposed to do. Waterhouse had refused to explain why Gibbs alone was exempt from Tevendon duties.

So, yes, Sellers was fed up, and he was happy to blame it on Polly and Jack's irritatingly flawless house. There was a peacock-feather fan laid out on the coffee table. It might, at a push, have been a very posh coaster, but Sellers suspected it wasn't. In which case there was no coaster, which also seemed unlikely, given the impressive, oiled gleam of the table. The polished wooden floor looked equally untouchable, and the white and gray rug seemed to scream out, "Stain me and I'll end you."

Sellers decided his only good option was to hold the mug of coffee Jack had given him in his hands and forget about putting it down anywhere. On arrival, he had removed his shoes without waiting to be asked, which had impressed Polly; she'd thanked him for his thoughtfulness. Maybe she'd been up since 4 a.m. too, creating this show-home effect. Sellers didn't think so, though. The perfection extended too far. There were no cobwebs in high corners, no scratches on skirting boards, no large bowls in the kitchen containing a shriveled apple, paperclips, broken bike lights and the white plastic handle of a long-dead feather duster. Sellers had considered eating the shriveled apple at 4 a.m. today before setting off, then decided he couldn't face it—not with this level of hangover.

He and Sondra had shared too many bottles of wine with dinner last night. Then they'd left the empty bottles on the kitchen table along with a splash or two of the wine itself. They'd also left their dinner plates, knives and forks unwashed in the sink, and the pans in which Sellers had cooked his new speciality—extra-hot vegetarian chili non carne with chili-flake rice—on the stovetop with the leftovers still in them. That kind of thing probably never happened in the McCallion household. Sellers couldn't imagine that part of Polly and Jack's morning routine was "stumble into the kitchen and swear loudly at the sight of last night's congealed food."

"You said you had questions for us?" Polly seemed eager to get going. She was sitting cross-legged on the rug. Sellers tried not to be distracted by her tanned feet and red-painted toenails. Jack sat behind her on a velvet sofa. It was the same color as the wine Sellers had drunk the previous night, which wasn't helping.

"Yeah, about the letter Lucy Dean sent you, like I said on the phone."

"Letters," said Jack. "We got one each. Lucky us."

"Can I see them?"

"Sure." Jack bounced up off the sofa. Less than a minute later he was back. He held out the two envelopes.

Sellers took them. Now he was in a predicament. He decided he'd rather ask than risk getting it wrong. "Where can I put my coffee down?" he asked.

Polly smiled. "That's so sweet of you to ask. Anywhere!"

"Really?"

"Really. This is a home, not a museum."

Sellers placed his mug down on the coffee table, avoiding the peacock fan, and read the contents of the two envelopes. They were exactly what Waterhouse had told him they would be. "What was your reaction when these arrived?" he asked.

"I was stunned," said Polly. "I couldn't believe she'd written the letter in the first place, to Jane's killer. It actually made me think . . . I mean, I know she wasn't, but—" She broke off.

"Wasn't what?" said Sellers.

"The one. She was with me when Jane was stabbed, so I know she didn't do it, but if it wasn't for that, I'd definitely suspect her. Any kind of odd behavior like these letters is a red flag for me."

"I *do* suspect her," said Jack. "Look, here's how I see it: we've been told that William couldn't have done it, right? I don't know if that's a solid fact—you guys are the experts—but if it is? And we know *we* all didn't do it, the rest of us, because we were together and could see each other the whole time. And no one could have got in from outside, which is another thing we've been told . . . You see what I'm saying? If everyone's in the clear, then no one is." Jack spread his arms, like a . . . what was that insult Sondra threw at Sellers whenever he thought he was right about something and tried to argue the point? It sounded like demigod. Demagogue, that was it. Jack McCallion sounded like a demagogue as he said, "It's so simple, it's unreal. Normally when we say, 'These three people, or these nine, or these twenty people can't have done X,' it's meaningful. Why? Because there are another twenty, or hundred, or thousand people who *could* have done it. Here, though, we have a case where there are how many people who might have done it, according to you guys? Zero! Zero viable suspects. Couldn't have been an inside job, couldn't have been an outside job. Well, that doesn't work, does it? Because someone, sure as eggs is eggs, murdered Jane Brinkwood. So, what's the obvious next question?"

"You tell me," said Sellers.

"Do we have any reason to think that the 'couldn't have done it' logic applies more strongly to Lucy than to any of the rest of us? None that I can see! And that's why I suspect her. She had the motive to end all motives, and Polly's right—who's the only known suspect acting more suspiciously than any of the others? Lucy."

"But your wife's just said Lucy Dean was there on the terrace with you the whole time," Sellers reminded him.

Jack threw back his head and groaned. "Have you forgotten the train of logic we've followed to get to this point? When every person on the planet has a 'but they can't have, because X' attached to them, then all of those statements lose their validity. We know one of those 'can't, because' rationalizations must be wrong. Which means it has to be possible that Lucy did it. Even though, yes, she was on the terrace with us the whole time. Look, don't ask me how she did it. I have no idea."

Polly frowned. "I *don't* think Lucy did it. In fact, I'm sure she didn't."

"Then who?" said Sellers.

"William?" She sounded tentative.

"He loved her," said Jack. "Lucy hated her. You've got to go back to basics with these things, Poll."

"Yes, but there are other basics. It's not only about who had the best motive. If motive were all that mattered, I'd have committed several murders myself by now. Including, probably, Jane Brinkwood's." Polly smiled, but it faded quickly. "Sorry, bad taste. I just mean that murderers kill because they're the kind of people who are willing to end someone else's life in a violent way. That's it. That's what separates murderers from non-murderers. And on that front, I'd say Lucy Dean is an extremely unlikely murderer. She's too thoughtful and too . . . verbal. Caroline Moyle-Jones, Susan Henry and William Gleave are all more likely candidates, I think, just going by personality. For different reasons in each case. Actually, maybe even Harriet. Maybe Harriet most of all. If Miss Marple were in charge, she'd say Harriet," Polly concluded.

Sellers nearly asked why, then realized he didn't care what a fictional old lady detective would think. "Why would you have killed Jane Brinkwood?" he asked Polly.

"I didn't. And I wouldn't have, because I'm not a murderer. This is my point."

"But you didn't like her much?"

"Like her?" Polly laughed. "God, no. She was a disgusting cow. The kind of unpleasant that you don't often meet. Like, willing to be openly, brazenly nasty."

"To you personally?"

"Yes. Though Lucy told me she was never like that before Tevendon. She was always friendly and charming on the surface and was really convincing as a nice, sweet, kind person, from what Lucy said. If that's true, then the mask well and truly slipped and Jane didn't even try to put it back on."

"And she was unpleasant and hostile to you personally?" said Sellers. "How?"

Polly looked at Jack. "Do I have to say? I mean, it won't help to solve the case."

"I've been a detective for nearly twenty years, Mrs. McCallion. I know it gets trotted out a lot on crime TV dramas, but it's true: you really never know what might help until you find it. Often it's the least significant-seeming thing that makes the difference."

"We could just tell him, Poll," said Jack. "I'm sure we could agree on a quid pro quo."

"How do you mean?" Sellers asked.

"Polly and I did something naughty. I was the one who did it, though we thought up the plan together. However officially naughty it was, it was a plan that had justice on its side. Natural justice. We saw to it that someone got their comeuppance. I don't regret it and I never will. No violence was involved, obviously."

"I slightly regret it." Polly looked anxious.

"Go on," said Sellers.

"Only if you promise no one else will ever get to hear about it. It could make serious trouble for me and Poll in our day-to-day lives. In our careers."

"I can't keep it from the other detectives investigating this case."

"Fine," said Jack. "But can you guarantee it won't go any further than that?"

"It probably won't, if it doesn't need to," said Sellers. What would Waterhouse tell him to say? Anything he had to, to get the information. "I'll do my best."

Jack chewed his lip as he considered it. Then he said, "Not good enough. Sorry." He didn't look sorry at all. "You'll have to settle for the juicy-details-redacted version. Which is this: Polly and I made a plan, and we enacted it. It worked. Sublimely well, in fact. The comeuppance was satisfactorily delivered. None of this happened at Tevendon or involved anyone from Tevendon. It was connected to our professional lives. But Jane Brinkwood found out about it, and she threatened us."

"How did she find out?"

"My best guess is that she earwigged on us talking about it one day. We discussed it more than we should have because Polly's never stopped worrying about it since it happened. So, yeah, on holiday, with more free time than usual, the subject kept coming up. Jane used to sit by the pool with earphones in, tapping her fingers on her lounger as if she was listening to music. I reckon most of the time she was spying on us. And then one day she appears in front of us when we're on our way to breakfast and accuses us of sending her an anonymous note telling her to beware. We just laugh at her. Obviously we haven't done any such thing. We tell her to get lost and leave us alone, but she won't have it. She starts saying she knows it must have been one of us, or both of us."

"Then she pulls the actual note out of her bathrobe pocket," said Polly. "Yeah, she's in her dressing gown and slippers, but wandering around outside. And she's obviously been crying. Her eyes are red and swollen."

"The note's handwritten on stiff card, with really neat capital letters on it," said Jack. " 'Beware'—that's all it said. It was so lame and silly, and the idea that Jane had got steamed up about it . . . I mean, if someone posted something like that through my letterbox I'd just have a good laugh, I think. Not Jane. She accused us of trying to drive her out of the resort, conspiring with Lucy to ruin her and William's honeymoon. She demanded that we admit to doing all these heinous things. So I told her to go fuck herself, and that's when she threatened us."

"How?" asked Sellers.

"She told us she'd heard us talking and she knew what we'd done. Regarding the comeuppance," said Jack. "If we didn't admit to everything—the sending of the note and the conspiring—then she said she'd . . . go to the relevant people and reveal all. I didn't believe her for a second, and I responded with an equally implausible threat of my own: I told her that, if she acted against me and Poll in any way whatsoever or ever bothered us again, I'd find a way of sneaking into her bedroom and I'd cut her throat from ear to ear." He grinned. Seeing Sellers's expression, he said, "Oh, come on, I didn't mean it! I deliberately chose the most gruesome and outlandish threat I could think of. I was trying to show her how ludicrous it was, us standing there hurling implausible threats at one another. Mine wasn't real. It was a parody, designed to make a point."

"How did Jane respond to it?" Sellers asked.

"Not well." Jack chuckled. "Not well at all. I said to Poll at the time: I genuinely find them fascinating, these people who are so committed to dishing it out without the slightest reservation or hesitation, who turn out to be utterly unable to take it when their shit gets flung back at them. Jane was a prime example. She grabbed her throat with both hands to protect it from my imaginary slashing razor, and kind of whimpered, then ran away. That was that. She didn't bother us again. Actively avoided us. Job done." Jack smiled.

"Making death threats is illegal," Sellers told him.

"Yeah, I don't do it every day," said Jack. "And as I said: not a threat. A parody. What's up, DC Sellers? You look as if you're deciding I'm a bad egg or a loose cannon or something of that ilk. I know that look. I've seen it in many people's eyes over the years. That's okay. I'm not going to be offended if you want to be wrong about me. I know I'm a good person."

Sellers was remembering what Polly had said earlier. *Murderers kill because they're the kind of people who are willing to end someone else's life in a violent way.* He thought about that statement in relation to Jack McCallion and found himself suspecting that this was a man who was capable of committing murder—not only if he had to, but also if he wanted to. And he'd have no trouble justifying it to himself. He might even boast about it.

"Jack's the loveliest man in the world," Polly said. "Honestly. Take it from me. I've been married to him since forever, so I ought to know."

25

Wednesday, January 15, 2020

"I need to ask you a strange question," Simon told Susan and Mick Henry. The three of them were in the Henrys' suite at the University Arms Hotel in Cambridge. Through a stained-glass window, there was an impressive view of a large, square expanse of green.

The first question Simon had asked was "Why Cambridge?" Susan had pursed her lips and said, "You have no good hotels in the Culver Valley. None. Why is that?"

"No idea," Simon had said.

"Also, we wanted to visit a beautiful place," she'd added with a smile. "Yesterday we saw the Chronophage—have you seen it? The golden time-eater? What a phenomenal work of art!"

Simon hadn't seen it. He was here to discuss more mundane things. "I need to ask you both a question," he said. "About snoring."

"Snoring?" Mick repeated, looking baffled.

"It's relevant, however beside the point it's going to sound. Does either of you snore?"

"Oh, me. Me!" Susan stuck her hand up in the air. "My snoring is legendary, right, Mick?"

Her husband nodded.

"What about you?" Simon asked him.

"No, Mick's a silent sleeper," Susan answered for him. "It's so unfair. He's huge, and a man. I'm a woman and half his size—he should be the snorer, if there's any justice in the world. How about you?" She nodded at Simon's wedding ring. "Is there a snorer in your marriage?"

Simon really disliked this woman. He had no intention of answering.

As if she'd read his mind, Susan said, "Oh, I'm so sorry. I keep forgetting: you Britishers hate real talk. It offends you. I only asked because, if there *is* a snorer in your marriage, Mick and I have a solution. A wonderful cure-all, as long as you have the square footage."

Now Simon was confused.

"Separate bedrooms." Susan beamed at him. "Mick and I swear by them. We visit each other, of course."

Keen to change the subject, Simon turned to Mick and said, "Mr. Henry, did you at any point have a conversation in the office at Tevendon about snoring? With Anita Khattou and Lucy Dean?"

"Yeah, kinda. And please, call me Mick."

"My snoring was a problem at Tevendon," said Susan. "We knew it might be, but we decided it was worth it anyway, after we read an amazing write-up of the resort in the *New York Times*. Turns out . . . yeah, it could have totally ruined our vacation. We'd happily have booked another cottage—what's money for if not to make life easier, right?—but the others were all occupied. Anita kindly let us have the one reserved for staff, Number 4. It was right next to ours, so it was perfect. Close together, but far enough away for Mick to get a good night's sleep without my snoring disturbing him."

"But that's not the conversation you had with Anita and Lucy in the office," Simon said to Mick. "You didn't tell them what your wife's just told me."

"No," Mick admitted.

"What?" Susan asked. "Mick? What am I missing?" She didn't like anything to escape her control, Simon guessed.

"I thanked Anita for letting us have Cottage 4, but . . . I kinda lied," said Mick. "And not only then. The first time I explained our problem to her, I lied then too. I figured it was harmless. It wasn't a lie that would hurt anybody, so what did it matter?"

"What lie?" said Susan.

"I pretended I was the one who snored."

"*What?* Why would you do that?" She laughed.

"I thought . . . I don't know. It would have felt ungallant to say it was you."

"Oh, my goodness." Susan looked up at the ceiling. "That's *insane*. I tell the whole world that I snore. You think I'm ashamed of it?"

"No, I know you're not."

"Are *you* ashamed of having a wife who snores?" Susan persisted.

"No, not at all."

"Then why lie about it?"

"Honestly, I couldn't tell you." Mick looked at Simon and shrugged helplessly. "I guess I'm old-fashioned in ways I don't really understand. I agree, it makes no sense."

Simon thought he could understand it. Snoring wasn't traditionally feminine. Mick had wanted to protect his wife from being seen by anyone as unwomanly.

What his admission didn't explain was why Anita Khattou had also lied. She'd told first Lucy Dean and then Simon that she had been kept awake, when she'd slept at Number 4, not only by the snoring, which might have been difficult to attribute to a specific person, but by loud arguments in which Susan had screamed at Mick about *his* snoring keeping *her* awake.

Assuming the Henrys were telling the truth now, Anita must

have lied about that. In reality, the arguments she had overheard must have been the other way around if they'd happened at all. Simon couldn't easily imagine Mick, or anyone, yelling at Susan Henry. Why would Anita lie? In his wildest imaginings, Simon couldn't believe Anita would care if Susan Henry were to be perceived as unfeminine by . . . who? Random guests at Tevendon? Lucy Dean? The police? No. It made no sense.

"Completely different question," he said. "Did Jane Brinkwood ever threaten either of you?"

"Hell, yes," said Susan.

"She did?"

"Sure. Let me tell you, Detective: that crazy lady had *been through our outdoor trash cans*. She'd trawled through them and found in our recycling the packaging for a medication I'm on: Lisinopril. For high blood pressure. I'd torn up the boxes into little pieces, put some of them inside other containers . . . and the thing is, I hadn't torn up any other packaging, so once she'd put my Lisinopril boxes back together again like a creepy jigsaw puzzle, she must have thought to herself, *Why's it only these little cardboard boxes that have been torn up?* What made it so infuriating was that she'd guessed correctly what I was up to. I *had* torn up the Lisinopril packaging and scattered it to the four corners of the recycling can in the hope of hiding it from Mick."

"She didn't want me to know she'd been diagnosed with high blood pressure," Mick explained.

"Until I got threatened by the Brinkwood bitch. Sorry, Detective Waterhouse, but that's what I call her. I thought: *I refuse to be this woman's victim*. I said, 'You do what you gotta do, honey-bunch.' Then I told Mick myself before she got the chance, soon as he got back from that day's freezing cold swim."

Mick chuckled. "I couldn't get enough of that swimming lake!"

"What exactly did Jane Brinkwood say to you?" Simon asked. "Did she overtly threaten you?"

"Uh-huh," said Susan. "First she told me she knew I'd sent her a note saying 'Beware.' In capital letters. I was like, 'I'm sorry, are we back in kindergarten?' She said I wanted to drive her away from her own honeymoon and destroy her happiness, or words to that effect. It was laughable, and laugh I did, right in her face. That's when she got all riled up. She asked if Mick knew I was on Lisinopril. If I wasn't trying to keep it secret from him, why had I torn up the boxes, etcetera etcetera? I've no idea how she knew I was the one on the medication. Why did she assume I was the box-tearer-upper and not Mick? She didn't seem to care a damn about admitting to having gone through our trash. I'm telling you: she *was* trash. I feel sorry for you and your colleagues, Detective—having to make as big a song and dance over the murder of someone like her as you would for a decent person. I mean, when you think what she did to Lucy Dean . . ." Susan winced.

"Yet you've come back here by choice, to help us solve her murder," said Simon.

"Not really," she said. "We've come because Lucy's 'letter to Jane's killer' mail-out was for sure gonna stir things up, and it felt important to be close by. Mick and I were part of it then, and we're part of it now."

"My wife doesn't like to be left out of whatever's going on," said Mick.

"No, I don't, if I'm part of it," Susan agreed. "But frankly, Detective? I could care less about Jane getting stabbed to death."

Silently, Simon corrected her: *You mean you couldn't care less.* Some things were reasonable variations—pavement and sidewalk, for instance—but in the case of couldn't versus could care less, the English version was obviously correct.

"Can I ask why you didn't tell me about this exchange you had with Jane until now?" said Simon.

"Sure." Susan smiled. "I didn't want to, and I knew it wouldn't make any difference. The only person that little episode furnished with a motive was me—maybe Mick too, if he wanted to defend my honor—and I knew we hadn't done it."

Simon turned to Mick. "Tell me about the bones you found," he said.

A tremor of shock passed across Mick's face.

"What bones?" said Susan.

"At Tevendon, on 30 June, your husband was overheard in the resort office, talking in an agitated way to Anita Khattou about some bones he'd found. He was worried they might be human."

"Mick, you never told me this."

"I didn't want to spoil your vacation, Suze." He put a hand on her arm. "I'm sorry. I should have told you."

"And me," said Simon. "I was investigating a murder. According to what was overheard, you'd found hidden bones two days previously. That was something I needed to know."

"I'm sorry, Detective. I would have told you if I'd thought . . . You see, Anita set my mind at rest, so I didn't think much about it after that. She said they were animal bones."

"But when you first found them you thought they were human. Why?"

"Look, I'm an antiques guy," said Mick. "Not a zoologist. I can't tell an animal's leg bone from a human's."

"Presumably you know animals live and die in wooded areas," said Simon.

Mick nodded.

"If you found bones in the woods behind Tevendon Mere, I don't see why it would even cross your mind that they might be human, or why you'd be agitated about it."

"I guess . . . I guess it was only that I'd never seen bones before." Mick looked a lot happier suddenly. *Why?* "It freaked me out, and I overreacted. Thankfully Anita, bless her heart, was able to set me straight, and that was the end of the problem."

"When you first saw the bones, why did you think they'd been deliberately hidden? The person who overheard your conversation with Anita said it was clear that was what had alarmed you most."

"No, the bones weren't especially hidden," said Mick. "I . . . I don't remember saying that." He seemed less confident now. "Or, if I did, I was probably assuming I'd found human remains. Humans don't just die in the woods in the way animals do. But someone might take human bones and stash them away in the woods hoping they'd never be found."

You're making it up as you go along.

Simon looked down at his notepad. "The day before, 29 June, Lucy Dean bumped into you in the woods while she was walking there. She said you seemed brusque and unfriendly. Didn't want to make conversation."

Mick looked puzzled. "I don't remember that at all. I was probably on my way to a swim in the lake or on my way back after one. I could easily have been in a hurry, in either direction. Detective, speaking of the swimming lake at Tevendon—"

"Mick, for goodness' sake." Susan rolled her eyes.

"I know the resort's closed, but . . . well, I'm figuring you and your guys have the keys? I wondered if there's any chance I could have a swim in my dear old friend while I'm over here?"

"No," said Simon.

"But here's the thing, Detective: the murder happened in the main part of the resort. The woods and the lake are right across the other side of the road. Separate entrances and everything. A whole separate area. The way I see it, the swimming lake's not really part of the crime scene. Do you think if I personally contacted Lord Brinkwood and—"

"Mick, stop, for Christ's sake," Susan snapped. "Watch the detective's face. He doesn't give a rat's ass about your swimming needs. Neither will His Lordship."

"Okay, okay." Mick held up his hands. "I thought it was worth a try, that's all."

"I've found you three other places to swim. *Three*." Susan counted it out on her fingers. "The Riverbank Club in Cambridge, Buckden Marina, and the country park in that village. What's it called? Milton."

"All right. I apologize if I was out of line, Detective. I sure hope Tevendon opens up again, though. I'd love to go back someday. It's funny: when Suze first told me about it, I'd never heard of Silsford or the Culver Valley. I was like, what do I wanna go visit some Podunk place halfway across the world for, when I can go to Maui or the Caymans? But Suze was right, as she always is: Tevendon's special."

"Podunk?" Simon had never heard the word before.

"He means a small town," said Susan.

"I'll take your word for it."

It had been Mick's word, in fact. Mick was the one who'd said it. *Podunk.*

Mick the antiques guy . . .

Simon felt a stirring of excitement as another piece of the puzzle teetered on the edge of falling into place. But was this one too much of a stretch? Was there a way to test it?

Eventually Simon said, "I need you to talk me through every single day of your holiday at Tevendon last summer. Both of you. I mean, each of you, one by one. Every day, every detail. What you did when, separately and together."

"Ooh! Like a kind of oral vacation diary?" said Susan.

"Yeah, like that, but . . . more as if you were giving a statement about your daily actions at Tevendon to the police. A formal one that might be read by anyone."

"You want us to write it down?" said Mick.

"No, I want you to talk me through it."

"Why?" asked Susan.

"Because I do."

"We might not remember every single thing we did and when we did it," she said.

"That's fine. Just do your best."

"Okay. But I warn you, Detective, there's going to be a lot of Mick swimming in that lake. One day he went twice, the crazy fool, crack of dawn and again midevening."

"Then I'd like him to tell me about that. And then you can tell me about what you did." If he let her, Susan Henry would do the narrating for both of them and that would make the exercise redundant.

"Should I go first, then?" said Mick. "Start with day one?"

Simon nodded. *This will be the test*, he thought.

26

Wednesday, January 15, 2020

Steep, Sam Kombothekra thought to himself. Everything about Caroline and Harriet Moyle-Jones's house in Sheffield was steep: the angle of the road it was on, the five steps leading up from the driveway to the front door, the staircase that you met as soon as you walked inside. Even its garden had three levels. From his position on the sofa, Sam could only see two of them; the third was too high, above where the window ended.

"Well?" said Caroline Moyle-Jones. She'd asked him a question. Evidently he wasn't responding fast enough for her liking. She was sitting next to him on the sofa. Harriet sat at the other end of the room in a square leather armchair, underneath a framed picture of a large pigeon standing on the deck of a much smaller ship. She had a mug of mint tea cupped in her hands and looked distressed. When Sam had arrived and introduced himself, she'd called out to Caroline, "The police are here!" as if it was a big shock and not a prearranged visit.

"It's definitely not harassment," he told Caroline. "And Lucy's letter to Jane Brinkwood's murderer can't be called slanderous because she's not aiming it at you or at anyone in particular. She explicitly wrote it to an unknown person. Her covering note makes that clear."

"So, what, she can just write creepy letters to unnamed

murderers and send them to us whenever she feels like it, and there's nothing we can do to stop it?" said Caroline.

"No, that's not how it works," said Sam. "You say you contacted her and told her never to send you anything similar again?"

"Too right I did."

"That's a reasonable request. Maybe Lucy'll think so too. Why don't you wait and see what happens? Do you really think she'll make a habit of it?"

"I want a guarantee that she won't," said Caroline. "Can't you at least talk to her? Tell her it's unacceptable, in a way that makes it clear there's some kind of muscle behind it? The muscle of the law?"

"I think that would be . . . unnecessary and unwise at this point," said Sam. "Lucy didn't break any law when she sent you both that letter. I can see why it wasn't pleasant to receive, but . . ." He did his best to look apologetic. "It's not up to the police to tell people what letters they can and can't send when no laws are being broken."

"I don't think she'll do it again," said Harriet hopefully, clearly wanting someone to agree with her.

"All that means is you don't want it to happen, Harri," said Caroline. "Anyone's capable of anything. We should have learned that lesson by now."

"I need to ask you both a question," said Sam. "We're asking everybody: At Tevendon, did Jane Brinkwood threaten either of you?"

Harriet immediately looked at Caroline, whose expression was wary. After a few seconds she said, "Yes, she did. How did you know that?"

"She threatened quite a few of the other guests. You should have told us at the time."

"And made you think I might have had a massive grudge

against Jane?" said Caroline scornfully. "No thanks. I didn't want to make it any easier for you to decide I was guilty of murder when I wasn't."

"Tell me what happened," said Sam. "What was Jane's threat to you? What prompted her to make it?"

"Nothing I'd done, that's for sure. She accosted me and told me I'd better stop trying to mess with her head or else she'd do worse to me. I didn't have a clue what she was on about, and I said so. She seemed to think I'd posted a note to her cottage telling her to beware. I told her I hadn't, and asked her how she knew it was intended for her and not William."

"What did she say?" Sam knew the answer, but it never hurt to check.

"It came in an envelope—her name on it, not his. She kept saying she knew it was me who'd sent it, and if I didn't admit it, she was going to . . ." Caroline stopped and shuddered. "I'm actually embarrassed for her, remembering it. She threatened to tell everyone my secret—to go on social media and trash my professional reputation by sharing my shameful secret as widely as she could. It might have been scary if I'd had a secret, but I didn't. I don't. Anything potentially reputation-damaging, I generally broadcast it myself, via my stand-up comedy. Like my criminal record for driving offenses: I've got six points on my license, three for looking at my phone while driving—only Google Maps, but still—and another three for bumping into some bikes outside a bike shop and then driving away, which Sheffield police chose to define as leaving the scene of an accident, even though I'd had no idea I'd bashed the bikes and paid for them to be fixed as soon as it was brought to my attention."

Caroline shook her head. "That's it. Those six points on my license have been fodder for my stand-up and my sketches for the past few years. That's what I'm known for: taking the mickey out of how shit a driver I am. I don't have any shameful secrets that anyone could expose."

"So, what did you say to Jane Brinkwood when she implied that you did and threatened to make it public?"

"I said, 'Er, what secret?' She couldn't come up with anything, obviously, so she said something lame like, 'You know what it is' and then wandered off awkwardly—but not before I'd told her to fuck off and never come near me again."

Sam turned to Harriet. "Did Jane threaten you too?"

"No." Harriet sounded uncertain. "Caro, you explain."

"Harri *did* have something she was hiding, and worrying about, and losing sleep over for months before we even got to Tevendon," said Caroline. "I knew nothing about it. I only found out when I told her Jane had threatened me and it had made no sense. She went beserk and assumed Jane was threatening to expose *her* secret. I told her that was ridiculous. If Jane had meant the threat for Harri, she'd have made it to Harri. It was obvious she was just trying her luck. Most people have got something, haven't they? Some kind of skeleton in the cupboard?"

"I don't know," said Sam truthfully. "I find it hard to imagine because, like you, I haven't."

"Most people have got . . . things," said Harriet quietly. "You two are the exception."

"Wait till you hear what Harri's shameful secret is." Caroline shook her head. "I have finally, *finally*, persuaded her it'll be okay to tell you. She won't lose her job or be banished from polite society. She was so terrified of it getting out, her first idea was to beg me to fake-confess to Jane that I'd sent the anonymous note and ask for her mercy and forgiveness. Uh, I don't fucking think so! For something I hadn't done? No way."

"I panicked," said Harriet.

"Harri's background, her family of origin, is very different from mine," Caroline told Sam. "Not to get too psychological, but she grew up believing that her survival depended on burying everything that was true for her and living a lie—pretending to want the kind of life her parents wanted for her. Her default tendency, growing up and even for most of her adult life, was to keep as much to herself as possible. It still is. When I opened Lucy's murderer letter, I knew Harriet must have got one too, but she'd said nothing about it, even knowing there was no way I wouldn't find out."

"I'm going to have therapy," Harriet told Sam. He couldn't work out if she sounded proud or defiant.

"It's a phobia, basically," said Caroline. "Harri has a crippling fear of telling the truth when it's in any way difficult, emotionally."

"I'm sorry, but I have to ask you, Harriet," said Sam. "What were you so afraid people might find out about you?"

"I have a Twitter account," Harriet muttered, staring down at the mug in her hands.

Sam waited. After a few seconds he said, "Lots of people have them. Why is it a problem?"

"This is going to take forever if she tells the story," said Caroline. "Sorry, I just haven't got the patience. Harriet had a secret Twitter account. She created it after she got a load of wrongly directed abuse on her main Twitter account, which is in her professional name, not our married name. Harriet Jones— like the supermodel Harriet Jones. Heard of her?"

"I haven't, I'm afraid," said Sam.

"She was a reality TV star and now she's a supermodel and an influencer. She's part of the clean makeup movement."

Sam didn't ask what that meant. He understood "makeup" and hoped that would be enough.

"She'd said something totally harmless and well intentioned about makeup. Someone got steamed up about it, and a handful of the hundreds of abusive messages that were sent to her got sent to Harri instead. It didn't last long. Harri explained that she was a different Harriet Jones and this bunch of absolute freakoids said, 'Oh, I'm so sorry to have troubled you, please accept my apologies and have a lovely day' before going off to resend their 'You evil bitch, the only makeover you need is a faceful of acid' abuse to the correct account. Harri was pretty traumatized by the experience, and she also spent some time researching the cause of all the fuss: what supermodel Harriet had said, what people had said back to her—"

"She'd done absolutely nothing wrong," said Harriet vehemently. "It wasn't right that she was getting attacked so viciously. I felt I had to do something."

"So she set up another Twitter account, a secret one, in the name @wordscanhurtus and started tweeting people—members of Twitter attack mobs—in order to try and persuade them to stop being so nasty on social media. Which, you have to admit, was a nice idea. If only something like that could work."

Caroline stood up and walked over to the sideboard that was standing against the wall. She opened the middle drawer and pulled out some sheets of paper, which she passed to Sam. "I've printed out all the tweets that were ever sent from the @wordscanhurtus account. This is it: the sum total of my wife's supposedly shameful secret."

It was around ten pages altogether. Sam skim-read the lot. To a different person each time, Harriet had tweeted messages such as, "I know you're angry, but can you please think about what you're saying?" and "Is this really who you want to be?" and "How is this torrent of aggression going to make the world a better place?" Sam's favorite was "Is this splurge of vitriol beneath you? I think it is. Will it make you feel worse rather than better in the long run? I think it will."

He looked up at Harriet. "So when Jane Brinkwood told

Caroline that she knew her secret and threatened to reveal it, you thought she was talking about these tweets of yours?"

She nodded. "I know it doesn't really make sense."

"Yes, it does," said Caroline. "People who suffer from excessive fear and anxiety interpret everything as meaning that the worst possible fate is about to befall them."

"You haven't tweeted anything illegal here." Sam looked again at the pages. "Social media allows us to make anonymous accounts, and you seem to have used yours to encourage people, not to be malicious. You've done nothing wrong, as far as I can see."

"Hallelujah. Of course she hasn't," Caroline agreed.

Sam said, "Is there anything else you want to tell me, either of you, about Jane Brinkwood or anything that happened at Tevendon? Maybe something you've been scared to say until now?"

A look passed between Harriet and Caroline. It lasted a fraction of a second, then it was over. Sam might have imagined it.

"No, nothing," they both said at the same time.

27

"Are you sure you're happy to fend for yourselves?" Anita waved the keys in the air. She had met Simon and Sam Kombothekra at the main gates of the resort. "I don't want Ian to be on his own. He can get really down if I leave him to his own devices for too long."

"It's absolutely fine with us." Sam took the keys from her. "As soon as we're finished, we'll drive over and return them."

"Thanks. That would be brilliant. All the keys are labeled individually, so you shouldn't have any trouble."

"One thing before you go," said Simon. "In the near future, I'm going to need to have everyone back here. Will Lord Brinkwood allow that, do you think?"

"Who's everyone?"

"The people who were here the night Jane died. I want to talk to them together, as a group. I was thinking maybe in the indoor dining room."

Anita looked worried. "I'm not sure how Ian would feel about that. He wants the place to be . . . unused, basically. Empty."

"You've just given us the keys," said Simon. "We're about to go in."

"That's different. From Ian's point of view, that's part of the investigation into Jane's murder."

"So would this meeting be. You want the murderer caught and behind bars? Let me do it my way."

"I'll talk to Ian," said Anita. "That's the best I can promise."

Once she had driven off and he and Simon were alone again, Sam said, "This plan to get all the Tevendon crowd together . . . does it mean what I think it means?"

"No. There are still gaps that need filling in."

Anyone else, at this point, would have asked Simon if he knew the answer to the main question: Who murdered Jane Brinkwood? Sam didn't ask. That was why he, and not Charlie, was here at Tevendon today. In many ways, Charlie would have been Simon's first choice—he'd have loved her to witness the discovery of what he strongly suspected he was about to find—but she'd have asked too many questions and complained too much when she didn't get the answers she wanted.

Sam followed Simon as he walked along the path: the main one, the long-way-around one that would take them past most of the cottages. Simon knew—how could he forget?—that there was a quicker way, through Number 1's garden and then the gate that led into the office building's garden, but he wanted to see each of the houses again.

He stopped in front of Number 6, the cottage that had so briefly been his and Charlie's. It looked neglected, as did the whole resort. Would it ever reopen? If it did, would some people come for the wrong reasons, because they knew it had been the site of a brutal murder?

Sam didn't ask why they were standing in front of Number 6. Eventually, Simon started to walk again, past Numbers 7, 3, and 2, then across the outdoor dining terrace past 5 and 4.

"I assumed we'd be heading over to the other side first," said Sam. "To the woods, to look for bones."

"Keys?" Simon held out his hand. They'd reached the front

door of the office building. The key was easy to find in the bunch Anita had given them, and they were soon in.

"You're right," Simon told Sam. "Bones is exactly what we're looking for."

"Here? In the resort office?"

"Here. Close the door behind you. Just in case someone's prowling around out there. I don't want anyone overhearing." The windows were all shut.

Once he was sure it was safe, Simon asked the question he'd been waiting for this moment to ask: "Where are the woods?" He couldn't help smiling at the prospect of the little show he was about to put on. He knew Sam wouldn't mind. Sam knew how to wait and he knew how to be a good audience. Unlike Charlie, he was never too proud to fall into that role: an audience of one, ready to be surprised and impressed.

Read the room. Thank goodness for Charlie spotting the significance of those words when she'd heard them from Lucy Dean. And then there was Simon's own contribution, after Mick Henry's use of the word "Podunk." It was mind-blowing to think of the number of deductions that might never have been made if all the various thought-chains had evolved and combined differently.

"Where are the woods?" Sam repeated the question. "They're on the other side of the road where we just met Anita."

"Now tell me again where the woods are, but without using the same words you used the first time."

Charlie would have been spluttering with impatience by this point. Not Sam, who had bowed his head and seemed to be applying himself to the task he'd been assigned.

"The woods are in the Culver Valley, in England."

"No, that's too general. Be specific. More like your first try but in different words."

"The woods are . . . just over there"—Sam indicated with his head—"behind Tevendon Mere."

"Yes!" said Simon. "The woods are behind Tevendon Mere. And that's what Liv heard Mick Henry say, right, about where he'd found the bones?"

"Right."

"Anita confirmed it and so did Mick himself. Animal bones. Here's the problem, though: Liv told Charlie and me that she wasn't really listening to the fine detail of what Mick said, because at a certain point Gibbs joined her outside the office and she started talking to him, to distract him. She didn't want him to hear that any bones had been found. She thought he might go 'all police-y' and let it spoil their holiday. So she was eavesdropping while talking. Don't you think there's a chance she might not have been able to hear what was said with one hundred percent accuracy?"

Sam nodded. "Yes. A good chance."

"So she could have misheard the part about finding bones in the woods behind Tevendon Mere?"

"I suppose so. Though if Anita and Mick both confirmed it later, maybe Liv heard right."

"In one sense, she heard very right. She heard the *sounds* she thought she heard."

"What do you mean, 'the sounds'?" asked Sam.

Simon pulled out a chair from behind Greg Summerell's desk near the office's front door. He sat down. "When I spoke to Mick and Susan Henry, Mick used the word 'Podunk.' Do you know what it means?"

"No," said Sam.

"I didn't either. The meaning's not important, but it made me think of something I hadn't really noticed until then, or only noticed subliminally. So I put it to the test. I asked Mick and Susan Henry to talk me through every detail of their Tevendon holiday: exactly what they did while they were there. Mick did a lot of swimming in Tevendon Mere. Every day, in fact. One day, he swam there twice, morning and evening. But do you know what he never did, this retired US-Navy-guy-turned-antiques-dealer who lives in Colorado?"

"Swam in the heated pool?" Sam guessed.

"This isn't about swimming. It's about words. Mick Henry did swim in the heated pool once or twice. But that's irrelevant."

"So what did he never do?"

"In more than a dozen mentions of his favorite swimming spot, Tevendon Mere, he never once called it Tevendon Mere, or the mere."

Sam frowned. "What? What did he call it, then?"

"The swimming lake. Every single time. His wife did too, whenever she mentioned it. Swimming lake, or lake. And guess what? Just like 'Podunk' is American and means nothing to a lot of English people, the word 'mere' as a name for a lake is hardly ever—maybe never, in fact—used in America. So it stands to reason that Mick and Susan Henry would call it the swimming lake. Personally I've always thought of it as the swimming pond, even though it's way too big to be a pond. When I drew a map of the resort, though, that was how I labeled it: 'Swimming Pond.'"

"I see." Sam nodded slowly. "So you're wondering, why would Mick Henry say 'Tevendon Mere' when describing where he'd found the bones if he'd never called it that previously?"

"Exactly. Liv said she heard him say 'Behind Tevendon Mere, in the woods.' I didn't think anything of it when she first told us because the woods *are* behind Tevendon Mere. Plus the woods seem like a likely place for someone to find bones. But after talking to Mick Henry and hearing him say 'swimming lake, swimming lake, swimming lake' over and over, I don't think it's likely he said 'Tevendon Mere' when talking to Anita."

"But—"

"Next question: Have you ever heard an American say the word 'mirror'?"

"Mirror . . . Right. Right!" Sam looked excited, which Simon appreciated. He was the opposite of a tough crowd. "That's what you meant about Liv hearing the sound she thought she heard. The right sound, but the wrong word."

He'd got it.

"To an English ear, an American saying 'mirror' sounds almost identical to the sound of anyone saying 'mere.' Mick Henry's an antiques specialist." Simon nodded at the far wall. "And look. As luck would have it, there's a mirror on the office wall that looks very much like an antique, don't you think? Ornate, gold, Brinkwood family crest at the top. Slight mottling, with the odd small black spot around the edges of the glass . . . I think Mick Henry, as an antiques dealer, might well be interested enough to take that mirror off the wall and have a really close look at it."

"Incredible," Sam breathed. "So—"

Simon stood up. "Whatever Liv thought she heard Mick telling Anita, I think she got it slightly wrong. I think what she actually heard was him saying that he'd found bones behind the *mirror*—this one." Simon pointed. "And not in the woods, but in the *wall*, which also begins with the letter 'w.' If Liv thought she'd just heard 'behind the mere' instead of 'behind the mirror,' her brain would have prepared her to hear the word she expected to hear next: 'woods,' not 'wall.' "

"If you're right, that would explain why Mick assumed they were human bones and wanted the police called," Sam said.

"Correct. Who would go to the trouble of hiding animal bones in a wall?"

"So . . . Mick and Anita must have lied."

"In a big way," said Simon. "That's if I'm right. Shall we have a look?" He walked over to the mirror. "Give us a hand.

This is likely to be heavy. Mick and Anita might have moved it together. Maybe he asked if he could take a closer look and she helped him lift it down off the wall. It seems likely that an antiques expert would want to see the back as well as the front."

"It does," Sam agreed. "Well, let's try and follow in their footsteps and see if we find what they found."

Together he and Simon lifted the mirror off the wall. "Over there." Simon pointed the way with his head. Sam had to walk backward. Once the mirror was securely propped up behind Greg Summerell's desk, they stood back and looked at what it had concealed: a large cavity in the expanse of white wall. The hole was about two feet wide and one foot high. Its edges were jagged, and its shape irregular. It reminded Simon of the shape of a small country on a map.

Simon didn't move towards it straight away. "What do we know for certain?" he said. "Someone, for some reason, smashed into the wall and tore away a large chunk of plasterboard. Why? To hide bones?" Slowly, he walked over to the hole. "It would have been easier to hide them in the woods—much easier, in fact. And . . . *shit*."

"What?"

"There are no bones in here."

"Are you sure?"

"Very. Wait, there's something else, though . . ." Simon reached down into the wall cavity. When he pulled his hand out, he saw that he was holding a small navy-blue hexagonal box and a piece of paper. The box had a green ribbon tied around it with a bow at the top, and gold lettering on its lid, which said "French's Handmade Jewelry." The ribbon wasn't real, Simon saw on closer inspection. It was made of something hard, and built into the box's design. No untying was necessary in order to open the box, which Simon did. Lying flat on a bed of green silk was an ugly white brooch made of some weird material. Was it papier-mâché? Simon didn't really have a clue what that was, though he'd heard the name. Not metal, anyway. It looked as if it was perhaps supposed to be a bolt of lightning but was doing a very bad job of resembling one. There was nothing else inside the box except for some grains of plaster dust from the smashed-up wall.

Simon turned his attention to the piece of paper, which was more interesting. "Look at this." He passed it to Sam. "A list of names. Twelve in total—six pairs." Simon started to read them aloud. "The McCallions, the Henrys, and the Moyle-Joneses, and then some unfamiliar ones: Lindsay James and Davina Slade. Imogen Dean and Bailey Rufo. Tommy and Fran Jordan—"

"Lindsay and Davina," Sam interrupted. "I've heard those names before. Why are they next to Caroline and Harriet Moyle-Jones like that? It's as if whoever wrote this wants to link the two pairs—Harriet and Caroline with Lindsay and Davina."

"And the same with the others," said Simon. Just as Lindsay James and Davina Slade's names were opposite Caroline's and Harriet's, Tommy and Fran Jordan's names were opposite the McCallions' on the list, and Imogen Dean and Bailey Rufo were opposite Susan and Mick Henry.

"I know where we've heard the names Lindsay and Davina before," said Simon. "Anita Khattou overheard Caroline and Harriet talking about them at dinner, after Gleave and Brinkwood had scuttled off back to their cottage."

"Of course," said Sam. "And didn't they say they'd played those characters in a parlor game?"

"I think so, yeah."

"Maybe the game involved the McCallions and the Henrys too," said Sam. "They might have played the roles of those other people: Tommy and Fran Jordan and Imogen Dean and Bailey Rufo. Dean is Lucy's surname, whatever that means."

"Where are the bones?" said Simon. He was also thinking about the white lightning brooch, and about the one Lord Brinkwood had worn the other day. Wasn't there an old song called "White Lightning"? "We need to get the woods searched," he told Sam. "And the lake, or the mere, or whatever you want to call it."

"You think that's where the bones are?"

"I don't know." Simon sighed. "I thought they'd be here, in the wall. Wherever they are, I doubt they're animal bones. When we find them and get a chance to look at them—which we will—they're going to turn out to be human."

28

Friday, January 17, 2020

"How soon could you get here?" Simon asked Charlie. He'd rung her from his car, which he'd parked on the far side of the road opposite Barrmore Nursery in Rawndesley. He could have put it in the official nursery car park, but that was dangerously close to the large rectangular yard in which around forty toddlers were screaming and running at each other like planes intent on crashing. Several young and middle-aged women in coats and hats wove cheerfully in and out of the swarms of children, smiling benignly and trying to make conversation with one another as if they hadn't noticed the anarchy all around that threatened to engulf them. Simon could hardly bear to watch.

"It doesn't matter how long it would take me to get there," said Charlie. "I'm not coming. They're *kids*, Simon. Tiny, harmless tots. Stop feeling sorry for yourself, get inside and do what you're there to do. Why *are* you at a nursery, by the way?"

"If you get down here and do this one thing for me, I'll fill you in on where we're up to."

"Is it Brinkwood-related?"

"Yes."

There was a short pause. Then Charlie said, "Is it the nursery that Lucy's daughter, Evin, goes to?"

"It is, but that's not why I'm here," Simon told her. "Not primarily, anyway."

"What's that supposed to m— No, I'm not going to ask that. You'll only promise to tell me as soon as I've driven over there and taken an unpleasant chore off your hands. But, I mean, how unpleasant can it be for a big strong policeman? These are *toddlers*, Simon. You can't be scared of them."

"I'm not scared. It just looks horrific. I don't fancy going in there. Much as I hate the scum we're used to dealing with, they make sense to me. These screaming munchkins don't."

"Maybe if you think of each of them as someone's beloved child, it'll help? I don't fancy it either, by the way. Do you think hanging out with snotty preschoolers is my favorite hobby? Ugh!"

"Let me have one last try at persuading you: What if I tell you everything you want to know upfront? Why I'm here, what's happened over the past few days. Would that make a difference to your willingness to help me out?"

"Almost definitely not," said Charlie. "But let's try it anyway. Who knows how accommodating I might feel if you really talk to me for a change instead of keeping me in the dark." She sounded more amused than resentful.

"I've been angry," said Simon.

"Yeah, I spotted that."

"You should have told me about Liv and Gibbs and Number 6. You're not stupid. Soon as we found Jane Brinkwood dead, there was no excuse for not telling me who Mr. and Mrs. Friendly were. Your secrecy actively impeded the investigation. What Liv told us helped. A *lot*. I could have done with having that help sooner."

"Don't forget Gibbs's secrecy," said Charlie. "I wasn't the only one who didn't tell you."

"I'm not married to Gibbs."

"And let's face it, there aren't many people who can say that."

Simon laughed, then worried Charlie had heard him. He was supposed to be telling her what she'd done wrong.

"I'm sorry," she said. "I've got no decent excuse apart from it makes me feel sick every time I think about those two—Mr. and Mrs. Bigamy. But you should have talked to me about how angry you were. You always just clam up."

"I suppose so."

"And I'm particularly reluctant to raise the subject of Liv and Gibbs with you because of what it might lead to. *Is* leading to. This right now is the lead-in."

"What do you mean?"

"Here's what I don't understand, Simon. We had a decision to make. We knew they were planning an illegal, bigamous wedding and we did nothing. You made us do nothing. I wanted to tell Liv to cut the crap and cancel the plans, threaten to report them. You wouldn't let me."

Simon was holding the phone away from his ear. He could still hear every word, and the distance helped.

"I went along with what you wanted," Charlie said. "I'm angry with myself more than you, I think. Every time I thought about the whole horrible mess, I got more confused, so I persuaded myself you were right: that we didn't know for sure that they were actually going to do it, that if we started to mind our own business and treated Liv and Gibbs as if we didn't suspect them at all, then we'd see no evidence that they'd done anything illegal. We'd be blissfully ignorant. It was the easy way out and I'm not blaming you, or rather I'm blaming myself just as much, but we did the wrong thing. We fucked up and . . . it really bothers me. And I can't believe I'm saying this but . . . if Gibbs is a bigamist and he's also willing to withhold important information in a murder case, he doesn't deserve your protection. Or mine. He should be out of a job."

"You think I'm protecting Gibbs's career?" said Simon. "I'm not. I'm protecting my own. I need him there so that I can keep turning up for work day in, day out. With Gibbs gone, I'd soon be gone too. If anything changed . . ."

How could he explain it? It wasn't about Gibbs. Simon didn't even particularly like him. "I couldn't and wouldn't stay in the job if Gibbs went," said Simon. "Same's true of Sellers, Sam, even the fucking Snowman. I couldn't do it. And without the job, how would I have any money? What would I do with my time?"

There was a long pause. Then Charlie said, "Am I missing something?"

"My attitude to work's changed in the last few years, Char. I used to be sure I wanted to do what I do. Even if a case went sideways or if Proust was a twat, I still had the conviction that I was in the right place and the right job, just a more ideal version of it. I thought I had a purpose in life and this was it."

"And that's changed?" said Charlie.

It had changed more than Simon could express. Should he tell her? Would the relief of saying it aloud to another person outweigh the hassle that Charlie, with her good intentions and her concern, might create for him once she knew?

"There's a big part of me that doesn't want to be a DC any more," he said.

"*What?* No, there isn't."

"There is."

"Oh, really? Then why are you driving yourself to the edge of exhaustion drawing endless maps of the Tevendon Estate Resort? Why haven't you heard most of what I've said to you since last July because you're too busy obsessing about Jane Brinkwood's murder?"

She didn't get it. Normally, Simon would have given up at this point. "I want to know who killed Jane Brinkwood more than I want anything else in this world," he said, "but that's different from wanting the job of being a police detective and all it entails. I *want* to want it, and I don't understand why I don't any more. I always used to think it was the perfect work for someone like me."

"It is."

"Then why am I constantly fighting off thoughts that tell me the opposite? Why do I spend so much time wishing I could sit at home and do nothing, with no one expecting anything from me? If there were a way of hearing about the tiny minority of interesting cases that come in and trying to figure them out without having to go to a place and be an employee, and fit in with all the other employees doing their drone work like the little ants we all are . . ." Simon stopped. He'd forgotten what he was trying to say. "The point is, I'm not adaptable any more, not like I used to be."

"Simon, you've never been at all adaptable, trust me."

"I have been. More than I am now, anyway. That's why everything needs to stay the same at work if I want to try and convince myself I'm the same too. You've all got to be there: you nearby, on a different floor. And Sam, Gibbs, Sellers, the Snowman. Nothing can change. Then maybe I can persuade myself I haven't changed."

Neither of them spoke for a few seconds.

"Charlie? You still there?"

"Yeah. I had no idea you felt that way. We need to talk about this properly, face-to-face. Ideally when you're not about to stroll into a seething pit full of toddlers."

Why would she say that? They'd just talked about it. Simon had been feeling quite a bit better too for finally getting it off his chest. The prospect of having to talk about it again threatened to bring on a gloomier mood. "Do you want a Brinkwood progress report or not?" he said.

"Always."

Simon talked Charlie through the latest developments, finishing with the discovery of the hole in the wall behind the mirror in Anita's office.

"So none of the bones you were expecting to find, but instead a posh-looking jewelry box containing a weird brooch and a piece of paper with a load of names on it," she summed up. "Six pairs of two, three of them being the McCallions, the Moyle-Joneses, and the Henrys."

"Right."

"Tell me again which pairs were assigned to which."

"Polly and Jack McCallion were paired with Tommy and Fran Jordan. Mick and Susan Henry were with Imogen Dean and Bailey Rufo, and Caroline and Harriet Moyle-Jones were with Lindsay James and Davina Slade. That's why I'm having to brave the toddlers. The real Lindsay and Davina both work at Barrmore Nursery in Rawndesley where Evin Shabani-Dean's a . . . pupil, I guess you'd have to say. Lindsay's the manager and Davina's a childcare assistant."

"Wait," said Charlie. "'The real Lindsay and Davina'? Who are the fake ones? Those names ring a bell."

"The fake Lindsay and Davina are characters from some kind of parlor game that Caroline and Harriet Moyle-Jones once played."

"Oh, right, I remember," said Charlie. "But, hold on . . . Why would the Moyle-Joneses ever play a parlor game that involved two staff members from Evin's nursery?"

"Good question," said Simon. "Maybe they're lying. That's what they said after Anita Khattou heard them talking about Lindsay and Davina the night Brinkwood was killed."

"I bet they're lying," said Charlie. "What about the other names on the list, the ones we don't know from Tevendon?"

"Imogen Dean and Bailey Rufo are Lucy's older sister and her husband. They live in Allen, Texas. In America."

"Yeah, I know where Texas is, thanks. How did you find out who all these people were?"

"I rang Lucy. I was going to ask her if she could shed any light. Pete Shabani answered her phone and told me who they all were. Tommy and Fran Jordan are the couple Brinkwood was booked to go and work for as a doula when she and Gleave decided to inflict her on Lucy instead, so that they could spend more time together under the same roof. Brinkwood let them down—left them completely in the lurch. I spoke to them this morning."

"How did Pete know the names of a random couple Jane Brinkwood had disappointed?" asked Charlie.

"Apparently it became part of her romantic story about how she and William were destined to be together—that she knew as soon as he offered her the chance to come and work for him and Lucy that she was going to drop everything, and Tommy and Fran Jordan would just have to manage. This was a story she told multiple times while out at dinner with Pete and Lucy. Beggars belief, doesn't it?"

"Understatement," Charlie muttered.

"I've also spoken briefly to Imogen Dean and Bailey Rufo. Woke them up by calling too early. Now I just need to speak to Lindsay James and Davina Slade and then I'm done."

"Something feels like it's missing," said Charlie. "Or . . . it's too neat, or something. You find a piece of paper in a hole in the wall with six previously unknown names on it, and then almost immediately you identify all six people and they all have a clear connection to the Jane Brinkwood case?"

"I only identified them almost immediately because Pete told me who they were," said Simon. "He also told me some other very useful things. For instance, he told me who he suspected of Brinkwood's murder."

"And?" This was Charlie's voice at its highest pitch.

"He was dead right."

"What? You mean you know who stabbed her?"

"Yeah. I'd worked it out before I spoke to Pete, but it was interesting to hear that he'd got there before me via a totally different route."

"Simon, if you don't tell me—"

"I will," he promised. "Soon."

Ten minutes later he was inside Barrmore Nursery, in a small room that was mercifully child-free. Lindsay James, an efficient middle-aged woman with green-framed glasses and a pleasant, round face, had sent someone off to find Davina Slade. "She'll be here in a sec," she told Simon. "In the meantime, can I make you a tea? Coffee?" She pointed to a kettle and mugs arrangement in the corner of the room behind her desk.

Simon didn't like the look of the half-full glass bottle of milk that was part of the display—like the kind the milkman used to deliver when he was a kid. It was cold enough outside but too warm in here for milk to stand unrefrigerated for long, and something about the bottle made Simon suspect it was an old-timer. "No, thanks," he said. "I'm fine. I've only got a few questions. It shouldn't take more than a minute."

The door opened and a woman of about thirty walked in. She had her hair tied back, apart from an overly long fringe that must have obscured her vision almost entirely. "Am I wanted?" she asked Lindsay James.

"This is DC Simon Waterhouse from the Culver Valley Police. He's here to ask us a few questions."

"About?" said the younger woman.

"Are you Davina Slade?" Simon asked her.

"Yeah, why? What's this about?"

He kept it as brief as he could, told her that both her name and Lindsay's had been written on a piece of paper that was found at the Tevendon Estate Resort, where a murder had been committed on 2 July last year.

"Jane Brinkwood, do you mean?" said Lindsay James.

Simon nodded.

"None of us at Barrmore could believe it," she said. "It was all over the news for weeks. We couldn't believe it was someone connected to one of our bubs. That's what we call them: our bubs." She smiled. "Evin's one of them, as I'm sure you know. Not that Evin was in any way close to Jane Brinkwood, but she was . . . well, you know."

"Did you know Evin used to be called Zoe?" Davina asked Simon.

"Davina, don't bother DC Waterhouse with all that." Lindsay looked embarrassed.

"No, I want to hear whatever you've got to tell me," Simon said. "That's why I'm here."

"Yeah, why *are* you here?" said Davina. "You couldn't have known we'd have anything to say that was worth your time, so why did you come?"

Simon gave a minimal explanation about the list he'd found at Tevendon.

"What?" Davina looked angry. "I don't like the idea of my name being on a list. Was it, like, a list of people the killer was targeting?"

"Oh dear." Lindsay looked upset.

"No, nothing like that at all," Simon reassured them. "You're not in the slightest danger, I promise you."

"How can you know that?" Davina challenged him. "Which other names were on the list apart from mine and Lindsay's?"

"You'd make a good detective," Simon told her. She looked unimpressed. "I'm sorry, I can't tell you any more than I have—but, take my word for it, you're safe."

"Now that you're here, do you want to know what I think about Jane Brinkwood getting murdered?" said Davina.

Simon indicated that he did.

"She had trouble coming to her, that one. Doesn't surprise me at all that she ended up with a knife in her back."

"Because she ran off with a married man?" said Simon.

Davina Slade shot him a scathing look. "No. For lurking on the street next to our playground all the time, like a dirty pervert in a mac."

"What? Are you saying that Jane Brinkwood . . ." Simon was too distracted by his own surprise to finish the question.

"Davina, that's not fair," Lindsay said. "She doesn't mean what you think she means, DC Waterhouse."

"I can speak for myself, actually. Lucy Dean's a funny one too, changing her daughter's name like that. Not only her surname, which I'd understand, but her actual name. You can't do that to a kid. It's not fair."

"Poor Lucy was very upset, and who can blame her," said Lindsay. "She decided to make some big changes in order to feel she was having a fresh start. I can understand it."

"I can't," said Davina. "It was like she wanted to brainwash us all—'Evin this, Evin that,' as if we were all supposed to forget she'd ever been called anything else. That's what pissed me off: the pretense. She wanted to act as if Evin Shabani-Dean had always been the kid's name and we'd never met anyone called Zoe Gleave. I remember, when I had to say to her, 'I'm afraid we've had some trouble today—from Evin's dad and his fiancée,' she made this whole show of looking at me all innocent and saying, 'I'm Evin's dad's fiancée. I haven't given you any trouble.' She knew I meant William Gleave and Jane Brinkwood."

"She was trying to impress on you how important it was to her that Pete should be perceived as Evin's father," said Lindsay.

"I'll perceive however I want, thank you very much," Davina snapped. "And I don't appreciate being lied to, right to my face. She knew what and who I meant."

"Did William Gleave and Jane Brinkwood come here and cause some kind of trouble?" Simon asked. "And what did you mean about her lurking by the playground?"

"She did use to hang around quite a lot," said Lindsay. "Trying to catch glimpses of Evin, I suppose. *Not* like a pervert, not like that at all," she clarified quickly. "There was nothing of that nature about it, nothing sexual at all. We had no idea who she was, this blonde, angelic-looking woman who stood and stared every day. Then one afternoon I saw her in the playground. That shocked me. She had no business being there. I knew she wasn't one of our parents, so she must have just walked in off the street. I saw her from my window, here. She was talking to Davina, who was outside sitting on that bench . . ." Lindsay pointed.

"I was reading a story to Evin," Davina took over. "Suddenly there's this blonde woman right in front of me, bending down to stroke Evin's hair. I said, 'Excuse me, please don't touch her.' She said, 'Oh, it's okay, there's nothing to worry about,' and laughed as if I was making a fuss about nothing. Then she told me who she was. She said to Evin, 'I'm going to be your second mummy soon.' I couldn't believe what I was hearing. I told her to get out of the playground."

"I'd come outside by this point," said Lindsay. "Jane was in mid–sob story by the time I arrived."

"Yeah, she was all, like, 'Zoe's evil mum forced William to give Zoe to her and her new boyfriend and now William's lost his daughter and it's not fair.' Silly cow. Then she started saying to Evin, 'Don't you want to be able to see your real daddy, Zoe?

Pete's not your real daddy.' Poor Evin was sobbing. It was horrible. Worst thing that's ever happened at Barrmore."

"We were frogmarching her towards the playground gates when who should turn up but William Gleave," said Lindsay. "I told him to take himself and Jane home and ensure nothing like that ever happened again. He was terribly apologetic, actually."

"Yeah, he'd been clueless," said Davina. "Stupid sod. He made an appointment to speak to Lindsay the next day, didn't he?"

Lindsay nodded.

"What did he say?" asked Simon.

"Oh, he couldn't grovel enough," said Lindsay. "He's a strange one, that man. Didn't seem remotely concerned about his daughter. Instead, he was full of guilt and shame because it wasn't fair to *Lucy*, what Jane had done. He kept saying that with real feeling, as if he hadn't treated Lucy incredibly shabbily himself. I got the sense that it was a very strange situation indeed. He sat where you're sitting now, DC Waterhouse, and told me all about his and Lucy's agreement: that he would have no further contact with Evin—he made sure to call her by her new name too. He said she was Pete's daughter, not his any more, and he was committed to keeping his promise to Lucy and staying well away. He claimed he'd made this very clear to Jane, who had obviously ignored him and decided to try and get him his lost daughter back. Well, apparently, he didn't want her back! All he wanted now, he said, was to live happily ever after with Jane, who was the love of his life—he said that quite openly, 'the love of my life'—and to be as fair to Lucy as he could in the circumstances."

"He's an arsehole," Davina contributed helpfully.

Simon chewed the end of his pencil and thought about what to ask next. This story felt as if it added quite a lot to the picture; at the same time, he couldn't see how it changed anything. Eventually he said, "So if William had no interest in being Evin's dad any more, why was Jane bothering to hang around here? Did he explain that?"

"Yes, he did," said Lindsay. "And a most unusual explanation it was too. I thought he was going to tell me something about Jane wanting children herself and not being able to have them, and maybe therefore wanting to play happy families with William and his daughter. But no, that's not what he said. He told me matter-of-factly that Jane had no time for kids and just really hated Lucy. She wanted to try and make Evin her daughter to punish Lucy."

"For what?" asked Simon.

"She was apparently very jealous of Lucy because she'd had William first, as it were. William said he wished Jane would stop being so silly and petty about it. He was very direct and didn't bother to defend Jane or anything."

"That's . . . quite a story." Simon shook his head.

"That's people for you," Davina muttered.

"When did this happen? What date? Do you remember?"

"Not offhand, no, but I can look it up. It's in our records."

"That'd be helpful, yeah. I don't suppose William told you why Jane hated Lucy so much? I mean, the other way round there'd be no explanation needed, but it seems a bit much to steal someone's husband and then hate them too. Was it just jealousy because Lucy was Wife Number 1?"

"If you hate the woman whose husband you've stolen, you don't need to worry about how you've destroyed her life," said Davina. "It's much easier."

"William did explain Jane's antipathy towards Lucy, come to think of it." Lindsay was looking thoughtful. "And that, also, was rather peculiar. A little later, of course, Lucy made a concerted effort to put things right and befriend William and Jane as a couple, bless her. They all became good friends for a while—Pete too. Lucy told me all about it. I have to say, I did admire her for making the effort. Anyway, we didn't have any trouble from Jane after that. The new friendship removed the cause of Jane's hatred in one fell swoop."

"How so?" asked Simon.

"Well, William said the only reason Jane hated Lucy so much was because Lucy loathed *her* as much as she did. Jane could be very black and white about life and about people, he said. If someone said mean things about her, that made them automatically the enemy."

"Even when they were the abandoned wife of the husband she'd run off with?"

Lindsay shrugged. "Apparently so."

Simon looked down at his scrawled notes. He knew he'd only be able to decipher roughly half of them later if he was lucky, and also that he wouldn't need to; he'd remember every word. He always did when it mattered.

"So . . . had William known that Jane had been hanging round here, staring at Evin in the playground?" he asked Lindsay.

"No, though he'd suspected she was up to something, he told me. So that day—the day she actually walked in through our gate and touched Evin's hair—he'd followed her and caught her in the act."

"And the reason he came back the next day was just to apologize again?"

"And to ask a favor," said Lindsay. "He wanted us not to tell Lucy what had happened. With Jane. He promised to ensure that she never bothered us or went near Evin again. I told him, 'Sorry, but I couldn't agree to that even if I wanted to.' I don't know about you but if someone behaved that way towards my child and a childcare professional withheld that information from me, I'd have something to say about it."

"So you told Lucy?"

"I'd already told her, the day before."

"The whole story?" said Simon. "The hair-stroking, the stuff about Pete not being Evin's real dad? Or did you trim it down to make it less upsetting?"

"No, we told her everything," Lindsay said. "I warned her to be on her guard. Frankly, even after William promised it would never happen again, I had concerns. I believed Jane might turn out to be dangerous and uncontrollable. Sorry to speak ill of the dead, but that was my sense of her."

"And mine," said Davina. "She was properly evil, if you ask me. When I heard she'd been murdered, I was like, 'Of course she has. Someone goes round acting the way she did? It was bound to happen.'"

Simon asked Lindsay, "How did Lucy react when you told her about Jane's behavior with Evin in the playground?"

"She was furious. At first. Then she started laughing in a slightly manic way. I asked her what was funny and she said, 'If Jane thinks she's the only one with secret plans, she's dead wrong.' And no, before you ask, she definitely wasn't planning to kill Jane."

"Sounds like she was planning something," said Simon.

"Oh, she was, but it wasn't murder. I know what it was: she told me. She was planning to ruin Jane and William's honeymoon by taking herself and Pete to the same resort at the same time."

"What? Are you sure?"

Lindsay nodded. "She'd booked the cottage already, she told me. And Jane would never be able to prove it was anything but a coincidence because Jane and William hadn't breathed a word to anyone about any honeymoon plans, and Jane had told Lucy dozens of times about how beautiful that particular resort was—so Lucy knew it could very plausibly be made to seem like a genuine coincidence."

"How had she found out where they were going if they hadn't told her?" Simon's mind was reeling. This felt momentous, but what did it mean? He was too deep in the finer details to be able to stand back and look at the overview, see how it was altered by all this new information.

"No idea, I'm afraid," said Lindsay. "I didn't ask how she knew. I just warned her to be very careful indeed."

"What did she say?" Simon asked.

"It gave me a bit of a shiver, her response did. I didn't know whether to be scared or impressed. She said, 'Don't worry, Lindsay, I'll be fine. My revenge will be extremely safe and exceedingly sweet.'"

29

Monday, January 20, 2020

LUCY

There are bones at the front of the room. On a table. Three of them. Whose are they? They're relatively small. I don't think they can have belonged to an adult, so either an animal or a child, which means they can't be . . .

No. Of course not. Jane's funeral was last October. She was cremated. I read about it in the news. It's not her.

Then who?

DC Simon Waterhouse is standing awkwardly next to the macabre display. I assume he's going to say something about the bones or else they wouldn't be here, and neither would we. I feel like a school kid waiting for the start of a sinister assembly. We're at Tevendon in the indoor dining room, which feels deserted in spite of our presence, and irreversibly cold even though there are waves of warmth coming from the radiator next to me. Everyone is here who was here last July. Apart from Jane.

I can't stop looking at William, who's sitting in front of me and can't see me watching him. What's he thinking? I'd give anything to know. It breaks my heart to see him there, at the table on his own. I hope he meets someone else one day, someone he can be happy with and who isn't a monster.

All day, knowing this bizarre gathering was scheduled for tonight, I've been wondering how it might feel to be here with William again, in the same place as before but with everything so different from how it was last year. I knew it would be difficult and feel jarring, but I didn't anticipate this silent, howling sadness that keeps welling up inside me.

Is this how endings feel when it's something that could so easily not have ended? The William I loved—before he met Jane and mutated into a different person—would have been distraught to know that he'd lost me forever. And he has. He truly has. It shocks me that not even a tiny part of me wants him any more, not even for the wrong reasons.

Someone will, though. He's bound to meet a woman in due course and start a new life.

If he doesn't have to go to prison.

Watching him now, I'm more certain than ever that he didn't do it, and yet not at all sure that the police won't decide he did. Maybe that's what DC Waterhouse is about to say and, somehow, try to justify. Mistakes like that happen all the time—often accidentally or because people don't care quite enough to get the detail right, or don't want to admit to their own fallibility.

Behind DC Waterhouse and the bones on the table, there's a row of seated police officers—DC Sellers and DS Kombothekra, whom I haven't seen since last July, Charlie Zailer and an older, bald man with chalky-pale skin and a piercing stare who looks like a malicious frozen lollipop in human form. I locked eyes with him a few seconds ago and I'll be happy if I never have to repeat the experience.

Charlie hasn't looked at me since we all arrived. She probably hasn't forgiven me for what I didn't tell her when we last met, despite the groveling letter I wrote her. Maybe she saw straight through it, like she saw through me in the baklava café when I pretended I'd told her everything. I'm not the world's best liar because I so hate having to do it, and it's almost impossible to get good at something you loathe. The idea of her having written me off as a liar with zero integrity makes me want to cry. I'm not that. I always tell the truth to myself, once I've worked out what it is. That has to count for something.

"I expect you're all wondering about these." DC Waterhouse points to the bones. "They're human, not animal."

"Whose are they?" asks Susan Henry.

"I can't give you a name. What we've managed to find out is that they belonged to a female child, name unknown. She ended up as a medical skeleton that used to be a training model for St. John Ambulance crews in the North West."

She ended up as a medical skeleton. What a horrible thing to hear. A chill prickles my skin.

"Someone bought these three bones, not the whole skeleton, on 15 June last year—seventeen days before Jane Brinkwood was murdered," says DC Waterhouse, watching all of us carefully as he speaks. This is far worse than I imagined. Not knowing what's going to come out of his mouth next is terrifying.

"The purchase was made online. Whoever it was, they went to great lengths to put several layers between themselves and the vendor so that they couldn't be traced. Which told me that they felt guilty about the purchase—or perhaps about what they intended to do with the bones, once bought."

"Is it legal to buy human bones?" asks Caroline Moyle-Jones, at the same time as Jack McCallion says, "What's this got to do with Jane Brinkwood's murder?"

"That's the trouble I've had with this case," says Waterhouse. "Working out how all the different parts are connected. It's especially hard when there are so many elements that might or might not be anything to do with how or why Jane was killed. For example, somebody moved the tables and chairs either the night before or early in the morning of 2 July, the day Jane was killed. The tables had been arranged differently the day before, you might remember. But when you all arrived at breakfast on 2 July, they were in their current arrangement." Waterhouse points at the view of the terrace from the window. "An outer circle of six tables and one table on its own in the center, on the raised bit. There was a key difference between the original arrangement and the new one. Originally, every single table was closer to one specific other table than to any of the rest. Whereas in the new arrangement, that wasn't true of any of the tables. The higher-up one in the middle was equidistant from all the others, and the ones in the lower circle were each equidistant from the one in front and the one behind."

Like in "Horace the Horse." I haven't thought about that song for years. My older sister, Imogen, used to sing it to me when I was little. Horace is upset about being the last horse on the merry-go-round, until he turns around and sees that all the other horses are behind him, not in front of him.

"Who rearranged the tables and why?" says DC Waterhouse. "That's only one element of the puzzle, though. Another one is: Who sent two anonymous notes to Jane—one the day after she arrived at Tevendon and one on the day she died? The first said 'Beware.' The second said 'Beware of the couple at the table nearest to yours.' Which makes the moving of the tables more interesting, doesn't it?"

"I assumed it was Anita and the staff who moved the tables, for aesthetic reasons," says Susan Henry. She looks at Anita, who shakes her head. "Why haven't we been told this before?"

"The police never tell you anything they don't have to," says Jack McCallion.

"I'm going to be telling you quite a lot before we all leave here today," Waterhouse says. "Maybe more than I need to. But I think you all need to hear all of it. And although I now know who murdered Jane Brinkwood, you won't be hearing the name of that person for some time. That's right: I'm going to make you wait."

"You say it as if it's a punishment," says Caroline.

"Maybe it is. Don't you all deserve a punishment? Let's face it, you're all guilty of something."

"What are you talking about?" Jack looks around, as if expecting the others to join him in objecting.

"You're all guilty of lying, impeding the investigation into Jane's death, and therefore of obstructing justice. Apart from one person: Pete Shabani."

Pete? I've been holding his hand under the table, but now I let it drop. What's he told Waterhouse? When? *Surely he wouldn't have . . .*

"I'm sorry," he mouths at me. "I had to." I don't know what he's apologizing for. How could he not have prepared me for this before we got here? I turn away from him and back to DC Waterhouse. If I start thinking about Pete possibly deceiving or manipulating me, I won't be able to get through the rest of this. He didn't; he can't have done. Pete Shabani is the loveliest person in the world. If I can't believe in him any more then I can't believe in anyone or anything.

"Before I go any further, does anybody else want to volunteer the truth about anything they've lied about up to now?" Waterhouse asks.

No one speaks.

"No? How about the person who moved the tables and sent the 'Beware' notes? Fancy owning up and explaining? Because the same person did both those things, but they didn't kill Jane. So maybe if we could get the tables and the notes out of the way first . . . No? No takers? I mean, 'Beware' on its own is quite straightforward if a little vague, but I'm sure there are lots of people here who'd love to understand why you issued that specific warning—'Beware of the couple at the table nearest to yours'—having first moved the tables to ensure that no one table or couple could be identified. Why would you want to give such a specific warning and make it refer to no one in particular?"

Waterhouse is looking from face to face as he speaks, so it's impossible to know who he's talking about. "Oh, I should have said: the intention of the notes wasn't to torment Jane or make her suffer. The opposite. They were genuinely intended to warn her that there was something to be scared of. You see, the note-writing table-mover was afraid on Jane's behalf. Weren't you? You can speak up. *I know who you are.* Tell me why you did what you did. Aren't you keen to skip to the point where everyone knows you're not a murderer?"

There's no response from anyone.

"I guess our note-sending table-mover's not feeling talkative yet," Waterhouse says. "Fair enough. How about the bones-buyer? I know who you are too. Are you ready to talk? Why not get it over with? I'd rather you tell me than I tell you."

Still nothing.

"Holding out to the bitter end." Waterhouse nods. "Can't say I blame you, bones-buyer, since you *are* the person who killed Jane. Never mind. Shall we hear about the finding of the bones instead, and the fact that the two people who found them didn't tell anybody, especially not the police?"

Anita stands up. "That was my fault completely," she says. "I found them, and I . . . I didn't tell the truth when you asked me about them, DC Waterhouse. And I was so sure they were animal bones. If I'd thought for a moment that they might be human bones, I'd have told you straight away." Lord Brinkwood, sitting at the table next to her, reached for her hand and made comforting noises.

"Anita and I found them together," says Mick Henry. "And it was my fault that we did. I feel responsible."

"Where did you find them?" Waterhouse is looking at Anita. "When I came to the Manor House to interview you and Lord Brinkwood, you told me you found them in the woods behind Tevendon Mere."

"That was a white lie," says Anita. "I didn't think it would matter. I'm sorry. I found the bones—Mick and I found them—in a hole in the wall behind the big mirror in the office. Mick wanted to take a closer look at the mirror, from behind as well, to see if there were any markings on the back—"

"Antiques enthusiast!" Mick chips in.

"He asked me if I could help him take it down off the wall. I said, 'Sure, no problem.' Next thing we knew, we were staring at this gaping hole that I'd had no idea was there. Mick peered into it and saw the bones."

"My first thought was, *Has some psychopath buried a body or something?*" Mick says.

"I take all the blame for us keeping quiet about it," Anita keeps trying to talk over him. She seems intent on protecting him. "Mick wanted to call the police and I begged him not to. There was already stress and tension from the first anonymous note, and between Jane and Lucy—everyone was feeling it, I think—and I just thought, *All I need is for everyone to get het up about bones in the office wall.*"

"And it didn't occur to you that the bones might be human?" Waterhouse's tone makes it plain that he finds this hard to believe.

"Not even for a second," says Anita. "Animal bones turn up in the woods all the time: small animals. These bones were small. I just . . . human bones being hidden in a wall was such an outlandish possibility, I didn't think it was possible. I persuaded Mick to stop worrying about it, and he offered to take the bones back to the woods."

"Which I did," says Mick.

"And that's where we found them—and we were able to distinguish them from animal bones very easily," says Waterhouse.

"And you didn't tell me?" Susan Henry snaps at Mick.

"No, I didn't," says Mick. "Once Anita had seemed so sure they were animal bones, I wasn't worried any more. There didn't seem a need to tell you. I didn't want you to worry either. I mean, Anita's the boss, right? If she didn't think it was anything worth looking into—" He breaks off with a shrug. "She's the one who works near the woods and knows animal bones when she sees them, I thought. And it's not like I wanted to be interviewed by the police, not even for a half hour. What I wanted was to enjoy my vacation."

"Of course," says Susan. "Cutting short a swim to tell your wife you'd found some bones would have been a terrible deprivation. I can see that."

"I'm sorry, honey."

"I'll *make* you sorry. So, what, did the two of you make some kind of dramatic pact to keep it secret?" She turns around and scowls at Anita. "Is that part of the five-star resort service now: conspiring with husbands to keep secrets from their wives?"

"No, of course not." Anita looks stricken. I don't blame her. The wrong side of Susan Henry wouldn't be a fun place to hang out.

"Susan, I promise you—I swear on my life—it wasn't like that. Really, genuinely."

Simpering and sucking up is a bad idea. A show of strength of some kind would impress Susan more.

"It was just something we agreed to forget about," says Mick. "There seemed no need to mention it to anyone."

To Anita, Waterhouse says, "Didn't you wonder why someone

had gone to the trouble of hiding animal bones in a hole in the wall?"

"I mean . . ." She seems to be trying to remember. "Not really. Maybe in passing, but there wasn't much point in wondering when I'd never know and they were only animal bones, or so I thought."

"It's not true that you'll never know." Waterhouse looks around the room. "Soon we'll all know everything."

Lord Brinkwood stands up. "DC Waterhouse, can I please clarify—are the bones Anita found in the wall connected to a past crime? You said they came from a medical skeleton—"

"They did. There's no crime associated with them or with Graves House as far as we've been able to find out."

"What's Graves House?" Polly McCallion asks.

"The resort office building. That was its original name," Waterhouse tells her. "*Graves House.*" He repeats it as if it's significant.

"Then Anita's little white lie hasn't mattered too much, has it?" says Lord Brinkwood. "I'm not saying it's ideal—and please don't forget, DC Waterhouse, that in this instance the murder victim is my daughter—"

"I haven't forgotten it for a second."

"—but Anita has now admitted to the part she played in making your investigation . . . run less smoothly than it otherwise might have, so I hope that you can be charitable towards her."

"I'll try, but it's hard to be charitable when no one tells you the truth about anything. Apart from Pete Shabani. He stopped lying in the end. The rest of you are still lying. Turns out Pete suspected all along that he might know who killed Jane. The problem was that he didn't trust himself. He should have. He was right."

What's Waterhouse talking about? Pete? He didn't suspect

anyone. He's been as clueless as I have, since July. Hasn't he? I try to catch his eye but he's staring down at his hands. He won't look at me, no matter how hard I will him to.

Why the hell would he not tell me if he thought he knew who'd killed Jane?

"But Pete believed something that wasn't true," Waterhouse goes on. "So did I. I believed all nine of you—all of you here apart from William Gleave and Lord Brinkwood—when you told me you were together on the restaurant terrace the whole time Sergeant Zailer and I were gone. That's what you all said. The truth is somewhat different. The truth is that, at the moment someone was fatally attacking Jane with a knife, none of you were out there on the terrace, sitting at your tables. *Not a single one of you.*"

Wait. If that's true . . .

Do I know who killed Jane now?

I can't work it out. Part of me is still expecting to hear Waterhouse say that William did it, that the blood pattern evidence was wrong.

"The terrace—that dining space out there"—Waterhouse points through the window—"was empty when the attack on Jane Brinkwood took place. Until Pete broke ranks, you were all protected by your unanimous commitment to dishonesty. It's kept you safe, hasn't it, for all these months? Impressive. But then Lucy sent out multiple copies of her letter to Jane's killer, and everyone started to feel the pressure a bit more. Suddenly most of you were willing to tell us a little bit or a lot more— about being threatened by Jane, or her accusing you of sending the anonymous letters, or, in Pete's case, about the suspicions you'd been trying to push away for so long—"

"That's nonsense," Lord Brinkwood protests. "My Jane would never have threatened anybody."

Waterhouse ignores him. "But even before Lucy posted those

letters and stirred everyone up, she'd helped us on our way to finding out the truth without realizing it. I missed it, but Sergeant Zailer spotted it."

I can't believe this is the same DC Simon Waterhouse as the one who was at Tevendon last July, or the one I spoke to outside Spilling police station more recently. How is he so fluent and certain? How can he hold the room like this, as if he's the only authority in the world? The Simon Waterhouse I knew before today was awkward and surly. Not a great talker. I'd never have imagined he'd be able to do this, what he's doing now.

"How did I help?" I ask him.

"You wrote the word 'room,'" he says.

30

Monday, January 20, 2020

Simon could see he had Lucy's attention. She didn't know what he was talking about, and very much wanted to. "In your letter to William, which you kindly gave me a copy of, you wrote the word 'room.' I didn't spot it. Luckily, Sergeant Zailer did, and when someone we were interviewing used the expression 'read the room,' she realized what had been bothering her about your letter. It was the presence of one word in one line: 'I was luckier than you, and able to eliminate all the people I was in a *room* with when the murder happened.'" Simon was easily able to recite it by heart. "That's what Lucy wrote to William, and it was a direct contradiction of what she'd told us: that when Jane was murdered, she was on the restaurant terrace, outside, with eight other people: Anita, Pete, Polly, Jack, Caroline, Harriet, Susan, and Mick.

"Interesting, isn't it? When Lucy wrote that letter to William last September, she didn't plan on it ever being read by any police. Bringing me a copy was an afterthought, four months later, after a surprise visit from William made her impatient to find out who killed Jane. But while she was writing the letter, mainly for therapeutic purposes, she thought there was a good chance no one would ever read it, and she allowed the truth to slip out: she was in a room. Not on the terrace. Also in that room with Lucy while Jane was being attacked were seven of the other eight people who had told us they'd been sitting outside on the terrace at their tables."

"Seven?" said Jack McCallion. Then he worked it out and said, "Oh, right."

"Right," Simon repeated. "Remember that lie you told, Jack? Forgot the details, did you? Let me jog your memory: like Lucy, you were one of the eight people in the room. Oh—if I haven't said already, it was this room, the one we're in now. There was one person who didn't follow the rest of you in here, though, wasn't there, on the evening of 2 July? That's who murdered Jane Brinkwood: that person. And that's why you all looked so devastated and tense when Sergeant Zailer and I returned to the terrace some time later. You'd all heard the police sirens by then. Faces and food, you see."

"What do you mean 'faces and food'?" Mick asked.

"It was obvious from your expressions that you were all scared. I should have trusted my instincts about that instead of talking myself out of what I knew I'd seen. You weren't concerned and curious, which would have been natural. You were frightened—the kind of fear you feel when you've got something to hide, which you all did, whether it was the sick game you'd played earlier in the day or the murder you'd just committed. Pete Shabani's the only one who had nothing to feel guilty about, though he was frightened for Lucy. Also, none of you had touched your main courses. That wasn't down to guilt. There was a much simpler explanation: none of you were at your tables, so you couldn't eat. You were all either in here or, in the case of one person, at Cottage Number 1 killing Jane Brinkwood."

"Please tell me who killed my wife," said William Gleave. "I've waited long enough."

"So have I," said Lord Brinkwood. "Tell us a name."

The questions hung in the air. Simon allowed the involuntary noises to subside before carrying on. "The rest of you, the other eight, unquestioningly gave the murderer an alibi by pretending they were on the terrace with you at the time, just as you all gave each other an alibi that was a lie: you said you were all sitting at your tables on the terrace too. No doubt you thought it didn't matter because you knew you were all in here together. It was so much easier, wasn't it, to say you'd stayed at your tables because what reason could you possibly have for coming in here? You were also, all eight of you, one hundred percent convinced that the ninth person—Jane's killer—was outside on the terrace the whole time. Apart from Pete Shabani, who had suspicions thanks to a train of logic he'd followed that turned out to be completely correct, you all believed—all eight of you—that all *nine* of you couldn't possibly have done it because you were all in the restaurant area at the relevant time."

"Who's number nine?" William asked again.

"Here's what happened," said Simon. "Sergeant Zailer and I left the terrace to go and check all was well at Cottage Number 1 after the trouble at dinner. You'd all witnessed the scene between William Gleave and Jane Brinkwood. I'm guessing none of you understood its significance any more than I did. Jane had lashed out at Lucy and Pete for supposedly stealing her champagne. Then William came out of the kitchen onto the terrace and within seconds he'd pulled the menu card out of Jane's hand and torn it into small pieces. Why? No one had a clue at the time apart from William himself. Then he went over to Jane and whispered something in her ear, and she pushed him away angrily. She said, 'Oh, my God, I can't believe it,' and ran away from him while he shouted apologies after her. At that point, no one understood any of it apart from William and Jane.

"You all saw them leave in a violently emotional state. You already knew Jane was in an angry and unpredictable mood from her strange behavior when she'd arrived at dinner, saying

'Didn't expect me to still be here, did you?' in a provocative way and accusing me and Sergeant Zailer of not being who we claimed to be. Then there was the champagne row, then the bizarre bust-up between William and Jane. Understandably, you were all on edge. And then you saw me and Sergeant Zailer abandon our dinners and head off the same way William and Jane had gone. You probably guessed we were on our way to check they weren't tearing each other to shreds behind closed doors. And you were worried, weren't you?"

"Anyone would have been concerned, in our position," said Polly. "Nothing felt safe that night. There was a real air of threat. We all felt it."

"Yes, but you had an extra reason to be nervous, didn't you?" said Simon. "You were all— Sorry, not all. Apart from Anita, who knew nothing about a certain drama that had been enacted that afternoon, you were all scared in the way that only people with a guilty conscience can be scared. Thanks to Pete, I know all about your supposedly fun little game: the one with the sole aim of intimidating and scaring Jane away from Tevendon and driving her out of her own honeymoon. Pete told me all about it."

Lucy was staring at Pete in horror. Simon felt sorry for him. He looked as if he'd been turned to stone, or wished he could be.

"Pete was feeling guilty because Lucy, by that point, had told him what you'd all done to Jane earlier that day."

"I can't bear this for much longer," said William. "What did they all do to Jane?"

"You won't have to wait much longer," Simon told him. "Going back to Pete . . . When Lucy told him about the game, he was horrified. He knew it was an awful thing to do to anyone, however much you disliked them, and that it had probably contributed to Jane's unhinged behavior at dinner. He felt guilty on Lucy's behalf, he told me, because she didn't seem to feel bad about it at all and because, as her fiancé, he felt responsible for her. And the rest of you who'd joined in with the game were terrified. Jane was clearly in the kind of mood where she might have said anything. What if she told me and Sergeant Zailer about the game? What might we do? At the very least we'd probably have recommended to Anita that she ask you all to leave immediately."

"And what about the fact that Jane had threatened us and accused us when we'd done nothing wrong to her?" said Caroline angrily. "She'd treated us all in a way that was utterly repugnant before we thought of striking back."

"She had," Simon agreed. "But you were still worried, weren't you? You really didn't want Sergeant Zailer and me to find out, and it seemed highly likely that we would. That's why, the minute we'd left the terrace, you all scuttled in here for an emergency damage-limitation summit. What could be done, if anything? What excuse could you all construct before Sergeant Zailer and I got back, to make what you'd done seem less appalling?"

To William, Simon said, "The people involved in this game were the Henrys, the McCallions, the Moyle-Joneses and Lucy."

"It was my idea," said Lucy. "I suggested it. Everyone else went along with it, but you can blame me, William. And DC Waterhouse is right, and so was Pete: I don't feel guilty about what we did. I . . ." She shrugged. "It's all very well saying I should but I don't. Jane did so many things that were way worse—not only to me but to Evin too."

"Hear hear," said Susan. Simon looked at Lord Brinkwood, who seemed to have shut down and retreated into himself. Anita had her arm around him.

"That's the one thing that justifies it most, for me," said Lucy. "Jane stalked my daughter's nursery, spied on a child who was nothing to do with her, none of her business. She told Evin that Pete wasn't her real dad. After she yelled at me outside the resort office, I thought, *If I don't take some kind of action against this . . . thing that pretends to be human, I'll never be able to look myself in the face again.*"

"We supported Lucy because we'd seen for ourselves what Jane was capable of," said Caroline. "Someone needed to stop her. You can't just go round threatening—"

"Let's talk about the threats." Simon cut her off. "Polly, Jack, you wouldn't tell DC Sellers what Jane threatened you with, but we did a bit of digging . . . asked a few of your colleagues, Jack, if they could think of anything someone might threaten you with, anything irregular."

"I bet you did," said Jack.

"I think I got there in the end. You arranged for a woman called Nina Lesser to be fired, didn't you? From her job as a PR consultant."

"I did, yeah," said Jack.

"She'd done some PR for your restaurant chain, ConnoisseurCuisine, and you were happy with her work at the time, according to all your colleagues. In fact"—Simon addressed the others—"Jack was so happy with Nina's work that he recommended her to Polly, who was starting a business of her own: an online healthy eating program. Polly had a meeting with Nina, but they never got further than that initial consultation. I wonder why not? Anyway, a few days later Jack put in a complaint to the PR company Nina worked for, accusing her of unprofessional and inappropriate behavior of various kinds. According to Jack's colleagues, that was all lies. He'd had no complaints about Nina's work for him. So tell us, Polly: What did Nina do in her consultation with you that inspired you and Jack to get her sacked on false pretenses? Did Jack have a fling with her while she was doing his PR, and she let it slip out by accident in her meeting with you? She denies that, incidentally. Claims to have no idea why Jack would lie about her like that, when she knows he was happy with the work she did for him."

Polly rolled her eyes. "How depressing that your imagination went straight to the most sexist stereotype imaginable. Just like Nina's did."

"What do you mean?" asked Simon.

Polly looked at Jack for permission. He didn't look happy about it, but he nodded. "Nina made it clear at our first meeting that she didn't think I deserved to make money from my business. Why? Because I'm a woman. Soon as I told her what I wanted to create—*have now succeeded in creating*, by the way— she said, 'I think we'll need a strategy for warding off any negative attention you might attract, given that you're going to be making money from this venture.' That's what she called it. Men have businesses, you see. Men found companies. Women have *ventures*—sweet little hobbies to keep them busy till hubby comes home. She said we'd need to think of ways to build in freebie offers and scholarship schemes to make it clear that what I cared about was helping women to lose weight, not just making money for myself. All the time I was thinking—excuse my language—*You sexist piece of shit*. I said to Jack: 'Did she tell you the first thing ConnoisseurCuisine needed to do was focus its PR energy on apologizing for selling food in your restaurants in exchange for money? Or did she take for granted that you were selling a commodity people would want to buy because it would improve their lives?'"

"So you decided to lie and get her fired," said Simon. "Understood."

"Actually, Polly tried telling Nina's bosses the truth," said Jack. "They gave her some mealy-mouthed bullshit. Didn't care. So, yeah, I rang up and lied, and within an hour Nina was gone—because a man who owned an already extremely successful business had complained. That mattered to them."

"I feel bad about the lies but not about the end result," said Polly.

Simon nodded. "I can see how the lies would be bad PR if they got out—for both your businesses. Jane Brinkwood over-heard you discussing it and threatened to go public with what she knew. She threatened everyone. She was a threatener. Remember that. It's going to be important later."

"The game," said William Gleave insistently.

"Yes, let's get back to it," said Simon. "The game that was designed to make Jane drop everything and run away from Tevendon in the middle of her honeymoon. I found one of its accessories in the same hole in the wall where the bones were: a piece of paper with names listed on it. Lindsay James and Davina Slade, for example. Those two names had been paired with Harriet and Caroline Moyle-Jones. The names Imogen Dean and Bailey Rufo had been paired with Susan and Mick Henry, and Polly and Jack McCallion had been paired with Tommy and Fran Jordan. I'd have been mystified by that piece of paper if Pete hadn't already told me about the game. Like I said: Pete wasn't a participant but Lucy had told him about it once it was over, wanting reassurance that it was an okay thing to have happened.

"It was a clever idea. Lucy, you said it was yours?"

She nodded.

"Do you want to explain it for the benefit of William, Anita, and Lord Brinkwood, the only people here who don't already know? Anita, I'm right, aren't I? Despite hearing snatches here and there, like Caroline and Harriet talking about Lindsay and Davina, you don't really know what happened, do you?"

"No," she said. "Not at all. But . . ." She looked around at the others. "Did the game take place after four thirty and before dinner on 2 July?"

A few people nodded.

"Right," said Anita. "That makes sense. Something had clearly happened to Jane before dinner, to make her so . . . unstable. I'd bumped into her in the gardens at four thirty-ish and she'd seemed in an okay mood at that point."

"DC Waterhouse—" William Gleave stood up.

"I know. The game," said Simon. "William's right. We've waited long enough. Lucy, do you want to explain, since it was your creation?"

Lucy sighed but she stood up. She and Pete were holding hands again, Simon noticed. William sat down as his ex-wife started to speak. "I wouldn't have had the idea if I hadn't imbibed too many detective novels and TV thrillers. After Jane yelled at me outside the office in that horrible, humiliating way, and after everything she'd done to me, I thought: if this were a satisfying thriller, it would turn out that all of us other guests at Tevendon aren't just random strangers who happen to be here at the same time. We'd all be secretly connected. We'd all have congregated at Tevendon under false names and with a shared aim: revenge on Jane. It sounds crazy, I know, but it really cheered me up, that idea. I mentioned it to Susan, only to make her laugh—"

"And I told her, 'I'd actually do that. It'd be hilarious,'" said Susan.

"And then before I knew it, I was saying, 'Should we? Should we actually do it?'" Lucy looked at William. "You can't blame me. The police can, Lord Brinkwood can—but not you, not after everything you've done." She turned to Simon. "Susan and Mick pretended to be my sister Imogen and her partner, Bailey. Polly and Jack—"

"Hold up," said Susan. "You're missing out the best part: we pretended to be Imogen and Bailey *pretending to be Susan and Mick Henry*. When all along, we were just plain old Susan and

Mick Henry. Come on, DC Waterhouse, you've gotta appreciate that on some level? The artistry. The *structure* of it."

"We loved the idea too much not to do it," said Caroline.

"And we all knew that Jane deserved it," said Jack. "There was no doubt in any of our minds about that."

"The real Imogen and Bailey were at Pete's and my house at the time, looking after Evin while we were away," Lucy told Simon. "Polly and Jack pretended to be Fran and Tommy Jordan, the couple who'd been banking on Jane being their doula. She let them down when William suggested to her that she should come and infiltrate our home and my pregnancy instead. Fran and Tommy had seen photos of Jane on the Doula UK website, but she had no idea what they looked like, luckily. So they were the characters played by Polly and Jack."

"And Harriet and I played Lindsay James and Davina Slade from Evin's nursery," said Caroline.

Lucy nodded. "Jane *had* met the real Lindsay and Davina but I was reasonably certain that neither of them had told her their names. I'd been so upset by her ambush of Evin, I'd made Lindsay tell me more than once what had happened that day— word for word, moment by moment. There had been no opportunity for introductions. I thought Jane would probably think, *Oh, these must be just two more people from the nursery.* It was a nice touch, I decided, to use Lindsay's and Davina's names—it wouldn't give anything away and it'd be a kind of tribute to the real Lindsay and Davina who were the ones who'd protected Evin from Jane."

"And you were yourself: Lucy Dean," said Simon. "You didn't need to pretend to be anyone else, did you?"

"No. I was plain old me."

"And the game happened at Number 3, right? Caroline and Harriet's cottage? Why there?"

"It's the furthest from Number 1," said Polly. "We thought it would be sensible to stage our little production as far away from William as possible."

"I went out looking for Jane once we were ready," said Caroline. "I found her easily enough, and told her I needed to talk to her urgently. Said I had something important to tell her. When she arrived at the house, the others were all there, waiting. We sat her down and we . . . we confessed. Well, fake-confessed, I suppose, since it wasn't true. We told her we'd been lying to her, and that we weren't just a collection of unconnected couples who all happened to book holidays at the same resort. We were an army of her enemies: people who knew she was evil and were on Lucy's side against her. And so we'd all come here, using false names—but she'd never be able to prove they were false, because we were cleverer, more powerful and more resourceful than she could possibly imagine."

"That was my line," said Polly proudly. "Cleverer, more powerful and more resourceful," she repeated.

"I loved that part!" said Susan.

"And you knew Jane could never prove you were there under false names because it wasn't true," said Simon.

"Exactly," said Polly.

"This is wicked," said Ian Brinkwood quietly.

"I'm sorry about how upsetting all this must be for you, Lord Brinkwood." Lucy seemed to mean it. "I truly am, but there's not much I can do about it. The problem with wickedness is that it usually produces more of itself. That's why it's so dangerous—not only because it creates victims, but because it creates more terrible people. I had no bad in me until Jane came into my life. And by saying that, I'm not blaming her for anything I've done. It's not as simple as that. I know my actions are my responsibility and not hers." For the first time since he'd met her, she seemed to Simon to be entirely calm—neither anxious nor in need of anything. Was it because the truth she'd craved since last July was so close to being presented to her?

"Why didn't Jane tell me that you'd all . . . done this to her?" said William. "I knew something had happened when she came back to our cottage in floods of tears, but she refused to say what it was."

"Shame, probably," said Caroline. "Didn't want you to think of her as a victim."

"So . . . you told Jane that you'd arranged for this army of enemies to come here, to Tevendon?" Simon said to Lucy. "Why? To do what?"

"To show her that this was how her life would be from now on. Wherever she went, whoever she met, she'd never know for sure that anyone was who they said they were. I asked her how many people she'd destroyed or betrayed in her life so far. Dozens, I was willing to bet, given how she was. How many people were there in the world who'd been wronged by her and hated her? And how many friends and relatives and allies did all those people have? I told her I was going to dedicate the rest of my life to making sure she could never again feel comfortable in *her* life. There would always be someone, or lots of someones. Enemies in disguise. Some of them would very convincingly pretend to be close friends, only in order to betray her later on."

"It was a chilling little speech Lucy gave," said Susan approvingly. "Even I had the heebie-jeebies and I wasn't the one on the receiving end. *And* I knew it was all made up. The truth is, we weren't going to do anything to Jane at all after we'd had our little game. That was going to be it: the full extent of our revenge."

"It was perfect." Polly looked anxiously at Simon, as if worried that he was insufficiently appreciative of what they'd done. "So clever and neat: a conspiracy to pretend there was a conspiracy. When all along there was no conspiracy—except suddenly, there was. If it had been any less conceptually impressive—" She broke off. "We all know that it was cruel too, but the cleverness of it somehow made it feel . . . I don't know."

"Elevated," said Harriet Moyle-Jones. It was the first time she'd spoken.

"Jane totally fell for it." Jack smiled at the memory, then tried to turn the smile into a neutral expression. "The 'Beware' notes had done all the hard work for us. She was fully ready to believe the world and everyone in it was out to get her."

"And your hope was that she'd pack up and leave Tevendon immediately?" Simon asked.

"Yeah, basically," said Lucy. "We thought she'd run away screaming and leave us to enjoy the rest of our holidays without her noxious presence, soon as we'd told her. Who wouldn't want to escape fast after hearing something like that? Turns out: Jane Brinkwood wouldn't. And didn't. Once we'd said our piece, she got up and left Number 3 without saying a single word, head held high. We weren't sure what she'd do next. After she'd underreacted rather than overreacted, my gut instinct told me that she probably wasn't going to be driven away that easily. She was too proud and stubborn."

Lucy looked at William. "It's okay. You can hate me if you want to."

He gave a small shrug, then turned away. His eyes were dull and unfocused.

"So, what, you went back to your cottage and told Pete what had just happened?" Simon asked Lucy.

She nodded. "I trust him and value his opinion more than anyone's. I had to know what he thought might happen next. He was obviously frantic and called me an idiot, asked me if I'd lost my marbles—all the things you'd imagine."

"And then, a bit later, it was time for dinner," said Simon.

"Presumably you were all on the edge of your seats, waiting to see if William and Jane would appear or not."

"By seven o'clock, I had a strong suspicion that they would," said Lucy. "I could . . . feel the heaviness of her still being around. I know that's not rational, but I could sense it: we weren't off the hook. I wondered if William might storm over to my table and start calling me every insult under the sun for what I'd done."

"We were all just sitting there waiting, wondering," said Mick Henry.

"Yeah, and also wondering about the 'Beware' notes because, come on, why wouldn't whichever of us had sent them admit it to the rest at that point?" said Caroline. "After what we'd all done together that afternoon? Surely it was time to fess up. But I asked everyone after the game, once Jane had gone, and still no one would admit it."

"That's because no one involved in the game sent those notes to Jane," said Simon. "Someone else did that. Someone different altogether."

31

Monday, January 20, 2020

The silence in the room was thick with expectation. Charlie had no idea what was coming next. In the old days, she would by now have been looking forward to sharing some of these goings-on, though by no means all of them, with Liv the next time they got together. "Ooh, tell me all the goss," Liv would have said. "Every stitch and detail." And Charlie would have had fun choosing what to reveal and what to withhold.

Maybe I'll ring her. Maybe I can see her sometimes and enjoy hanging out with her even while disapproving of her.

"William?" said Simon. "Who do you think wrote and sent the two 'Beware' notes to Jane?"

"I don't know," William snapped.

"Really? No idea at all?"

"None."

Simon turned away in apparent annoyance, muttering something under his breath. Charlie didn't understand why he was still treating William Gleave, a person of utmost twattishness, as a source of potential help when he was quite obviously a wife-murderer. *Look how he treated his first wife.* If that wasn't a form of murder, Charlie didn't know what was. If there was such a thing as soul-murder, William Gleave could be said to have attempted it. Not to mention abandoning his two-week-old daughter, having betrayed her before she was even born. If it hadn't been for sweet, kind Pete Shabani, who came along and saved the day . . .

Charlie shuddered as it struck her that, for Chris Gibbs's wife, Liv was the Jane Brinkwood figure, though the poor woman didn't know Liv existed, let alone that she'd been sleeping with her husband for a decade and been married to him, bigamously, for part of it. How could Charlie have any kind of relationship with Liv, knowing all that?

"Let's get back to dinner on 2 July," Simon said. "We've established that, with the tables arranged as they were that night, no table could have been *closest* to whichever one William and Jane chose. There would always have been at least two that were equally close. As it happened, there was only one table free when they arrived late: the raised one in the middle. So, as a warning to Jane, 'Beware of the couple at the table nearest to yours' was meaningless. But remember, the word 'yours' in the note had been written above something else that had been crossed out. And each table was, in fact, nearer to *something* than any of the others was. Lucy and Pete were nearest to the kitchen. Polly and Jack were nearest to this room. Anita's table was closest to the office and to the big tree near the entrance to the office building's garden. Mick and Susan were closest to the car park, Caroline and Harriet were closest to Cottage 4, and Charlie and me? Cottage 5. You don't need to remember all the specifics. Just keep in mind: every table was nearest to something—a different thing in each case. At first I thought one of those things might have been what was originally written in the note, but that didn't work because the note-writer couldn't have predicted where everyone would sit that night. So what *did* the writer write initially, after 'Beware of the couple at the table nearest to . . .' and then obliterate later and replace with 'yours'?"

Charlie wondered what would happen if she stood up and

said, "No one knows, Simon. No one apart from you. Just fucking tell us."

Everyone was staring at him blankly.

"The answer starts to be obvious when you think about what actually happened at dinner. Play it back in your mind, incident by incident. Shall I talk you through it? Try and picture it, as if it's happening now. First Jane sends William inside to get their special bottle of champagne that's been chilling in the restaurant's fridge. She's determined not to let the bastards—that's most of you lot—grind her down. She's decided to stay, drink, be merry, prove that she can't be defeated that easily.

"While William's inside, Jane notices that her posh champagne's already out and open, on Lucy and Pete's table. They're halfway through drinking it. She goes ballistic, accuses them of theft. An unpleasant argument follows, and at a certain point Lucy loses her patience and says something like, 'Are you still going on about the champagne? It's only a drink, stop making such a fuss.' That's when Jane loses it. She yells, 'It wasn't yours! It was ours!'—which of course Lucy has never denied. All Lucy's said is that the mix-up was made by the waiters and she and Pete had no idea the bottle they were drinking was Jane's.

"Immediately after Jane had finished yelling at Lucy, in the silence that followed, I heard a door bang shut," Simon went on. "I turned and looked: it was William. He'd emerged from the kitchen building. The door had swung shut behind him. I didn't hear him open it to come out, though, and I would have if that had also happened during the silence . . . which told me that William had opened the door and come outside while Jane was still screaming. When I worked out what this meant, everything fell into place."

"What did it mean?" asked Lucy.

"It meant there was a good chance William had heard Jane

yell, while very upset, 'It wasn't yours! It was ours!' Now, remember, he's only just rejoined us all, so he has no clue that there's been a row about a champagne bottle. He doesn't know what Jane's screaming about.

"She turns and starts walking towards him and he sees she's got a menu card in her hand—except I'm guessing the menu side's facing Jane's dress and the side William can see is the blank one. Just a small rectangular piece of white card. *Exactly the same size as the two cards on which the anonymous notes to Jane had been written.*"

"Whoa, wait a second," said Mick Henry. "I'm confused."

So was Charlie.

"You won't be if you let me carry on," said Simon. "Unless you'd rather take over and explain why you wrote those two notes, William?"

William shakes his head.

"But you admit that you wrote the 'Beware' notes to Jane?"

"Not much point denying it now, is there? You've worked it out."

A murmur of astonishment spread around the room. Simon looked furious for a moment, then weary. If anyone else had noticed, they would assume he was angry with William for all those months of lying. Charlie knew better: what had angered Simon was that his audience had only reacted to the discovery that William was the note-writer once he'd admitted it. They hadn't trusted Simon enough to take his word for it.

"Most people wouldn't have seen that card in Jane's hand and thought, *Anonymous note*," said Simon. "Most of us would have thought either *What's that? Don't know*, or *Maybe it's a menu card*, since we were at dinner and each table had one of that exact size and shape. But William wasn't most people. He had a guilty conscience and a secret he was keeping from his wife: that he'd been the one ruining their honeymoon by sending her sinister anonymous communications. He hadn't meant them as an attack on her, but as a genuine warning. He was trying to protect her, in fact. I'll come to that in a second.

"Point is, William knew better than anyone that Jane had interpreted the notes as an attack and wouldn't readily forgive the sender if she were to find out who it was. He also knew something pretty bad must have happened to Jane in the afternoon and she was refusing to tell him what it was. Maybe he was afraid she'd worked out that the notes were his handiwork and was secretly planning some awful revenge. No wonder he was unhappy and full of dread when they arrived at dinner. Fast forward to a bit later when he emerged from the kitchen building. He heard Jane scream those particular words—'It wasn't yours! It was ours!'—and then two things happened. First, Jane said directly to him words to the effect of 'Aren't you going to say anything?' She probably meant 'Aren't you going to stick up for me in this champagne fight?' but he didn't know that. He'd been inside and had missed the fight. Second, and maybe simultaneously, he saw the small card in Jane's hand. That's when his brain made a completely false connection that seemed to him as if it had to be true. He assumed the card in Jane's hand was the second anonymous note and that he was the object and cause of her angry screams."

"Why on earth would he assume that?" asked Harriet.

"Because before he'd crossed out the last word and replaced it with 'yours,' the note had originally said, 'Beware of the couple at the table nearest to *ours*.' When William heard Jane scream, 'It wasn't yours! It was ours!' he put it together with her snapping at him—'Aren't you going to say anything?'—and the small card in her hand, and assumed she'd worked out the truth. That's why he ran over to her and started to whisper to her. I can imagine him saying something like, 'Please forgive me. I didn't mean for the notes to scare you . . .' And *that's* when Jane found out that the note-sender was the one person at Tevendon she'd totally trusted: her husband. No wonder she wanted to run away from him at that moment."

Simon started to walk slowly towards the table where William sat alone. When he reached it, he said, "I understand why you wanted to warn Jane. Lucy had turned up on your honeymoon. You had a bad feeling about the way things might go."

William nodded. "Hard as I tried, I couldn't shake off the dread," he said. "Turned out I was right."

"You wanted you and Jane to leave Tevendon and go and have a more relaxing honeymoon somewhere else, but Jane wasn't easily talked into changing her plans. You knew she wouldn't agree to leave just because Lucy was there—that would have felt to her like letting Lucy win. But you really didn't want to stay. You'd had a frightening dream about you and Jane at Tevendon, hadn't you? Before you arrived."

"But . . . what did the note mean, William?" asked Lucy. "Why 'Beware of the couple at the table nearest to yours'? And why did you write 'ours' first time round? None of it makes any sense."

Keeping his eyes on the table, William said quietly, "The words came from my dream."

"Interesting," said Simon. "I was going to ask the same thing. It was the only unanswered question I had left."

William looked at Lucy. "I didn't mention the . . . soundtrack when I told you about the dream. It would have sounded too stupid. The words were almost the scariest part. And it was me saying them to Jane: 'Beware of the couple at the table nearest to ours.' It was my voice and I was trying to warn her, saying it over and over again but it wasn't working. She couldn't hear me because we were both dead. And . . . it makes no sense apart from in the twisted logic of nightmares, but I knew I was warning her about *us*. We were the couple at the table nearest to ours. I woke up in an ice-cold sweat. I'd have canceled Tevendon on the spot if I'd thought Jane would agree to it, but I knew she wouldn't. And then we arrived and you were here, my ex-wife of all people, and I thought, *This honeymoon's cursed. I have to get Jane out before something terrible happens.*"

"That was your guilty conscience talking," Susan told him.

"All right, so the words came from your dream, but why put them in a note when they didn't mean anything concrete?" asked Lucy.

"I didn't know what else to write," said William. "I needed Jane to be as worried as I was so that we could leave. In the dream, those words terrified me. I thought they might scare her too—maybe even more so because they made no logical sense."

"But as soon as you'd written them down on the card, you spotted your mistake," said Simon. "'The table nearest to ours'—which implies very strongly that Jane and her anonymous correspondent are going to be sharing a table."

William nodded. "I only realized when Jane was already on her way downstairs. I had about four seconds to play with. I couldn't believe I'd not thought of it before, even when I was moving the tables."

"That was you too?" said Lucy.

He gave her a look that seemed to say, *Haven't I just said so?*

"He moved the tables to make sure 'the couple at the table nearest to ours' didn't implicate any couple in particular," said Simon.

"I don't think my brain was working properly," said William. "All the stress had clouded my judgment. I remembered to avoid the security cameras, moved all the tables really carefully . . ."

"Your brain was working the way a madman's brain works," said Lucy, though she sounded sympathetic. "Cryptic notes, messing around with tables in the middle of the night? It's . . . worrying, William."

"I nearly had it all under control," he said. There was an edge of desperation to his voice. "I just didn't think of the problem with the word 'ours' until it was nearly too late. As quickly as I could, I scribbled it out, wrote 'yours' over the top of it and dropped it on the mat by the front door."

"That must have bothered you, the messiness of it," said Simon. "You're naturally tidy. No dust on the ornaments in your house."

"I didn't have time to start from scratch. Jane was coming down the stairs." William looked up at Simon. "How the hell did you work it out? I don't see how you could possibly know everything you know."

"It was the only explanation there could be, once I'd put all the elements together," said Simon. "Jane screaming 'It wasn't yours! It was ours!' and the only other thing that might mean besides what it actually did mean. And you tearing up the menu, and the terrified look on your face. When you first came outside after going to the kitchen, you looked miserable as anything but not frightened. Then Jane looked at you and said, 'Aren't you going to say anything?' and suddenly you were . . . as scared as I'd ever seen anyone. And then you apologizing and her acting as if she'd had the shock of a lifetime and suddenly couldn't stand you. It seemed the only possible explanation."

Simon walked back to the front of the room. "Here's another question for you, since you're talking at last: Are you sure it was Jane you were frightened for?"

William looked wary. "What do you mean?"

"I saw myself what she was capable of. The way she behaved at dinner that night, accusing me and Charlie—Sergeant Zailer—who she'd never met before. The chaos she caused over the champagne. She didn't hold back. And when she arrived at Tevendon and found Lucy here, she didn't like it, did she? I heard her screaming at Lucy like a demon, saying horrible things most people'd never say to anyone."

"Yes, she had a temper," said William quietly.

"So maybe you were scared she'd do some damage, rather than be on the receiving end of it. Was that why you were desperate to take her away?"

"I don't know. All I know is that I couldn't get away from the dread. After that dream it was like . . . I felt disconnected from reality. I can't really describe it."

"It's called depression," Susan told him. "That can happen when you're trying to kid yourself that you haven't just demolished your wonderful family for the sake of a manipulative psychopath. Prozac might help."

"We can do without the commentary, thanks," said Simon. To William he said, "Has it occurred to you since Jane's death that there was no way she could have read the word 'ours' on the note after you'd scribbled it out so thoroughly?"

William nodded. "There's no way she could have known unless I'd told her, which I hadn't. No one else knew."

"But we tend to believe our worst fears more than our rational deductions, don't we?" said Simon. "That's why you took the menu from Jane's hand and tore it to pieces to destroy the evidence of your guilt, even though you thought she knew already. Still, you couldn't bear for that note you'd written and then lied about to exist, could you, once she knew the truth?"

William offered no resistance to Simon's interpretation. He said nothing.

"So what happened when you got back to your holiday cottage?" Simon asked. "Shall I tell you how I think it played out? I think you started off trying to make Jane see how sorry you were, but she wasn't having any of it. She carried on verbally attacking you. Eventually, you couldn't take it any more. You gave up. Sat down in that chair where Sergeant Zailer and I found you, facing away from Jane and kind of tuned out. Went numb. I can't be sure of this next part, but I think Jane probably didn't like it when you stopped reacting. Did her anger escalate at that point?"

A small nod from William was the only response. Charlie might even have imagined it.

"Did she tell you the marriage was over and that she hated you, and could never trust you again? Did she threaten some kind of physical violence?"

This time there was no movement, no hint of confirmation.

"I think that's what happened," Simon said again. "Luckily for you, though, a savior was nearby, or at least near enough to hear Jane shouting. This savior knew there was a quicker route to Number 1 than the path Sergeant Zailer and I had taken, and she was sitting very near to that route. *Nearer to the tree, and therefore to the entrance to the office building's garden, than any of the other tables.* That would have made getting to Number 1 even easier and faster." Simon looked at Proust as he said this. Charlie knew why: the Snowman had poured scorn on his "Nearer to" theory when Simon had first offered it as a possibility.

"She also knew the gate between the office building's garden and Number 1's garden was unlocked," Simon went on. "She must have heard Jane screaming at William, after the revenge-game conspirators had come in here to have their emergency meeting. Jane's angry voice would have carried on a still night in the middle of the countryside, especially if the people in here were keeping their voices down. We all heard how loud Jane could be when she was in a rage."

She? Charlie knew he'd described William's savior as "she" deliberately. So that surely had to mean . . .

"William's rescuer headed straight for Number 1, via the quick route." Simon had started to walk a wide circle around the room. "As she approached the open back door of the house, she must have heard what Jane was threatening to do in more detail—she might well have heard a death threat. I think at that point she realized William might be in more danger than she'd originally feared."

"You keep saying 'she,'" said Jack McCallion.

"That's because the killer's a woman," Simon told him. He turned to Anita. "Do you want to take over now?" he asked her. "Or shall I carry on, and explain to everyone why you murdered Jane Brinkwood?"

32

Monday, January 20, 2020

LUCY

Anita? Is Waterhouse asking us to believe that Anita would kill someone? Sorry, but I don't believe it. She didn't hate Jane like the rest of us. She was the only one who didn't. Even Pete, who'd forgive anyone anything, had more antipathy towards Jane than Anita did. And if DC Waterhouse is right about Jane screaming threats at William, and Anita dashing to his rescue, then surely that's self-defense. If Jane had a knife and was about to use it on William, and Anita ended up wrestling it out of her hands and somehow things got out of control, then surely it's self-defense. Or defense of another person. That must be a category in law. It's definitely not murder, so why does Waterhouse keep calling it that?

Lord Brinkwood clears his throat. He says, "You're surely not trying to suggest that Anita murdered my daughter, DC Waterhouse?"

"I'm doing more than suggest it, Lord Brinkwood. I'm saying it's what happened. Anita, tell him."

This suspended moment is unbearable. No one speaks. Anita has pushed her chair back from the table and is staring down at the floor. For a moment, I imagine that we might all stay frozen like this forever. Waiting. Still not knowing.

I look up and see Charlie watching me. I want to smile at her but I can't. It's probably not true, but I imagine that she's asking me a question in her head. *Did you know? Did you know all along, and were you protecting her?*

No. No, I didn't. I couldn't have, because it wasn't her. Anita was on the terrace the whole time—I know she was. I saw her there, through the window. So it can't have been her. I could believe it of anyone else more easily. Pete believes it, I can tell. I wish, more than anything, that he'd been honest with me about his suspicions. Then we could have discussed it, just the two of us, before being dropped into this hellish situation where neither of us knows what the other is thinking.

How long is this silence going to last?

After a few more seconds, Anita says, "It wasn't murder."

"But you admit that you killed her?" says Waterhouse.

"Yes."

Lord Brinkwood rises slowly to his feet. He's looking at Anita as if he's never seen her before.

"You're expecting me to say how sorry I am, Ian, and beg you to forgive me," she says in a dull voice. "In a way I'm sorry and in a way I'm not. I think I'll let DC Waterhouse tell you about it. It's less effort that way, and after hearing everything he's said so far, I'm in no doubt that he's worked out exactly why I did what I did."

"Darling, if Jane attacked you," says Lord Brinkwood. "If it was self-defense . . ."

Anita's face changes: from resigned to her fate to something sharper. That's when I start to believe it, when I see that shift. She really did do it.

And she's just decided that lying about her reason for doing it might be worth a try. Seemingly in a rush to get the words out, she says, "Yes, it was defense. Not of me but of William. She was going to kill him if I didn't stop her, Ian. We struggled, and the next thing I knew . . . I didn't *mean* for her to die. I just had to get the knife off her before she killed him."

"She's lying," says Waterhouse. "Not only to avoid prison but also, mainly, because if you believe her, Lord Brinkwood, then her plan can still work. Even now. Take my word for it, it was murder. Opportunistic rather than premeditated, and with the bonus of believing she was saving William's life—which, who knows, maybe she did—but Anita very much meant to kill your daughter. Jane dying was an essential part of her hastily made plan."

"But before, you said Anita heard Jane threatening William and that's why she went the quick way to Number 1," Polly McCallion points out.

"True," says Waterhouse. "That all happened. And when Anita arrived and heard Jane threatening and verbally abusing William, she decided, probably in a split second, that this was the perfect moment to commit a murder that hadn't even occurred to her as a possibility until then. This was her perfect chance. I think she might have entered the house just in time to hear Jane say something like, 'I'm going to go and get a knife from the kitchen drawer and stab you with it.' I don't believe Jane was holding the knife over William already or that Anita struggled with her and got it off her. The crime scene didn't indicate that at all. What the evidence suggested was a killer who quietly took a knife out of a drawer, approached her victim from behind and stabbed her as hard as she could, twice, in the back. William, perhaps you can help us here. Did Jane have a knife in her hand?"

"I don't think so," William says. "She wanted me to turn around and I wouldn't. Couldn't. She told me I was going to have to, or else what was to stop her grabbing the sharpest kitchen knife and cutting my throat from ear to ear? I remember she said that. From ear to ear."

"Interesting," says Waterhouse. "That's what Jack McCallion said he'd do to her, when she threatened him and Polly."

"She's a threat plagiarist," Jack says with a snigger.

"But, DC Waterhouse, Anita must have been on the terrace with the others when Jane was killed, so she can't have done it," Lord Brinkwood blurts out. Then he frowns. "I mean . . . in this room with the others."

"Keep up, will you?" Jack snaps at him. "Anita's just admitted to having killed Jane, so how can she have been here with us?"

"Jack, for fuck's sake." Polly scowls at him. "He's an old man. He's Jane's dad."

Lord Brinkwood makes a sweeping gesture with his arm, one that includes all of us. "But . . . but . . . you all said you were together when Jane died. All of you, together."

"Yes, they did, didn't they?" says Waterhouse. "And here's the strangest part: with the exception of Pete, I think they all truly believed Anita was in the clear and couldn't have done it."

"We did," I tell him. "After the eight of us had finished having our ultimately pointless damage-control discussion in here, we went back out onto the terrace and heard police sirens that sounded like they were really close. Like, inside the resort. At the same moment, I noticed Anita, who was sitting at her table exactly where we'd left her. Of course I assumed she'd been there all along. She looked straight at us and said to the whole group, 'I'm sorry, but I can't pretend I didn't hear most of that.' And I thought, *Shit, what happened to keeping our voices down?* Our discussion had got quite . . . animated."

"Yeah, some people wanted to confess all to anyone who'd listen and receive absolution, and others were refusing and insisting we tough it out," says Susan.

"All the windows had been open like they are now," I tell Waterhouse. "I thought we'd been quite tactful in what we mentioned and what we didn't. Apart from anything else, Pete had been there in the room with us and none of us really wanted him to know quite how . . . vicious and venal we'd been to Jane. I certainly didn't. But we'd discussed her threats to us all quite openly, and Anita seemed to know all about Nina Lesser getting sacked for something she hadn't done, and Harriet's secret Twitter account, and that Caroline and Harriet had impersonated two people called Lindsay and Davina. She'd heard enough to seem really shocked. And the thing is, I'd *seen* her. At the beginning and at the end—I mean, I don't remember exactly, but I saw her a couple of times as I moved around the room, sitting at her table."

"She was extremely convincing when she told us she'd been there the whole time and heard every word," Susan tells Waterhouse. "None of us doubted it."

"I did," says Pete. "We were all together in here, and the forensics proved William hadn't done it. How could it not have been Anita? Except . . . I was never *sure* it was, and Lucy told me categorically that it wasn't—I could see she was convinced. She said she'd seen Anita sitting outside on the terrace the whole time. I'd been facing the other way, so I just . . . believed her."

"Big mistake," says Waterhouse. "As we now know, Anita overheard plenty, but she picked it all up in probably the first three minutes of your discussion and the last ten. The rest of the time she was busy killing Jane."

"But she had—*has*—no motive," I say.

Waterhouse nods. "I'm sure you all thought that, didn't you? That Anita couldn't have done it, that she had no reason to. That's why you lied so quickly and easily, Lucy, when Sergeant Zailer and I finally got back to the restaurant terrace and told you a serious incident had occurred. It was you who immediately volunteered the information that you'd all been together on the terrace the whole time. And everyone was quick to corroborate. Let's face it, it suited you all—gave you all a solid alibi, the eight game-players and Anita. She didn't want to admit she'd been at Number 1 killing Jane, and you all didn't want to have to explain why you all decided to move in here for an impromptu meeting. So the lie solidifies and gets endlessly repeated and reinforced, and everybody's happy— except for our usual exception."

"Saint Pete!" Susan purses her lips as if she disapproves of Pete's aversion to deceiving the police.

"And when you found out that the crime scene evidence had ruled William out as the killer?" Waterhouse looks around at each of us in turn. "I could be wrong but I'm betting most of you, deep down, thought, *Yeah, right. How could it be anyone but him? He was with her in the house. That evidence must be wrong.*"

"DC Waterhouse, will you please tell me why Anita stabbed my wife if it wasn't to defend me?" William asks.

"I will. I'm getting there. First I need to tell you why she made a hole in the office wall behind the mirror in order to hide a dead child's bones that she'd bought off the internet."

"What the fuck?" murmurs Caroline.

"That's sick," says Jack. "In the old sense of the word," he adds quickly. "Sick as in depraved."

Waterhouse, at the front of the room, picks up a bone and points it towards the ceiling. "Did someone help you move the mirror to hide the bones, Anita? DS Kombothekra and I managed it easily, but we're two strong men."

"I'm strong too," says Anita. Her voice sounds hoarse. "It's easy enough if you know the right technique. You need to be careful and not rush it."

"Anita, why the *fuck* did you buy little kid bones and hide them in your office wall?" Susan asks her.

"Ah, the *wall*," says Waterhouse. "The all-important wall."

"Meaning?" Susan snaps at him.

"DS Kombothekra and I found two other things in the same hiding place: a small jewelry box and a sheet of paper. The paper had all the names on it from the game—Lindsay James, Davina Slade and the rest. The jewelry box contained what I assumed at first was a brooch in the shape of a white bolt of lightning. A brooch is a piece of jewelry, right? So: belongs in a jewelry box. And there it lay: dead flat, on a bed of what looked like silk or satin.

"Almost immediately after I'd closed the box, though, I thought, *Hang on: brooches have pins*. That's how you attach them to clothes. Not too long before, I'd interviewed you, Lord Brinkwood, and you were wearing a kind of brooch or badge on your lapel, and it was leaning forward on its pin, not lying flat on the fabric. I thought, *Where's the pin for this brooch?*, the one in the jewelry box in the wall. So I checked it again later and there was no pin."

"All brooches have pins," Polly tells him.

"Agreed. But this wasn't a brooch. It was something else. That's when I remembered that the jewelry box had also contained what looked very much like white, powdery dust. Plaster dust, from the wall. But how would that have got in there, inside a closed box? Did someone place the white lightning-shaped thing inside the box at the very moment that the wall was being smashed into? Seemed unlikely. And then I saw how obvious it was and knew exactly what the non-brooch was."

"Well?" says Susan.

"It was a small piece of the wall of the office building," says Waterhouse. "The smashed-up wall with the hole in it. Someone had taken a piece of that broken wall and carefully—lovingly, you might say—placed it inside a jewelry box for safekeeping. No one would do that, though, I thought. Not unless they had a strong, emotional attachment to that building, a building that was due to be demolished in the very near future to make way for a fancy hotel."

Anita has started to cry.

I don't understand. Does anyone else? Or is Waterhouse still the only person who knows what he's talking about?

"Before the Tevendon resort existed and that building became just 'the office building,' it was called Graves House," he says, half sitting on the edge of the bones table at the front of the room. "One of two Edwardian villas in the grounds of the Tevendon Estate. When Jane Brinkwood and her father, Ian, rescued Anita from her parents' clutches, it was where she lived—in Graves House. It quickly became her place of refuge and the only happy home she'd ever known. Then, when the resort was created, she was able to work there. And then disaster struck: Ian Brinkwood decided that he wanted to make some changes to the resort, maybe to bring in more profit, and he had the idea of a hotel. All the other resort buildings were new, no doubt energy-efficient, few repairs needed. It made perfect sense to Lord Brinkwood to demolish the two older buildings that needed a lot of maintenance and maybe didn't have the right green credentials—you have to think about things like that these days. Neither Graves House nor Number 1, Heaversedge House, were listed buildings so nothing could stop Lord Brinkwood's tearing them down—least of all Anita, who wasn't his fiancée then. She was just an employee, maybe a friend, someone he'd rescued. Point is, she had no say in anything and Lord Brinkwood, like his daughter Jane, was accustomed to getting his own way.

"So Anita, in desperation, had an idea. She'd probably seen crime shows on TV where buildings have to be kept intact because bones are found there, and if there's an unsolved crime associated with a building, then you can't knock it down, can you? It might contain vital evidence. That was how Anita hoped she could save the life of Graves House—by buying human bones, which is unfortunately all too easy to do, and hiding them in the wall. It was a ridiculous plan. It would only have halted the demolition for a matter of days—that's how long it took me to establish that these bones weren't connected to anything the police would be interested in.

"Here's a mystery, though. When Mick Henry wants to look at the antique mirror and he and Anita find the bones together— her pretending to be as surprised by the discovery as he was—why didn't she take her chance and agree with Mick that it was suspicious and that the police should be called? That's what she wanted, that was the plan, so why not go for it? I'm guessing it's because of the jewelry box that was also in the wall, and which presumably Mick saw. Couldn't have him telling the police about that—together with the bones, that box and its contents might have told a very different story from the one Anita wanted it to tell. And her fingerprints were probably all over the bones. She'd been planning to clean them up, I expect, before 'finding' them at a time that suited her, once she'd moved the jewelry box out of the way. So when Mick suddenly wanted to look at the mirror and the bone-finding happened too soon, she panicked. She decided to reassure Mick they were only animal bones, so no cause for alarm. He agreed to take them and put them back in the woods where Anita had told him they must have come from. Where animal bones belong."

"If she didn't want the bones found when they were found, why did she agree to take the mirror off the wall for Mick?" asks Susan. "Couldn't she have said it was screwed in there and wouldn't come off?"

"Mick was already standing by the wall," Anita says. "He could see it wasn't fixed in place. I didn't know how to put him off, so I just prayed he'd only look at the mirror, not at what was inside the hole."

"I should probably confess . . ." Mick glances nervously at Susan. "The list of names from the game wasn't there when I looked that day with Anita. I'm afraid that was me. I put it in there later. I found it outside Caroline and Harriet's place, just lying in the garden after the game was over."

"On 2 July?" Waterhouse asks him.

He nods. "I picked it up and thought, *What do I do with this?* Throwing it in the trash or destroying it felt wrong, given the significance of what we'd all done. It was . . . well, it was a little piece of our history. A day we'd never forget. I thought it ought to survive. Later, before dinner, I walked past the office and it was empty. I didn't want to keep the list on me—it was kinda burning a hole in my pocket—"

"So you thought you'd scoot in, move a mirror and stick it in the wall cavity?" Susan shakes her head. "You're a mighty strange man, Mick Henry."

Anita isn't denying anything Waterhouse is saying about her, so I suppose it must be true. "How did you know?" I ask him. "About Anita's attachment to Graves House and her determination to save it? Did you really get all that from one little jewelry box with a piece of wall in it?"

"Not only from that, no. There were three other things that told me I was on the right track. One is what Lucy told Sergeant Zailer about Anita sometimes referring to Lord Brinkwood as 'Lordian' in a scathing tone, as if she resented him. Why would she, if he rescued her, and if she later accepted his proposal of marriage? Because she had a quite separate reason to feel bitter towards him," Waterhouse answers his own question. "Thanks to his orders, the building she loved was scheduled for demolition. The second thing involves your snoring, Susan. Anita said she'd been sleeping in the office building because she'd needed to give you and Mick Number 4, to resolve your snoring issue. In telling the story to Lucy, she mentioned having her nights disrupted by rows in which you yelled at Mick for snoring. Not true. Anita didn't know it wasn't true, though, or that Mick doesn't snore, because she never spent a single night in Number 4 even before she handed the keys over to Mick. Why would she sleep there when she could sleep in the house she loves and regards as her true and only home: Graves House?

"And the third thing: when I spoke to Lord Brinkwood's lawyers some time after Jane's murder and after he and Anita got engaged, they mentioned something about her not needing or wanting to inherit the Brinkwood family millions or any of the houses. They made a passing comment that didn't register as significant at the time. They said, 'All Anita wants from Lord Brinkwood after he dies is a normal-sized house that feels like home.' Clearly they were talking about Graves House. To them it seemed as if Anita was asking for next to nothing, given who she was planning to marry, so that's how they presented it to me. But to Anita, Graves House was everything. I spoke to the lawyers again this morning and they confirmed it: Lord Brinkwood told them on 4 July last year, two days after Jane's death, that he wanted to make a new will and bequeath Graves House to Anita. He very likely was never going to reopen the resort now that he associated it with the tragic death of his daughter, he told them, and even if he did, there would be no new hotel and Graves House was to remain untouched. It was earmarked, suddenly, to be Anita's home after his death."

"Fast worker," mutters Susan, looking sideways at Anita.

"Oh, my God." Caroline turns to face Anita, who's sitting behind her. "That's why you did it. Right? You knew that if you killed Jane, Lord Brinkwood would shut down the resort, abandon the plan to build the hotel . . . You knew you could take advantage of a lonely, bereaved old man and make him give you that house you'd always wanted. And, even better, you were standing there behind Jane listening to her threaten William and talk about sharp knives in the kitchen, and you knew that if you killed her then, right that second, you'd always be able to kid yourself that you did it for a noble reason—for William's sake."

"Couldn't have put it better myself," says Waterhouse.

Anita shakes her head as if he and Caroline have both missed the point. She looks at me suddenly. "Haven't you ever wanted to save a life?" she says. "To *save* something, something that's precious to you?"

I have. My marriage.

"Except you can't. You're powerless." Anita turns to Waterhouse. "And then, one day, you're not. You see a way. The bones in the wall was a ludicrous idea, maybe, but . . . this wasn't. William would be safer and, ultimately, happier. Ian would be less lonely married to me than he would living alone for the rest of his life—a widower who'd lost his daughter as well as his wife."

"And you'd have your house," says Waterhouse. "So simple. All you had to do was murder Jane, comfort her father, somehow persuade him to propose marriage—"

"Anita loves me," says Lord Brinkwood gruffly. "Yes, she loves that old building—I'm still not quite sure why—but she also loves me. Don't you, darling?"

"Yes, Ian. I do. How could I not? You were the one who made the decision to save Graves House. I'll always be grateful to you for that. Promise me that when they send me to prison, you'll look after it for me."

"Prison?" Ian Brinkwood responds to the word as if it's an absurd suggestion. He says to Waterhouse, "Surely Anita won't be locked up? There were clear mitigating circumstances. I mean . . . the house really had nothing to do with it."

"It had everything to do with it," says Anita.

"Yes, but Jane was upset. She wasn't in her right mind. She might have killed William. All you did was stop her."

"No," Anita says angrily. "Let me have my true reason. Please."

"You've gone off the 'defending William' lie, then?" says Waterhouse. "I'm assuming that's why you put the knife on the carpet between him and Jane once you'd cleaned it to within an inch of its life, instead of back in the drawer—to leave us with the idea that maybe Jane had it in her hand at some point."

"That's what I hoped you might think, yes," says Anita. "That Jane had been about to stab William with that knife and that the killer had stopped her by stabbing her with a different one. I washed the knife really thoroughly to make it look as if it hadn't been used but was maybe about to be."

"You cleaned it so thoroughly that you wiped off all fingerprints, which means we found none of Jane's. So that was never going to work," Waterhouse tells her. "And you could so easily have been caught. If William had been less traumatized, he'd have turned round, maybe, and seen you. You were very lucky that he didn't register your presence."

"He was in a state of shock," Anita says. "Like a dead man, but sitting up—that's what I thought at the time. Yes, I was lucky. I didn't care at that point. I was desperate, and I knew I wasn't going to get a chance like that again."

"How could you be sure that you'd be able to persuade Lord Brinkwood to propose to you?"

"I wasn't sure at all," she says. "But I knew he wouldn't be building any fancy hotels on that spot any time soon. That was good enough. And again, I was lucky. Things went better than I'd hoped. I started to wonder if maybe someone up there"—she looks up at the ceiling—"wanted my house to be saved as much as I did."

"What about the blood on your clothes?" Waterhouse asks. "There must have been some."

She nods. "I stopped at Graves and got changed into a clean version of the same outfit—one of my other work uniforms, as I call them. They're all pretty much identical. I stuffed the bloody clothes into the hole behind the mirror, then went back to the restaurant terrace. Then a few days later, as soon as you and your colleagues and all the guests had gone and I thought it was safe, I burned them in the stove."

So you never hated Jane anywhere near as much as I did. It was never about that.

No, I'm not going to do this. I'm not going to allow myself to feel deserted by Anita. We have more in common than anyone might think. All right, so we didn't both loathe Jane Brinkwood and want to wipe her off the face of the planet—Anita had other things she cared more about—but we both know what it feels like to lose, or imagine you're about to lose, something that's unbearably dear to you.

I'm not going to feel deserted by Jane Brinkwood's murderer. And I'm not going to desert her either.

"What is it?" Waterhouse asks me.

I'm on my feet before I've decided what I want to say. "The right legal team could make a decent case in mitigation" is what comes out eventually.

"I agree with you," says Lord Brinkwood.

Waterhouse is the one I need to persuade. It's going to be hard. "Look at it this way," I say. "Anita could have murdered Jane in her holiday house at any point that week, if her true motive was saving Graves House. She didn't, though. So what changed? Hearing her screaming death threats at William. That's what made the difference. If she stands up in court and says that she did it because she was afraid he'd be killed otherwise, and if we all back her up and say how dangerous and on the edge Jane seemed that night—" I break off. Does everyone think I've lost my mind? Pete's looking as if he does. But then, he thought that anyway.

"Give up, Lucy," says Waterhouse.

Never. "I'm just saying, what proof have you got that'd stand up in court? A bit of wall in a jewelry box and some stories about snoring?"

"He's got what five police officers have just heard Anita confess to," says Charlie. Her face is a picture. She can't believe I'm trying this. Neither can I. But whether it works or not, it's worth it. Anita's shaky smile makes it worth it.

She killed Jane. And she knows I'm on her side.

33

Saturday, February 22, 2020

"So you're going to the wedding?" Liv clapped her hands together. "Ooh, goody. There'll be tons of goss, I bet."

She and Charlie were eating pita bread, tzatziki, and tara-mosalata at the same Greek café where Charlie had met Lucy Dean all those weeks ago.

Liv giggled. "Weddings, eh? Ha!"

"I'm glad you think it's so funny," said Charlie.

"Oh, come on, Char, you have to see the funny side. You really, seriously, thought Chris and I were going to have an *illegal marriage?*"

"Yes, Liv, because—wait, why was it, again? Oh, that's right: because I caught you in the act of *planning an illegal, bigamous wedding.*"

"Yeah, but I was never going to do it, not IRL, as they say. In real life," she clarified.

"I know what IRL means."

"A girl can dream." Liv looked serious suddenly. "Dream, and fantasize."

"About bigamy?" Charlie would never understand her sister. She wanted to keep trying, though. It was such a relief to have Liv back in her life and being in every detail the Liv that Charlie remembered.

"Yes, about bigamy," said Liv. "Romance *and* a crime! What could be more enticing?"

"You're a nutter."

"Er, excuse me. I'm not the one going to Lucy Dean and Pete Shabani's wedding."

"What's nutty about that? Don't answer." Charlie sighed. "I know it's . . . irregular. Simon doesn't want me to go."

"Of course he doesn't. I'm on his side."

"It's not till September, anyway. I can decide later. Like, *much* later." Charlie scooped up a bit of taramosalata with a strip of bread and stuffed it into her mouth.

"Do you *want* to be friends with Lucy?" Liv asked. "She sounds quite warped. That game with the false identities? No one who was right in the head would think of something like that."

"Says the woman who planned a bigamous wedding."

"How many times? It was a fantasy. A bit of fun. Lucy sounds dodgy, Char. She's literally setting out to befriend and champion the cause of a *murderer*."

"I know. Maybe that's why I said yes to going to the wedding."

"What do you mean?" said Liv.

"When Simon told me no charges were going to be brought against anyone but Anita, I had a strange thought. It was like a sentence that appeared randomly in my brain: *She's going to get away with it*. 'She' being Lucy."

"Get away with what?"

"All the obvious things: lying to us from start to end, almost. The fucked-up game. I think there's probably still some stuff we don't know. Not sure what it could be but . . . my intuition tells me there's something. Maybe if I keep in touch with her and go to the wedding, I'll find out one day. Also—and this is going to sound like a contradiction—I *like* Lucy. I find her interesting. You know William's going to be at the wedding?"

Liv's eyes widened. "That's gross," she said.

"You're pretty judgmental for a massive adulterer, aren't you?"

Liv chuckled. "Cheek! But seriously, your first husband at your second wedding? Big no from me. Though you should probably go because something exciting might happen and then you can tell me. And intuition isn't nothing. You should take it seriously. It's the voice of all the wisdom your soul has accumulated throughout the ages. I'm reading this book at the moment by Abraham-Hicks—have you heard of them?"

"No."

"They're a collection of spirits."

"*What?*"

"Yeah, they're a group of nonphysical energetic entities," said Liv enthusiastically. "Really, you've never heard of them? They're amazing. Let me tell you . . ."

Charlie, who had been unaware until this moment that nonphysical energetic entities could write and publish books, settled in to listen.

Tuesday, July 2, 2019

JANE

They've put something heavy up against the door. Maybe more than one thing. I've heard quite a bit of dragging. A few seconds ago there was some give and now there isn't, which means they're serious about not letting me out of here. And suddenly I can't get the door to budge even a fraction, however hard I push with all my weight.

The ringleaders are standing right outside talking about what they're going to do to me, not caring that I can hear them. Why would they care? I'm not a person to them. I don't matter. Nothing about me is worthy of respect or compassion.

I'm tempted to let rip, let them know how much I despise them, but I won't give them the satisfaction. I'll stay silent, make them wonder what I'm getting up to in here. There's no chance I can escape. This room has only the tiniest window. Should I open it and start screaming? No. That would give Jack the best possible reason to come in here and hurt me, as he's clearly longing to.

They have no plan—that much is apparent. It was a spur of the moment impulse on Jack's part to shove me in here when I was on my way to the front door. It's pathetic. It's not even his holiday cottage. If I were Harriet and Caroline, I'd be outraged. Sorry, I keep forgetting: those aren't their real names. If I were Lindsay and Davina, I should have said.

They're all pathetic, hiding away under false identities. That's why they've had to resort to discussing whether or not they ought to kill me. They were hoping they could scare me away from Tevendon, my own father's property. Ha! They soon saw I wasn't afraid of them. I made it clear I had no intention of going anywhere.

Jack's pride couldn't take it, clearly. He couldn't let me walk out of the house having won, so he pushed me in here, which is really pathetic because this isn't some dark scary dungeon full of torture weapons. If he does end up cutting my throat from ear to ear, as he keeps suggesting to Lucy, Caroline, and Susan that he should—sorry, Lucy, Davina, and Imogen—then no one in prison will be impressed to hear him boast that the murder happened in the well-appointed utility room of a luxury holiday cottage at a five-star resort.

"In theory I'm in favor. I *want* to want to do it," Lucy says apologetically to Jack, whose real name is Tommy Jordan. I can't manage to think of them as who they are. I might just stick to their fake-liar names. It makes life easier—which is sensible, given that I might not have much life left, depending on what they choose to do with me. *To* me.

I have some power, though, whatever they decide to do. I can think scared thoughts or brave, defiant ones.

No contest. They're not going to defeat me where it matters, which is in my mind.

"But in practice . . ." Lucy sounds worried.

"I'm also in favor in theory, but I don't like the throat-cutting idea," says Susan. "And I'm put off by never having done anything like this before. Realistically, what are the chances we'd get away with it? Lucy, what do you think?"

"I don't know," says the bitch that used to be married to my husband. "I just . . . I can't imagine what any part of the future will look like if we do it. I'm fairly sure we'd be making the world a better place by removing her from it—"

"No doubt about that," says Caroline.

"—but we'd be turning ourselves into much worse people. Let's not kid ourselves about that. And I'd have to keep it secret from Pete. He'd be horrified if he knew we were even contemplating it."

"That's because he's sweet," says Susan. "And that's okay. The world needs sweet people."

"And it also needs people like us," says Jack.

"Urgently," Susan agrees.

Caroline laughs. I hope she drops dead. I hope they all do.

"My worry is the others," says Lucy. "Harriet, Mick, Polly. They don't want it to happen. Not genuinely."

"They know exactly what we're discussing," Jack says. "None of them's out here trying to stop us."

"No, but I think Lucy's right," says Susan. "All three of them are secretly hoping we'll decide not to go through with it."

"Guys, come on . . . ," says Lucy.

"What?" Susan asks her.

"This is madness. Isn't it? I mean, we don't know what we're doing. We can't do something like this without . . . I don't know. I just don't think we can do it."

Ugh. I don't want it to be Bitchface Lucy who saves my life. Any of the others, fine. Not her.

"Don't we pretty much have to now?" Caroline asks. "She's listening to every word we're saying."

"If she tells anyone, we just deny it," says Susan.

"You're really proposing to *let her go*?" Jack can't believe it.

"What would we do with her body, Jack? Hide it? Burn it? Bury it in the woods?" Bitchface is on a roll.

"What about if we chopped—"

"No," say all the women. Then Caroline says, "For God's sake! I'm with Lucy. We're just not people who can do this kind of thing. Look, we'll probably wake up tomorrow and be *so relieved* we changed our minds."

"I can kinda feel some of that relief already," says Susan.

"Fine," Jack concedes. "I'm not going to hold out if I'm the only one."

I hear more scraping of furniture across the floor. *Thank God. They're letting me out.* If they think I'm going to run sniveling to William or my dad or the police, they've got another think coming. I refuse to play the role of their victim. I'm going to treat this like the joke it is, all of it: their pathetic debate about whether or not to murder me, their suggestion that from now on secret enemies will be waiting to attack me wherever I go. Bullshit. They're just trying to scare me, and I wasn't particularly scared, not even when the topic of maybe killing me came up. I knew they wouldn't go through with it, the stupid cowards.

I'm Jane Brinkwood, daughter of Lord Brinkwood. I have a husband who adores me and we're just about to start an amazing life together. Nothing and no one is going to get in our way.

ACKNOWLEDGMENTS

I am hugely grateful to my brilliant Hodder publishers and pals, especially my awesome editor Carolyn Mays. Thank you to Peter Straus, my wonderful agent, and all at Rogers, Coleridge & White. Massive thanks to Kate Jones, Faith Tilleray, and Naomi Adams for constant help and support on all fronts. Thanks to my family—Dan, Phoebe, Guy, and Brewster, and also Adele and Jenny Geras—and to Emily Winslow, whose editorial advice improves each book enormously and who went above and beyond this time by lending me a suite of rooms to finish this novel in! Thank you to my Dream Authors, who are a constant source of inspiration, fun, and creativity. And, as always, thanks to all my readers who send lovely emails and messages—it's so wonderful to know you're loving the books!

The New Hercule Poirot Mysteries
by Sophie Hannah

"I was thrilled to see the Belgian detective in such very, very good hands."
—Gillian Flynn, #1 *New York Times* bestselling author of *Gone Girl*

Hercule Poirot's Silent Night: The New Hercule Poirot Mystery

The world's greatest detective, Hercule Poirot, puts his little grey cells to work solving a baffling Christmas mystery.

The Killings at Kingfisher Hill: The New Hercule Poirot Mystery

The world's most beloved detective, Hercule Poirot, races to save an innocent woman from the gallows—but then why has she confessed to being a murderer?

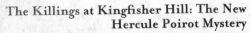

The Mystery of Three Quarters: The New Hercule Poirot Mystery

Exerting his little grey cells, Poirot must solve an elaborate puzzle involving a tangled web of relationships, scandalous secrets, and past misdeeds.

Closed Casket: A Hercule Poirot Mystery

A diabolically clever mystery soaked in period atmosphere and loaded with clues, suspense, and danger.

The Monogram Murders: The New Hercule Poirot Mystery

Poirot must unveil a murderer at the home of a celebrated Irish author.

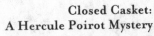